MW01711695

The Belize File

By

Harold R. Miller

The Belize File

Taylor-Dth Publishing
87 Piper Lane
Fairfax, CA 94930

ISBN: 0-9712923-5-3
Library of Congress Control Number: 2002095566

Manufactured in the United States of America

Dedication

Thank you Nancy, Ana, and
"___" (she knows who she is.)

ΨΨΨ

Other books by Harold R. Miller

The Emerald Head Caper
The Philippine File
The Australian File
Thai Moon Saloon

by Harold R. Miller & Nancy Cardinali
NITWIT

Published exclusively by
Taylor-Dth Publishing

Also available at
www.taylor-dth.com

Chapter 1

The searchlights streaked across the water, piercing the moonless night, slicing the darkness like cleavers, baring everything, and yet nothing. The engines on the patrol boats roared in synchronous tempo as the three of them plowed through the swells on their hunt, like wolves bounding across the fallen snow after a rabbit, they smelled the scent of their prey and pushed on past the point of reason, nearly past the point of safety.

The driver of the ocean racer dodged the lights and bounced over the swells, keeping an eye behind him lest the lights play across him as he crested each mound of water. He cinched his seat belt tighter, and reached for his SCUBA mouthpiece. He was getting close to the cay. He smiled against the wind blasting his face. "One of these days," he laughed aloud in exhilaration, in the pleasure of knowing he was again eluding the patrol boats. It was a game of cat and mouse he enjoyed, so long as the cats continued to be careless and inept.

He raced into a cove at the end of the sandy cay, clamped his teeth around the SCUBA mouthpiece, and reached down for the scuttling lever. He throttled back the engines, not too much, but just enough to stop the high speed porpoising of the 40 foot boat. He braced himself and yanked on the lever as he cut the engines off.

The ocean racer nose dived into the water at over 90 miles an hour. The forward inertia threw the driver against the tension of his seatbelts. The water rushed over him, pushing at his face, pushing back on his head. Four seconds was all it took, he knew, for the boat to decelerate to a manageable slow sinking rate to the sand bottom, but it seemed to take forever each time he went through the procedure. But, it was better than the alternative, he rationalized.

When the boat settled on the bottom, he peered upward at the hulls of the patrol boats roaring over head, the white of their wakes agitating the plankton enough to provide light for reading a newspaper, if one were trying to read a newspaper at the time. He grinned around his mouthpiece, thinking how absurd it would be to try reading a newspaper on the deck of the patrol boats while chasing him.

The patrol boats sped off in different directions, continuing their hunt, as he released his seat belt. With his SCUBA tank casually slung over his shoulder, he slowly rose the twenty feet to the surface.

The patrol boats were no longer around, so he took his time in a leisurely ten yard swim to the shore where he would uncover his camouflaged 14 foot outboard runabout, hide the SCUBA, and be on his way.

The moon was an emerging golden glowing ball to the east as he started his outboard and slowly motored out into the Caribbean on his way back to the mainland. The patrol boats could stop him now, if they spotted him. He was certainly not in the boat they were looking for, so he couldn't be the smuggler they hunted.

As he neared the mainland, he began wondering why the arrangements didn't include covering up his boat runs. He frowned. Someday he was going to have to demand protection from the Coast Guard for his runs.

* * * *

The morning's sun shimmered through the wood slats of the window jalousies on the best honeymoon cottage in San Pedro, Belize.

The rays fell on a quick-witted gecko, the tiny green

lizard believed by the natives to be a lucky omen, as it eyed a common cockroach nearby. It made its lunge, but the cockroach was too elusive, and scurried through a crack in the wood floor, out of reach.

The rays continued their encroachment. As certain and indisputable as sand through an hourglass, they inched their way across the bed to land on the face of the new bride and heighten the fairness of her skin.

She stirred. She moaned in complaint at the intrusion, and tried to brush away the annoyance. Suddenly she screamed. She bolted upright and startled her husband, who had been sleeping peacefully beside her, tired from the late night party given by the hotel's staff.

"Allie?" he asked, sitting up, barely awake.

"Gerald?" she responded, reaching for him, reassuring herself he was there. "Oh, God," she said as she felt his warmth. "It... It was a dream.... No, it was a nightmare. I was standing in... in water. I was looking at you and suddenly you disappeared. It was awful!"

Gerald stroked his new wife's red hair. "Well, you're awake now, and I'm here." He kissed her fears away. "It sounds like you were having a classic dream. You know, where you want something so much that the thought of it being taken away from you is traumatic. Lots of people have bad dreams like that."

She leaned back on the pillows. She sighed with relief, fully in control of herself once again. "I suppose you're right," she agreed. "Just a bad dream." She smiled up at him. "It's true, I do want you so much." She smiled. "I couldn't bear to lose you now, not when it took me so long to get you."

"You're so beautiful," Gerald said, reaching his arm under his new bride's head, lifting her to gaze into her eyes, to kiss her gently.

She laughed lightly. "If you keep complimenting me like that, I'm liable to get an ego you can't deal with."

"Only suiting," he responded as his other hand reached around her waist, pulling her closer to him. "This is the spot," he grinned, gently kissing her on the side of her neck. "This is what made me fall in love with you."

She leaned her head back and sighed, enjoying his touch.

His hand moved across her waist, slowly caressing, lightly touching her. He cupped her breast, and turned his head down to gaze at her soft, inviting form.

"How can anyone have such beauty?" he asked, running his thumb across her nipple, gently massaging it with his thumb and fingers.

"I love it when you do that," she sighed. She closed her eyes, as if in a dream. She took a slight gasp of breath and held it in, fearing that to release it would cause the dream to fade.

He kissed her on the ear, and tugged on her earlobe. Her responses urged him on. He gently thrust his tongue into her ear, and pulled her closer to him, knowing the slight trembling of her body came from her excitement.

He kissed her throat. He ran his tongue down her neck, and between her breasts in little circular motions. He brushed his lips across her nipple, then took it in his mouth, massaging it between his lips, brushing it with his tongue, sucking it gently.

She buried her head in his hair. She parted her legs and pushed herself against his knee, wrapping her arms around his head.

He slid his hands across her hips. He massaged them, squeezed them, aiding her thrust against his body. Slowly, softly, he moved his head down across the gentle curve of her belly, kissing, caressing with his tongue.

She drew a sharp breath and held it as he nibbled on her thigh.

"Oh, God," she moaned, thrusting her body against him. "God," she moaned again, longer, drawing the word out in her pleasure. She could hold her passion no longer. She rolled him over onto his back, then pulled herself on top of him.

The sun played across her cinnamon colored hair as she threw back her head in mounting pleasure. Tiny beads of sweat formed on her forehead. Her breasts swayed with her every movement, exciting him even more as they brushed across his chest when she leaned forward and wrapped her arms around his neck. She pushed her mouth onto his. She probed his mouth with her tongue, thrusting it into him, meeting his. And she exploded in rapture.

"Allie," he gently called as she lay on top of him for several minutes, taking pleasure in the stillness, in his presence inside her.

"Umm," she moaned, not wanting to move, needing to feel him.

He wanted to say more, so much more.

Her touch sent a warm thrill though him. He reached for her. He held her close to him, as though he needed her to be inside him, to be a part of him, to be his soul.

She moved again, molding her body against him, and kissed him on the cheek. She sighed as he rolled onto her. She wrapped her legs around him, and probed the warmth of his mouth with her tongue, caressing his in rhythmic response.

She exploded once more when she felt his release. She held him close to her trembling body until he finally rolled over beside her, exhausted and spent in pleasure, their bodies glistening in the morning's sun.

"It's going to be a lovely day," she said, at length, in the comfort of his closeness. "And us with nothing to do, but..."

"Nothing to do but what?" he asked, grinning.

"You know," she teased.

"Come on," he protested. "We can't, now. We have to get up. We have things to do." He glanced at the travel clock on the nightstand. "It's almost eight," he added with some urgency. "Come on. We have to get dressed."

She brushed against his legs as he forced himself out of bed, frowned lightly, playfully, and sat up. "Well," she said. "This was the best honeymoon I've ever had, and already I'm being rejected?"

"The best honeymoon?" He laughed. "And just when have you ever had any others?"

"Ummmmh, well…"

He turned to her, and took her face in his hands. He kissed her once more, then peered into her eyes. "Any regrets?" He asked.

"Well, not yet," she smiled, again reaching for him.

"Ah, umm, no," he said, after several seconds, resisting her touch. "Look. We have to get dressed. We're expected at the charter office in twenty minutes."

"So soon? You mean we can't...?" He voice trailed off suggestively. The soft splashing of the Caribbean waves enhanced her seductive ploy.

"Look, we wouldn't be so late if you hadn't kept me awake all night," he grinned.

"It wasn't me. It couldn't have been. I think I was done in by all the Cuba Libre's we drank," she said. "No, I think it must have been one of the maids. I hear they have excellent maid service in these Caribbean hotels."

"Yeah? Funny you should say that. That's what I heard, too."

"And you?" she asked.

"And me what?"

"Any regrets?" She reached for him and put her arms around his neck.

"Nope. You're fantastic " He gently removed her arms, and got out of bed. "We have to get a move on," he added as he strode to the shower.

She playfully pouted, then she rose from the bed and rushed to join him, pushing an unreasonable and sudden sense of foreboding from her mind.

At the time Gerald and Allie played in San Pedro Town, on Ambegris Cay in northern Belize, it hadn't yet been discovered by throngs of cheap vacation seekers, like most of the Caribbean countries.

The cay, or key, as it's often spelled in English, is located just around the corner, south of Cancun, Mexico, and faces the largest reef in the western hemisphere.

The sleepy village has twelve hotels, all with back doors on the beach and front doors opening on sand streets. The inhabitants, an ethnic mixture of Garifuna, Creoles and Mexicans, are less affluent than their neighbors to the north, and are proud of their literacy rate, boasting that over 95% of the population can read a newspaper with some comprehension. They have a cultural history of piracy, thievery, and petty wickedness, which, it has been said, carries over to the present.

The hotel where Allie and her husband played on their honeymoon night had adequate accommodations, and maintained a well-established yacht chartering service. The Eden like setting appealed to the rich Gringos who loved spending their winters under the hot Caribbean sun, until, of course, they discovered the best kept secret of the entire Caribbean; the insidious, biting, nearly invisible insect known as the Caribbean Sand Fly.

To handle the charter business, the hotel owners built a pier that protruded into the small lagoon created by the reef. The water in the lagoon was so clear it belied its depths, and the assortment of charter yachts tied stern-to along the pier seemed to be floating on air. The boats varied in size from twenty feet long for an economy one day excursion, to fifty feet long for the ramblings of the rich and famous. They sparkled in the hot morning's sun, bright in their white paint and blue sail covers.

The charter office, with the bamboo roof, rattan furniture and Formica counter top, was perched at the beginning of the pier. The matron of the office was an overly tanned, overly bleached blonde who mostly bulged out of her faded red bikini. The woman's sole responsibility was the chartering business, and this morning she was idling away her time waiting for customers when she spied the approach of Gerald and Allie. When they entered the office she reached behind the counter and retrieved the charter file.

"You must be Mr. and Mrs. Levine," she greeted them. "I can tell from the honeymooner look. It's refreshing, ain't it? To see people such as you two, actually in love, these days. I mean, there ain't many people down here on honeymoons. Real honeymoons, that is. Most are just playing. You can tell, you know, mostly by the way the girl looks, all bored, and such." She completed her remark while feigning dismay at a cockroach scrambling across the counter top. She grabbed a fly swatter from under the counter and took a swing at the insect. "Guess them cockroaches are going to be the death of us one of these days," she exclaimed, returning her attention to her customers, ignoring their grimaces.

"Well," Gerald said with forced politeness. "We did the play thing for a while, and I chased her 'til she caught me."

"And am I ever going to make him pay for it," Allie chimed in, laughing.

"Well, you really caught him good, honey," the blonde said "Two weeks on a Westsail 42 charter with full insurance and food ain't a bad catch. I've seen girls down here get friendly with any man who could spring for a cruise like that, and without getting the lifetime benefits you snagged."

Allie wasn't impressed by the directness of the woman, but she overlooked the style, thinking it must have been developed over years of being one of those friendly girls the woman described. "Yeah. It wasn't easy," she responded, then pinched Gerald in the side to keep him from making any snide remark.

By eleven in the morning Gerald and Allie were checked out of their cottage, and safely loaded aboard the Westsail. Then, while they motored out of the harbor past the pleasure yachts tied to the pier, and past other not so pleasurable workboats anchored about in no particular order, Gerald taught Allie how to raise the mainsail.

"Not bad for your first day out," Gerald called from the cockpit. "For a girl past her prime you learn quickly enough."

She playfully signaled her response with the middle finger of her right hand.

"Now, once the main is raised," he continued, undaunted, "and the halyard is secured, you can..." then he paused. "Ah, you do know what secured means?"

"Smart ass," she called back to him. "I'm not exactly a land lubber."

"Well, all right! Good Girl!"

She glared at him.

"After the main halyard is secured," he continued, "you can raise the staysail. Be careful about the club-foot boom. It's going to swing over, so be sure you stand to windward, that's the upwind side, when you hoist it."

Allie shot a glance of disdain at her husband, then laughed.

"Hey," he defended himself. "A few bits of maritime vocabulary thrown in here and there won't do any harm." He adjusted the main sheet. "The main and staysail are all I think we're going to use this afternoon," he continued. "There's a little freshness in the afternoon winds, and as soon as we clear the cut in the reef we'll follow it south along the coast before turning east. It should be an easy sail." He paused to check the sail. "And that'll be good, 'cause it won't give us any trouble, and I don't want to break in a new hand too saltily." He grinned.

Allie's mind flashed on her nightmare as he said the word 'trouble', but she quickly pushed her fears out of her mind with a shrug that came from her practical upbringing. Then she made her way back to the cockpit to take up a reclining position on the leeward cushion. “New hand? Saltily?” she chided. “My, Don't you become the Captain Bligh when the wind gets in your hair?”

“Better Captain Bligh than Captain Queeg,” he joked.

“I don't know about that. At least Captain Queeg got back to land after the mutiny.”

“Ah hah!” he quipped. “I can see you don't know your maritime history. So did Captain Bligh.”

“I thought he was thrown overboard during the mutiny.”

“Nope. Not thrown overboard. In fact, if you've ever read the Bounty Trilogy you would know that he was put overboard with a twenty three foot longboat which he sailed for 72 days to the French Society Islands to safety. It was a remarkable feat of seamanship.”

“No use talking about either of them, then. No one's going to get put overboard on this cruise,” she said. “I hope,” she added as an afterthought, feeling uneasy with the words.

Several hours passed in the silent rapture of sun and sea, with the gentle swells rolling the boat gently, and with an occasional coral island to look at in the distance. Gerald was at the helm, guiding the smooth cutter, and Allie was seated beside him, glorying in the peace and beauty of the day.

“Time to locate some protected anchorage near one of these cays for the night,” Gerald said, breaking the rhapsody. “I don't want to try sailing among these reefs after dark.”

The wind had turned to blow more steadily off the port beam by then, and the wheel required constant attention. He coaxed Allie into tending the wheel so that he could go below to check the charts. With little effort, he located a suitable anchorage among the numerous cays about an hour's sailing time away. It was in an inlet on the leeward side of a small island named Nose Cay.

As they sailed near the cay, Gerald started the engine to bring the boat up into the wind so he could drop the sails. Then they motored to less than fifty yards from the beach to drop the anchor. The boat drifted around to gently tug on the line and set the anchor in the sandy bottom.

Allie went below to busy herself in the galley, and a minute or so later she tossed a can of cold beer up to Gerald, sitting in the cockpit enjoying the mood of the late afternoon.

He popped open the can, then gazed at Allie. He watched her movements, savoring the fullness of her shape. Her breasts stood proud and boasting as they held out the tiny patches of bikini top above her stomach, a flat stomach ending in the gentle rise of her Mound of Venus. She was 5'4" tall, weighed 115 pounds, and was twenty six at her last birthday, just before their marriage. "I just can't get over it," he said, appraising her.

"Over what?"

"How beautiful you are. I guess you know that bikini you're wearing is driving me nuts."

"Why, thank you," she beamed. "How about some coffee, and...?" she added suggestively.

"And what?" Gerald chuckled as he set his beer aside and descended the ladder into the main salon.

Allie watched the rise in his emotions showing in his swimsuit as he approached her. She felt goose bumps again, all over, like a child in puberty. "God," she said. "I hope this paradise never ends," she added as he reached around her to untie the bikini.

The next morning dawned as orange and blue as was ever described in all the tour and travel brochures ever printed.

Gerald, the old salt, cooked the first breakfast at sea.

Then Allie, with energy renewed by food, delayed the anchor weighing long enough to satisfy another hunger.

By mind-morning they were again citizens of the sea. Gerald started the four cylinder diesel engine and gave the wheel to Allie as he walked forward to retrieve the anchor.

He landed the anchor with ease, and glanced into the water. There was something there that attracted his attention. Still standing on the bow, he directed Allie to motor forward slowly. There was something on the sandy bottom. "Come ahead just a bit farther," he called, looking down through the water. He peered closely at the sight, then whistled.

Below him, in less than twenty feet of water, beside a coral ledge, was a powerboat.

On closer inspection the powerboat looked as though it had not been under the water for very long. Some drifting sand formed rivulets across the deck, stirred up by a passing shark. Nothing was yet growing on it, as would have been the case with anything that had been in the Caribbean water for more than a month.

"It's a high speed ocean racing powerboat," Gerald commented to Allie as she came forward to look. "It has three inboard-outboard drives. Just like the type used in the Miami to Nassau races held yearly off Florida."

"It must have had trouble at some time," Allie said.

"Maybe," Gerald said. "I can't imagine it just being left where it sank."

"Maybe it was stolen," Allie suggested, turning her attention back to their now idly drifting sailboat. "Maybe we better mark this spot on our chart so we can report it when we get back."

"Good idea," Gerald agreed, reluctantly returning to the cabin to mark the chart.

In the mean time, Allie motored out to the open sea,

and it wasn't long before Gerald was again whistling, immersed in the joy of the Caribbean freshness and the excitement felt by anyone who has ever sailed a warm weather passage.

The day passed to near its zenith, and the boat had all three sails set full-and-by before Allie noticed another boat in the distance.

"See that? Over there!" she called to Gerald. "That boat. I've been watching it for about a half hour, and it hasn't moved."

Gerald peered in the direction she pointed, then got a pair of binoculars. He trained them on the older fishing trawler that was floating aimlessly just inside the horizon. "They have an American flag flying upside down on the cabin mast," he said. "That means distress."

"You mean they're in trouble?" Allie asked. "We have to help them if they are."

"I'm not so sure," Gerald responded pensively. "Remember what the chartering people told us? Don't be too anxious to help another boat. It might not really be in any trouble, and the people on board might have something else in mind than a need for being rescued."

"Well, it wouldn't hurt to just get a little closer to them, to get a better look, would it?"

"I suppose not," Gerald answered. "Better trim in and head in their direction. We can at least check on them. Better start the engine, too. It will give us better control, if we need it."

The sails were trimmed in and the engine was started. With the help of the mechanical wind they cautiously motor-sailed over to render aid.

"That looks like a woman on deck," Allie said when they got closer. "She's waiving her arms. What's that mean?"

"That's the international distress signal for boats without any radio."

"We are going to help, aren't we?" Allie made the question sound more like a demand.

"I guess, if we have to," Gerald relented, turning their craft to head directly for the trawler, pushing the engine throttle forward some more to give them greater headway as they pointed higher into the wind.

They came within hailing distance and Gerald studied the trawler. "La Cucaracha?" He read the name on the bow. "Something's not right here," he added on further study. "That woman on top of the cabin looks more like a man..."

"Oh, my God!" Allie exclaimed, as she came to the same conclusion. "You're right!"

"Why is he up on deck doing the signaling when there are two men in the wheel house?" Gerald asked. "I don't like this," he added as he throttled back the engine.

A man with long black hair and a mustache that flowed over his mouth, stepped around from behind the wheelhouse with an automatic rifle. He fired a short burst in the direction of the Westsail, just clearing the mainsail.

"Heave to!" Someone shouted the demand from the loudspeaker on the phony distressed trawler.

"Jesus!" Gerald yelled as he spun the wheel. " Pirates! We have to get the hell out of here!"

Allie reached for the sheets to pay off so they could sail away from the trap.

"Heave to now!" Came the second order. "Heave to, or we shoot!"

"Duck!" Gerald shouted to Allie.

Those were his last words. A second burst of gunfire caught him in the chest. The impact threw him over the rail into the water.

"Gerald!" Allie screamed as she ran to the boat's side. Hysteria sent icy chills through her. She reached over the rail in a futile attempt to grab Gerald, now face down in the water, drifting away.

The trawler pulled alongside the sailboat. Three men stepped up to the gunwale carrying grappling hooks, and lashed the boats together.

The captain emerged from the trawler cabin carrying a half-full bottle of whiskey. He tipped the bottle to his lips, and leaned his head back to take a deep swallow from it, baring his bulging belly under his diesel stained T-shirt.

He wiped his mouth on the back of his arm, and leered at Allie. He tossed the whiskey bottle into the sea while grinning broadly at his helpless victim. Her screams excited him as he climbed over the gunwale onto the sailboat's decks. He laughed, thinking of the pleasure he would get from this woman.

Allie's last consciousness was of two rough hands grasping her about her waist, throwing her to the deck.

Chapter 2

"It's what? I thought you dudes said you were going to rent a truck for this caper? You gotta be out of your ever lovin' minds to rip off a rental truck! Man, the first cop we pass is gonna pick us off. Shit, man. Why don't you hang a sign on the back sayin', 'Hey! We stole this. Here it is!' A stolen rental truck? Man!"

"Cool it, will you, Hauke? Nobody's going to know this truck's hot. There's gotta be a thousand U-Hauls in this city, and they all look alike. That be the beauty of it, Man. They ain't even going to miss it for two, three days. I got it from the storage yard. Nobody goes there for days at a time, and that's just for when they run out of trucks at the office. Like I say, that be the beauty of it. Besides, we don't look no different'n any dudes changing pads. Ain't that right, Carl?"

"Right on!" Carl said. "We be just a couple a bloods moving 'cross town. Yeah, just a couple a bloods and one honky, all squeezed into the front of this van hoping to make a little easy money. Like I say to the man, if he stops us. I say, 'No, Ossifer, I ain't knowed this hyar truck warn't got by no rights. No, Suh. Me and Josh and Hauke, hyar, we thunk it was all nice and legal like. Yassuh, Massa Policemans, Suh. Yas, Suh! And 'sides, Suh, that's why this hyar piece is hyar. Jes' to show yuh how as we's gonna make it all work like as how it's 'sposed to, Suh. And here: Bang! Bang!' That's what I say to any fuzz tryin' to stop us, man. Then what happens? There's one less muthah fuckin' cop to give us a hard time, that's what."

"Carl You jiving me?" Josh asked. "Tell me you don't

got no piece with you. I told you this has gotta be a clean job. Quick in and quick out. No fucking around, and no shootin', man!"

"Look, Josh," Carl retorted. "I don't go nowhere without my piece, man. I ain't going to be throwed in no slammer. Not me! If I got to, I'm gonna fight my way out. man, just take one shot at a cop and he craps his pants. And while he's worried about the mess, you make it out the back."

"Hold on a minute, Carl!" Interrupted Hauke. "Josh's right. There's no way I want to get caught in this job with you ready to blow away a cop. No way can I get messed up with a dude like you. That's all I need, burglary, assault with a deadly weapon, murder! man, they're the hardest raps to do time for. There ain't no way I want any part of this if you're gonna burn a cop. You can let me out at the next corner, Josh, and I don't know nothing about nothing, hear?"

"What's the matter, White Nigger?" Carl taunted Hauke. "You scared? You jive us bloods in the daytime, trick our bitches at night, but you got no guts for a good gig? You yellow, man?"

"Easy, Sucker," Hauke bristled. "You go easy. You don't be making noises like that with me. I'll show you where to put that fucking piece."

"Okay! Okay!" Josh shouted. "You two got to quit hassling. Either we do it, or we don't. Sheeeeit, man!" He slammed his fist against the truck's steering wheel. "I go through the trouble of setting up this God damn sweet job, and you two are going to blow it. You're going to blow it right down the tubes. And why? 'Cause you're nothing but a bunch of jive-ass dudes, that's why."

"Carl!" Josh continued. "I'm saying this one time. You keep that piece in your pocket. I ain't gonna be no part of no murder rap, neither. You hear?"

He turned his head back to the street. "Hauke," he

went on. “You just cool down, man. Carl don't mean nothing. He just gets edgy, know what I mean? He don't mean nothing by it. We just play it cool, nice and easy, like I said. We walk in the back door, and out again with the goods, and drive off. Nobody catches on, no hassles. Somebody see us, they think we're just shucking for the man, dig? Nobody's gonna stop us, nobody’s gonna to ask questions. Like I said, that be the beauty of it.”

Fucking great! Hauke thought. How in hell did I get into this screwed up plan? Two dudes so coked up most of the time they don't know if they're coming or going, and I got to be mixed up with them on a job like this. If I'd a known they were this stupid.... He let the sentence drop. Ah, what the hell? It's easy bread, I guess, but Josh's right about one thing. Nobody's gonna get hurt on this job. We get busted,? First thing I do is jam that piece of Carl's down his mutha throat. A little rip off is all right, but man, burning people ain't my style.

“This is it,” Josh said as he turned into a quiet street in a residential area. “The yellow house on the corner. I'll back up the driveway and open the rear doors. You two go around to the back of the house, like I said, and look for the key on top of the gas meter. Inside, one of you go for the front room for stuff that’ll be easy fencing. The other look in the kitchen for silver and stuff. Just take things one dude can carry, unless there’s some big antiques that maybe we can take the chance with, and two of us can carry’em. I'll take the bedroom. Two trips, maybe three, each, in and out, and we split. Make it cool! Don't take more'n twenty, thirty minutes, on the outside.”

Josh finished his orders as he backed the van into the driveway.

* * * * *

Lawrence Lattimer was sitting in the front room of his house directly across the street from the yellow house, reading his daily San Francisco Chronicle. He glanced out his window and noted the truck being backed into his neighbor's driveway. "Martha!" he called to his wife. "Come here for a minute, will you? Look at Parrish's place across the street. Aren't they on vacation?"

"They left on Wednesday, I think. Why?" Martha answered as she entered the room, wiping potting soil from her hands onto her smock.

"Then what's that U-Haul truck doing in their driveway? Three men just got out of it." He watched the activity. "Look at that! They parked in the driveway and walked right around into the rear yard, like they were doing something they're supposed to do."

"Well, maybe George Parrish wanted some work done while they were away, or something," was Martha's evaluation, tending to cast aside a problem with a solution she thought too obvious.

"I wonder," continued Lawrence. "Doesn't it seem strange to you that George would have strangers in his house while he was away? Two black men, at that. You know George. He's worse than Archie Bunker. I have a bad feeling about all this. Get me the phone. I think this should be reported, especially with all the burglaries that have been happening around here lately."

* * * * *

"Damn it!" cried Hauke. "Two cops just pulled around the corner. I told you dudes this was a bad gig!" Damn, he added under his breath. With me standing right here at the side of the truck. Jeeesus! There's gotta be a way out. Maybe I can get around to the front and to the sidewalk before they get too close. I can tell them I don't know nothing about this gig. He stepped away from the truck.

That was when he saw Josh running. "Hey" he yelled. "Where the fuck're you running to?" He looked back at the cop car. Damn, he said again under his breath. That cop car's faster'n I thought.

Josh never made it as far as the sidewalk before the

police were out of the car.

Hauke saw one cop start chasing Josh. Good! I hope he catches the mutha', he added, sneaking around the rear of the truck. Maybe I can make it across the back yard and over the fence.

He stopped. Hey? There's Carl. What's he up to, jumping back behind the corner of the house like that? Jesus! He's got his gun out! He's gonna shoot that cop! Shit! I gotta stop him! I gotta get to that cop before Carl gets a bead on him.

He raced toward the cop. He lunged, hitting him with a full running tackle. "Look out! He's got a gun!" he shouted.

BAHWAM!

Hauke saw the side flash from Carl's .44 Magnum as he and the cop went head over heels down the driveway, just under the whining bullet. "Jesus! That was close," he complained, conscious of the ringing in his ears. "That God damn cannon! man, if the slug don't get you, the fucking noise will!"

He sat up as the cop scrambled to stand over him. Now you've done it, he said to himself. You blew your only chance to make it out of here, no one ever knowing you were mixed up in this shit. But no! You had to go and play hero. What the fuck are you doing, anyway? You could have let Carl smoke the cop, could have gotten out, and nobody'd know. He shook his head, trying to wring out the ringing. Hell. Who are you trying to kid, Hauke, you stupid bastard? You ain't ever smoked nobody yet, and nobody ever gets smoked when you work a gig, remember? Not even the cops. Hell, Slammersville, here I come, again, I guess.

* * * * *

Bob Miller's secretary opened her boss's office door, and with an apologetic expression, stuck her head inside. "Mr. Miller?" she said, "There's a man in the outer office that says his name is...is..." She let her voice trail off in confusion.

"Yes?" responded Bob Miller gently, seated at his desk. "Yes?" he asked again, with stronger emphasis, noting her lack of confidence.

"A Mr. Bear? Mr. Mikel Bear?" The name seemed to confuse her. "Yes," she said at length, reassuring herself. "Mr. Mikel Bear."

"Un-hunh," Bob Miller said. "And just what shall we do with Mr. Bear?"

"Oh," she blushed. She caught herself, suddenly realizing what was expected of her. "Of course! I'll show him right in."

Mikel Bear, often called Bear, depending on which side of his disposition you happened to be on at the moment, looked around the outer office. "Crap," he muttered as he made a careful assessment of the office and its furnishings. "Some nice office for a state employee. No wonder taxes are so damn high." He paused. "For those that are dumb enough to pay taxes, that is," he chuckled.

He scanned the office some more in idle curiosity. And that secretary, he continued. That mouth, and smile! I bet I know how she keeps her job.

His obtrusive cynicism dominated his thoughts; his cynicism which decimated his respect for people. But, oddly enough, that very cynicism supported his overwhelming charisma. It was a perverse charisma that attracted the less accomplished man on whose plane he could feel superior, and therefore comfortable. It also attracted the attention of those men in the most responsible positions who often got themselves into the problems that his expertise as a private investigator could resolve.

Just what in hell would a man of Bob Miller's reputation want with a P.I., Bear asked himself. I'm supposed to help put the bad asses in the jails around this state, not worry about them after they get out. That's the job of the specialists like Bob Miller. They're the Parole Department. They're the specialists. Specialists? The thought amused him. Specialists in failure! The whole damn parole system is nothing but an expensive failure.

That was as far as he got with his thoughts before the door behind the secretary's desk opened. In the middle of the doorway stood the secretary, beckoning him to enter the inner sanctum of the parole office.

Don't you wish she was beckoning to you like that for other reasons, he chuckled to himself as he strode past her. His amusement was heightened by the added consternation his self-satisfied grin caused her.

The secretary shut the door, leaving Mikel facing the man who he considered was probably the most successful parole officer in the State of California. That can't be saying too much, though, he considered.

"Glad you could come," said the graying father figure. "I'll get to the point. There's a particular problem I want to talk to you about. It's one that I think is just too far out of my style to do anything with. That's why I need a man of your reputation to handle the job I have in mind; a man with your ability to get things done, an ability to mold circumstances, so to speak, and people."

"Well," responded Mikel, sitting in the chair facing the desk. "Your opening statement sure as hell makes me sit up and take notice. Now that you've given out the honey, where's the vinegar?Who do you want me to help you control?"

Bob Miller frowned. He reached for his faux Meerschaum pipe from a stand on the desk in front of him. "The vinegar, as you call it," he began, tamping some tobacco down in the pipe, "is this: The man's name is Beaulleiu. Mantee Hauke Beaulleiu. He goes by his middle name, Hauke. He's 26 years old, and has already spent eleven of those 26 years behind bars for one crime or another. One of the unusual things about him is that he has completely rejected the white race. He's white, but he walks, talks, and totally acts like a black man."

"A nigger," Bear rudely interjected.

The parole officer's gaze showed his disdain for the term. "Like a nigger, if you prefer," he said. "But he's white. He was raised with blacks, and he went to school with blacks. That is, through the first two years of high school before he quit. His mannerisms are totally those typically characteristic of the stylized black sociology. He possesses a perfect example of what you would call black worship. As a matter of fact, whenever there is a mixing of the two races, you will find Hauke standing up with, and for, the black people." The parole officer completed his remarks and struck a match to light his pipe. "Not that I'm trying to say that black is bad," he quickly added.

"Black is beautiful. Ain't you heard?" Bear said with sarcasm.

"Uh. Yes. The problem is, these particular black people that are his peers are the criminal type. They're no Martin Luther Kings. They're the kind who hate the idea of authority, and totally reject it, fight it. They have no sense of decency, no respect for anyone, not even themselves. Hauke copies their mannerisms, their style, and joins most of their activities just to display his particular brand of rejection for authority. And, I should add, to gain recognition for his own peculiar ego. Then, as a result, those peer pressures force him into situations where he meets trouble."

"Yeah. I heard it before. The same old story. My boy ain't bad, it's just the company he keeps. Come on. There must be more to this problem, as you call it, then the fact that this guy loves black people."

"Look, Mr. Bear," the parole officer said. He was losing his temper. "If you have any reservations about taking this job because of the man's social preferences, then we might as well forget the whole damn operation. I don't care for your racism."

Mikel Bear smiled. He knew he had gotten though to this man. He now had control of the conversation. "Reservations?" he said. "Social preferences? What the hell are you talking about? If he had the proper social preferences in the first place, he wouldn't be where he is now, would he? And I wouldn't be here having my time wasted with bull bleep about the excuses for his crimes. Now, let's get one thing straight. If I'm going to do a job for you, I want the facts, clear and simple. I couldn't care less if the guy is black, yellow, white, blue or green. He is what he is. A nigger is a nigger, and a honky is a honky. There's no derogation in either term, understand?"

The parole officer relaxed and leaned back in his chair. Again he tried to light his pipe. It seemed to be the plague of all pipe smokers that their pipes never stayed lit. His was no exception. "I have to admit, when you were recommended I was warned you had a way of taking charge. I think you just put me in the place you wanted me. For some reason, though, I don't feel offended. I feel as though I just let go of the tiger's tail without being bitten."

"I'd have to call that a compliment," Mikel said with a satisfied grin. "Okay. You told me one of the several unusual things about Mr. Hauke. What are the others? You gave me a name, now give me the facts behind the name. What was he sent up for? What are his priors? Why is this problem one you can't handle, and why, for Christ sakes, do you think that, as an investigator, I can be a hand holder for someone I don't even know?"

Bob Miller lit yet another match to hold over his seemingly non-burnable pipe tobacco. He took another puff to keep the mixture glowing, then continued his story.

"First, I want you to take an interest in this case

because I've been told you have a reputation for getting things done. When you agree to do them, that is. Secondly, because of Mr. Hauke." Bob Miller began the tale.

Bear listened to the typical tale of background circumstances. This time there were a few points of interest that cornered his attention, like the way Hauke never caused physical harm to any of his victims in all the petty, and felony, crimes he committed. And how, although often extensively interrogated, he never revealed the names of those who were suspected to have been with him.

Bear listened to the entire tale of the childhood background of a mother who didn't know who the father of the boy was. How the mother was selling herself to support her lover, and her lover's habit, when she conceived the child. The real surprise, he thought, was how Hauke's mother managed to impart any speck of decency in the man. Hell, no wonder he only associated with bums. He never knew any other types.

"But that doesn't explain the rejection of his race," Mikel said as he tuned back in on the recitation. The officer was just coming to the answer for that particular question.

"It's my belief," the officer said, in an attempt to emphasize his point, "that Hauke has never had any examples, or role models of a decent person, or of what a decent person is. He has never had a role model of honorable character with which to identify. Most of his concepts of right and wrong seem to lie somewhere in the realm of those common to the questioning development seen in teenagers from fifteen to seventeen. As for his rejection of whites, that, I think, is related to the fact that since he didn't know who his father was, and had no earthly way of finding out who it might be. He felt it easier to reject that hurt by rejecting anything that made him think of his father. Ergo, whites, and all models of white behavioral patterns."

"As for his priors," the officer continued after a short puff and resultant pause. "You can take a look at his rap sheet, if you want to, later. His last arrest was when he was caught with two black men burglarizing a home out in the avenues. One of the other men pulled a gun, and Hauke saved the life of one of the arresting officers by tackling the officer before the gun went off. The judge saw that as a sign of some redeeming social value, and had the charge reduced to Criminal Trespassing."

"Criminal Trespassing? Just what the hell is that?"

"Being where you aren't supposed to be, for the purpose of committing a crime. Anyway, he drew a three year probation, in spite of his priors."

"And you need someone to help this poor little kid, right? Is that where I come in?"

"Not quite yet. Just as Hauke was on his way to report here for his first parole interview, he was intercepted by one of the sergeants of the city police department, who has to remain nameless, and asked to do something to help the local police combat the pushers working the Hallidae Plaza area. He agreed, but why he agreed is somewhat of a mystery."

"Not really, if what you say about him is true. I'll bet the sergeant was that overzealous new transferee, McIvers."

Bob Miller let the question of McIvers' name pass. "But what ever the reason, he agreed to lend a hand by setting himself up as an undercover buyer..."

"A snitch."

"I believe that's the term. He agreed to become a snitch for the sergeant, and talked the sergeant out of some small time money, about five hundred dollars, to make the opening buy of some marijuana from one of the pushers in the area."

"Don't tell me. I can fill in the details myself. The cop gave the snitch the dough, and he disappeared. Right? Or, better yet, the snitch talked some of his buddies out of a joint or two, which he then gave to the sergeant as a come on, along with a phony name and address of the seller. Right?"

"So far you've shown me that you're every bit as smart as they say you are," the parole officer said with a weak smile. "That's almost the way it happened."

"That cop deserved to be taken. Nobody should be stupid enough to give a snitch enough money for an unsupervised buy. So, again, where do I come in?"

"There's a little more to the story," Bob Miller said as he again lit his pipe. "In the process of giving the sergeant the phony name, Hauke talked him out of another five hundred. To make the deal tighter, I believe was the phrase. Then he disappeared, ah, split."

Mikel grinned. "Now you're beginning to sound like me, using my language. So he split. Now the sergeant is madder than a creosoted cat, and swears the next time he lays eyes on the snitch he's going to bust him, or worse, smoke him, even if he has to use a drop gun to do it. Right?"

"That, I'm afraid, is right. Except that I don't think the word smoking was part of his expression," the officer conceded.

"So, I'm to take this snitch and keep him out of sight for a while, 'til the cop cools off. Right again?"

"Within reason. I want you to fulfill my functions on this one case as a parole officer. To protect Hauke, and to supervise his activities as any other parolee, but with the special sanction of the Adult Authority, in an area completely away from any possibility of his being found by Sergeant McI...er, what's his name, if possible. And for that, the state will take care of your fee."

Mikel 's plan was quickly formed. "Nope. No deal," he

said as he took a cigarette from his pocket and lit it, appreciating the fact that he wasn't a pipe smoker. At least with cigarettes, he joked with himself, you don't have to work so hard to get lung cancer. He quickly took a pack of Viceroys out of his pocket, extracted one from the pack, popped it into his mouth, and lit it, borrowing matches from Bob Miller's desk.

"What? Why?" responded the parole officer, surprised by the Bear's refusal.

"Because, I'm not a parole officer. As a matter of fact, as far as I'm concerned, the entire parole board and their system is lousy. The parole system, the way it is now, won't work. It hasn't yet, and it never will."

"Why is that?"

"Why? Because, you take a man out of his environment, which was bad enough to begin with to get him into trouble, and you send him up for a couple of years in an environment one hell of a lot worse, full of hardened criminals. Then you get him out of the slammer on parole, and put him right back into his original environment, but now as a much more hardened man. The only possible end result of that is to create another situation worse than the first one. Then, zap! Right back into the slammer again for the next round of fun and games. It's an endless cycle. You specialists, and I use the term loosely, should have been able to figure that out by now. But then, since you spend more time studying your psychology and sociology books than in studying people and the real world, I suppose it's no surprise that the answer escapes you." He paused long enough to take a puff on his cigarette. "Another thing that stinks about the system is the way it's funded. The money given the parole system is based on how many men it has out on parole in any given district at any given time. That's wrong! That's an incentive to let people out on parole according to numbers, not according to the person. Financing should be based on how many parolees get back into society successfully. By the number of parolees who break the chain, not by those who perpetuate it. And another thing, get some God damn parole officers who have had some experience on the streets, someone who knows the type of people they're dealing with. Four or five years in college and a degree in something as ridiculous as Sociology doesn't mean a damn thing without the reality of seeing the world."

Bear took the last puff on his burning weed before continuing. "If you want me to help this guy Hauke, then I'll do it my way, without your system, and I'll give you back a man who is proud to be a man." Mikel wondered if this story would be believed. He considered that the sentimentality might be a bit much. He didn't particularly need to be stuck with someone he didn't know, and be held responsible for his rehabilitation, but the fact that the state was going to pay his fee meant that his fee could be just about any damn amount he wanted it to be. That part he liked.

"You'll turn him around?"

"I'll turn him around," Mikel affirmed. "Assuming, of course, that you know where to find him?"

"I have my secrets."

"You gonna let me in on'em?"

"Actually, Hauke called me yesterday. He asked what I thought he should do."

"And?"

"I took the liberty of giving him your telephone number at the time. I told him to call you this evening."

"That's a bit presumptuous, ain't it?"

"I, too, must know the people I deal with, Mr. Bear. I believed, quite correctly so, it would seem, that you would jump at the chance presented here."

"Quite rightly so," the Bear said, realizing the game had been played. He got up. "I'll be in touch," he said. He snuffed out his cigarette on the desk ashtray, and left the room.

The parole officer smiled, nodded his good-bye without getting up, and returned to the task of lighting his pipe.

Mikel gave the secretary another leer as he exited the office.

I wonder, he muttered to himself as he approached the elevator, why having been given an opportunity to control a man like this guy Hauke makes me feel as though the fox has been given the key to the hen house? Hauke is just the man I need to help me run things down in Belize.

He grinned as he began his ride down. "Now to see a certain sergeant in the good old SFPD," he said to the elevator walls. "But not for a few days," he added.

Three days later Mikel strutted between officers engaged in typical vice squad work in the San Francisco Police Vice Squad Operations room.

He laughed at what the captain would have to say if it was known that he was virtually harboring the man who had made such a fool out of one of his department's sergeants. "But, then," he mused. "I doubt if Captain Giddings even knew about the farce played out between Hauke and McIvers."

Mikel was right in guessing that the sergeant had done his damnedest to squelch that story before it got too widely known. Mikel 's contacts in the department had supported his guess.

"Sure. You can use my office to talk with Sergeant McIvers, if you want," the captain said to Mikel. "Lord knows, I owe you bigger favors than that. I got the feeling that this meeting between you and McIvers is going to end up with my owing you another favor, right?"

"Just might be," replied Bear. He knew that was the way to keep himself in the clear, by keeping the local police owing him favors. He used his position as an investigator to work both sides of the fence to his greatest advantage. "If they only knew," he often said to himself.

After a few minutes the sergeant entered the small office and glared at Mikel who was seated in the captain's swivel chair, his feet up on the captain's desk. His greeting showed some of the professional jealousy he felt. "Well, well, well. Mr. Bear," he said. "What's a hot shot in the drug busting game have to say to a little man like me?"

Mikel ignored the sarcastic reference to his operations as a part time confidential informant for the DEA. "I can say," he responded, "that the love lost between us isn't going to be dispelled by wasted amenities. So, I'll give it to you straight. A few weeks ago you were taken for a couple hundred bucks by a small time kid just out on probation."

"So? How'd you know about that?"

"It's my business to know things," retorted the Bear. "And I know a lot more."

"Like what?"

"Like how you bragged to a few of your friends that you'd give anything to put that man back in the slammer. You still feel that way?"

"What's it to you?"

"If you still feel that way, then it's nothing to me, and I don't have anything more to say to you. But, if you can swallow your pride, then I can put you in a good position for those lieutenant's bars you've wanted for so long, and you won't owe me anything for the help."

The sergeant stared at Mikel. He wasn't sure he heard correctly. It was obvious that the part about not wanting anything in return was pure bull, but the risk might be worth it. "And why would you do this for me?" he asked as he finally sat in the oak chair across from the captain's desk. "I've never shown you any special consideration."

Bear smiled inwardly before answering. "Because I know enough about this department to know you're one of the hardest working cops in town," he responded. "I know that your lateral transfer from Homicide to Vice kept you out of the promotions slot. And I know that's been causing you a lot of frustration, which, I think, was directed at, shall we say, one of my clients."

"Hauke is one of your clients?" the sergeant asked with surprise. He stared at the presumptuous and officious Mikel Bear. He considered his position, his options. "Okay," he said at length. "I know your reputation. You have enough pull around here, so maybe I can vent my anger with that two bit chiseler in some other direction. What's your deal?"

Perfect, thought Bear. He knew the man could be netted. All that was needed was to play the line the right way, using the right bait.

Mikel began reciting the rehearsed scenario. He related a story of how he discovered a coke dealing ring that had strong connections with the Russian River S & M activities scene. He recited events pointing to the step in his investigations which involved the need for a scam, a sting type scam that would bring all the forces of an alleged international sex, drug, and violence ring into play. Every detail was laid out for a certain vice officer to rope in, thereby making a national name for himself, to say nothing of having cut the cancerous aberration from society's core.

Jesus, Mikel thought as he finished his recitation. If that's not enough for this cop, nothing will be. Of course, he left out certain details of the plan, details that he didn't want the sergeant to know. The sergeant's knowing about them just might interrupt them. Mikel didn't want that to happen.

"What I need from you," Mikel continued. "At this point, at least, is all the information you have in your files concerning the Russian River resort area pornography producers, the S & M murder cases, and the files concerning our fair city's most famous porno actress, Marena, and her associations with Manny Bolton."

"Manny Bolton, the artist?" the sergeant asked in surprise.

"The one and same," Mikel answered. "Also her association with a certain private investigator named Elzee Taylor. And, come to think of it, while you're looking, check for anything that might associate either of them with the disappearance of Kerry Kevins, or with the Kollin Kevins Foundation."

"Christ!" the sergeant said. "You might just as well ask for the complete file section of the department. Some of that information relates to still active police work, you know."

"Of course I know that. That's why this is so big. Big enough to almost get you your own department, not just your lieutenant's bars." Lay it on thick, thought Mikel.

"The Russian River S & M case files?"

"Got to have them, too."

"Well," the sergeant shrugged. "I guess if it gets us what we want, and manages to solve that mess, too, then nothing would be hurt by letting you see those files."

"Deal?"

"Deal. When?"

"I'll get in touch with you. Just get the copies as soon as possible. Maybe as early as next week."

With a nod, the sergeant got up and walked out of the office, leaving the glass panel door open.

"Everything as good as you hoped?" Captain Giddings asked as he returned to his small office.

Mikel was just getting up from the comfortable chair. "I think I'll get a chair like that for my office." He said, avoiding the question, offering a friendly wink on his way out, instead

Chapter 3

Penn Gwinn wrapped his legs around the barstool and ran his hand through his thinning blonde hair. He finished the gesture with an absent minded stroke of his well trimmed blonde beard.

"Damn it, but I hate funerals," he said to PZ on the adjacent stool as he readjusted his 190 pounds on the cushion. His five foot nine inch frame was well muscled, and it never seemed to fit a barstool comfortably, in spite of the many hours he spent on one.

PZ nodded his agreement, shaking his curly black hair out of his eyes in his usual fashion.

Penn glanced at PZ and forced a wry smile. PZ was an enigma. His hair always seemed to look like the infamous Pig Pen in the Peanuts comic strip. No sooner would he comb it then it would be back in scattered disarray, almost as though it was planned that way.

PZ was an enigma in other ways, too. He wasn't the educated, suave, yet macho, type investigator of television fantasy. He was much more of a street person type. He was a hustler, a person who could play the streets, who knew where and how to get along in that environment.

Not too surprising, Penn mused. PZ was practically raised on the streets of New York before coming to California in his late teens. Penn took another sip from his drink. That certainly is in contrast to me. You'd think I would know him by now, but that's hardly so. Six years; for six years we've been partners. I guess you really never get to know your friends. Penn took another sip from his drink. He's a good investigator, though. In spite of his penchant for booze and for smoking pot now and then;

maybe a snort or two of coke, too. But that's the way he is, I guess. He's just an enigma.

Then, I'm sort of an enigma, too. Maybe I don't really know myself as well as I thought. If I did, why would I put up with a partner who is so much into the sleazy side of life?

"I suppose you know," Penn said to PZ, returning to their discussion. "Now we're going to have to find the son of a bitch who killed him."

PZ frowned, but didn't reply. Instead, he called to the bartender, "Hey, Sue. Give us another fuckin' round, unh?"

Sue, the bartender, nodded in recognition and mixed another two drinks. A Myers's Rum straight up with a squeeze of lime for Penn, and a Black Russian for PZ. Those were the favorite drinks of the two from the Flyin' Penguin Detective Agency, and today they needed something to dilute their sorrows. They had just attended a friend's funeral, and that was why Sue mixed the drinks a lot stronger than the bar's owner, Sam 'The man' Chivano, allowed.

Penn gazed at his drink for several minutes in silence, then re-squeezed the lime. More to break the mood than for any other reason, he offered PZ a challenge. "I'll bet you dollar you can't spell the name of the rum she makes my drinks with," he said.

PZ looked up. "Fuck you mean? The rum she puts in your drink?" He asked. "You got a bet," he added, sliding a dollar from his change on the bar over toward Penn.

"I'll even give you three tries," Penn said, picking up the dollar.

"Hey! You ain't won yet," PZ cautioned. "M-Y-E-R-'-S," he said.

"That's one," Penn smiled.

PZ glanced at him. "Oh. Yeah. M-E-Y-E-R-S," he re-spelled.

"That's two," Penn grinned.

PZ looked pensive for another moment or two. 'M-A-Y-A-E-R- fuckin' apostrophe S," he said, less confident.

"My dollar," Penn chuckled. "It's M-Y-E-R-S-apostrophe - S," he spelled. "That's S apostrophe. Ask Sue for the bottle if you don't believe me. It's one of the few words in the English language that has an S followed by an apostrophe and another S. It's a good bar bet."

"Fuckin' chicken bet," PZ concluded.

"Aren't all bar bets chicken bets?"

"When you fuckin' lose, they are." PZ responded.

Several long minutes of silence ensued, broken only by an occasional blaring of the mechanical voice of the automatic jukebox demanding someone play some more music.

Someone finally obeyed by plugging some quarters into the machine and the noise it belched stirred Penn to speak. "Markham was a good investigator," he said.

PZ again nodded as he sipped his drink.

"The police haven't gotten anywhere," Penn added between sips, expressing his disappointment with the progress in finding the killer.

"Well, Captain Giddings is good, and I know he's your friend and all that," PZ said. "But I don't think he's got what it takes to solve this one."

It was Penn's turn to nod in agreement. He lifted his head from the drink, and let his eyes roam about the bar until they rested on Sue, behind the chrome and Formica counter. He watched her reflection in the back bar mirrors, an image fragmented by the stems of the many glasses stacked on the shelves. Her movements played across the glasses, bouncing back and forth from mirror to glass as she efficiently mixed and served the drink orders.

Sam Chivano was a fan of Don Johnson of Miami Vice fame, and his devotion to the program that played out its repetitious melodrama every Friday night on the television sets of the nation showed in the bar's decor.

Only, Sam's version of the pink and blue color scheme seemed grotesquely depressing to Penn for such an afternoon. To him the colors were glaring in spite of the smoky haze that permeated the room, a haze generated by the sticks of pseudo-sophistication held between brown stained fingers of the patrons.

"Who the hell would want to put a .45 slug through Markham's head, anyway," Penn asked gloomily, returning to the topic after the third sip from his drink. He savored the flavor of the rich brown liquid for several seconds before swallowing. "And why?" he added. "What the hell's the motive?"

"Maybe he was working on somethin' too fuckin' big for 'im," PZ suggested.

Penn grunted his agreement. "That's obvious. Only it's hard to believe. He's no two-bit gumshoe. Or wasn't, anyway. He knew his way around. The only way I can figure that someone got to him was that whoever did it was a friend, or someone he knew, at least, and didn't think was a danger."

It was PZ's turn to grunt an agreement, although he didn't show much enthusiasm with his effort.

The color, the noise, the haze and the bumpa rumpa rhythm of the 50's style music from the jukebox mixed together in Penn's mind like a nightmare. "Let's get out of here," he said at length, showing his melancholy mood. "If we don't do something about Markham's murder, and do it now, we're not going to be able to call ourselves detectives anymore."

"How'd I know you'd say that?" PZ commented. "Don't you think we oughta get some idea of where we're going before we go?"

Penn had no quick and easy answer. He subverted hisfrustration by glancing at the blonde woman in the nearby booth. He watched the way her peroxided hair bounced about her shoulders as she laughed with her companion, her suitor, the guy who had been feeding her drinks for the last hour. He flashed on the question of how long it was going to take for the greasy looking character to hustle her full enough of Gin Rickeys to twist her sober objections into drunken compliance.

He shook his head. "Your favorite blonde is back," he said to PZ, as though changing the subject might offer some clues to where they should start their investigation.

PZ glanced at the blonde. "Yeah," he responded. "Canal carp."

"Canal carp?" Penn asked.

"Yeah. She lives on Canal Street. Nothing down there but trash." He emphasized his rejection of the woman by taking another sip of his drink without another glance in her direction.

"Marena," Penn said without explaining what was to him an idea of inspiration. "Marena Bloeswell."

"Marena?" PZ was surprised by the unexpected mention of her name. "What the fucka 'bout her?"

"That's where we start."

"Why her?"

"She was a good friend of Markham's, wasn't she? As a matter of fact, it seems to me that he was on his way to see her the last time we saw him."

"Yeah, but the cops checked her out already, remember?"

"They asked her a lot of questions, that's true. But if I know them, none of the questions were the right ones."

"So now you're better'n the cops?" PZ quipped.

Penn studied him. He was confused by the remark, but he let it pass. "Look," he said. "You know how much time Markham spent in the Mitchell Brother's theater. What the hell, maybe something he was working on rubbed off on her."

"More like the other way around," PZ said with

sarcasm.

"We should go through his files, too," Penn added.

"What're you gonna find the cops ain't found?"

"It's the same old thing, PZ. Damn it! They have to have missed something. Besides, they didn't know him the way we did. Maybe we can interpret those files in a different way."

"Worth a try," PZ said with a shrug. "But I still think it'd be a waste of time."

"There's one thing we should do first, though," Penn added. "We have to get some answers from Marena before we look though Markham's files."

"Hey, now. That could be fun," PZ perked up.

"Then finish your drink and let's get going," Penn directed. They passed through the glass doors of the dim lit bar into a sudden bright shaft of sunlight that streaked through a break in the rain clouds overhead. The thumpa thump of the jukebox faded into the distance as the doors closed.

"Maybe this is a good omen," Penn commented while looking at the sky, subconsciously quickening his pace as he headed for the parking lot. "Might as well take the Red Beast," he said as they approached his car. "It's my turn to drive, anyway."

"So? I'm gonna argue?" PZ said as he opened the passenger side door and plopped inside Penn's 1978 Pontiac, the two-door hardtop with the specially installed 454 cubic inch Trans-Am engine.

With a roar the overpowered car was maneuvered out of the parking lot, bound for San Francisco, with only a little slipping and sliding on the dampened streets.

* * * * *

Marena Bloeswell trotted out of the Mitchell Brother's Blue Movie Mansion, commonly known as the palace of porn, at the corner of Polk Street and Geary Boulevard in San Francisco. "God damn rain," she swore while she pulled her long overcoat tighter around her. She hadn't expected the sprinkling. She stepped off the curb and flagged down the first cab that passed. It turned out to be a Veteran's Cab.

"Thanks," she called to the driver after she got into the rear seat. "You guys sure are a lot better than that damn Yellow Cab Company."

The cab driver looked at her in his rear view mirror as he put his cab in gear. "Yeah? Why's that?" he asked.

"Did you know that they won't stop for you if you try to hail them on the God damn street corner? Something about a company rule of theirs that says they can't pick up a fare unless they're dispatched from Central, first. Damn bunch of twerps. Now you gotta have a damn appointment to get a cab. Everything's run by appointment now days, hunh? God damn it."

The cab driver cast another glance at his fare through his rear view mirror. He seemed amused by the sudden seemingly endless tirade, and when he got a full look at her, he was even more interested in her. "Jesus," he gasped. "You're..."

"Yeah. Marena, the famous porno actress. Don't that beat all?" She smiled at the driver, enjoying his awe of her. "But don't worry none. I'm not going to try to work out the fare, or nothing. I got the money to God damn pay you." She hoped the driver would see the suggestion in her challenge.

"Hey," he returned. "I don't mean that. I mean, can I have your autograph, or something? I saw your last flick three times, and man, it was hot."

"Yeah?" She was pleased. "You really saw it three God damn times?"

"Yeah."

"What part did you like the best?"

"Hey. I liked all of it the best. All of it that showed you, all of you, that is."

"Yeah?"

"Yeah."

"What else? I mean, any special part you liked the best?"

"Well, yeah. I really liked the part where you did that, sort of, well, you know, that strip in front of that priest. Where you got him all hot and bothered, you know? man, that was hot, what you did with yourself."

"That right? Well, maybe, if you liked it that God damn much, I could show you some more? Like some of the stuff they cut out of the movie? Maybe, no fare then, hunh?" She decided she was going to talk her way out of paying the fare, after all, since he had taken her suggestion.

"Yeah!" the driver responded with enthusiasm, his expectations showing through a missing tooth grin. "You damn betcha. Where you wanna go? For a good long look at you, you know what I mean? I'll take you anywhere in this God damn city."

The driver pulled the cab over to the curb in the first red zone he found, and turned to face the woman, making no effort to hide the awkwardness with which he unzipped his pants and grabbed himself.

Marena giggled, then laughed, and leaned back in the seat to open her coat. She had just left one of her nude dancing routines, and she had been in such a hurry that she hadn't the time, nor the inclination, to get fully dressed before leaving the theater. She wet her fingers, spread her legs, and began slowly massaging herself. She closed her eyes, tilted her head back, and giggled again. She enjoyed the scene she formed in her mind of the driver enjoying himself while watching her. It was exhilarating for her, exhibiting herself to a stranger on a busy downtown street.

Several minutes passed before the incessant horn honking by the short tempered driver of the municipal bus trying to get into the red curbed bus zone completed their escapades of self indulgence. The cab driver hurriedly wiped himself off, zipped up his fly, and put his cab into gear. He pulled away from the curb and yielded the space to the blue smoke belching motorized behemoth.

Marena hadn't finished, but she decided that wasn't so important at the moment. She would have time for satisfaction later. She sat up, pulled her coat around her again, and gave directions to be dropped off in front of the 2000 Filbert Street apartments at the top of Pacific Heights. Once there, she hopped out without so much as a follow up thank you to the cab driver for the ride.

"Good afternoon, ain't it?" she said in greeting the doorman. She gave him a friendly wink as she tossed her short cut platinum blonde hair with a flip of her head, and paced through the glass paned, brass trimmed doors into the foyer of the most expensive apartment building in San Francisco.

She hadn't time to luxuriate in the splendor of the surroundings, though. Elzee Taylor suddenly emerged from one of the building's three elevators and confronted her with a broad grin. He was dressed in his usual attire of jeans, brogans, chambray shirt, and a worn Navy aviator flight jacket fashionably mod in its outdatedness. It was the type of dress he always wore when he was heading for the Russian River area. She was glad she had hurried. He hated it when he had to wait for her.

"Hey, hey, Babe," he greeted her. "My car's being brought around. Shall we go?" He grabbed her elbow and escorted her back outside without waiting for her reply.

Marena smiled again at the doorman for opening the car door for her, and flashed a bit of her nakedness for his enjoyment in return. Then, as she got into the car and sat on the plush leather rear seat, she wondered how it was that Elzee always seemed to possess the right amount of assertiveness with casual gentleness to persuade her to do anything he wanted. Normally she would insist on being the dominant one in her relationships, but with Elzee things were different.

Elzee was different.

Elzee Taylor was the man she had become accustomed to, that she had become dependent upon, that she relied upon. He was the man who had introduced her to the big time. He was the man who had met her in the bus station three years ago when she was an aspiring novice in the world of show business. It was Elzee who had made her a name with almost international recognition in such a short time.

It was Elzee who talked her into doing pornography. She objected at first, but when she discovered the pleasures of showing herself to others, to men she didn't even know, to men who she could never even see. It excited her. She really got into it. She discovered that through the media of motion pictures and video tapes she could watch her own performances, and she could also watch the men as they eyed her movements with leering grins. The thrill of being wanted so much urged her on to more. Urged her to do more, to do things more kinky, things more exciting, things that developed with each twist of sexual deviation that she acted out. Then, when she discovered the pleasures of making specialty pornography movies, movies that displayed her special talent for sadistic pleasures, her cash flow grew almost as quickly as her addiction to the art.

Although Elzee had sold her contract to an investigator friend of his, and no longer had the option of deciding her career development, he still enjoyed seeing her, and still offered her advice. She still enjoyed that.

On this day Elzee was making the trip to the Russian River area in Guerneville to see his investigator friend and collect another payment due on the sale of her acting contract. He agreed to deliver Marena there on that day, and he was pleased that she was on time. He was also pleased that he would be able to get her to their Center for Motion Picture Production, as he called it, well in time for an evening's shooting.

"The river's a nice place," Marena said as she made herself comfortable beside Elzee, resting her hand on his leg. She briefly considered turning him on during the ride, but decided against it on watching his expression. "Especially in the summertime," she added with childish afterthought.

Marena turned her thoughts to summertime in the Russian River area. It was in the summertime that practically any closeted form of perversity was practiced in the area. If what you wanted couldn't be openly acknowledged, there were many places that it would be practiced in secret, in guarded rooms where guilt could be hidden in dimly lit surroundings.

It was where the boys from the Castro Street and the south of Market Street S & M clubs would congregate in the summertime. It was where they went to get some sun, to play and take their pleasures. It was a place away from the prying eyes of those hypocritical big city dwellers, from those who repressed their desire to dabble in the same pleasures.

Marena engaged Elzee with small talk for the first half-hour of the trip as they left the city, crossed the Golden Gate Bridge, and to wend the way northward along Highway 101.

Once through San Rafael, the conversation drifted onto their present project. It was a movie that, in spite of her great range of experiences with almost everything and anything sexual in nature, would involve some scenes she had never yet performed.

It was an S & M movie. She liked performing in S & M movies, generally, but it was the particularly sadistic scenes of this latest script that she had at first been reluctant to do. She remembered the last movie she made several months earlier under the auspices of the new producer, the investigator who bought her contract. And she remembered the stranger who was putting up some of the money for her performances. She also remembered that "sick God damn little artist," as she called Manny Bolton, the male lead in that film.

She remembered how Manny and that other man from Belize, who she called a creep, who played the other sadist in the movie, got so involved with their part that the cute little guy got hurt. He never recovered from the electric shock treatment they gave him. He died playing the part of the masochist.

Everyone thought that was great for the movie, though. They thought it was the ultimate in S & M. A true snuff film, they called it. But she thought it was too much. She swore she wouldn't play in another movie like that unless she got to talk to the guys with the money, first, to make sure that didn't happen again. "After all," she had told Elzee. "I have a God damn reputation to protect, ain't I?" That was part of her reason for going with Elzee this afternoon, to resolve just such a problem before the start of the upcoming three days' filming.

That was also why, when they arrived in front of their filming location, the house in the woods on Old River Road, that they both hurried into the building without worrying whether or not the limousine was left parked where it was exposed to curious passers by.

** * * *

"She might not be here, Chief," PZ said as he climbed out of the Red Beast.

Penn parked near the intersection of Polk and O'Farrel streets in San Francisco. He ignored the suggested restraints put forth by PZ, and paid no attention to the suggestive glances of the two black men sporting long earrings in their left ears who leaned against the corner of the building nearby. With PZ close behind, he threaded his way through the street loungers and legitimate pedestrians to the entrance of the blue movie capital of the West coast, at the same time wondering just how many of the bums sprawled on the sidewalk were really undercover vice squad detectives.

"I suppose it is a possibility that she won't be here," Penn finally responded to PZ's comment as he slipped a twenty dollar bill through the slot under the glass in the cashier's cage to purchase two tickets. "But it's worth a try."

The young girl with the dyed red hair grinned from behind the bulletproof plastic of the cage. It was obvious what was on her mind, and Penn wondered if she was one of the performers during her off cashiering hours. The buzzer that she pushed signaled their right to pass through the steel faced doors to enter the dark interior of the Palace of Porn. Penn went through the doors, and again PZ followed, not the least reluctant this time.

"Jeez," PZ said after they passed through a second door that protected the dim interior from the interrupting light of the outer door. What he faced was clearly delighted him.

A stage was located less than thirty feet away from the entrance, across a dozen or so half occupied rows of theater seats. The room was completely dark save for the red colored spotlights that shined on the undulating pair of forms on the black velvet padded stage.

PZ, the most lecherous of lechers, was forced to stare at the antics of the pair of nubile bodies moving about on the stage. "No fuckin' way that's possible," he said in awe.

"Come on," Penn commanded. "Christ. You'd think you never saw a couple go at it before."

"Not that way, I ain't," PZ said, defending himself, while trying to keep his attention on the performers while at the same time following Penn's progress.

"This must be the way to the back room," Penn said as

he led the way down the center aisle, then across the space between the seats and the stage. He ignored the 'down in front' yells of the male audience, and passed through the curtain beside the stage. He had to reach back to grab PZ by the collar and pull him away from the close up view of the performers, and that was why he failed to see the monstrously huge man standing behind the curtain that covered a small room.

"Where d'ya think you guys are goin'?" the man growled.

Penn turned in surprise. The man towered over him by more than a foot, was nearly twice his size around the chest, and had arms like piano legs. He hoped this monster man wasn't as unfriendly as his question implied.

"Jeez," PZ exclaimed when he cleared the curtain.

"He ain't gonna help ya none," the monster rasped. "I said where d'ya think you're goin'?" He stepped in front of the two detectives, and standing defiantly with his hands on his hips, he glared at them. "Ya got two seconds to come up with the answer, or you're tossed out."

Penn backed away, while PZ moved to Penn's left.

"We're here to see Marena," Penn stated. He hoped he sounded authoritative enough.

"Yeah? You, and everybody else. She ain't here," the monster said.

"Says who?" Penn challenged. Apparently he hadn't sounded like he had any authority at all.

"Jeez-sus," PZ whispered quietly.

"Fuck youse," the monster bellowed as he stepped towards Penn. At the same time he threw a punch with his ham-sized right fist directed at Penn's chin.

Penn expected just such a move. "Says me," he quipped as he stepped to the side, stuck out his right foot, and grabbed the man's right arm at the wrist in a grip from Ju Jitsu training. He pulled forward, adding to the man's thrust.

The move surprised the man, and he was off balance before he realized what happened. He tried to recover while stumbling past Penn with his neck outstretched and his other arm out in front of him, but his arm was no protection. He slammed into the wall, face first.

The thud echoed through the building, but no one in the audotorium paid any attnetion to it. They were too wrapped up in the stage show.

To complete his defense, Penn raised his arm and brought it down hard, with his elbow aimed right at the back of the monster's barrel sized neck.

"Jeez-sus kariste," PZ muttered as he heard the crunch of bone hitting bone.

The monster hit the floor face down with a thud, and didn't move.

Penn watched the monster for several seconds, expecting him to get up. He saw no movement, except the slow and labored breathing of an unconscious man.

"Fuckin' dead?" PZ asked, nonchalantly. He recovered his poise when the big man hit the floor.

"No, fortunately," Penn replied, "but, he's going to have one hell of a head ache when he wakes up. Come on." He opened the door near the end of the small room, and stepped through it into another hall that fronted several dressing rooms. Staring him in the face were two women. From their mode of attire, Penn surmised they were some of the stage performers, relaxing between acts.

The first woman had purple hair, and wore a sheer, thin black robe untied at the front, which hung loosely over breasts that any sensible man could see were surgically augmented. She stood in purple high heeled shoes that added four inches to her height, with her arms crossed, smoking an unfiltered cigarette. She peered at Penn through ringlets of smoke wafting up in front of her face.

The second woman had blonde hair, wore even less than the purple haired one, and her breasts would have been as well shaped as the other woman's, had she worn something to support them.

"Tell me where I can find Marena," Penn ordered, as he approached the two women.

The purple haired woman inhaled a puff of smoke in thought. "Who're you?" she asked coarsely, letting the smoke filter out through her words.

"Someone who wants to see Marena," Penn replied with force. "And I want to see her now," he added.

"Bullshit," she said with a sneer.

The other woman stepped back, refusing the challenge.

Penn approached the smoker. He stood in front of her, only inches between their eyes. "Look, sweetheart," he growled, wondering if he might sound a little too much like Bogart. "One more smart answer like that and you'll find yourself face down on the floor with your overgrown monster pal in the other room. Now where the hell is she?"

The woman stared in Penn's eyes, and calmly took another puff from her cigarette.

Penn had to step back to avoid being burned.

"Okay," the woman said as she turned her head in last minute consideration, and exhaled the smoke. "So, what's it to me? She's not here. She went to the Russian River."

"That's a big place, sweetheart," Penn retorted. He definitely sounded too much like Bogart, but what the hell?

"I don't know where," she said with a shrug. "She does a movie thing up there once in a while. Today was one of her days. That's all I know."

"Who would know?"

"She's got some guy, a manager she calls him, that takes her there sometimes."

"Who?"

"Some guy named Elwood... Elz... or something like

that. No, Elzee. E-l-z-e-e. Yeah. That's his name, Elzee Taylor."

"And?" he asked, pushing for more information, and withholding his surprise at hearing the name.

"Hey! That's all I know," she said in defiance. "So, get lost." She joined her friend who was standing to one side, took another puff off her cigarette, and turned her back on Penn.

PZ kept his eyes on the two barely covered torsos during the interchange, and he had a hard time taking his eyes off them when it was time to leave.

"Some things never change," Penn commented, glancing at PZ.

"Good thing, too," PZ said, continuing his ogling.

"I was talking about you, Turkey," Penn said, "not them. Anyway, I think we got want we wanted. Let's get the hell out of here."

PZ had a second chance to eye to oddly coupling couple on the stage, and bumped into a patron standing in the doorway on the way out. "Now what?" he asked Penn as he recovered his poise and shielded his eyes from the bright afternoon's sun he and Penn faced on reaching the street.

"Well," Penn answered, as he and PZ threaded their way through the crowd forming a line for the matinee show at the Great American Music Hall half a block down Geary Street. "Now we find Elzee Taylor."

Chapter 4

Shafts of afternoon sunlight played off the surrounding storefronts, and formed facades of mysterious imagery as the two detectives walked down the street.

"I have to admit," Penn said, glancing up at the sky on their way back to the Red Beast. "I don't think much of Elzee Taylor. He was always too slippery for me. The last time I talked to him he lived up on Filbert Street in a nice part of town. The 2000 block, I think."

"Yeah. I think I heard that, too," PZ agreed as they got into the car.

"I never did understand how he could afford that place on what he had to be making in the P.I. business," Penn commented, as he started the engine.

"Come on," PZ said. "You tryin' to tell me you don't know what he's been doing?"

Penn looked at his partner with surprise. "No, not for certain. I've heard a lot, though. I suppose it's all true?"

"That he's mixed up in the fuckin' porno racket? No pun intended. I've even seen a few of 'em. Not so fuckin' great."

"Not kinky enough for you?" Penn kidded, amused by his partner's confessions..

"Hey. Everybody to their own, okay?"

"You're not answering," Penn persisted.

"Yeah? Okay. No, they weren't up to my fuckin' standards, okay? I passed over that stuff when I was a kid in New York."

Penn chuckled with PZ's explanation, and pulled out into traffic.

"Now, there is where you get some flicks," PZ went on with an impish grin.

"You're not getting on another of your everything in New York is better speeches, are you?" Penn responded.

"Hey," PZ said. "I can't help it if things are more lively where I come from?"

"If things are more lively and always better in New York, then what the hell are you doing here?"

"I'm here because that's the problem. Things are a lot more lively. Too fuckin' lively, know what I mean? And too fuckin' many people."

"If you mean too many New Yorkers, yes, I know what you mean."

"S now you're a comedian," PZ responded.

Penn smiled as he threaded the car through the heavy Polk Street traffic heading North, and turned East on Sacramento to Van Ness, and then onto Filbert Street, thinking it would be the quickest route. But Filbert Street developed into a turtle-way of stop signs and cross traffic. Occasionally a skateboarder or two would come flying through an intersection on the way to an early grave. Luckily Penn missed them.

"One a them guys is gonna get it, one a these days," PZ remarked to Penn, approaching the crest of the hill and pulling to the curb. He parked in front of the prestigious white stucco and marble-sided twenty story apartment building in the Pacific Heights area of San Francisco, the 2000 Filbert Street Apartments.

"Jeez. What a fuckin' view," PZ said as he got out of the car to peer down the hill at the bay, lying smooth and flat in the afternoon's sun. "You can see all the way to Sausalito."

Penn said nothing as he came around the front of the car to join his partner. He ignored the view and stared at the building, making a mental note of the brass nameplate on the building's façade. He also noted the doorman, who was an African American in a full length brown coat with cut away tails, bright green slacks, white shirt, green bow tie, and a chauffeur's cap. He was drying and polishing the building's nameplate with a handkerchief.

After a few final rubs, one cautious look of inspection, another rub, and a satisfied grin, the doorman turned around. He tucked the cloth into his coat pocket and peered at the two recent arrivals.

"The dude there is looking at us," PZ said, sticking his hands in his pockets, leaning back against the car.

"That's probably because we don't look like the usual residents of this place," Penn responded. "Frankly, I don't think you look like you have enough couth," he added in jest.

"Couth?" PZ raised to the challenge. "man. I got more fuckin' couth then that dude ever had," he added as he walked towards the doorman. . "Hey, my man," he greeted. "What's the word?"

The doorman coolly stared down his nose at PZ without answering.

"What's happen-nen?" PZ said.

"You have some problem?" the doorman stiffly responded, as he brushed off his sleeve with his white gloved hand. His tone showed his impatience with the man who would confront him in such low brow English.

"Problem?" PZ responded. "Hey. No problem, my man. It's your world. I'm just livin' in it."

"Then may I suggest that you live in it somewhere else, Sir? Unless, and I doubt this, that someone here is expecting you?"

By that time, Penn had enough of the charade. He approached the doorman. "I have to apologize for my friend, here," he said.

The doorman interrupted him. "The question still stands. Do you have an appointment with anyone here?" His manner changed from patient oblige to calm irritation.

"Ah, no, we don't actually have an appointment. But, I'm sure that if you rang Elzee Taylor's bell, he would invite us in."

The doorman gazed at Penn, taking his time in responding. "Mr. Taylor is out," he replied at length.

"Out?" Penn asked pensively. "Ah, I don't suppose," he added as he reached in his pants pocket to retrieve a folded stack of twenty dollar bills, "that you know where he is out to?"

The doorman looked at the money in Penn's hand, and back at Penn's face. "I might," he said with a developing smile.

"Would, say, a Jackson be enough to come under the heading of the word 'might'?" Penn asked, taking a bill from the stack in his hand.

"Now, Mr. Jackson," the doorman said with a widening grin, now using the characteristic slang that PZ had tried to use. "Why, Suh, he be my most favorite white man." He paused to show his pearly white teeth in a broad grin. "There's only one thing that I likes better," he added.

"I bet that's two Jacksons," Penn said while unfolding another bill.

"Oh. You're good," the doorman said in even more heavily accented Ebonics slanguage. "You're mighty good. Now, two Jacksons just might be able to get me to forget myself and mention where Mr. Taylor went. For three Jacksons? Well, now. For three Jacksons I jes' might be able to tell a fella who he went along with."

Penn laughed and peeled off another twenty. He folded the money, stuck it into the doorman's coat pocket, and asked, "Where and who?"

The doorman returned to his officious demeanor. "The Russian River," he said. "Every Wednesday Mr. Taylor goes to Guerneville to take care of business. And this time he had that blonde bombshell with him. The porno queen, Marena."

"When did he leave?" Penn asked, after glancing at the chagrined PZ.

"Less than two hours ago," the doorman replied. "And now, if you will excuse me, I have other things to take care of." He turned and walked back inside the building lobby.

"You don't have to rub it in, Buzzard," PZ volunteered, after he got back into the car, and after Penn pulled the car out into traffic.

"Hey! Did I say anything?" Penn said, grinning.

"You were thinking it," PZ complained as he reached for a cigarette in his coat pocket.

Penn again thought of chastising his partner for smoking, but decided against it, and nothing more was said until they had returned to downtown Market Street by way of Columbus Street, and managed to get caught up in the afternoon's heavy traffic.

"You know where the fuck you're going?" PZ asked, taking the last drag from his unfiltered Pall Mall.

Penn nodded.

"Where?" He asked, tossing the cigarette out the window.

"To take a stroll through Markham's office," Penn answered, shaking his head at PZ's blatant avoidance of anti-litter etiquette. "Since it appears that we're not going to be able to speak with either Elzee or Marena today."

"I don't think that's good idea," PZ said.

"Why not?" Penn asked, surprised. "What do you have against it?"

"I got nothin' against it," PZ explained. "But his fuckin' office is probably locked, being the subject of a police investigation, and everything. We ain't gonna be able to get in. That's all."

Penn wondered if PZ's answer sounded a bit too strained. "I think we can handle the getting in problem well enough," he said. "Besides. There might be something there that the cops missed. He may have hidden a few things somewhere."

PZ shrugged his shoulders in silence.

Penn turned onto Market Street and headed for the 700 block. "795 Market Street, wasn't it?" Penn asked, for no other reason than to re-open the dialogue. He knew the address well enough.

"Yeah," PZ responded. "Office number 642. The parking's gonna be damn impossible, you know."

"Hey," Penn chided as he wound his way along the street, avoiding streetcars and pedestrians unsafely caught on the street-center safety islands. "What do you mean? Aren't you the one with the parking karma?"

PZ shrugged his shoulders again, only with a little more enthusiasm as the result of the compliment.

"It must be working already," Penn added as he passed the building and turned the corner onto Kearny Street. "There's a space right there. How do you do it?"

Again PZ shrugged. "Just my style," he said.

Penn parked, and after PZ plugged the meter with several of his 3/8ths inch S.A.E. washers, they both walked back to Market Street, dodging drunks and an occasional panhandler.

"Typical," Penn commented as they entered the lobby of the 795 Market Street Building. A bag lady was busily trying to push a shopping cart with her entire stock of possessions in it through the old-fashioned glass door. She finally managed, but only because the two P.I.'s held it open for her.

"What's so typical about a bag lady?" PZ asked, watching the ancient woman push her cart off down the street.

"Not the bag lady," Penn frowned. "I'm talking about the building. High class 1930's, rundown 1990's. Once a shining example of hope in the future, now a shoddy reminder of that future's despair."

"You want to tell me about it?" PZ said as they

entered the building's lobby and made their way to the elevator.

"About what?" Penn responded, not sure he understood PZ's question.

"About what's bothering you. You're philosophizing again."

"Am I?" Penn said. "I guess I still can't make any sense out of killing one of the good guys. That's what's bothering me. Why was he killed? What was he onto? Something big? What? And who did it?"

"Ain't that what we're here to find out?" PZ asked dryly. "If we can get in, that is. I still don't think we can."

After numerous rattles, squeaks and groans, the elevator slowly reached the sixth floor. The doors ground open. At one time they would have swished open on oily slides, but the rollers had long since worn through.

"The hallway's got new recarp," PZ said as they stepped out of the elevator. He was forcing himself to say something positive about the ambiance.

"Right. It's not more than five or six years old, by the looks of it," Penn said with a touch of sarcasm as they set out to search for room number 642.

"Here it is," PZ said after turning the last corner in the hallway. "Locked, too," he added as he tried the doorknob. "Just like I said."

"Turkey," Penn said as he retrieved his wallet from his pocket. "You thought it was going to be wide open? But, not to worry. I have the key."

"The what?"

"The key. The magic all lock opening key," he said as he pulled a plastic credit card from the wallet. "Watch."

"Oh, I get it, Chief," PZ began to chuckle. "You're going to use your credit card and charge right in?"

"Funny," Penn commented as he carefully slid the flexible card down the doorjamb while grasping the doorknob with his other hand. As the plastic pushed back the door bolt, he gently pushed open the door.

"Now," he said in a whisper that reflected his feeling guilty over the illegal entry. "Let's see if we can find anything that's going to be helpful."

With PZ following, Penn stepped quietly into the reception area of the two-room office suite. "Jeez-sus," he said, slowly shutting the door behind them and scanning the room. "A tornado hit the place! Files are all over."

"A mess, ain't it?" a man with a gruff voice growled while stepping into the front office from the back room.

The unexpected voice startled Penn. PZ jumped nearly a foot. They stared at the man.

Penn's first observation was of the man's size. His second was of the size of the barrel on the revolver the man held.

His third observation was how the man held the portable cannon with an ease that meant he was used to holding it, and probably knew how to use it.

"Welcome," the man said sarcastically, displaying a crooked smile. "I wasn't expecting no company, but that's okay. We was just leaving anyways."

"Who the hell are you?" Penn asked, controlled his surprise.

"The name's Martin, if it means anything to you. Which it don't."

"Martin?" Penn repeated the name as a diversion while reaching for the front door.

"Ah, ah, ah," Martin cautioned. "Leave the door alone and just move to the wall, there." He pointed to the bare space of wall nearly ten feet away from the door.

Penn cautiously followed the directions while commanding PZ with a glance, telling him to follow.

"That's good. Now turn around and say hello to that wall," the man said, "and nobody's gonna get hurt."

Penn and PZ did turn around, but Penn didn't quite face the wall. Instead, he kept his head turned to the side enough to keep his eye on the man's movements. He soon found those movements not to his liking.

"I said, watch the wall, Sucker," Martin growled as he stepped up and swung the butt of his revolver into Penn's kidney.

Penn grimaced, then turned his nose more to the wall, but he still watched Martin out of the corner of his eye.

Martin gloated sadistically on seeing Penn wince with pain, and he relaxed his gun hand, letting the gun point downward ever so slightly. That was his error.

Penn kicked his right heel up and backward with amazing quickness, catching Martin in the groin. As the man doubled over in pain, he added a swift kick in the face with his other foot.

PZ joined the action and pounded his fist into Martin's mid-section.

The man again doubled over, and Penn followed up by slamming the back of his elbow down on Martin's neck.

Martin hit the floor with a resounding thud.

"I always knew you were good for something," Penn kidded PZ while rubbing his left side where Martin had hit him.

"Only, not good enough," another voice said from the doorway leading to the rear office. This voice was polished, but with an accent, and the accent was unquestionably Texan.

Penn and PZ quickly turned toward the voice. What they focused on was another gun. This time it was a .45 caliber automatic, a military handgun like the officers carried during the war, and it looked menacing as it pointed at them.

Penn quickly summed up the situation and this second man. The voice was a Texas drawl, and the body was well dressed in a suit and tie, not in slacks, short jacket and polyester shirt like Martin. This man had a professional look. He was much more professional than Martin, who was too gaudily dressed to be have had enough training to be a professional. The total came to one organization man and one flunky. That translated to brains and power, and the combination spelled a need to be careful, very careful.

Penn was very careful. He leaned back against the wall, and with his outstretched arm, pushed PZ back with him.

"Wise. Very wise," the man from Texas said, as he stepped over to help his associate to his feet. "Now, if you'll get on your knees and place your hands together on the backs of your heads, I promise you no one will get hurt. Oh, and by the way, I'm much quicker with this .45 than my, ah, associate."

Penn presumed that to be true. He had faced this type of man before in his intelligence agency years. He knew the man would be well trained and not have the slightest reluctance to shoot anyone who stood in his way. He and PZ did as they were told.

That was when Martin, who had now regained his awareness, decided to take advantage of Penn's weakness. He placed a well aimed kick in Penn's stomach. "That's a pay back," he sneered when Penn doubled over in pain. "It's a bitch, ain't it?"

"You're lucky I don't have the time to let him do as he would like," the Texan said with a smile. "Ordinarily I would, but right now I have more important things on my mind."

He walked to the door and waited while his associate exited first. "By the way," he added on his way out, "you should know that you don't have to waste your time here. There's nothing around that would interest to you. We saw to that." With a smile, he stepped through the door and quietly shut it behind him.

"Sons a bitches," PZ swore as he scampered to his feet and headed for the door, drawing his Colt .44 Magnum from his shoulder holster. "I'm gonna fuckin' kill the bastard."

"Don't be stupid," Penn wheezed, getting to his feet. "Step outside that door right now and you're likely to get your head blown off. A man with his training is going to be waiting with a clear view of the door until the elevator arrives. Then he'll make a dash for it. By the time you got there you'd have to follow by the stairs. There's no chance."

PZ recognized the wisdom of Penn's words, and stopped. With a shrug he put his .44 back in his shoulder holster. "But he's a dead man. If I ever see him again, he's dead," he said.

"Sure," Penn said as he began his second look around the room. "But I'll be damned if we're going to take his word for there not being anything interesting in here. There's got to be something around, or else they wouldn't have been here looking for it."

"Whatever the so called 'it' is," PZ added.

"Whatever the so called 'it' is," Penn echoed.

"You got any idea who those guys were?"

"No," Penn responded, shaking his head pensively. "But I do know they're pretty high powered, judging from the looks of them. Markham must have been in it up to his eyeballs."

"No kidding," PZ agreed.

"You want the rear office or this one?" Penn asked while heading for the rear one.

"Some choice," PZ commented. "I'll take this one," he added with a sly grin. "The file drawers are already dumped all over the place. This'll be the hardest. You take the easy one, okay?"

"Sure," Penn responded as he passed through the inner office doorway. He was already surveying Markham's collection of things in the private office.

Only the office hadn't recently been so private. The first intruders had done a good job. There were files spread across the floor where the file cabinet had been thrown over. Each file had been opened and searched.

Penn threaded his way through the strewn files to reach the desk. The drawers were removed and dumped over on the top. Their assorted contents were scattered about. "Where to start?" he mused, as he pushed aside the office chair and stood behind the desk on top of several file folders that had been searched and thrown on the floor. He ignored the slippery piles of loose papers.

Suddenly his left foot went out from underneath him. "Damn it!" he yelled, landing with a loud thump, finding himself flat on his back looking up at the bottom of the desk, into the area where the drawers normally fit.

PZ rushed into the room. "Now what?" he asked as Penn struggled, trying to get up.

"Nothing. I slipped, that's all," Penn replied. "Hey, wait a minute," he added as he peered more closely at the underside of the desk. "What's this?"

A manila envelope was taped to the underside of the desk in a spot that would be above the center drawer and hidden from view unless the center drawer was removed.

"I'll be damned," Penn said as he ripped off the tape and removed the envelope. "Look what I found." He turned the envelope over and opened the flap. After getting up and clearing the mess off the top of the desk, he poured out the contents of the envelope.

The first thing that caught his attention was a photograph. "Well, well. Look at this," he said as he recognized the characters in the picture.

"That's Marena," PZ commented.

The sound of sirens suddenly pierced the room.

Penn glanced at the window. He hurried over to peer out the window at the street below. "I don't think we want to be here right now," he said as he returned to the desk and hurriedly stuffed the pictures back into the envelope. "There must be a dozen squad cars down there, all heading for this building. I'm willing to bet that guy Martin and that Texan reported something fishy taking place in this office. That would be just the trick to make sure we didn't find anything they might have missed."

"You got that one right, Chief," PZ agreed as he crossed to the window and peered down at the street. "We try explaining our way out of this we'll lose that envelope."

"Only if we're caught," Penn said as he stuck the envelope into his belt under his shirt and headed for the door.

PZ quickly followed, carefully shutting the office door behind their exit.

"I'll say one thing, though," Penn said as they entered the elevator that had finally reached their floor. "It's nice of them to announce their coming like that."

"Best sirens in the business, hunh?" PZ joked.

By the time they had arrived on the second floor level, Penn considered that they had ridden long enough for the police to have entered the lobby. The stopped the elevator and got out. As they entered the stairway leading to the first floor, the contraption resumed its groaning descent.

They quickly and quietly descended the stairs to the ground floor and hurried through the door to the lobby. Across the room were six policemen cramming themselves into the elevator, so they strolled across the lobby with forced nonchalance, while the elevator doors closed. Outside the building, they hurried back to their car.

"Close," PZ commented, as Penn pulled into traffic.

"Close, but no cigar," Penn smiled in return. "I just hope it all goes well without getting any closer."

Chapter 5

Penn and PZ returned to the Portobello Lounge and secured their favorite booth in the corner. It was the booth that enabled them to watch the bar crowd without having their conversations overheard.

Their drink order was taken by the very efficient, mini skirted cocktail waitress who saw them enter, and Penn turned his attention to the envelope from Markham's office. With care, he extracted the photo they had seen earlier, and placed it on the table.

"That's Marena, there, with the whip," PZ said, peering at the photo. "Who's the guy trussed up like a hog going to market?"

Penn shook his head in silent answer to the question, and turned the photo over. On the back were some scribbled notes. He read them aloud. "Left to right, Marena, Bund, Bolton, cameraman unknown."

PZ coughed lightly, as though taken back by the names, but Penn ignored the response as he put the photo aside and reached into the envelope again. "And here," he said as he extracted some papers. "Here we have what?" He began perusing the notes, remaining quiet as the cocktail waitress returned with their drinks, set them on the table, and took PZ's proffered five-dollar bill.

Penn studied the notes for several minutes. "It says the Guerneville location is a cover for the Belize Ring."

"Belize Ring?" PZ asked. "What's a Belize Ring?"

"Or who?" Penn corrected.

"Hunh?"

"Who is the Belize Ring?" Penn asked, as he picked up another note. "That's more the question," he said.

"Someone in Belize, apparently," he added as he looked at the second note. "Listen to this one: 'man from Belize City important big time.' And look at this, a photo of the smokestack of a large yacht. There's a symbol on the smokestack. It looks like a big square with the letter C in each corner."

"That makes as much sense as the Belize Ring thing," PZ said as he reached for the last piece of paper from the envelope. "This here's some sort of list," he said as he began to read the scribbling. "More names. This one you know. Mikel Bear."

"What?"

"Yeah. Listen. 'Marena, Bolton, Bund, Bear, Taylor, Hauke, McIvers, unknown, unknown, someone nearby who's in charge of distribution.' All in numbered order. And what's this scribbling? It looks like something Nostra. Cosa Nostra, maybe? Coca Nostra? No. It has got to be Cosa Nostra. "he thought for a few seconds, then added, "Jeez-sus. The Mafia."

"Mikel Bear is on that list?" Penn asked, ignoring the Mafia comment. Mikel Bear was more interesting and closer to home for Penn than the Mafia at the moment.

"Ain't that what I read?" PZ confirmed.

"What's he got to do with this?" Penn asked.

"Hey, Chief," PZ responded. "Ain't that what we're supposed to find out?"

"I'll be damned," Penn muttered as he read the list for himself. "Mikel Bear. I'd love to learn he had something to do with Markham's murder."

"Just what you been waiting for, hunh, Chief? To nail that guy."

"You can say that again. But just how does he fit in, I wonder?"

PZ looked back at the note. "Or McIvers? Ain't he one of your buddy, Captain Giddings, vice squad detectives? What's he got to do with this?"

"What's Belize got to do with it, for that matter?"

"Or, Belize. Yeah."

"Have you ever heard of the other two? Bund, or Bolton?" Penn asked.

"Bolton? It might mean Manny Bolton," PZ replied pensively. "An artist in Mill Valley. He does sick stuff, I hear."

"What do you mean sick stuff?" Penn asked.

"Bodies, parts of bodies, S & M themes. Things like that."

"He paints crap like that?"

"And makes good bread doing it, too, I been told," PZ affirmed.

"Good God," Penn said, slowly shaking his head. "Well, how about Bund?" he asked, returning to the list. "Do you know that name?"

"Bund? Maybe Markham meant Bond. You know, like James Bond," PZ grinned with his answer.

Penn let the attempt at humor pass without comment. "Taylor must be Elzee Taylor. And Hauke is Bear's sidekick."

"Yeah. Or used to be. Ain't heard much of him the last year, though."

"Well, there's one thing for sure. They're all connected. And they're also all connected with Belize, apparently."

"You think this is what those guys were looking for in Markham's office?"

"Probably," Penn answered as he took a sip from the drink he had been ignoring up to this time.

"Then those guys are connected to it?"

"That's a good possibility."

"They're big time," PZ said as though he was making an off hand remark, not wanting to appear intimidated by the recent escapade in Markham's office.

"That, unfortunately, is also a good possibility."

"They coulda done it, killed Markham, I mean," PZ

suggested.

"No. I don't think so."

"Why?"

"Because, if they had, they wouldn't have been back to go looking through his office. They would have gotten what they wanted out of Markham before they killed him."

"That does seem logical," PZ said as he sat back, looking somewhat disappointed. "But, ain't you taking this thing in the wrong direction?"

"So now you're the logical one, like Mr. Spock?" Penn asked in jest, secretly wondering why his partner was trying to change the subject.

"Sure," PZ responded. "If you're going to trek this investigation where no man has gone before, then I want to play Mr. Spock."

"Well, one thing's for sure," Penn said as he returned the photos and notes to the envelope. "Someone has gone there before us, and I don't think it was the Klingons. Otherwise, Markham would still be alive."

PZ chuckled, and turned to watch the bar crowd, as though the entire subject was put out of his mind.

"You know what," Penn said, speaking to the rear of PZ's head and taking only his second sip from his drink. "I think it's about time we did a little looking at our old friend."

"Old friend?" PZ responded as he turned back to face Penn. "You mean Bear?"

"I mean Mikel Bear."

"You fuckin' kiddin'? What with? He'd spot us in a minute."

"Us, true, but I don't think he knows Yanks that well. He's never seen him, as far as I know."

"Hah!" PZ laughed. "But, Yanks sure as hell has seen Bear."

"What do you mean?"

"Yanks has been dickin' Bear's wife."

"That's a little hard to believe. How do you know so much about what goes on with Bear's wife, anyway?"

"I got my sources," PZ bragged.

"Yes," Penn thoughtfully said. "I suppose you do. Anyway, sit tight for a few minutes. I'm going use the pay phone to give him a call."

"Pay phone? What're you paying fifty bucks a month for your cell phone, for?

"You know I don't like using a cell phone for sensitive calls. They can be monitoed by anyone with a scanner in the area. Any way, stay here."

"Hey! I ain't going nowhere, except maybe over there to say hello to Denise and Donna."

Penn left the table and ignored PZ's last comment. He knew PZ would start playing the minute he had a chance to ignore the investigation. He wondered why the man even bothered to mention his intentions.

The public telephone was in the back hallway. For once it wasn't busy, and Penn acknowledged that fact as one of the little miracles of the day. He even was surprised by the fact that the armless bandit functioned correctly on the first try, taking the quarter smoothly without the expected mechanical stuttering and coin regurgitating process it usually went through for the first several tries.

Penn listened for the ringing on the other end to be answered, and finally after the twelfth ring, a harried voice answered, "Yeah?"

"Yanks. This is Penn."

"Penn?" Yanks responded. "Hey. What's up, buddy?" it continued, cheerfully, recognizing Penn's voice.

Penn felt a twinge of flattery on hearing the change in response caused by mentioning his own name. He realized that was one of the things he liked about this part time operative named Yankovits, or Yanks, for short. The man always responded with cheerfulness. Even after failing some assignments he remained in the best of spirits. Even after having to spend four years in federal prison for being associated with the famous Watergate break-in, he was still enthusiastic about everything he did.

"Yanks, I think I got a job for you," Penn responded.

"Hey. Great!"

There's that enthusiasm again, Penn thought.

"You want me to meet you somewhere?" Yanks continued.

"No. I think I can give you this assignment over the phone. It's simple enough."

"Yeah? Great. What is it?"

"I want you to find out as much as you can about what Bear's up to."

There was a slight pause on the line before Yanks answered. "Bear? You mean Mikel Bear?" The concern was obvious.

"Yeah. Mikel Bear. You think you can do that? I mean, it wouldn't be a conflict of interest, or anything, would it?" Penn kidded, remembering PZ's comments

"Hey," Yanks responded after a short pause. "A man's got to do what he's got to do, right? Sometimes you got to put a little excitement in your life, right?" he chuckled.

"Excitement?" Penn laughed. "If you're doing what PZ says you're doing, that isn't putting excitement in your life, that's courting the Grim Reaper."

"Nah. Piece of cake," Yanks again chuckled. "Pretty good cake, too," he added.

"Well, at any rate, I'm going to be out of town for a couple of days, a week maybe. I'll call you when I get back. Is that enough time to pin him down?"

"Sure. What are you looking for?"

"Something between him and McIvers, maybe. Or the Russian River, or Elzee Taylor. Anything along that line."

"Hell, you want a book?"

"Sure, if you can dig up that much."

"Okay. You got it."

"Thanks, Yanks. See you." Penn hung up the phone. He turned to go back to the lounge, and without watching where he was going, he nearly ran into Denise Dela Tuna. She was in the hallway heading for the Lady's Room.

She smiled seductively at him. "Hey," she said. "If you got a wrong number I can give you a good one." She threw her chest forward for emphasis.

Penn laughed. "I bet you can," he said. "But not now. I've got things to do. Maybe later," he added as he walked down the hallway.

"Anytime," she called to him.

Penn felt her eyes watching him until he turned the corner of the hallway leading back to the bar.

When he returned to the booth he had to squeeze in beside Denise's girlfriend, Donna. She was sitting beside PZ, massaging his thighs with her hands. This would have been embarrassing for anyone other than PZ, but for him it was obviously pleasing.

"Hey," Penn interrupted Donna as she began nibbling on PZ's ear lobe. "If you don't mind? PZ and I have something to talk about in private."

Donna frowned. "I don't hear PZ complaining," she said.

PZ took the hint. He removed Donna's hands. "Later," he told her. "Right now we got business to tend."

"Well. Okay," she said as she scooted out from the booth. "But I might not be free later."

"Are you ever?" Penn said. "Bye," he added in response to her glare.

"You get hold of Yanks?" PZ asked as he straightened himself up and reached for his drink.

"Yep. I told him to get as much information on Bear as he could, including anything he could on the McIver's connection and on the Russian River tie-in."

"You think he can handle that?" PZ asked with a

frown.

Penn was about to say something about PZ's negativity, but his thoughts were interrupted by the bartender.

"Telephone call from Colonel Wilkins for someone from the Flyin' Penguin Detective Agency," Sue called from behind the counter where the house phone was connected. "Anyone here associated with that place?" she continued, waiting for a response. It was her practice to act as screening agent for the detectives when they were there. She did this for good will. It enabled the two to spend their off hours in the lounge and sustain the attraction they were to most of the crowd.

And, they did attract a crowd of admirers. Especially when PZ was in one of his story telling moods. Although the truth was usually far from what he related to the gathering of mostly female admirers, the exploits as he related them never ceased to be entertaining.

Sue repeated her question and looked at the two, waiting for their response. If either one of them shook their head, she would tell the caller that they didn't respond to the paging. Otherwise, she would put the phone on the bar for their use.

Penn and PZ usually would decline the calls when in the lounge, and the only person that they would always accept a call from was Lara, their secretary. But then, when she called, she never asked whether or not they were there, she simply ordered Sue to get one of the two to the phone. Usually it was Penn she wanted to speak with, since she was Penn's live-in girlfriend, as well as being the most proficient secretary the two ever had.

This time, though the caller wasn't Lara. It was Colonel Gerald Wilkins, an old friend of Penn's from his Defense Intelligence Service days, from the more serious days of fighting for their country in Southeast Asia. "Duty, honor, and all that," Penn often said to rationalize his military career whenever he was confronted by the sheepish uninformed groupies mislead by Hanoi Jane.

"Damn rights, I'm here," Penn shouted to Sue as he rose from the table, hurried to the bar and took the phone she held out.

"Hello," he said with enthusiasm. "I'll be God damn," he said after he heard the first response. "Gerald Wilkins! What are you up to?"

Then before the caller had a chance to reply, Penn added, "Hey. I'm sorry I couldn't make Allie's wedding, but I was in the Philippines, on a damn tough case. Did she get my present, though, last month? I sent it by, what was it... UPS. Yeah. What? Okay, I'll slow down and listen. Where are you, anyway?....At the Bermuda Palms? Yes...Of course I will.....Yeah. Okay. We'll be right over...Yeah, we. My partner and... What? Okay. We'll be right over. Okay...Yeah...Bye." Penn gave the phone back to Sue and returned to the table, looking pensive and dodging Denise once more along the way.

"Anything wrong, Chief?" PZ greeted his return.

"I'm not sure. That was my old buddy, Gerald Wilkins. You remember me talking about him? He's over at the Bermuda Palms Motel, right now. He's waiting for us."

"I thought he lived in New York," PZ said, surprised.

"He does, but he came out here to ask us for help."

"Help? On what?"

"I'm not sure about that, either. He didn't say. But about the only thing that would get him so upset is something about his daughter. I have a feeling that might be it."

"Then we better get movin'," PZ said. "We can get back to this thing later."

Penn was surprised by PZ's willingness to sidetrack any further discussion about Mikel Bear, or of Markham's murder, but he hadn't time to worry about that at the moment. Instead, he picked up the envelope, stuck it in his belt, finished his drink, and got up from the booth.

PZ quickly followed.

Neither of them took the time to explain their departure, but the friends who had gathered around the booth in Penn's absence had heard the conversation, and knew something was up that promised to be another good story from PZ at some later date.

The double glass doors of the lounge once again shut off the bumble bump of the fifties romp as they left, walking quickly to Penn's well worn Red Beast parked at the curb.

The roar of the oversized engine was barely lessened when Penn dropped the car into gear. The turbo automatic transmission turned that roar into squealing tires as Penn made a U-turn leaving the curb, ignoring the Volvo that was forced into a sudden stop.

“Jeez-sus!” PZ shouted as he was thrown against the passenger side door. “Get there in one piece, okay?”

Chapter 6

"If he's staying here at the Bermuda Palms, he does have a problem," PZ said as they arrived the almost famous establishment on Francisco Boulevard in downtown San Rafael. "The whores in this place have no mercy."

"Leave it to you to think of that angle," Penn commented as he parked the Red Beast in the parking lot in front of room number twelve

Hey," PZ responded defensively. "I was just trying to lighten things up a bit."

Penn gave that some thought. "Yeah I know," he relented while getting out of the car. "I suppose I should apologize for being so short tempered."

Penn noted the value of PZ's remark, though. The motel seemed to be the only one in Southern Marin County where prostitution was a thriving trade without police interruption. That fact did nothing to heighten what little respect Penn already felt for the San Rafael Police Department.

As he knocked on the door to the room, he noted the seedy appearance of two girls standing on the curbside, obviously looking for customers. He turned to face the door in preference to responding to their gestures.

A siren wailed along the freeway just across the fence from the frontage road that lead to the motel as Colonel Gerald R. Wilkins, U.S. Army Retired, opened the door. He grimaced against the noise, but the grimace quickly changed to a smile as he recognized Penn, who was already offering his hand in greeting.

He pumped Penn's hand vigorously. "Glad you came,

Penn. Come in," he said, standing aside to let his two visitors inside. "Can I offer you a drink?" he added with forced enthusiasm.

Penn nodded a thanks and stepped into the room with PZ right behind.

"This must be your partner, Mr. Thomas?" Colonel Wilkins said as he greeted PZ.

"That's me," PZ smiled. "Glad to know you, Colonel."

"Care for a drink?" the colonel again asked.

Penn shrugged his shoulders in affirmation, noting the colonel's repetition. The colonel seldom repeated himself unless he was worried about something.

PZ responded favorably, although Penn doubted that PZ would drink what was offered. Colonel Wilkins was a devoted Southern Comfort and soda drinker, while PZ was a Black Russian fan.

A moment or two of quiet followed, interrupted only by the sounds of cars passing on the freeway, while Colonel Wilkins took two hopefully clean plastic glasses from the coffee table in the center of the room. He plopped a few ice cubes in each of them, and poured in most of the contents that were left from an already half-emptied pint of his favorite whiskey. He added the final ounce or two to his own glass, and handed the other two to his guests while turning with a smile.

"Here's to old friends," the colonel said as he nodded towards Penn while taking a sip. "Now, here's the problem," he continued as he turned to take a seat in one of the wood and black Naugahyde armchairs that were supposed to suggest elegance.

Penn sat in the matching chair while PZ stood, staring disconsolately at the drink. He noticed how the colonel lost the jubilation first expressed with their greeting, and replaced it with other feelings, feelings that Penn didn't enjoy. The colonel had already consumed more whiskey than normal, and the lines in his brow evidenced his long hours of concern.

The story the colonel related was one much too familiar to Penn, and it was the problem that he suspected. It was a story of a missing daughter as told by an overwrought father. The girl had recently gotten married and had left on her honeymoon for the Caribbean. They planned to spend a few nights on Ambergris Cay, in Belize, then charter a yacht for a few weeks of leisurely sailing around on the clearest waters of the world before returning to the realities of everyday life in the Big City. Only they were more than a month overdue, and this tale had one twist to it. The girl was Penn's Goddaughter.

"I don't think," the colonel was saying. "No. I know, it's not like Gerald Levine to be late for anything."

"Gerald?" Penn softly interrupted his friend's tale.

"What?" The colonel paused.

"His name is Gerald?" Penn interrupted. He wanted to be sure the colonel wasn't confusing names and facts as a result of too much drinking.

"Oh, yeah. His first name is the same as mine," the colonel said before pausing long enough to take another swallow from his glass.

"It isn't like him to be so totally unreliable," the colonel went on. "It certainly isn't like Allie to be this lax in her responsibilities. That isn't how I brought her up to be. I guess I don't have to tell you how worried I am. How frightened I am. Which is something new for me."

"You've tried the Coast Guard?" Penn asked, knowing that the man had. Of course he had. Of course he had tried everything in his means to find his daughter. That's why he had resorted to calling on his old friend. Penn was his last hope. The colonel had a lot of trust in him. It was a trust based on their past years as fellow intelligence agency officers.

The colonel was also wise enough to realize outside help was needed when it came to looking for someone as close to him as his own daughter. He knew that to try to look for her himself would not be fruitful. There were too many hard questions to be asked, too many hard facts to be dug up. It wasn't possible to maintain the objectivity needed when the investigation involved a family member.

Penn, though, could work from that objective position. "Okay," he said after the colonel finished his story. "Look. I don't even have to tell you that I'll take this case. You know how much I owe you. But even if I owed you nothing, I'd take the case because you're a friend."

The colonel looked relieved. He sighed, then asked about the costs for such an investigation.

"Don't offend me," Penn responded gently. "We don't need the money. In the insurance end of the business we make five hundred a day plus expenses. That's what we bill insurance companies because they have more money than God. But I won't take money from you, not even if I needed it." He hoped PZ felt the same way, but he doubted it.

Nevertheless, he forced PZ to accept the arrangement, like it or not. A hard glance stopped PZ from mouthing any objection that might be forming in his mind, but Penn expected to hear from him on the topic later when they were alone.

"We'll start on this thing right away," Penn continued. "In the meantime, you know you can trust me, so take my advice. Go back home, lighten up on the booze for awhile, and try to relax. We'll take it from here, and I'll keep in touch. Okay?"

The colonel heaved another sigh of relief. "Thanks," was all he could say. That was more than he needed to say to Penn.

Penn motioned to PZ to follow as he got out of his chair and walked to the door, then the colonel thanked them both and agreed to take the first flight out that evening, back to his home.

Penn and PZ rode back to the Portobello Lounge in silence. He appreciated the fact that PZ hadn't made any comment about the fact that they weren't charging for the investigation. He did wonder what PZ was thinking, though.

Once more the raucous rambling of the semi-tonal 1950's style amplified guitars greeted them as they opened the doors to their favorite bar.

Only by this time there was the added noise of a dozen or so more patrons, all talking at once, all trying to carve their own breath's worth of air from the smoky haze in the room. The number of miscellaneous coughs heard from the various tables signaled their lack of success.

The two detectives forsook their usual booth for two places at the bar, and reached their destination safely after first skirting the playful grabbing made at them by the ever present Denise and Donna.

As Penn expected, PZ had some comment to make about the two. "Are you sure we don't have some extra time before we start working on this Allie thing?" he asked wistfully.

Penn glanced at him, then at the two girls smiling back. "I would think you'd have better sense than to tangle with those two," he said, knowing how meaningless his comment was to a man like PZ.

"That's just the point," PZ responded with a grin.

"What?"

"Those two. I mean both at the same time. Doesn't that sound interesting?"

Penn shook his head. "Only to you, it does. Catching two doses of the incurable at the same time? That doesn't sound too interesting to me."

PZ shrugged his shoulders and resigned himself to the reality of the moment. "It's obvious you're busy with the wheels turning on this thing for the colonel. What've you got in mind?"

"I don't really know at this point," Penn responded, once again noting how eager PZ was to replace the Markham murder investigation with this latest problem. "There is one thing I found most intriguing, though."

"You got to mean the part about Ambergris Cay being part of Belize?"

"Exactly. Look. We were going to have to go to Belize anyway on this Markham thing, right?"

"I didn't know we were planning to get into Markham's murder question quite that extensively. I mean, we're not getting paid for that, either. All this free work and we'll be looking for free meals before long."

"Look," Penn responded emphatically. "I'm going to Belize. I've got to find Allie, and while I'm down there, I'm going to look around with regard to Markham. Now, you don't have to go along, but I damn well expect you will."

"Well, since you put it that way, Chief." PZ reluctantly capitulated, as Penn reached over the counter to get the bar phone in favor of the mechanical monster in the back hallway, or his cell phone, which had a dead battery, again, because he was always forgetting to put it on the charger.

He dialed the number for the Fly Oakland Travel Service, paused while the phone rang, then made the necessary reservations for the very next flight to Belize City from Oakland International Airport.

"Fantastic," PZ complained after Penn hung up the phone. "Do you know anything about that place? From what I heard there's nothing happening down there this time of year but rain and heat, wet and humid and all that crap. To say nothing about the bugs, the mosquitoes, the spiders and all the other creepy crawlies."

"How do you know so much about Belize, anyway?" Penn asked. "And since when have you been afraid of a few bugs? Besides, I'm not sure we'll be down there all that long."

PZ stared at Penn, but never asked for clarification. He shrugged his shoulders instead, and called for Sue to send over another two drinks.

Nothing was said in the intervening lull, and PZ turned to stare at the crowd in the bar.

When the drinks came, PZ turned around. "Hah," he said glancing at Penn. "I see the wheels turning, again."

Penn affirmed the supposition with a nod. "Who do we know, who might know anything about Belize?" he asked.

"You mean, what does Captain Giddings, of the PD know about Belize?" PZ read Penn's mind. "You said he spends a lot of his vacation time rooting around in that part of the world, sifting through old Mayan ruins and all that, didn't you?"

"Sometimes you're pretty good at guessing," Penn said. "Now, guess this: What is the most profitable cash crop in that part of the world?"

PZ was silent for a minute, then answered. "You got to mean most profitably exported crop because of the location, don't you?" he asked.

"Exactly. It's probably not more than nine hundred miles or so straight north from Colombia. Does that give you any clues?"

"It gives me a lot of clues, but how's that fit with the missing girl?"

"Don't play naive."

PZ thought some more, then half smiled. "Okay. So where do they get all those boats they use for smuggling coke? Right?"

"Exactly."

"They sure as hell don't buy 'em off the shelf."

"Exactly. And that is what worries me."

"Especially with all the trouble they been having down there. If Allie's boat was ripped off by smugglers, then we got no reason to go down there. She's as good as gone, that's for sure."

Penn glared at his partner.

"Hey," PZ offered defensively. "I'm only pointing out the facts here. You know that, and you know I'm probably right."

Penn frowned. "Yes. I know you're probably right, but that doesn't release me from the responsibility of finding out what happened to her, does it?"

PZ shrugged again, clearly the loser in the confrontation. "Guess not," he said.

Penn did know that PZ was probably right, and he didn't like it. He didn't like the entire picture that was forming, and if the picture was a true one, if PZ was right, his friend Colonel Wilkins could start the obituary. The other thing that Penn didn't like was PZ's reluctance to pursue the investigation. The last concern was put out of his mind, though, as he finished his drink and got to his feet. "You coming?" he asked, as he sidestepped Dense and Donna on his way out.

"I guess," PZ answered, reluctantly following, but not before patting Denise on her rear.

PZ was quiet during the short ride from the lounge to the office in the Red Beast, and he said nothing when Penn asked for the second key that was required to unlock the two key safe in the office. Nor did he say anything when Penn took out both passports and then extracted several thousand dollars for expenses from the money they kept there for just such after banking hours emergencies.

The only thing he did say was to remind Penn to call Lara, and tell her where they were going, but the reminder wasn't necessary. Penn was already locking the safe and reaching for the phone when PZ mentioned it.

Penn spent a few minutes explaining the need for hurrying to the airport, and that he would take the bag he always kept packed in the office, also for just such emergencies, instead of taking the time to come home to their boat to put some things together.

He appreciated how Lara said she understood the life of a private investigator wasn't always the nine to five job she would like it to be, and wished him God speed. He knew she would be upset about his leaving on such short notice, and that she would be lonely during his absence. He also knew that he could look forward to coming back to her, and that made the parting easier, somehow.

PZ was a little more lively and conversant on the way to the airport, and he spent most of the time relating some of his past female exploiting experiences, as was typical of him.

Penn often considered that if PZ had really engaged in as many escapades as he bragged about, he would have to have been more active than Casanova had been in life and in fiction.

At the airport Penn parked the Red Beast in one of the long term parking spaces, and after confirming their direct flight to Belize City with TACA Airlines inside the terminal, went to the nearby public telephones to place a call to his friend, Captain Giddings. PZ headed for the departure waiting lounge.

"Hello Cap'n," Penn greeted the captain in his customary manner when the familiar voice eventually came on the other end of the line. "What are you doing in the Records Division? I thought once someone made Captain, all they had to do was sit around and wait for the phone to ring."

"Screw you too, buddy," was the familiar friendly response.

"Look," Penn said after letting out a chuckle. "What can you tell me about what's going on in Belize?"

"Belize? What are you poking your nose around in Belize for?" the captain responded in surprise.

"Just like a cop," Penn said, expecting the question. "You have to know everything about a question before you can answer it. I was hoping you could tell me something about the place. Is there anything going down? Or is it just your normal, quiet banana republic?"

"Quiet? Oh, sure. It's quiet, and normal, if you consider being the main trade route for cocaine smuggling normal. A lot of stuff passes through there. If you're going down there you'd better be careful. A lot of bad stuff goes on down there. And I do mean bad."

"Any names?"

The captain was silent for a few minutes, then said, "Yeah. One I can think of. I don't know how reliable it is, though."

"Yeah? Who?"

"A guy who calls himself El Tigre."

"El Tigre? Come on, you got to be kidding, that's straight out of Hollywood. No one plays the game with names like that, not since the thirty's. Are you sure someone's not pulling your leg?"

"You don't have to believe me, but you asked, so that's the answer. If you don't want to take my word for it, then give this person a call when you get down there. I've got a name here somewhere." The captain put down the phone. The rustling of papers could be heard in the background. "Here," he said when he picked up the phone again. "Here's a name. Baletta. Morgan Baletta. Baletta's a permanent resident, it says here."

"Baletta?" Penn asked. "Who is this guy, Baletta, anyway?"

"One of the DEA's most effective field operatives, or so I've been told. Not the Chief Agent, though. That's a guy named Bund, Morri Bund."

"Bund?" This time was unable to contain his surprise. "Did you say Bund?"

"Yeah. Why?"

"Oh, ah, nothing," Penn contrived to make his response ring true. He hoped his lie was successful as his mind raced and he controlled his answer. “I, ah, was just trying to write this down, and you were going a bit too fast for me, that's all. Ah, where's this guy Bund from?”

“From around here, sent down there on assignment a few years ago. He wasn't well liked in the San Francisco office. Anyway, it isn't supposed to be known by Bund that Baletta is down there.” He paused for a few seconds. “As a matter of fact,” he continued with a serious tone. “I probably shouldn't have told you, now that I look at this paper a little more thoroughly. So damn it, don't let anyone know where you got it, okay? And for God's sake, don't let Bund know about Baletta.”

“Look, Cap'n,” Penn said. “You know I don't have a loose tongue, so I don't know where I got that information. I guess it just came to me as rumors from the street if anyone asks.”

“Bust your ass, then,” the captain said, which was his manner of saying good luck.

Penn hung up the phone, hoping his ass didn't get busted at all, this trip. He glanced at his watch and headed for the boarding ramp to catch the flight, with the name Bund ringing in his ears.

PZ was already on board, and was already trying to make time with the flight attendant.

“Nothing ever changes much, does it?” Penn asked as he took a seat beside PZ next to the window.

“Nope,” PZ answered. “Great, ain't it? It stirs the senses. Keeps them alert.”

“Yeah? Well here's something else to stir your senses. Bund! Remember that name?”

PZ glanced at Penn with a slightly startled look.

“Morri Bund is the DEA agent in Belize City,” Penn stated.

“You're kidding,” PZ said. “Where'd you hear that?”

“From someone who shall remain nameless.”

“Captain Giddings?”

Penn shrugged his shoulders.

"What the hell's going on? It can't be..." PZ let the sentence drop.

"That the Bund in Markham's list is the Bund in Belize?" Penn continued the sentence for him. "And that they're connected with Allie's disappearance?" Penn thought about the association. "That is reaching a bit, isn't it? It has to be a coincidence," he said. "Doesn't it?" he asked as an afterthought while he sat back and buckled his seat belt. The engines on the jet began their whining warm up for departure, and he prepared himself for their nap inducing effect.

Chapter 7

"Major! The group's running into strong resistance at the South Channel!"

"Okay, lieutenant. Get the Com Chief on the horn for me."

The lieutenant grabbed for the field phone as the shrill of incoming mortar shells drowned out any hope of further communication with the officer ten yards away.

The first mortar exploded nearly on top of the major. When he looked up again there was a hole where the lieutenant had been. Pieces of camouflage uniform were spread out in a short arc thirty feet away. But there weren't enough pieces.

Suddenly: blackness.

"Captain! Four LCI's sunk near the entrance to the bay!"

"Okay, Ensign Merkle. Take this underwater scow right next to the reef. We can unload these Sneaky Petes in there before the moon comes up. If the waves keep breaking as high as they are it should give them good cover."

A half dozen rafts bobbing on a rolling surf.

"Incoming!" someone screamed from one of the rafts. "Shore guns by the sound of them, Major." It was Sergeant Trindle's voice. The sergeant had been in combat enough to recognize the sounds of field cannon. "They must have known we were coming. They have our range already. Oh, Christ!"

A flash of light. Blinding white, glaring light.

The submarine took a direct hit just below the conning tower, and smoke billowed upwards. It shook as another shell smashed into the stern section. The submarine exploded.

The shock waves swelled the breakers over the reef. The rushing, foaming water threw the helpless rubber rafts like walnut shells across the sharp coral, tearing the neoprene, shredding them like paper.

And all the while more explosions, water shooting upward to cascade down in eerie moonlit rainbows; coral pieces, equipment pieces, raft pieces and human pieces, all caught in the slow motion of shock recalled visions.

Sunlight shined in the major's eyes. The afternoon sunlight seeped into his slowly developing consciousness. Sand invaded his mouth as he lay face down among the palms that sprouted at the edge of the narrow beach. This wasn't the Mekong Delta. This was another place, another time, another war.

Then the very air turned red with fire. The fire turned to ice, and snow. Bitter cold. Mind numbing cold. He wasn't on a beach, now.

Suddenly he was hot. He was in the jungles of someplace called Laos. He never heard of Laos before, but they were there to keep the peace. It was before he received his field commission, a decision that was later justified by his working up the ladder of officer's status during the rest of the little, unknown, secret war. It was the precursor to the second war we lost: the Viet Nam War.

Somebody screamed off to the left. Explosions tore the trees out by their roots. It was the Tonkin Gulf, now.

"Colonel! We got to hurry if we expect to get those nurses off that island and in this submarine before Charley sees them."

"Charley. The Viet Cong." Who said that?

"I know, Major Gwinn. I know."

He was a major again, now, under the command of Colonel Gerald Wilkins.

"I'm doing all I can, Major. I can't get the captain to

move this pig-boat any faster. He knows what he's doing."

Major Gwinn looked down the wide stretch of sandy beach. How did he suddenly get back on the beach? Never mind. Too confusing.

Satan is running across the waves towards him. The water is the color of fire, of sulfur, glowing blue orange and white edged. He's chasing a rundown fishing boat, three boats, a sailboat, all the same boat. He's chasing them with blood thirsty vengeance, with salivating lust. But the boats keep evading him. He gets near one and it fades into the sea. It burns and disappears, only to re-appear somewhere else.

He's in the water. He's sinking. He's drowning. Drowning?

The jungle again.

"Okay, men. Here's the trip. We have four Aussies trapped just inside the entrance to one of the Viet Cong tunnels. We have less than three hours before Charley returns to this area, according to recon, so we have to move fast."

A blinding flash. A mind tearing explosion.

"Christ! Where did that grenade come from?"

Blackness!

"Damage report! Damn it! Get a damage report, Captain." In the submarine? How'd I get back in the submarine? Forget it. I don't have time for foolish questions.

"Look! This is my boat Major Gwinn. My orders are to deliver you near the coast where you want, but I'm going to get to wherever that is, my way. Got it?"

"What's that?"

"A cloud."

"A cloud? No. It's all red. It's a, no, it's changing shape. It's a devil. It's Satan, again. He's got a gun in his hand. He's pointing it at.... No, he's changing."

"What?"

"He's changing."

"Changing? Changing into what?"

"He's changing.... He's a boat, a, a fishing boat? Yeah, a fishing boat."

"Major Gwinn? Is that you? I guess I didn't watch where I was putting my big feet down again, hunh? God damn mines."

Those were the last words the Special Forces trained medical doctor, one year out of internship, ever whispered. God damn war. God damn waste.

"Pirates? What the hell do you mean, pirates?" the major asked, standing in the middle of a devoid, watery plain. "How can there be pirates in the middle of the Delta? You're nuts!"

"No. You're nuts, remember?"

Four green tinged men crawled out of the waves. They trudged up the beach. As they drew closer they changed shape, from men in dirty rags to loose shaped blobs. Then they changed colors; gray, fading, becoming transparent. They faded into nothingness as they trudged nearer, with the leering grins on their faces; grins showing rotten, stained teeth.

And all the time they grinned. They grinned and faded into cloudy wisps, never to be found. But they would come back. They always came back.

"And the girl?"

The grinning things always laughed at that question. They always laughed, and grinned, as they faded away.

* * * * *

Penn jumped up in his seat, his eyes wide. The alarm clock in his mind had gone off with an ear piercing ringing.

Penn Arthur Gwinn, ex-Major in the U. S. Army Intelligence Services, ex-Defense Intelligence Agency

Field Agent, ex-everything, sat up as the ringing flooded out his mind. Sweat fell from his forehead. His nap had been nothing but nightmares and bad dreams.

He had the same dreams before, many times. Only this time it was different. There was a different twist. There hadn't been the question about the girl before, nor had there been the grinning green men on the beach.

Penn got up and walked down the airplane's aisle to the lavatory. He looked at himself in the mirror. He ran his fingers through his thinning hair, wondering if it needed trimming again, what there was left of it. He decided he didn't need another trimming, yet, even though it was getting shaggy around the edges.

Around the edges, he smiled inwardly with sarcasm. Once there was enough hair on top to get shaggy, too, but that was a long time ago. He turned on the faucets and rinsed his face.

He thought about the dreams. At times he would be back in the jungle, waiting for the inevitability of death. One by one his team mates, the members of the Special Forces team, the specially trained little group of American manhood that had been assigned for his use, were being killed, destroyed, wasted in that God damn useless mess of a politically strategic non-war.

He knew the reason for the dreams, but he couldn't deal with their cause. He had to get into himself to release the trauma, but he couldn't, yet. It was still too real.

There were always pirates, in one form or another. There were always nurses to save. There was always death. There were always broken pieces of the seven years in Southeast Asia. He had been a specialist in killing. He was an agent trained in super secret agency field tactics. He had been a specialist in the jobs even the CIA couldn't handle. A specialist in jobs that meant dealing out death in one on one doses, if necessary. He was a specialist in locating and arranging for the elimination of those Special

Agents who began seeing the war as a money grabbing opportunity, not as a defense of Americanism.

Now Allie and her new husband had to be located. He had learned enough in his lifetime to locate just about anyone, anywhere. And now, at least, the endings were different when he found the person he looked for. The methods were the same, but the ending was one hell of a lot better.

He thought about Allie. He expected that if she were really anything like her father, the first two weeks of being late was just her way of getting lost for a while. It was her way of telling the world that she and her man were something special, that they did not have to return to the demands of society until they wanted to get reinvolved.

Penn wished that to be true, but he knew it couldn't be. He knew she was too responsible to let her career fade out as she lolled around in the decadence of the rich warm white beaches of the Caribbean. Something had gone wrong, unplanned, just as her father had said.

Penn also knew, as the Colonel had also said, that the Coast Guard operating in that area wouldn't help. "We're sorry, Sir," they always responded. "But we cannot put them on the emergency locate status until we have some indication that there is imminent threat to life or property, or that you have proof that they have disappeared."

Proof that they have disappeared? God damn bureaucracy, Penn complained against the incessant whine of the jets as he made his way back to his seat. That's like proving a negative. You can show something tangible, something positive, but how do you show something that's a negative, something that isn't there, that has disappeared?

That was their stock answer, though. Ever since Congress cut their budget they've been taking it out on the little people who need them the most. How in hell can they tell whether or not there's an immediate threat to life or property if they don't try to find out what happened?

What's the use, he mumbled before trying to drift off to sleep again. He knew the red tape of the bureaucracy. He knew if his Goddaughter was going to be found, he was the only person who could find her, just as he promised.

Less than two hours later, after several repeated, useless attempts to grab some more nap time, Penn felt the twin engine jet bounce along the worn concrete runway of the Belize City International Airport. Less than twenty minutes later, he and PZ had rambled their way through the careless visa stamping of Immigration, the bumbling bag inspection of Customs, and found themselves facing a line of run down taxi cabs in front of the airport, with half a dozen cab drivers beckoning to them.

"Well," PZ remarked as he scanned the line of taxis. "One thing's for sure. It's a lot easier to grab a cab here than it is back home."

"That's a fact," Penn agreed as he stepped off the small curb towards the first cab in line. "Come on," he called, getting into the front seat without waiting for PZ.

"Where to, mon?" the cab driver asked in his very best English accented Creole dialect typical of the country.

"Can you take us to the Fort George Hotel?" Penn asked.

"Yes, mon," the driver grinned as he put the 1975 model Ford station wagon in gear and bounced out of the parking lot along the poorly improved, twenty year old asphalt, two lane highway.

Several minutes passed. Penn became curious about the river that flowed quietly along the side of the road.

"Dat's da Haul Over Creek, mon," the driver said, perceiving Penn's curiosity.

"How did you know what I was thinking?" Penn asked.

"Dat be da first question anyone new to Belize asks

along here, mon," the driver said with a grin.

Penn glanced at the driver. "What makes you think we're new here?" he asked.

"Yeah," PZ chimed in from the rear seat.

"Because, mon," the driver turned and grinned with the whitest teeth Penn had ever seen. "Nobody ever ask can I go to da Fort George when dey be in Belize City before, mon. Dey know. Any cab driver can take anybody to da Fort George, mon. Dat be da only good hotel in da Belize City, mon. Dat's for true."

"Is that right, mon?" Penn replied, returning a grin.

"Hey, mon," the driver joked. "You be da Belize less dan one hour and now you sound mos' like da native. You gwan like Belize, I t'ink, mon."

PZ chuckled.

"You be fa da City long, mon?" the driver asked as he swerved to avoid a group of camouflage clad soldiers jogging along the roadside.

Penn peered at the formation of soldiers. "Belizean army?" he asked, ignoring the driver's question.

"Dem, mon? No. Dey be da British, mon. For true da Brits keep da army in Belize. We gwan independence from da English, mon, but dey be charge wid da defense fa da country. Da Belizean army, da Belizean Defense Force, dey not so well trained, mon."

"Independence?" PZ asked.

"Belize used to be British Honduras," Penn responded before the driver could. "It was a British colony."

Ten minutes later, after a rough and bumpy ride through the downtown area of the ramshackle Belize City, the driver pulled the cab to a stop in front of a two story, semi-modern, half European, half freeway motel, style building. It was built on the jetty formed by the intersection of Haul Over Creek and the Caribbean Sea.

"Here you be, mon," the driver said, as he got out to open the passenger side door for Penn. "Twelve dollars, mon," he added as Penn stepped out.

"You gotta mean Belizean dollars," PZ said. "It can't be that much American for that short ride."

"That be twelve miles, mon," the driver said with his ever present grin. "One dollar American for da mile, mon."

Penn shrugged his shoulders as he dug through his pockets and brought out an American twenty-dollar bill. "Tell you what," he said, as he handed the bill to the driver. "You can keep the change if you can be back here by eight in the morning to take us to the Municipal airport to catch a flight to Ambergris Cay."

"Sure t'ing, mon," the driver responded with glee. "I be da man here, for true! Don't worry. Be happy, mon."

"Sure t'ing, mon," PZ mimicked the driver as he and Penn made their way into the open-air lobby of the hotel. "You're a bit trusting, ain't you, mon?" he chided.

Penn ignored the remark. Instead, he made his way to the registration counter. After showing both their passports and posting half of the expected room rent in advance for both rooms, he called to the first porter who wasn't striving to look busy, and requested their bags be delivered to their rooms. He gave the man a five-dollar bill, American, for an advance tip.

"Come on," he said to PZ as he headed for the nearby lounge. "It's still early. Let's see what this country has to offer in the way of night life."

PZ followed happily.

Three black Russians and four rum and ginger ales later, they staggered up the stairs to their rooms.

"Jeez-sus, where'd the time go?" PZ asked as he looked at his watch just before entering his room. "Eleven thirty. Hey, mon," he chuckled. "Wake me up in the morning, mon."

Penn ignored the mirth and shut the door, quickly finding the bed and falling asleep on the top of it without bothering to undress. He did have to do that, though, before long. The air conditioner went off just after midnight.

The cab driver was waiting for Penn and PZ in the hotel lobby at eight the next morning, just as expected. When he saw the two take a seat at the table in the dining room for breakfast, he took the liberty of joining them.

"Nice day for a trip to San Pedro Town, mon," he greeted as he sat at their table.

"Yes, isn't it?" Penn said. "Have a cup of coffee. We'll be ready to go in just a minute or two."

Ten minutes later found them in the cab heading for the Municipal Airport, which was only four miles from the hotel on the opposite side of the town from the International Airport.

Within another ten minutes, after the driver let them off, they had boarded the single engine Cessna 305 six-passenger airplane of Tropic Air for the short trip to San Pedro, Ambergris Cay. Twenty-two minutes after that they touched down on the sand runway of San Pedro. Since they were the only two passengers in the plane, the pilot dumped them unceremoniously in front of the shack that served the San Pedro Airport terminal building before quickly turning around to roar down the runway in the opposite direction, heading back to Belize City with a downwind takeoff.

Penn watched the plane. "No traffic pattern to worry about, I suspect," he said, curious that the plane took off in the opposite direction in which it landed. "No wind to think of, either, this time of day."

They grabbed what served as one of the three taxis in town, and with little conversation from this driver, they found themselves deposited in front of the Nose Cay Charter Office.

"Well," PZ said as they faced the office. "I guess you were right. The Nose Cay chartering office is on

Ambergris Cay, like you said."

Penn turned to his partner while opening the door. "You still doubt my abilities?" he asked in jest while entering the office.

The brassy blond in the too small bikini stood behind the counter. She smiled at the two newcomers.

PZ was his typical leering self. He could only stand back and eye the woman, so Penn had to ask all the questions.

"Good body moves," PZ said later.

"You can be God damn embarrassing sometimes, you know that, PZ?" Penn responded. "Can't you ever be serious?"

"Hey. She looked like she could be real serious if she wanted to." PZ evaded the criticism.

"Nothing ever changes with you, does it, Turkey? I wonder how I ever got mixed up with you in the first place."

PZ let the remark go unchallenged, which was fortunate, in Penn's opinion. He was reaching the limits of his patience with his partner for dragging his heels in the investigation. He presumed the heel dragging was the reason PZ never helped in the questioning of the blonde.

Also, for the following three days, while they chased around Ambergris Cay looking for leads, while they flew back to Belize City to the office of the Prefecture of Police, while they visited the local U.S. Embassy, while they went to all the harbors and yacht basins, and while they went everywhere else they could think of where there might be a clue to be found, it seemed to Penn that PZ exhibited a lack of interest in anything Belizean.

The fact that no clues to the whereabouts of Allie and her husband could be found anywhere made Penn also wonder if perhaps PZ's lack of interest might not be the wisest position to take. Allie seemed to have disappeared from the face of the earth. Just like the many other people who had disappeared in that part of the world since the druggies and the pushers became such a prominent part of the American way of life.

By the fourth day Penn was beginning to think that maybe Allie was going to be added to the statistics. That's why, when he and PZ returned to the Fort George Hotel at noontime, he felt in need of the drink PZ offered to buy.

They placed themselves in a table on the verandah, and while they waited for the never rushed waiter to take their order, Penn's attention was drawn to the bar where he saw an overweight American woman tourist typically dressed in too tight white shorts and halter top. She climbed off her barstool, loudly uttered a complaint about something or other to her sunglasses bedecked, underweight husband, and sauntered over to the nearby telephone booth. No wonder the American tourist is not an enjoyed commodity any longer, he mused.

He was going to make some general comment about tourists who couldn't stop complaining long enough to start touring, when the waiter finally arrived.

"Myers's Rum and ginger ale," Penn said to the man.

"A black Russian," PZ added.

The waiter repeated the order in his slightly British colonial accent, and retreated to the bar.

"I'm not feeling very good about this case, PZ," Penn finally said at about the same time that the waiter returned with their drinks.

"I was feeling the same," PZ said without expression.

"That's the one thing I've always liked about you, PZ," Penn said with a sardonic grin. "You're so damn positive."

"Hey! You expect me to be jumping with joy? This case couldn't get any worse.?"

Chapter 8

On the first ring, Mikel Bear's eyes popped open. On the second he covered his head with his pillow, hoping it was just a dream. By the fifth ring he knew the telephone on his beside table was not going to stop ringing until he answered it.

He looked at the clock. "God damn it!" He complained. "Whoever it is had better have a God damn reason for waking me up at three in the morning." He reached for the telephone and lifted the handset in the middle of the seventh ring. "Yeah?" he bellowed into it.

"Mister Bear, Suh. You fa da get here mos' quick," the caller said. It was Manuel, one of the men who worked under Hauke's direction in the logging part of Bear's special importing enterprise in Belize. "She no gwan fa da let us go, true!" Manuel nervously added in his Caribbean Creole dialect that had as much English in it as his sixth grade education allowed.

Bear wondered why Manuel would be calling instead of Hauke, and a host of other questions about the call ran through his mind, too, but he side tracked them. He didn't want to talk about sensitive business matters over a phone that could be tapped. He paused for a minute or two, to think.

"Listen," he said at last. "Today is Wednesday. Get to the other phone. I'll call you back." Bear carefully worded his sentence. The code phrase told Manuel to go to a specific telephone, the one that was on the list to be used for that particular day of the week. He would then call from a pay telephone he would select at random. That way, none of their telephone conversations could be monitored.

Bear got out of bed and changed clothes with a quickness that belied his girth. He retrieved his telephone number code book from under his bedside table lower drawer, and on his way out the door he found the number for the phone booth where Manuel would be waiting.

He drove across town to Walnut Creek, to the phones outside Emile Villa's Barbecue House on South Main Street. He selected one of the three in private booths, entered, and pulled out a roll of quarters to feed the mechanical thief when the operator came on the line to demand the ransom for the call.

After only a surprisingly few minutes delay, the connection to the phone number the operator had dialed for him was made, and Manuel responded quickly.

"Okay. What the hell is so important that you got to call me at this hour up here? It's three thirty in the morning?" Bear growled.

"I knowed it, Suh. But, like I say, she no fa da gwan let us go noways," came Manuel's repeated excuse.

Mikel knew how to interpret the man's language. It was a cross between Carribe Indian and Spanish. 'She' meant either he, she or they, and from the context of the statement Bear knew it meant 'they'. Bear also knew that the 'they' Manuel talked about would be the local Belize customs agents, and that 'noways' meant detention. In other words, Manuel was saying he had been stopped, or detained for questioning. In Belize a person could be held indefinitely on suspicion, without charges being filed, but Manuel hadn't been that unlucky.

For Bear that meant an immediate trip to Belize to contact his connections, to lean on those who owed him favors. People like the DEA agent for the area, Morri Bund. Mikel thought about Bund. There's no sense paying the guy if I can't use him when I need him, he continued his thoughts, planning his move while Manuel waited patiently for directions.

"Listen, Manuel," Mikel said at length. "Stay put. Don't try anything. Just listen to what you're told, and do it, hear? And I'll be there first thing to smooth things out."

"Okay, Suh. Like as not I be doin' like you be sayin'," Manuel answered. He was relieved that something was going to be done. He then hung up the phone.

Bear listened to his end for a few minutes after the hang up, listening for any barely audible clicks that would indicate someone else was listening. Hearing none, he, too, hung up, and sauntered back to his Jaguar XJS V-12 sedan, lighting a cigarette on the way.

"Damn it!" he complained as he stared at his initialed gold plated lighter for a few minutes, thinking about the call. He absentmindedly diverted his frustration by reading the initials and the inscription on the lighter. "To one hell of an agent," the engraving read. The initials A.R.S. were for his former name. The name he used all his prior life. All his life before becoming embroiled in the workings of the inner circle of drug rings in New York. Before he had to enter the Federal Witness Protection program to guarantee his future safety. "That was before I developed the sweet set-up I've got going now," he concluded, tiring of the nostalgia.

"Damn it," he swore again as he put away the personal memento from by-gone good days and climbed back into his car for his return home. "Now I gotta go to Belize to straighten out this damn mess."

He roared into the intersection in anger and made a U-turn. He didn't see the cop car until the flashing lights came up behind him, forcing him to the side of the road.

"God damn it!" he swore for the third time that night. He took the ticket without further comment, knowing he couldn't waste time arguing. There were more important things to do.

The plane Mikel Bear boarded left San Francisco International only two days behind the Flyin' Penguin

Detective Agency's flight. His arrival was somewhat more notable, though. As he got off the plane in Belize International Airport, he was greeted by two Belizean customs agents and escorted to a limousine waiting outside.

The rear door was opened for him, and he was ushered into the interior with something less than a gentle push.

"Hello, old friend," came the greeting from the darkened interior.

The men who unceremoniously escorted Mikel got into the front seats, then raised the privacy window between the front and rear seats.

"Well, God damn it," Mikel responded, recognizing the voice. "Just what the hell is this all about, you old faggot?" He camouflaged his relief with an attempt at humor.

Agent Morri Bund, Chief of Operations for the Belize Area, United States Drug Enforcement agency, responded to the question, "So nice to see you, too. I knew you would drop everything and come down here if the signs of a crisis were presented the right way. You didn't let me down."

Bear stared at him. "What are you talking about?" he demanded, at length.

The agent smiled. "I do hope you forgive Manuel for that little white lie. I made him call you with that trumped up message."

Mikel felt his anger rising. He was relieved that there wasn't really any crisis, but at the same time he was angered by such a ploy. "Why in hell did you have to risk exposing the telephone code system by calling me from here when there's nothing going on but monkey business?" he demanded.

"Hey, calm down, Amigo," the agent consoled the Bear. "That was the only way I could get you here, like I said, and I know you'd want to handle this thing, yourself, rather than let that wimp of a Creole handle it. I mean, he's got a nice ass, but really, he's not much for smarts."

Bear looked at the agent again. "How the hell did they ever let a fag like you get in charge of operations anywhere?" he asked with sneering contempt. Then, without waiting for an answer, which he knew wouldn't be forthcoming, he continued, "And just what the hell is this crisis? It had better be damned important."

"Some P.I.'s from the states arrived a couple of days ago. They've been asking questions. A lot of questions. I think you should be the one to re-direct their attention, so to speak."

"You mean to say," Bear responded in rising anger, his face full of disbelief, "that you got me out of bed at three a.m. and made me fly two thousand miles just to tell a couple of private dicks where to get off?"

The agent raised his eyebrows with the choice of words.

"Don't make anything funny out of my words," Mikel commanded. "I want a straight answer. If you're capable of doing anything straight, that is. What the hell is so important?"

"I don't think I should be the one to mis-direct their inquiries," the agent said, ignoring the intended barb. "After all, I am a federal employee. I have to maintain some decorum. Anyway, it's important to you because of the questions they've been asking."

The engine on the car was running to power the air conditioning system. Variations in the idling speed caused by the air compressor switching on and off filled the awkward silence that followed Bund's statement.

"What questions?" Bear asked at length, bracing himself against the expected bad news.

"Questions about a certain girl who disappeared in the Nose Cay area about a month ago," Bund said.

Bear again glared at the man. "What the hell does that

have to do with me?"

"The girl and her new husband were on a charter sailboat," the agent answered.

"So?"

"The same type of sailboat that Milagro got rid of when he found that couple who had anchored near your ocean racer."

"The same type of boat, or the same boat?" Bear phrased the question very carefully.

"That, unfortunately, is not possible to determine, since Milagro sunk the boat in deep water."

Bear waited for a delivery truck to rumble by before he continued. "Is it going to pass?" he asked.

The agent smiled a self-satisfied smile. "I think so. Those, dicks, ah, your words, Honey, not mine, don't know anything about that, yet. Not as far as I can tell."

"Who are these nosy dicks?" Bear asked more intently. He repeated the double entendre to purposely pique the agent.

The agent let the remark pass without reaction. "Some guys that go by the name of the Flyin' Penguin Detective Agency."

The Bear sat upright with a jerk. "You're putting me on," he retorted.

"I wish that were true," the agent said. "I wish it, because then they wouldn't become a thorn in my side, in our sides."

"He's always been a thorn in my side," Mikel responded, sitting back in the soft leather seat to re-think the situation.

"He? Who?"

"Penn Gwinn, the boss of that outfit," Mikel answered with vehemence.

"Then, I guess I did the right thing by calling you down here to make sure you handled this problem all by yourself, right?"

"Yeah, I guess so," Bear reluctantly agreed.

"You might say I did you a favor?"

"I suppose you could say that," Mikel responded. He was careful with his choice of words. He knew what would be asked next.

"Then," the agent said with a softer tone that implied he was going to ask for something, "you might be inclined to see your way clear to do me a favor in return?"

"What kind of favor?"

"Well," the man began. "I do have to go to San Francisco again for a few days, and I was wondering if your contacts, some of the people you, ah, know, ah, might introduce me, ah, might make arrangements for me to..."

"For Christ sakes, you're so God damn predictable. Just say want you want. Oh, never mind, I know damn well what you want. But listen, this time don't be so God damn messy."

"You're still mad about that? I told you it wasn't my fault. It was an, ah, a little accident. Besides it was all supposed to be part of that gross little movie you wanted to make. I think it just got a bit out of hand."

"I don't give a damn what you think it was. The fact is, it was damned expensive for me. Do you have any idea the amount of money, to say nothing of the amount of coke, I had to spread around to keep everybody off my back on that one? To keep things pointed in other directions? Jesus Christ! Dead bodies aren't that easy to conceal in San Francisco, you know. Even if it is in the South of Market Street area."

"To be frank, I don't know," the agent responded more aggressively. "And also, I don't care to know, but I do know that if it wasn't for me steering things in other directions, as you say, down here, you would have one hell of a lot more trouble."

The Bear shot a glance of contempt at the man.

"Okay. So you don't like me," the agent went on. "But

nonetheless, you can't operate without me and without my protection. So, I'm not really asking, I guess. I am requesting, that you find me another, shall we say, subject for my trip. I might even be willing to make another movie."

Subject? With disgust Mikel re-phrased the term in his mind. To the agent he responded, "Okay. I'll have it set up. Now, where's Hauke? I want to talk to him."

The agent smiled with his triumph. "The last time I spoke with him he was staying at his little retreat West of town on the Hummingbird Highway. Only, now you'll probably find him in the bar at the Fort George Hotel, or in one of the side rooms with one of his disgusting little black tarts. God, but that man is so gauche."

"Why? Because he likes women?" Mikel tried to make the question sound like an indictment of the agent, not of Hauke's lifestyle.

"Well, Dearie," the agent said with exaggeration. "You said it, not me."

"Don't fucking dearie me, friend," Bear growled. "And never mind about Hauke right now. I want to go to the hotel first."

The agent directed his driver to take them to the Fort George Hotel, where Bear got out, slammed the car door without courtesy, and strode into the lobby to get a room.

He made sure the agent would make the limousine available for his use later in the day, but he first wanted to get cleaned up. Then he would contact Hauke. He had some questions about the couple and the boat that Milagro sank. He shook his head. "Who the hell told Milagro to do anything that stupid, anyway? It sure as hell better not have been Hauke, or there's going to be hell to pay."

The desk clerk's greeting interrupted his thoughts, and after registering, he made his way down the hallway to his room on the first floor. It wasn't until he got to his room that he remembered Hauke had a run that afternoon.

Chapter 9

"Sir!" the radar Yeoman called. "I been watching a blip. I think you better check it out."

"Okay, Yeoman," Lieutenant Nelson responded. "Where is it? Oh, there. Yes, I see it. Not a very large item, though, is it?"

"No, Sir, but we're over ten miles away. Could be another small boat."

"What's the speed?"

"I'd say it's moving about six or seven knots. It's slow. Maybe a sailboat, or a fishing boat."

"Good, Yeoman. I'll take it to the Old man."

Lt. Nelson left the radar room to report the sighting to Commander Sealag, the skipper of the U.S. Coast Guard Cutter # 237. They were cruising the southwest Caribbean area between the Yucatan and the coast of Honduras, near a group of islands called Islas De La Bahia, and any boats seen in the area would be of interest to their mission. The cutter was assigned to look for drug runners, contraband smugglers, or any ships of U.S. registry that might be in the area. They were to stop any such vessels and search them for contraband.

Their function was a small cog in the Drug Enforcement Administration's use of the Coast Guard in their stepped up efforts to curtail the unbelievably lucrative commercial enterprise of running the high money stuff into the U.S. via any method the smuggler's ingenuity could devise.

"Skipper," the lieutenant addressed his superior once he found the man in the ward room. "Radar's spotted a blip."

"Radar, hunh? Who spotted it?"

"Yeoman Yellman."

"Yellman? Isn't he the man that gave us so much trouble with the last sighting?"

"I'm not sure I know what you mean, Sir."

"Isn't Yeoman Yellman the man who kept insisting the regulations required a search of the last boat we stopped? Even though my decision was to not search it?"

"Yes, Sir," answered the lieutenant. "That's the man. But, I do believe he was right on the regulations thing, Sir."

"Now, don't tell me that you're going to harangue me on that point, Lieutenant?"

"No, Sir," the lieutenant replied with strictest military courtesy. He had realized his breach of military etiquette.

"I had my reasons, you know," the skipper added.

"I don't doubt that, Sir."

"Fine. Then let's go up and see what this sighting is all about. Oh, and I don't want Yellman on deck. As a matter of fact," the skipper added as he looked at his wristwatch, "I believe his watch is about over anyway, is it not?"

The lieutenant confirmed the hour of the day, and agreed that the Yeoman's watch was about over.

"Then assign his replacement to watch before we get to the boat you've spotted, and tell the chief that Yellman's not to be included in the search party, if I use one, that is. I want Yellman below decks during this stop."

The lieutenant stared briefly at his superior. To place an active crewman on technical restriction on a boat as small as a cutter was tantamount to placing him under house arrest. The only excitement on a boat the size of a cutter was to volunteer in the unusual assignments. That was all there was that could break the monotony of routine duty, providing the man didn't enjoy playing poker all night. To restrict the man's deck access, too, was nothing short of punishment.

The lieutenant considered questioning his Commander's decision, but thought better of it. "Yes, Sir." he replied.

The two then ascended to the bridge where the executive officer was in command as Officer of the Day. The skipper took command, and the executive officer took the opportunity to stand down long enough to grab a cup of coffee from the wardroom before returning to the bridge. When he got back, he found the lieutenant had gone to tend to other duties, but was just returning.

"I hear we have another sighting," the executive officer said to the lieutenant as a conversation opener.

"Yes, Sir," responded the lieutenant.

"Sailboat?"

"Possibly. Or, more likely, a fishing trawler. It's not much of a blip. Can't be an all steel hull, we're probably seeing the metal gear on board. And, she's moving slow."

The skipper looked at his two junior officers, and asked them, "Has anyone given the helm a heading to that blip you're doing so much talking about?"

"Uh, no, Sir," answered the executive officer.

"Don't you think it would be a good idea to do so, Mister?"

"Yes, Sir. Right away, Sir," replied the executive officer as he reached for the bulkhead mounted intercom. "Bridge to radar," he called.

He got his response, then requested the heading to the latest blip. After receiving the compass azimuth, he relayed it to the man at the helm.

"Ask Radar what the distance is, if you will, Mister," the skipper directed his second in command.

The executive officer responded by transferring the request through the intercom to the radar room, and after receiving his reply, told the skipper the distance was less than ten miles.

"The thing should be in view pretty soon, then," said

the skipper.

It came into view within fifteen minutes.

"There she is, Sir," the executive officer said. He was the first to spot the vessel, even before the bridge look out made the observation.

The boat was a fishing trawler, and it was flying an American Ensign. They were approaching it from astern.

The skipper grumbled some remark about the efficiency of the look outs, then directed the executive officer to retrieve the Registry of U.S. Vessels which was kept on the bridge, while he trained his eyes on the trawler becoming clearer in view.

Twelve minutes later the cutter approached close enough to the stern of the trawler to enable the skipper to read the boat's name.

"Cucaracha," the executive officer said as he, too, read the name on the stern.

"And?" the skipper asked, expecting all the information from the Registry to be read to him.

"She's a commercial fisher of 51 tons. United States registry. Owner's name: Jonathan Ploven. Built in 1965, non-owner operated. The serial number is..."

"That's enough, thank you," the skipper abruptly interjected.

"Shall we board, Sir?" the executive officer asked with some anticipation.

"No, we shall not," the skipper answered sternly. "Call the vessel and ask if they are in need of any assistance."

"In need of assistance, Sir?" the executive officer asked, confused by the contradiction of sailing orders the captain was proffering.

"I believe you heard me," was the captain's ever-stern reply.

"Very good, Sir," came the response.

"You have the bridge, Mister," thc skipper abruptly said as he headed for the companion-way. He left thc bridge without waiting to hear any of the conversation between the executive officer and the observed vessel.

Thirty minutes later the executive officer knocked on the door to the skipper's quarters.

"Yes?" came the response from within.

"May I come in?" the executive officer asked.

"You may," was the reply.

The executive officer stepped through the door as the captain shut the untitled blue book on his desk.

"May I have a few words with you, Sir?" asked the junior officer.

"Certainly," the skipper responded in a surprisingly friendly tone. It was in response to the executive officer's initial friendly approach. "What about?" he asked as he turned to face the man.

"Well, Sir," the officer began. "We have been at sea for just less than twenty days, and as we are a medium duty class boat, we will be out another thirty before this tour ends. During the time that we've been out so far we've stopped seven boats, and have failed to search two of them. As I understand it, our written orders were to search all vessels of American registry, and apply the zero tolerance standards for contraband and vessel seizure. Is that not right?"

The skipper nodded. He didn't respond, because he knew the question to come.

"Then, why did we not search those two?"

"Have you considered," countered the skipper, "that your question borders on impertinence?"

"Yes, Sir, I have. But I don't think, after having served under you for three tours, that you'd deny me the right to such questions. Particularly in this case, and particularly in view of the level of tolerance you have shown in the past for questions of similar nature from someone in my position."

"And it is just your position that allows me to respond

to that question," the skipper said, after relaxing in his chair.

The answer was not what the junior officer expected, and his frown displayed his disappointment.

The skipper peered at the executive officer. "Very well," he said at length. "Again, because of your position, I will answer your question. But remember this, everything you hear in this room does not go beyond the door. This is top secret cryptologic level information I am about to impart to you. As a matter of fact, the information is so sensitive, I have been instructed to divulge it to my second in command only under special circumstances. And then only after I receive a pledge to honor the sensitivity of the material. Do I have that pledge?"

"Of course," the executive officer replied, sure of his response, but not sure of his part in the intrigue.

"Here. Read this." The skipper lifted the book he had shut on the executive officer's entrance, and handed it over.

The executive officer lifted the book, opened it to the first page, and while the overhead fluorescent lights buzzed their 60 cycle song, he read aloud. "Top Secret Cryptologic clearance required." He turned the page and read more. "The following registry is of vessels under direct protection of the United States White House. They are not to be stopped, searched, or in any other way impeded. Their location when sighted is to be reported through Channel Z, immediately."

The executive officer looked through several of the following pages. Each page had names of vessels listed alphabetically. There were five pages of double spaced lines giving the vessel names and identification numbers, as well as a complete description of shape and size of the vessel. There were a total of 25 vessels listed.

Most of the vessels were less than Class 3 in size,

which meant they were under sixty five feet in length, and the names of either the owners or operators of the vessels were included.

The executive officer shut the book, looked at it for several seconds, then gazed at the skipper with uncertainty.

"I think you'll see the names of the last two vessels we stopped but did not search, in that book," the skipper stated.

The executive officer didn't bother to look up the names. He realized they would be there. "Are you trying to tell me...?" he began his question, then paused as he set the book on the table.

The skipper took advantage of the pause to interrupt the man's question. "I'm not trying to tell you anything that is not in that book, and in the orders it gives," he said. "You read our sailing orders this tour, and you read the part about superseding instructions. That book contains our superseding instructions."

The executive officer stared at his skipper for several seconds, thinking of how to phrase his next question.

"There are no more questions, Mister," the skipper interjected, "because there are no more answers. Do you understand that?"

"Yes, Sir," the executive officer slowly replied. "I do."

"Good. I'm sure you do," came the response. "Now, if you will please allow me to catch up on some paperwork, I would be grateful."

The executive officer turned on his heels, and left the room, trying not to slam the door in his frustration.

What the hell is going on here, he asked himself as he trod down the metal corridor. What the hell are we doing protecting suspicious boats instead of inspecting them? Especially since our tours out here have been assigned specifically to assist the DEA. Does the DEA know what we're doing, or what we're not doing, I wonder?

His further thoughts on the subject were interrupted by the call from the bridge that requested his presence. It was time to redirect the course for the continuation of the zig zag patrol patterns, and navigation needed the approval of the Officer of the Day.

The executive officer decided he would return to this problem when he had more time.

Chapter 10

Hauke reached for the telephone and retrieved it in the middle of the fourth ring. “Yeah?” he barked into the receiver.

“El Tigre will be giving an interview,” the caller said.

“Yeah?” Hauke again responded. “When's he want the interview to take place?”

“At three thirty Thursday, there.”

“Tell him I'll meet him,” Hauke said before quietly hanging up the receiver.

He looked at his watch. It was exactly noon, the precise time the call was expected. The cryptic message was exactly what he expected, except for the mention of the time. That was part of the coded message that he didn't know in advance. In fact, that time note was the entire purpose for the call.

He rose from his chair and crossed his small bedroom without noticing the gecko in the corner on the wall. He pushed aside the mosquito netting over his bed and sat down. He pulled open the drawer on his nightstand, then retrieved a notebook that was filled with telephone numbers interspersed with names and dates.

All the names and dates were phony entries. They were entered just to make the notebook look like a personal telephone directory, like a personal notebook containing the miscellaneous scraps of information that any tourist would collect on an extended trip in a foreign country.

The telephone numbers, though, were relevant. They were the coded numbers which, when matched with the time and day just received from the telephone call, would give the telephone number and location of the telephone booth in which he was to receive his call. It would be the booth that would provide him with the details of the upcoming smuggling run.

He located the telephone number he was looking for on the third page. It was for the telephone in the lobby near the lounge of the Fort George Hotel in Belize City.

He always felt uncomfortable at that phone. He suspected that most of the drug dealers who aspired to be big time international dealers, for which Belize was fast becoming famous, would be using it. And if he could think of that, then the DEA most certainly could. And that meant a high degree of probability that the telephone would be bugged.

However, the code stated that was the telephone where he was to receive the call, and he had to be there, so he stalked across the room and out the front door. He had to walk half a block to get to the small shed where he kept his locally registered Toyota. He paid no attention to the collection of birds and small animals flitting about in the semi-jungle canopy overhead, complaining of his passage through their domain. After reaching his Toyota, he found he had to fight the recalcitrant engine, finally bested it, and backed out onto the Hummingbird Highway heading for Belize City thirty miles to the north.

Half an hour later he parked in the lot for the Fort George Hotel. He had managed to find a parking space at the end of the lot nearest the hotel entrance, which meant he could make a hasty departure later. "It ain't so smart staying around to get tagged, if anybody has a mind to ask questions," he reminded himself, as he crammed the Toyota's standard transmission into reverse, shut off the engine, and got out, purposely leaving the keys in the ignition for hasty starting later.

In the hotel he made his way to the telephone just as a female American tourist raced for it. But Hauke, being the quickest and much more agile, won the race. He shut the old fashioned glass doors of the booth in her face, smiled in response to her threatening expression, then turned his back and ignored her while waiting without lifting the receiver.

The woman grew more impatient and angry with each passing second. Then, with a shaking of her fist, she retreated to sit in one of the lobby couches, carefully eyeing the man who had usurped her need to talk to her baby sitter.

Also in the Fortt George Hotel, were Penn and PZ. They were having their first drink of the day in the lounge, seated at one of the centrally located tables, surrounded by luxuriously padded chairs. They sipped on their drinks, talked, and rambled on verbally without much direction.

"You know," PZ said. "We ain't gettin' nowhere with this mess. Right?"

Penn looked up, studied PZ's hopeful expression for several seconds, then decided an answer was justified. Not to PZ's question, but to his attitude. "What is it, PZ?"

"What's what?"

"Look. You haven't had any stomach for this job since before we left the states. I almost think you didn't want us to look for Allie. And on top of that, now that I think of it, you were even dragging your heels on looking for Markham's murderer. How come?"

PZ looked surprised at the chastisement. He shook his head defensively before answering. "I ain't dragging my heels at all, even on the Markham thing. But the truth is, since you mentioned Markham's murder, we just ain't got the power to solve that puzzle. We oughta let the P.D. handle it. But on this Allie thing, I'm just as anxious as you are to find her. I just don't see how we made any progress, that's all. Besides..." He let the sentence drop and took a sip of his Black Russian.

Penn glanced up over the top of his glass of Myers's.

"Besides what?"

PZ shrugged in deference to answering.

"Oh. I see. What you mean is, that besides all that, the women around here aren't your type?"

PZ shrugged a second time, adding a negative grimace.

"PZ. The problem with you is that you're more interested in women than you are in getting the job done. How the hell you ever acquired even enough experience in this business to get your own license is beyond me. Besides, there are other things to stimulate the mind besides women."

"Hey. So I'm a New Yorker. If I want mental stimulation, I'll go to a library."

Penn never bothered to continue the worthless argument. They had the same discussions many times in the past, and the truth always revealed itself. PZ was hopelessly biased and bigoted, to say nothing of being a whore-monger. There was nothing anyone could do about it. He decided to change the subject, just as much out of boredom as out of disgust for his partner's ideals. "Belize used to be British Honduras," he said. "This is where a lot of the Honduras Mahogany comes from."

PZ responded to the change in attitude and relaxed. "Don't Honduras Mahogany come from Honduras?"

"It probably comes from both countries. Didn't you see all the logs being loaded on that freighter in Haul Over Creek as we came in on the taxi?"

"Hey. I saw so many boats in the last three days I wouldn't know the difference between a freighter and a scowl."

"The word is scow, Turkey," Penn said with a grin.

"Scowl, scow. What's the difference if you can't tell 'em apart? They're the same to me."

"Oh well, never mind. To bc honest, I think I agree with you. The scows we've seen have only caused scowls, not to mention what we learned from the brassy blonde at the chartering office. Or what we didn't learn, actually."

"Yeah, that's for sure," PZ said, happy to be joining in the criticism of someone other than himself for a change. "Would you believe somebody could be that loose in their chartering records? I mean, if you owned the boat you were chartering out, wouldn't you want to know where the boat was going before you let it out?"

"Sort of a binding note on where it was bound?" Penn said with a grin.

"Got to make a joke, hunh? Yeah, that's what I mean."

"Not a joke, really. The comment, I mean. That chartering company, though, is a joke."

"The blonde wasn't."

"Are you ever going to grow up, PZ?"

"Why? I have more fun this way. Besides, I don't want to worry like you do. It'll just make me lose my hair. Then I'd have to look like you."

"I didn't lose my..."

"I know," PZ quickly interrupted. "You grew up through it."

"I purposely keep it cut this short," Penn responded after pausing. "Anyway, if you were going to charter a sailboat in this part of the world, where would you go?"

"Me? I'd go to the nearest hotel, beach the boat, and spend my sailing time in the bar. You know how I feel about boats."

"Okay. Wrong question. Where do you suppose they went? Don't you think it odd that they didn't even tell the charter office their destination?"

"They did, remember? They said they were going south for a few days and skunk hole about."

"Gunkhole."

"Hunh?"

"The word is gunkhole, not skunk hole."

"Whatever. Gunkhole about some cays for a few days,

then head back."

"But that isn't what happened."

"That's for sure. Hey, let's have another one. It's damned hot in this country." PZ called out the order for two more drinks.

The bartender nodded his head. The lone waiter, who depended solely on tips for his income, cast a hopeful glance in their direction.

"Anyway," PZ went on. "I guess that's why the blonde broad sent us back here to talk to the perfecture of Police."

"Christ, PZ," Penn interjected with a shaking of the head. "When in hell are you ever going to learn some English? The word is Prefecture, not perfecture."

"What the hell? Whatever. You knew what I meant."

"Only because I know you."

"Then, that's what words are for, ain't it? To transgress meaning."

"Trans what? Oh, you mean to transmit meaning."

"Listen, Buzzard. We gonna to set here and go through this all day?"

"Sit here, not set here. We'll sit here as long as it takes to teach you the language."

"Bull bleep," PZ frowned.

"You mean bull s..." Penn began with a sly grin.

"Stick it," PZ hastily interrupted.

Penn laughed.

PZ showed his annoyance with Penn's superior attitude until the drinks came, then he was forced to dig in his pockets for money. The diversion changed his mood.

After the waiter formally thanked PZ for what was a mere pittance of a tip, Penn returned to the topic at hand. "Just what did the Prefecture tell us, anyway?" he asked, hoping to renew PZ's interest.

"Far as I can tell," PZ said as he perked up, "he didn't tell us a damn thing. All he said was to take a look around, and if we see the boat, tell him. Otherwise, he thinks he's got too many other things to do. He wasn't too anxious to help."

"That's about all I got from his discourse on the wonders of this little coastal country, too."

"So?"

"So, I guess we have to look around some more, by ourselves."

"Mind if we finish the drink first?" PZ asked, half heartily objecting to the suggestion that he be forced to go outside again during the heat of the afternoon.

"After the drink," Penn agreed. He actually wanted to get going at that very minute, to get some questions answered, but decided to let PZ finish his drink in peace.

A minute or two later, someone put some money into the old-fashioned juke box, and it spewed forth with some new-fashioned reggae music.

An indeterminable time later, the fat woman in the lobby again approached the phone booth, since Hauke seemed to be doing nothing more than just standing inside it, taking up space, and her time. As she was about to pound on the booth to remind him that occupying the booth meant using the telephone, his expected call came.

"Yeah?" he barked into the receiver while turning to throw a triumphant grin at the woman.

"El Tigre changed his mind about the interview," the caller said.

"Yeah?"

"It's to be given at five, Friday."

"Tell him I'll make it," Hauke responded before hanging up the phone.

Back in the lounge PZ began tapping his fingers in time to the music.

Penn shook his head once again, leaning back in his chair. He listened to the punctuated rhythms and let his gaze wander about the room. He casually took inventory of the few other tourists in the area, including the thin man that was left at the table by his oversized wife who had headed for the telephone booth in the lobby some time ago.

Hauke finally opened the doors to the phone booth and stepped out with deliberate slowness. He was ready to dodge the fat woman's onslaught, if any came about, but she wasn't about to hinder him. She wanted to get to the phone. She squeezed her considerable bulk into the booth almost before Hauke left it, and struggled to shut the doors behind her entry as he quickened his pace through the lobby, headed for his car.

A movement near the entrance to the lobby caught Penn's eye. He stared at the lobby, not sure he had seen what he thought he had. "God damn!" he exclaimed, sitting up with a jerk.

"What?" PZ responded, following Penn's wide eyed stare.

"Hauke! Mikel Bear's minion. I just saw Hauke hurrying through the lobby!"

"Bear's what?"

"Minion. You know, go-for. Come on!" He said as he hurriedly slid back his chair and got up.

PZ pushed back his chair to follow. In his haste he bounced the chair backward. As he turned to see what was happening with the chair, he knocked against the cocktail table, knocking it over, and the drinks spewed across the varnished and well polished Honduras Mahogany floor with a crashing of glass and splashing of booze. "God damn it," he swore as he turned back to chase after Penn, ignoring the mess he made.

Hauke's car started with amazing speed, considering all the objections it presented earlier, and he was off down the road in less than a minute after leaving the telephone.

PZ reached the lobby and stopped at the head of the stairs just behind Penn, who was staring at the rear of a Hauke's departing gray Toyota that was already half a block away.

"Damn it!" Penn swore. "I swear that was Hauke!" He looked for a taxi. "And no God damn taxi in sight. Where the hell are all the taxis when you need one?" At any other time, it seemed to Penn, there were at least half dozen parked about with their drivers beckoning. "Well, hell," he said, as he turned back to the lobby. "There's no way to catch him now."

The waiter was in the midst of cleaning up their spilled drinks when they returned to the lounge, so they sat at the bar.

Penn ordered and paid for the round.

* * * *

Hauke parked his Toyota in front of the office for Hard Loggers Exporting Company, on the Belmopan Road, just South of Haul Over Creek. He had the information that indicated the time and place to make his next rendezvous. The code name El Tigre meant Honduras was to be the starting place for the positioning, and that meant also that the coastal charts were to be used. The phrase about El Tigre changing his mind meant there was no change in plans from the preset routine. The 'five Friday' code words meant that the rendezvous was to be at the point on the chart where the fifth latitude line down from the top of the chart met the fifth longitude line from the left hand side.

The time of the rendezvous was correlated with the addition of the two numbers provided in the code phrase. Five and fifth, therefore, would be ten. The times were always during dark hours, so it would be ten P.M. That location, if his memory served him, was about 80 degrees west longitude by 17 degrees north latitude.

Chapter 11

Hauke made his way to the marina near the Hard Loggers yard. It was nearly 3:00 p.m., and time to ready his outboard runabout for the pickup run. He rigged his fishing poles, checked his SCUBA gear, and generally made the boat appear as though he was going out on another one of his overnight fishing trips.

He had gone through this routine often enough to make it appear a common occurrence to the locals working on the docks. They paid little attention, other than to say hello on seeing the familiar face. Nor did the port officials pay any attention. They had seen him come and go many times, and he usually returned with a fish catch of some sort, so they considered he was honestly enjoying his avid interest in the sport while taking time off from the heavy responsibilities of running the log exporting company.

They were sure he was not related to any illicit activities, especially in a boat as small as his. Such a boat, they knew, could never make it past the outlying islands and cays, let alone as far across the gulf as to reach another country to import anything suspicious. They considered him harmless enough from their positions of authority.

Besides, they knew that the Prefecture of Police gave him preferential treatment. "Hauke is an American," the Prefecture said, justifying his position. "All Americans were to be given preferential treatment when their operations brings so much needed money into the economy."

Within an hour on the water Hauke passed the

freighter that had loaded the shipment of specially prepared logs from the Hard Loggers yard and was on its way to San Francisco. He glanced at the ship with an inward grin, and pushed the throttle of his outboard all the way forward to race across the whitecaps forming in the freshening breeze. He leaned back in the cockpit seat and enjoyed the wind as it streamed through his long black hair. He looked forward to the three hours the ride was going to take.

Back at the Hard Logger's office, Manuel had watched his boss clear the harbor in the small open boat. With a smile he turned back to the yard. "Well, mon, she be all your'n, now, true," he said to himself. He enjoyed these periods when Hauke was out of the yard, for that meant he was the big man in control of the operation for a while. His pride swelled, in spite of the envy he had for Hauke's position. The pride came from the power of being boss. The envy stemmed from wishing he could be the boss all the time.

"Sometime, mon," he said to himself as he looked over the yard. "Sometime, maybe she no come back from de trip, true?" He chuckled as he walked back to the yard office with the casual swagger of a straw boss. "Someday, maybe, Mr. Hauke for true no fa da come back da trip. Da trip she be mighty dangerous, what wit da boat she be da small and all. Yessuh. Some day, true. May be."

The Hard Logger's yard was typical of any small lumbering operation. There was an intake rack where the logs that were floated down Haul Over Creek were stored after they were hauled out of the water. There were also the other operations stations; the cutoff saws, the scales, and the loading cranes for putting the logs onto the freighter.

Then there were the grading and numbering racks where the logs were numbered with the pertinent code numbers that indicated their moisture content at the time of shipping. The tags also showed the coded shipper's name and various other bits of information incidental to identifying the soon to be lumber.

One of the numbers of the code markings on certain logs was the code that indicated a particular log was specially prepared.

Part of Manuel's job was to select a mahogany log of a certain diameter from those stacked in the yard. He then drilled a certain number of holes of a specified diameter and depth in one end of the log to accommodate the plastic wrapped bags of cocaine tar that were later placed in the holes by Hauke. Manuel had to have all the logs in the yard checked, and all the holes drilled, before Hauke returned from the coca run.

Manuel had been preparing and marking these special logs when Hauke explained about making another run, but now that Hauke was gone, he was too important to work at that task all day. He would maybe take it up later, but right now he decided it was time for a nice cold beer.

He felt a certain loyalty to Hauke, for it was Hauke who had given him the job as Assistant Manager of the operation, but his sense of loyalty was lost in his self confidence with Hauke gone. It was also Hauke who always stood up for him against the big man, the man named Bear, from the states. Manuel was terrified of Bear. Although he had never seen a live bear, he considered that Mikel Bear sounded and acted like what he guessed something as nasty and awful as a live bear must be like.

That was why, whenever he learned that Bear was in Belize, he would lay low until the man was gone. Manuel hated it when the Bear showed up at the logging operation, but he knew the man was The man, and had to come around to check on things. "To make sure all the parts of the operation were operating," as Bear had explained to him.

Sometimes Bear wasn't able to come, and he would send one or two men in his place to take care of his business. These men would show up at the logging company office looking rushed, busy, and all-important. They always wanted to talk to Hauke. They'd go into the private office with Hauke for a few minutes, or a few hours, then they'd leave, still all rushed, busy, and all-important looking.

Once or twice Manuel was invited to sit in on the meetings, but only when they dealt with topics within the scope of things that Manuel could handle. He felt truly important when that happened.

So, when the two visitors from the states arrived just after Hauke left, and asked for him by name, it was easy for Manuel to believe that they, too, were messengers from Bear.

This was an especially easy presumption because of the telephone call Morri Bund had ordered him to make to Bear. He knew something was up and someone was sure to show up because of that call.

"I'm sorry, Suh, ah...Suhs," Manuel responded to Penn's request to speak with Hauke. "But Mr. Hauke she be out on da fishing trip, again, true."

Penn and PZ were standing in front of the Hard Logger's office addressing Manuel. They were both somewhat on edge, slightly rushed and wary as the result of their sudden location of Hauke in Belize. They were suffering from their surprise with the sudden change in events. Also, they hadn't expected to find the place where Hauke spent his time, and probably couldn't have found it, if the Prefecture of Police hadn't been so cooperative and informative.

As a result, they appeared to Manuel to be two persons rushed, busy, and all-important, who wanted to speak with Hauke. He knew they could be nothing but on business for the Bear.

Then, when Penn asked about the fishing trip Hauke was on, Manuel was sure the two were Bear's men. He was sure enough to be able to engage in certain confidential discussions with them and impress them with his importance.

"You know, Suh," Manuel continued with busting pride. "She be on da coca run fish trip."

"Coca Run?" Penn pronounced the words with a questioning tone.

"Yessuh," Manuel answered. "You knows. The run she be set by El Tigre, so he gotta go. Beside a which noway Hauke knowed I was who call fa da Bear, as how Mr. Bund she tell me no way fa da make no word fa da she 'bout me be fa da call."

Penn glanced at PZ, wondering if he understood what the man was trying to say, but PZ was staring at the man with opened mouth, as though utterly surprised.

"Dat call she be fa da mighty important, as Mr. Bear she send you so soon like."

"Yeah," Penn quickly responded, catching himself, sensing the man's error in identifying them. "That's true. Ah, when will Hauke get back from his run?"

"Maybe one, maybe two day, I expect," Manuel replied, his self-importance becoming more evident. "Like as how she gone, might be you leave your words fa da me. She be get it soons she come back, fa true!"

"Ah, no," Penn replied. "Our message is for Hauke. And look, we want to surprise him, okay? So don't tell him were here. We'll see him later. Okay?"

"Well, okay," Manuel responded. He was somewhat disappointed.

"Good," Penn said as he turned to leave. "Come on, Turk," he called to PZ, thinking it would be a good idea to leave some sort of name with Manuel to throw off suspicions during later questioning by Hauke, which he was certain would be forthcoming. Unfortunately, the shortened form of what he always called PZ when he was mad, was all he could think of at the moment.

"Ah, sure thing, Buzz," PZ answered, following Penn's lead.

Manuel watched the two return to their waiting taxi, thinking he made a suitable impression, judging from their expressions. "Well, maybe I be da big man more soon den I t'ink. May be."

Less than five minutes later, still feeling satisfied with himself, his mind turned to the beer that was stashed in the office refrigerator. He strode over to the refrigerator, and with his preoccupation with the beer, left the office door partially open.

Wiping his brow with the back of his bare arm, he juggled open the door of the old fashioned Frigidaire that hummed incessantly in its struggle to protect its precious contents of cold beer. He held the refrigerator door for a few minutes and stared inside while trying to decide between a clear Corona from Mexico, or a bland Budweiser from California.

He opted for the tangy flavor of the Corona, even without the benefit of a fresh squeezed lime to add to it. He grabbed the bottle, then reached for the opener on top of the refrigerator and snapped open the bottle. He gulped down half the beer as he stood facing the refrigerator and absorbing the cold air, with his back to the office door. His attention was so intently focused on his drink that he didn't hear the office door swing open and then close with a slight click of the latch.

"Where's Hauke?" Bear suddenly growled.

Manuel jumped, dropping his beer bottle in surprise. He ignored the plop of the breaking bottle and overlooked the pieces of broken glass scattering across the floor as he quickly turned around to face the man he feared most.

The surprise brought a lump to his throat, and he swallowed several times to regain control of his speech.

"What the hell's the matter with you?" Bear growled again before Manuel could summon up enough courage to say something. "You seen a ghost or something?" Bear added. He sensed Manuel's fear of him, and he loved playing on that fear for his own perverted ego ingratiating pleasure.

"Mistuh Bear, Suh," Manuel finally gulped out. "I thunk, I means, like as how two men... I mean... I thunk might be you wasn't coming, dem men, dey be your'n."

Mikel gazed heavily at Manuel. "Manuel," he growled. "Get a grip. What in hell are you so excited about? What men?"

"Dem two," he said. "Dey was just right here. Dey want Mister Hauke, too. I thunk dey be your'n mens, what wid dat telephone call and all. Like you sent 'em." Manuel's reasoning power was gaining momentum. He furrowed his brow in fear of the answer of his next question. "Ah...you like as not didn't send dem?" he stammered.

"What the fuck are you talking about?" Bear bellowed. "What two men?"

"Dems' dat was here," Manuel nearly whispered, fearful of the response the confession was sure to evoke.

"Look," Bear said menacingly. "This is not the time for games. What two men? What were their names?"

"Two white mens, Suh," Manuel nearly whispered his response as he stepped backward, back until he was stopped by the refrigerator that was still open. The cold air sent shivers up his back. He was trapped, but he knew he had to answer. "Gawd, Suh. Dey... I... dey..."

Mikel glared at Manuel.

Manuel gulped once more. "Dey... one about dis here tall," he quickly held his right hand to the approximation of Penn's height. "Wit most no hair, kinda light colored," he added. "And da other she be maybe so, with all curly hair." He held up his left hand at the same time to indicate

PZ's height. "Da tall one, she have da beard," he stammered in definition, hoping the honesty in his efforts would be recognized.

Several seconds passed in silence with Manuel holding his hands in the air in front of him, leaning back against the refrigerator. He half expected he would be attacked at any second.

Bear only continued his glare, though. He let several more seconds pass before speaking. "The one with no hair," he finally asked calmly. "Did he have glasses?"

"Yessuh. Fa true!" Manuel hastily answered without moving his hands.

"Did they have names? Now think hard. Did they give you their names?"

"Yessuh. One she be call fa da Turk, and da other, she be call Buzz."

"Did they say anything about coming back or not?" Bear demanded.

"Mistuh Bear, Suh. Dey wanted to fa da see Mistuh Hauke. I say she be da come back maybe tomorrow. So day say dey be here den."

It took Bear several seconds to translate Manuel's words into intelligible English, and after contemplating the meaning, made his decision. He didn't want the two men, whom he now recognized as his two adversaries, to find him in Belize. "Look," he said. "I'm going to leave. You haven't seen me, understand? And when you see Hauke, you tell him about those two guys. He'll know who they are, especially if you tell him their names are Penn and PZ. Got that?"

"Mistuh Penn and Mistuh PZ," Manuel repeated. "Yessuh. I got dat. Fa true," he added, fervently nodding his head and still keeping his hands out in front of him.

"You damn well had better 'got that'," Bear threatened. "And tell Hauke that they got to be taken care of. You got that, too? I said taken care of."

Manuel repeated his head nodding without speaking.

"Good," Bear said as he turned and strode out of the office, slamming the door behind him.

Manuel waited for several seconds more before letting his hands fall. When he heard the car door slam and the vehicle pull away from the yard, he began to breath easier. He turned to get another beer from the refrigerator with shaking hands.

Mikel stalked out of the Hard Logger's office feeling his anger rising. The heat of the afternoon was stifling, and it was especially troubling for a man of his bulk. The sweat ran down his neck and soaked his open shirt collar before he got safely ensconced into the back seat of the limousine loaned him by Agent Morri Bund. "God damn it!" he swore. "All I God damn need is the fucking Flyin' Penguin Detective Agency breathing down my neck down here. One thing is for God damn sure. It's time to get rid of those worms for good."

He tried to get Penn Arthur Gwinn at least three times over the past ten years. Each time his plan seemed to backfire for some unknown reason. "But this time," he mused, "they're out of their element. They're in my web, my control. If Hauke can't take care of them this time, for good, then I'll get somebody like Luigi and Pasqualli down here to pay a call on them." He leaned back to relax once more, thinking he would get rid of Penn Gwinn at last. "Hey," he yelled at the limousine driver, regaining his temperament. "You got the God damn air conditioning on in this thing or not?"

After being reassured his comfort was being seen to, he returned to his thoughts of his enemy. Yeah. Down here's the place to take care of Penn. And it'd be a good thing to get rid of his twerp sidekick, too, before too much of that thing about Markham gets out. He reached for a cigarette from his shirt pocket with his right hand and at the same time reached into his left pants pocket with his other hand to retrieve his favorite lighter. He had the lighter struck and burning, almost up to his face to light the cigarette he put there, before he realized the cigarette was soaked with sweat.

"God damn it!" he swore as he flung the soggy nicotine stick on the carpeted floor. "I must have been madder'n I thought. I'm sweating like a pig." He turned his attentions on the driver. "Hey," he called. "You got any smokes up there? Give me one, will you? Mine are all wet."

The limousine driver shrugged, pulled a pack from the seat beside him, and tossed it back through the now open privacy window, which when closed, separated the front seat from the rear.

"Thanks," Bear said grudgingly as he took one out of the pack before tossing the pack back. Yeah, he continued with his thoughts, after happily taking a deep puff from the cigarette. Who's to know if another tourist wanders off down here in the jungle? It happens all the time. Their bones might be found in a year or two, maybe.

He chuckled as he agreed with himself. "Maybe I should arrange a back up plan for their elimination before I leave," he said aloud to no one in particular. He re-considered the idea. "Yeah," he affirmed. "It'll only take a minute, and the back up makes the job guaranteed."

Chapter 12

Back at the Fort George Hotel, Penn and PZ had once again taken their favorite table. Then Penn signaled the waiter to take their drink order.

"Just what in hell is going on here, anyway?" Penn asked thoughtfully as the waiter approached.

"Sir?" the waiter asked, thinking the question was directed at him and wondering what he had done to disturb the Terrible Two Tourists, as he had decided to call them by this time.

But Penn was deep in thought, and didn't respond.

PZ, though, was always ready for a drink. "He ain't talking about you," he said in reassurance. "But we'll take the usual."

"Very good, Sir," the waiter responded, now quite familiar with what the usual was for these two.

"What the hell?" Penn repeated his question. "Let's get this thing straight. Hauke is down here running a company named Hard Loggers that has something to do with our old buddy, Bear."

"And we got mistook..." PZ added.

"Mistaken," Penn interrupted.

"Whatever," PZ said. "We got mistaken for two of Bear's messengers. And Hauke, Bear's right hand man, is right now out on a coca run fishing trip, what ever that is."

"That's what I heard," Penn agreed.

"Just what the hell is a coca run fishing trip?" PZ asked.

"What do you think it might be?" Penn countered.

"Coca? Cocaine," PZ responded, emphasizing the last syllables of each word.

"A cocaine run fishing trip," Penn said.

"Hauke is smuggling coke?" PZ asked the obvious.

"And if Hauke is, you can bet it's at Bear's direction," Penn added.

"Wait a minute," PZ began in a sarcastic tone. "Is this the same Mikel Bear that's supposed to be such an fucki' good DEA snitch? The same Mikel Bear that a couple of years ago tried to set you and your girlfriend up on a phony coke dealing bust?"

Penn chuckled, "Yeah. The same one and only."

"That's a bit like a Tricky Dick, ain't it?" PZ responded, referring to a former president for whom he had little admiration.

"Tricky Dick?" Penn asked in amusement. "More like pestilent prick, if you ask me." He paused to ponder. "Now, that means," Penn went on. "That Bear is smuggling coke into the states from Belize, and the only way I can see that he'd be able to do that is through a cover, a strong cover. A cover, maybe. Like Hard Loggers. Right?"

PZ shrugged his agreement.

"Exactly," Penn continued. "And, how does he get supplied?"

Again PZ shrugged.

"From boats," Penn said. "That's what Hauke's fishing trips are. He picks up the stuff from boats that come from... From where?" He stared at PZ, expecting more than a shrug. Finding no help, he answered his own question. "From boats that come in from Colombia. Venezuela, or maybe Panama. Or Nicaragua, Honduras, any country in the South or Central American coastal area that needs the money the coke dealing brings in." He paused. "And Hauke meets the boats and brings the stuff on into Belize."

It was easy for Penn to understand how a man in Mikel Bear's position could have access to the personal needs of various customs inspectors and be able to develop the requisite bribery set ups. Particularly so, if the Bear had as much access to the DEA operations as he was reputed to have through his cover of being a DEA snitch.

"Yeah? Whatever it is, it's a nice little coke thing they have here," PZ commented as he leaned back in his chair.

"Coke thing?" Penn perked up as he repeated PZ's words. "Good Christ, PZ. You hit the nail on the head."

"I did?"

"Right. Cosa Nostra, our thing. Coca Nostra, our coke. That was Coca Nostra in Markham's notes, just like it was spelled."

"Coca Nostra?"

"Exactly," Penn continued with exuberance. "And Markham must have been onto Bear's drug smuggling. That's why Bear's name was on the list along with Bund here in Belize."

"That's possible," PZ reluctantly agreed.

The waiter delivered their drinks while Penn was deep in thought.

"Then the dudes we saw in Markham's office were Bear's men?"

"No," Penn said. "I don't think so. Bear's not cool enough to hire someone that efficient and smooth. They were big time. Bear would like to be big time, but the truth is, he's still nothing more than a New York cowboy, mostly show and no go, no substance. I just don't see him being the brains behind those two. Bear's methods just don't fit in with those two."

"Oh," PZ said. "That's just a fucky ducky," he added. "The way I see it, big time means big guns, and we ain't got a bebe gun between us down here. I wish I'da brought my hog leg 44."

"There's another question," Penn went on. "If the cocaine gets shipped out of here through Bear's operation, how does he get it in here?"

"I thought we just decided it was through Hauke and his little fishing trips."

"How does Hauke get his hands on it?" Penn continued his line of reasoning.

PZ shrugged his shoulders again without answering.

"Well, simple," Penn again answered his own question. "Hauke meets the supply boat on his little fishing trips. And, if the Bear likes to cover his tracks, that supply boat is probably a different boat each time."

PZ paused for a few seconds, considering the scenario. "then where would he get all the different supply boats?" he asked after considerable thought.

"Hell," Penn said in response. "Boats end up missing all the time..." He suddenly realized what he had said. He stopped, stared at PZ, and stated the supposition they simultaneously formed. "You don't suppose that Allie's charter was..."

"Pirated," PZ butted in.

"That means Mikel Bear could have had a hand, I mean, might have been the cause, even remotely, for the piracy?" Penn asked.

PZ didn't answer.

"I hope not," Penn said. "If Allie's boat was pirated there's no chance we'll ever see her again. The guys that do that sort of thing are famous for eliminating any witnesses."

"Wait a minute, Chief," PZ said. "Ain't you over reacting a bit? We don't know anything like that, for sure. And besides, even if Bear was behind half the boats that end up missing in the Caribbean, or even in just this part of the place, ain't it kind of slim he would be responsible for the one boat we're looking for? I mean, what would the odds be for that?"

Penn took a long sip of his drink before he answered. "I hope you're right. I hope the odds are too damn slim."

"Yeah," PZ responded as he slid down a little more in

his wood backed chair and reached for his drink.

"But, you know what?" Penn sounded a little more positive.

"No," PZ answered as he perked up. "I don't know what. If I did know what, I'd be back home doing something, or somebody, maybe, I enjoyed. But no, I don't know what. That's why I'm down here sweating my ass off."

Penn glared at his partner for a few seconds. "What I'm talking about, Turkey," he said, "is that we should pay a visit to the one person we forgot about down here."

"Who?"

"The guy that Giddings told me about. Baletta, Morgan Baletta. Captain Giddings said that if we wanted to know anything about what goes down around here, we should talk to Morgan Baletta."

PZ caught on to the idea with more enthusiasm then he had been recently displaying. "I think you're right, Nero," he kidded. "Let's wolf down the drinks and solve this mystery."

Penn grinned. "Good idea," he said. "But there's one thing I want to do first."

"Yeah?"

"Yeah. I think we want to call on our old buddy, Yanks. I think I'd like to know what he found out about the McIvers and Bear connection. Then I think I would like to have him put a tail on Mikel Bear."

Penn got up from the table and made his way to the public telephone booth in the lobby. After a short discussion with the Belizean Bell telephone operator with the heavily accented Caribbean version of the English Language, he heard his destined number ringing on the other end.

"Yanks?" Penn asked when the hello resounded through the handset.

"Yeah? Hey, Penn?" Yanks responded. "Hey, what's

up? Where you two been? Lara won't tell me a damn thing. She said something about you being out of town somewhere, didn't know where. And I know damn well that's a bag of carp, I mean crap. You ain't never been anywhere she don't know about. What are you, I mean, where are you? What're you up to?"

Yanks excitement was making his mouth precede his thoughts by a word or two. Whenever he got nervous or excited his speech was a dead giveaway. That was why he never won at playing poker. Half the time his bets would emerge in confusion.

"Well, old buddy," Penn began. "You won't believe this, but we're in Belize."

"You're in believe? I don't Belize it, I mean..."

"Never mind," Penn interrupted. "I know what you mean. But look, I have something for you."

"Great. What?"

"The last time we talked, you said you heard something about a McIvers, Bear connection. Remember?"

"Sure."

"Did you do anything about that?"

"Yep."

"Well?"

"Well? Oh, you mean, did I find out anything? Yeah, I found out a lot. McIvers' been feeding Bear information from some of the working homicide files from the city, but I ain't been able to get a file on which fingers, I mean, a finger on which files, yet, though."

"No kidding? I sure as hell would like to know more about that. Can you keep on that?"

"Sure."

"Good. And here's something else I'd like you to do. I want you to put a tail on Bear."

"What?"

"You heard me. I want you to put a tail on Bear?"

"Pin a tail on the bear?"

"Put, God damn it. Put a tail on Bear!"

"Put a tail on Bear. Oh, yeah. I can do that. When?"

"Right now."

"Can't"

"Can't? Why not?"

"He ain't in town."

"Where is he?"

"Somewhere down south, I think. Maybe L.A. Or maybe San Diego. Somewhere. Mexico, maybe, even."

"Jesus. You don't mean Belize? He couldn't be in Belize, could he?"

"Don't know. Where the hell is Belize, anyway?"

"One country south of Mexico, sort of."

"Well, I guess that's where he could be."

"Damn," Penn said quietly. Then he continued his orders to Yanks. "Watch his house. I want to know when he gets back. And when he does get back, tail him. Keep on him for as long as you can. I'll get back to you as soon as I can. Tomorrow, maybe. Get it?"

"Got it."

"Good. Okay. See you."

"Yup. Bye."

Penn hung up the phone and emerged from the telephone booth. He returned to the table deep in thought.

"You look upset, Chief," PZ greeted as Penn sat down.

"Bear's down here," he responded flatly as he reached for his drink.

"You're fuckin' kidding!" PZ was astonished.

Penn glanced at his partner. He knew there was no need to repeat his statement.

"Well, Chief. What now?"

"For one thing, I would rather not have Bear know where we are. For the second, we find Morgan Baletta."

"I agree with the first one. But how we gonna do the second? Where?"

"If I knew that It wouldn't be a question of finding, would it, Turkey?"

PZ let the challenge pass good naturedly. "Try the telephone book," he suggested instead. "Or maybe you could try your new found friend, the Perfecture of Police." He accented the 'Per' part of Perfecture for Penn's sake.

Penn again glared at his partner. "Do you really think Baletta's going to be listed in the Belize telephone book?" he asked with disdain. "What do we look under? Secret agent?"

"Now who's the Turkey?" PZ responded with a grin. "You look under Baletta, M."

Penn glared again. He had bad feelings about the suggestion. It was one of those feelings you get when you realize how stupid you've been. "PZ, you son of a bitch," he quipped. "You had better not be right."

"Hey," PZ said with a shrug of his shoulders, responding to Penn's challenge as he got up and headed for the telephone booth to prove his theory.

Penn was deep in thought when PZ returned with a grin.

"Guess what?" PZ asked as he sat back down at the table.

"You son of a bitch. You didn't...?" Penn let the question drop.

"Morgan Baletta. Telephone number 08-2504," PZ's grin broadened.

"I'll be damned," Penn said with a shaking of his head. "How do you do it?"

"Do what?"

"Always find the simplest means to do anything?"

"Maybe I'm smarter'n you."

"I sometimes wonder if you aren't."

"So, what now, Chief?"

Penn responded with an amusing smile. "I take it back. You're not that smart," he said. "Now we go to the

Prefecture of Police, get him to tell us the physical location of that telephone number, and we pay a visit on Morgan Baletta."

"Why not just call Baletta and talk to him?"

"Why not? Now that is a dumb question. Would you talk to someone about this over the phone if you didn't know the person calling?"

"Yeah I see what you mean."

"So, it'd be best to pay a surprise visit to this man Baletta, wouldn't it?"

"I guess."

"Good. Then let's go." Penn got up from the table and strode from the room with PZ not far behind. He wondered what surprises were next in store for them with this Baletta person.

Chapter 13

A taxi was waiting just outside the hotel entrance, and after explaining their desire to first go to the police station, Penn and PZ got into the rear seat. The cab driver then pulled out into traffic. The traffic wasn't much, though. It consisted mostly of bicycles and pedestrians with an occasional car or truck.

It took less than ten minutes to secure the directions to Baletta's small villa from the Prefecture of Police. It took another forty minutes of driving through alleys, over chuck holes, and over the ruts and mud puddles of the Western Highway after crossing the Swing Bridge over Haul Out creek, to get there.

"Well," PZ quipped after they had reached a spot in front of a broad, six foot high stucco and brick fence that the cab driver said was their destination. "This must be the place, 'cause their ain't no other place near this place like this place."

"Looks like it," Penn agreed as he got out of the taxi and handed over the exorbitant, ten-dollar fare the driver demanded. "Park over there," he directed the driver. "About a block down the road, and wait for us, okay? Here," he added as he pulled out another ten dollar bill. "This is for your waiting time, and there's another ten in it if you're still here when we get back."

The driver returned a knowing smile to silently acknowledge his agreement to wait, and put the cab in gear.

As the driver drove off, Penn turned to face the building. "It's supposed to be the only green painted cement block house on this part of the road before the big turn," he said to PZ in confirmation.

"And that sure looks like a big turn," PZ said as he looked at the part of the Western Highway, the only highway, that ran in a Westerly direction out of Belize City. It made one long turn across the flatlands before winding its way through the jungle on its way to the Belizean capital of Belmopan more than seventy miles away.

Penn motioned PZ to follow as he crossed the few steps from the road to the front gate of wrought iron that joined the two ends of the cement block fence. He gazed inside at the house that was set behind the fortress like fence. It was well maintained, and sat amid a plethora of jungle bushes, vines, trees, and Bougainvillea of the brightest red he had ever seen.

They opened the gate, dodged the falling Bougainvillea blossoms, and walked into the courtyard surrounded by flowers of every color imaginable.

In the corner, perched on a shoulder high stand, was a parrot. It squawked an objection to the intrusion into its solitude, as nearby a green iguana lunged for cover under the front porch. The yard was full of birds bounding among the bushes and tree limbs above the brightly tiled patio., The parrot's warning squawk set off a myriad of chirps, tweets and squeals.

"Jeez-us," PZ said. "What the hell did you do?"

"Nothing that I know of," Penn replied, watching the excited birds.

"One hell of a watch dog." PZ said. "Better'n geese, I'll bet."

The birds kept the attention of the two long enough for the front door of the cottage to be opened by a woman dressed in white shorts and a short sleeved white blouse. The blouse was knotted in the center of the waist in a midriff style. She stared at the two men while they were absorbed in their bird watching.

"What do you want?" she asked at last. Her voice was soft and velvety, but strong, with the clarity and forcefulness common to someone used to being in control.

Penn and PZ were startled by the woman's voice that suddenly contrasted with the squawks of the courtyard. They turned to face her. Neither had expected to be greeted by a woman, and even more of a surprise was the .357 Magnum she pointed in their direction.

"I don't think that's necessary," Penn quickly responded.

"I'll be the judge of that," the woman said, as she raised her left hand to brush aside one of her long blonde tresses that fell out of her overhead knotted bun to land across her left eye and partially obscure her vision. "What do you want?" she repeated.

"We would like to speak with Morgan Baletta," Penn answered, showing as much control over the unexpected as could be expected.

"Why?"

"I think that's between him and us," Penn replied.

The woman chuckled. "I'll be the judge of that, too," she added. "What about?" she repeated her question.

Penn decided he had to reveal at least part of their purpose to this formidable female obstacle if he and PZ were going to attain their goal, so he explained how it had been suggested by the San Francisco Police Department to contact the special agent.

"What makes you think Baletta is a special agent for anything?" the woman asked with suspicion.

Penn decided to answer the question with directness and with reason, since the woman was obviously not in the mood for playing games.

"Look," he began. "If you can put that thing down, then maybe we can relax enough to explain our purpose. Then, once you can see we're legitimate, you can take us to Morgan, okay?"

The woman relaxed slightly, and lowered the stainless steel Colt to point at the ground in front of the two, rather than at their mid sections. She then leaned against the door post to listen to Penn's explanation. "So?" she asked, in a tone that continued to show her confidence and her belief in her ability to control the situation.

"So," Penn began, glancing at PZ. He wondered why the man had been so inactive so far. Then he saw that PZ was staring intently at the woman.

It wasn't until that moment, when Penn returned his gaze to the woman, that he realized how fantastically beautiful she was. She stood at least five foot seven inches tall, with hips that were narrow, but which curved inward to her even narrower waist in luscious gentleness, revealing sensually sculptured thighs and legs under her tight fitting white shorts.

Penn shook his head at PZ's ogling, but he hadn't the time to admonish the man. He had to come up with an explanation for their knowing who Morgan Baletta was, or, he feared, this woman who was so beautiful in appearance was likely to become ugly in her disposition.

"I'm not going to stand here in the open and discuss sensitive information," he said at last, trying for a bluff. "We're private investigators from California, and we were sent here to discuss certain problems with Morgan Baletta which only Morgan and the people who sent us would know about."

"What kind of problems?" she asked sternly.

"The kind that deal with the special work Morgan does," Penn parried.

"And what kind is that?" the woman persisted.

"Look. Let's stop playing games," Penn countered. "Our problem deals with a guy named Mikel Bear, the Hard Loggers importing business, a guy named Hauke, and a certain method of importing things to the U.S. without their being known."

The woman became interested when the names were presented.

"And why should those names mean anything to Morgan?" she asked, still wary.

Penn decided he was going to have to let it all out.

"Because," he said. "Morgan is the special agent sent here to look into the same problems that we're looking into. Or rather, the same problems that we have uncovered while we were looking into another problem. We're hoping that we and Morgan can be mutually helpful in getting our jobs done."

The woman scrutinized the two for several more seconds before responding. Then, just as PZ was starting to grow restless, she said, "All right. Come on. Have a seat." She stepped out through the door as she tucked the revolver into the waistline of her shorts, and led the way into the cool shaded area of the porch just in front of a propane powered refrigerator.

She opened the door of the faded porcelain fixture, extracted three cold Coronas, and sat at the table as she reached for the bottle opener placed in the center of it.

Without comment Penn and PZ accepted the change in hospitality, and sat down. They each took one of the opened bottles, and after taking a deep swallow, Penn asked, "I assume we can speak to Morgan now?"

"That's a pretty good assumption," she said after completing her second swallow of the brew.

"Well?" PZ finally said. His impatience, to say little of his chauvinism, was getting the best of him.

"Well? Well what?" the woman responded.

"Well, where the hell is this Morgan Baletta?" he demanded.

"You're looking at her," she replied as she sat back in her chair and smiled.

PZ almost dropped his bottle in his surprise. Had he been taking a drink, he would have spewed it all over the table. "You?" he sputtered. "You're the guy? But, you can't be him. You're a woman."

"I'm a female, yes. And whether or not you like it, I am Morgan Baletta."

PZ was dumbfounded. He had so surely expected Morgan to be a male. After all, weren't all special field agents men?

It was obvious to Penn that PZ had a hard time handling the problem. For the problem to be such a damn attractive one, at that, caused even more consternation in the chauvinistic PZ. How could he reconcile such important work being done by someone like a woman? It might have easier for him to deal with the recognition of the woman's playing the game if she were more butch, more the masculine Russian woman type, but not someone as soft, alluring and luscious as this woman. For once PZ was overcome by the situation. Normally he could talk his way out of any encounter, but this one seemed to burden his imagination.

"Well," Penn said to Morgan after the initial shock wore off. "Then let's see how we can help each other." He opened the discussion with a friendly challenge.

"First," she countered, "you are going to tell me what you know, or what you think you know, about me."

Penn smiled at the gambit and returned the play. "What we know," he said, "is that you're a special field agent for the DEA, sent down here to keep watch on a certain other field agent."

"What other field agent?"

"Morri Bund."

"Where did you get such information?"

"From someone you don't need to know about," Penn decided he would add his own game plan.

It was checkmate. The woman realized she was not going to get anywhere with her approach, and Penn knew he had blunted her thrust.

"All right," Morgan said, compromising. "Since only those people who would have a need to know would possibly know who or what I am, you must be one of those."

"That is true," Penn had to return to his role playing on that point. He couldn't let the woman know that he had learned her identity through something as mundane as a mistake by Captain Giddings.

"Here's what we have to offer," he went on. "It might be of some use to you." He leaned back to take another swallow of his beer before talking. He did this more for effect than for a need to gather his thoughts. "We have had," he began his offering, "...a very interesting interview with Hauke's man, Manuel. It seems that Manuel mistook us for some type of messengers from the Big man in the states who runs the operation called Hard Loggers. He let it slip that Hauke is, at this very hour, engaged in picking up some contraband from somewhere out on the Gulf. The contraband, we have reason to believe, is cocaine. And the logging importation business, we also have reason to believe, is the method by which they import the stuff into the U.S."

Morgan's eyes widened slightly, then quickly returned to the cautious inquisitive stare. "Who is this so called Big man you mentioned?"

Penn caught the change in expression, and noted how smoothly she veiled her surprise. He considered that the information was of more than passing interest to her. He assumed it was because she hadn't yet put that piece of evidence together. He felt sure that he was offering something genuine in the bargain. "Mikel Bear," he stated.

"Mikel Bear?"

"Right. He's a private investigator from California. He's one slippery person. He has so many ties with the law enforcement agencies, as well as with the less than legitimate side of many operations, that you don't know for sure what he's doing. At least he thinks we don't know what he's doing."

Morgan offered no change in expression this time as she received the information. "I know the name," she replied. "He is supposed to be a big time snitch, isn't he?" Her question was more a statement in agreement than a point of curiosity.

"That's him," Penn said.

"Then," she continued, "what you're telling me is that you think Mikel Bear is the wheel behind the Hauke operation?"

"As best we can determine so far," Penn replied. "And what's more, I'm quite sure that the guy you're interested in, Morri Bund, is tied in with it. I can't see Hauke making all the boat runs that he must make without Bund having to look the other way."

A few minutes of silence followed as all three completed their beer. She then extracted three more from the well stocked refrigerator, with PZ leering at her every move. She opened the beer as one of the pet parrots sailed over to land on the top of the refrigerator, demanding attention.

"Scram!" Morgan ordered the green and yellow bird, waiving her arm around as though to brush it off the machine.

The bird let out a squawk that excited the other birds for several minutes, and flew back across the courtyard to join one of its soul mates on another perch.

"Ever hear of the Quad Lateral Council?" Morgan asked as she returned her attentions to Penn.

Penn was more curious about the sudden change in topics than in the topic itself. "Don't think so," was his cautious reply. "Who's the Quadrilateral Council?"

"Not Quadrilateral. Quad Lateral," Morgan corrected as she took another swallow from her bottle.

"I don't think I've ever heard of any Quad Lateral Council," Penn replied when Morgan finished her swallow of beer. He glanced at PZ. He noticed that PZ was still awed by the beauty of the woman who was also an agent, and he sensed that the woman agent was somewhat amused by PZ's gawking.

"You said that Hauke is out on one of his runs right now?" Morgan returned to the main subject with no further reference to the Quad Lateral Council.

Penn was confused by that tactic. He wondered if she was trying to reveal some other players in the game without revealing the part they played, or if she was merely tossing out the name as a gambit to divert his interest, to make him think there were other players.

"According to Manuel, he is," Penn responded without showing his curiosity in the tactics.

"It was yesterday that Milagro put to sea from Honduras in the Cucaracha, a fishing trawler," Morgan proffered at last.

"Then this Milagro is the contact for Hauke?" Penn asked, surprised at the suddenness with which she revealed the important clue.

"I haven't been able to prove that, but for the last several months, every time Hauke makes one of his little fishing trips, which he sometimes does as many as three times a month, Milagro sets out one day earlier. The pattern is consistent."

"That seems pretty clear to me." It was PZ who added the conclusion after finally regaining his self-control and showing interest in the conversation.

Penn smiled inwardly at the admission in her statement. She had revealed that she was well aware of Hauke's movements, and had been for at least the past several months. What he had told her was not any surprise to her.

"Yes, it would seem so," Morgan responded to PZ's

statement. "But there's one very big problem with that."

"What?" PZ and Penn asked simultaneously.

"The time and mileage figures don't match. When you track the time Milagro is out on his fishing run, match that to his boat speed, and come up with the maximum amount of miles he can cover, he couldn't possibly get anywhere closer than three hundred miles from the maximum range of Hauke's boat. How could they make any kind of exchange from two hundred miles apart?"

"Good point," Penn conceded.

"Not really," PZ interjected.

Penn turned to his partner. "What do you mean?" he asked.

PZ wanted to impress the female agent, and he had decided to join the meeting by jumping in with what he hoped would be some remarkable analysis. "I mean," he said. "If the figures don't fit, then you got the wrong figures."

Penn glared at his partner. Once more he had expected something more astute, and was disappointed. "Right," he said in exasperation.

"Really," PZ confirmed his statement. "The figures gotta be wrong. Either Milagro's boat, or Hauke's boat, goes a hell of a lot faster'n we think, that's all."

The other two stared at PZ. His conjecture was too simple to not be of some value. It was too witless to be worthless.

"Out of the mouths of babes," Penn said with a slight grin.

"Except," interjected Morgan. "The Coast Guard has sent tracking reports of both boats, at my request, which shows their speed."

"How can the Coast Guard track a wooden boat?" Penn asked, recognizing a fallacy among the apparent facts. "Radar won't reflect off a wood boat."

"They're not wood. I mean, the Cucaracha is wood,

but it has large fish tanks, fuel tanks, and other gear that are made of steel. Hauke's boat, though, is aluminum.

"What?" PZ asked for explanation.

"Radar is the only spotting and tracking equipment available to the Coast Guard. Radar goes through wood and fiberglass, so they can't track boats not made of metallic substance, or without a lot of metal in them."

"Oh," PZ said. Then, apparently undaunted by the reasoning, he added, "So, maybe there's another boat?"

"I thought of that," Morgan quickly replied. "If there was another boat, then why would Hauke have to go out at all in his small aluminum boat? It doesn't follow."

"Yeah, I guess that's a point," PZ conceded.

Penn wondered if the woman was telling all she knew about the subject. It seemed to him that she was pointing out the obvious only to show that it led to a blank wall.

"Wait a minute," PZ continued in support of his train of thought. "Is there anywhere out there, some little island, or something, where Hauke could have another boat, a fiberglass boat, stashed, to use in place of his slower runabout?"

"I'm ahead of you on that one, too," Morgan replied. "I searched the entire area, all the islands and cays. No other boat anchored near, or on, any of them.

"Oh," PZ was again momentarily defeated.

"There has to be some other factor," Penn tossed in. "If this guy Milagro is running the stuff out of Honduras at the same time Hauke is bringing it into Belize, then there has to be some tie, somewhere. We just have to find it."

"You're forgetting that we don't know for sure that Milagro's boat is carrying anything contraband when he leaves on his fishing trips," Morgan cautioned.

Penn gazed directly at Morgan's eyes after that statement. He knew damn well she had lied. If Milagro carried anything at all when he left port, the contacts that the DEA and Coast Guard have would certainly file a report on it. And if Milagro didn't carry anything of importance, than why would the DEA and Coast Guard have been keeping track of him when he left port at all?

"Why," Penn asked pointedly, "hasn't the Coast Guard intercepted Milagro's boat?" He knew the answer to the question as soon as he asked it, and to save the others the trouble of answering, did so himself. "Because it's not an American registry boat, that's why," he said.

"No," Morgan replied. "It actually is of American registry. According to reports, the coasties have inspected it, and have given it clearance. More than once, too, supposedly."

"Supposedly?" Penn noted the qualification.

"Well, that's what the reports say."

"I see," Penn said, returning to his beer. That was a little monkey wrench in his analysis.

Silence again pervaded the late afternoon. As the sun began fading behind the mountains, the collected assortment of animals in the nearby jungle began singing their night songs.

The melodic noises infused their quieting effect for several minutes before Penn realized the purpose of their visit hadn't yet been discussed. "But," he said, interrupting everyone's reverie. "That's not why we're here. What we need from you, in return for our little tidbits of intelligence, is some of your information on the pirates that frequent the Caribbean."

"Pirates?" Morgan asked with surprise. "You mean boat robbing, and the like?"

"Precisely," Penn responded, trying not to sound too much like Sherlock Holmes. "More exactly, are there any known to be operating in the area, and if so, where are they? And what are our chances of catching up with them?"

"Well," Morgan replied pensively. "There are several

names that float about every once in a while in that line, if you'll pardon the expression. And, come to think of it, Milagro has been reported to be associated with such people."

Penn and PZ exchanged glances. "The same Milagro?" Penn asked with doubt.

"The same. But we haven't heard anything about him actually doing any pirating himself. Then there's some guy that's been working north of Ambergris Cay, but he only comes to this region about once or twice every five years or so. Then there's supposed to be some character that calls himself El Tigre."

"El Tigre?" Penn asked in surprise.

"Yes. But that's only rumor," she responded, looking intently at Penn's expression. "There are probably others, but who really knows? If they're successful, no one knows about them."

Penn felt a sudden uneasiness. "How much more do you know about this Milagro, anyway?" he asked.

"Why?" Morgan responded. "I mean, other than for his association with Hauke, why would I be interested in him?"

"Our client, whom I can't name, is missing his daughter down here, somewhere. We believe her boat was pirated. It had to have been right in this area, the same area which you claim Hauke and Milagro would be in if they sailed directly towards each other, as you point out."

The woman thought for a moment before continuing. "Then I gather you think Milagro had something to do with this girl turning up missing? The same Milagro that is tied in with this Mikel Bear that you know, and with the same Hauke that is in the smuggling business?" Her expression showed genuine concern after her triple question.

Penn wondered why. "It looks like it's something like that, yeah," he responded guardedly.

"That sounds like a very slim thread to me," she commented.

"At least it's a thread. That's more than we've had to go on lately," Penn argued. "The vilest of spiders have the darkest and strongest threads in their webs," he added as he sat back, not feeling anything nearly so sage as he sounded.

The twilight had now turned to evening, and the songsters of the jungle were in full concert, their melodies having been rehearsed through eons of development to this one end. The chortles and chuckles of the nearby monkeys seemed to Penn to be some hidden mockery

The sounds played reverently on the group, until Morgan intruded on the mood by reaching behind her to turn on some yard lights.

"We had better go inside now," she said. "The mosquitoes are going to be invading the territory in about two minutes, and if you don't want to get carried away by the biggest Texas state birds you ever saw, you better be protected by walls."

Penn declined the offer. "I think it'd be a better idea if we hit the road now, Morgan," he said. "We'll let you know if we come up with anything else of interest to you."

Morgan nodded her assent as Penn and PZ got up in unison, and she arose to head for her front door. She closed it sharply as the two men passed through the front gate, deep in thought, also intent on reaching their four wheeled fortress before the descending attack of the buzzing hordes.

The ride back to town along the narrow semi-paved two lane road was uneventful. Both men spent the trip deep in thought.

It wasn't until they had once again taken their familiar seats in the cocktail lounge of the Fort George Hotel that they opened their conversation.

It was Penn who first approached the subject. "Did

you get a feeling during that entire episode with that woman that she was taking in our information about the Bear and Hauke thing without so much as a raised eyebrow? It didn't seem to be much of a surprise to her."

PZ pondered the question, then admitted he hadn't given that concept much thought. "There's one thing I thought of, though."

"What's that?"

"It looks like we hit a dead end."

"Why?" Penn wondered why PZ was suddenly so anxious to call it quits on this case.

"Look at the facts. The girl is gone without any trace, the only lead we have is damn slim, and even it if wasn't, all the circumstances surrounding the lead have been looked into without anything developing."

"You mean the Hauke-Milagro connection?"

"Yep."

"Then you think Allie's dead?"

"Well," PZ answered guardedly. "Maybe so."

"But not definitely so," Penn said flatly in contradiction. "So we have to follow what ever leads we have, no matter how slim."

PZ thought a while before responding. "I guess so," he said again, disconsolately.

"So how do we do that?" Penn asked, hoping to renew PZ's interest.

PZ glanced at Penn, then took another sip of his recently served drink before answering. "You mean we gotta follow Hauke on one of his runs?"

"Looks that way," Penn confirmed.

"The trouble with that," PZ objected. "Is that we don't know when Hauke makes his runs. I mean, we do know, from Morgan, that he makes at least one run, sometimes as many as three, in a month, but we don't know when the next one is. We could be waitin' around here for another two or three weeks to catch him going out."

"Possibly," Penn agreed with a slight frown.

"I can't get into that idea," PZ concluded after evaluating the possibility of waiting. "Unless, of course, we might be able to stay at the house of a certain woman we just met."

Penn glared at PZ. "Same God damn old PZ," he said with impatience. "Don't you ever think of anything else besides sex?"

"Sure," PZ bounced back with a grin.

"What?"

"Looking for it."

Penn shook his head. "PZ," he said. "I believe you'd expect conjugal rights on judgment day, if you had the chance."

"Probably," PZ responded said with his grin widening. "But I got an idea. Want to hear it?"

"Not if it has anything to do with your last one."

"It don't."

"What, then?"

"Why not bug Hauke's boat? That way, at least, we won't have to keep an eye on it while we're waiting. When it moves we can check on it by triangling it."

"You mean triangulating it?"

"Yeah, that's the word. Triangulate it. Then we'd be free to do whatever we wanted to while we're waiting."

Penn caught on to the idea behind the suggestion. "You mean, then you'd be free to try hustling Morgan Baletta."

"Well," PZ shrugged his shoulders. "I got to admit it's a good idea."

"The bugging part might be a good idea, but the hustling part is a joke. I doubt if you have that much talent. Morgan Baletta is not your average canal carp."

"Hey," PZ responded defensively. "There ain't been a woman yet that can resist."

"Oh? I know a certain former secretary...."

"She didn't like men," PZ interrupted. "Besides, I was too busy with something else at the time, if you recall."

"Running from someone's husband, I do recall."

"A little vacation, I recall."

"You skipped the county for a while, I recall."

"Whatever."

"Well, we can give the bugging idea some thought, as I said. But right now, I think I'll go to my room and take a shower. I'd like to clean up a bit." He finished his drink and got up from the table.

PZ followed up the stairs, obviously thinking about the Morgan Baletta part of his idea, not expecting his reverie to be as rudely revoked as it would be.

Chapter 14

Allie fought against the chains binding her to the bunk. Her wrists bled from the chaffing. How long had she been here? One week? Two weeks? A month? Time eluded her in her pain. She hadn't seen land since he first brought her on board and raped her. That pain was even greater than what the chains could ever do to her wrists.

"I'm going to kill that bastard," she kept saying to herself, repeating it in her mind whenever he came near her, every time he grabbed her, forced her submission. She knew she would be free one day, and she would kill him for what he was doing to her. Knowing that was her only solace.

She hated him. She had never known hate before.

Gerald was gone. And she had never known such fright, such loneliness. She could never forget that this monster had killed him.

Like an animal trapped, alone, watching the predator come close, she felt fear.

But she would never let him see her fear. She would never let him know that he frightened her as no other animal ever could. To let him see her fear would give him power over her. It would give him the means to destroy her very being. She was not going to let that happen.

Yes, she repeated to herself when she saw him descend the ladder into the cabin where he kept her chained. "I will kill you," she repeated over and over in her mind as he grabbed her partially clad body, forced her back on the bunk, and raped her again.

* * * *

Hauke bounced across the shimmering sea in his outboard runabout just inside the Belizean Reef. It took about three hours at his top speed of 20 miles per hour to reach his destination, a group of small sandy cays clustered south of Turneffe Island.

When he reached the area it was nearing sundown, so he hurriedly drove his run-a-bout onto the shore, and into the palm frond covered ditch he made in the beach.

He donned his SCUBA gear, and with an eye for any sharks which might be in the area, he waded into the water for the short swim to the ocean racer.

When he got to the boat he reached over the low gunwale to retrieve the end of a double hose which was fitted with a valve. He turned the valve and listened to the rush of air from the compressed air tanks as it began pushing water out of the buoyancy tanks built into the sides of the boat.

The tanks filled with air, and the ocean racer began its ascent to the cool evening's air of the Belizean Gulf.

It took another ten minutes to unseal the waterproof cover on the switch panel of the ocean racer, make sure the self-sealing waterproof gas tank vents were again open, close the quick scuttling scoop in the bottom of the hull, and open the engine compartment air vents. All this was necessary before starting the engines.

After a quick check on fuel levels, battery conditions, and engine oil, he started up each of the three Mercruiser V-8 engines to let them warm up in preparation for the night's run.

He was glad he had filled the fuel tanks after the last run, so no additional fuel would be needed for this trip. That meant he wouldn't have to cart those heavy five gallon gas cans from the outboard to the racer for the fill up, and as soon as the engines were warmed up, he would be ready for his exciting, high speed trip.

Ten minutes later Hauke was on his way out of the cove at half throttle. All three engines ran smoothly, so he opened them up, and once he was clear of the cay, he accelerated to just under sixty knots over the silvery Caribbean.

The boat was designed for ocean racing, and running along in the rolling swells that were usually seen on the trips between Belize and Honduras was a pleasure to someone who knew the boat's purpose. On this trip, however, the swells were unusually light. The night that settled down around Hauke was almost windless. The sea was flat and wide like a prairie. The whole surface as far as he could see was undulating slowly, gently, as though its power was simmering in one ominous, controlled motion, ready for something to burst forth, to explode from underneath.

Hauke listened intently to the smooth roaring of the three boat engines. He wasn't sure he liked the feeling he was getting from the sea, but he had to make the run that night. That was what the plan dictated. He had no choice.

After an hour on a generally southerly course, he opened the sealed cover over the satellite navigation instrument, turned it on, and plotted his course for the next two hour's run to take him to the latitude and longitude called for by El Tigre's phone call. He checked his position on the electronic Satnav navigation instrument every fifteen minutes as the late evening developed into early night time. At ten p.m. he reached the coordinates of the assigned meeting.

He slowly throttled back the powerful engines to an idle, then turned them off. He waited patiently, listening for the familiar heavy drone of a large diesel engine that would signal the arrival of his contact's boat.

Settling back in the rear cockpit seat, he lit a cigarette and glanced around. The moonlight played off the still flat sea, and an occasional flying fish would jump from the surface and splash back down, leaving ringlets circling outward like the wave from a pebble tossed in a pond.

The sudden solitude of the silence came over him, and in spite of the warmth of the Caribbean night, he pulled his short jacket closer around himself, listening, yet hearing nothing but the gentle slapping of wavelets against the waterline of the bobbing 40 foot ocean racer.

Another twenty minutes passed. It was 10:32, according to the lighted dial of his LED watch, when he first heard the far off rumble of the large diesel engine he was expecting. It was another ten minutes before he could see the form of the fishing trawler he knew would be coming from the west, running without lights.

Five minutes later Hauke retrieved the waterproof cased six cell flashlight, and turned the ray-o-vacs on to direct a concentrated beam of light half a hundred yards or so across the water to outline the bow of the fishing trawler, and to light up its name. With a slight shudder that he couldn't explain, he read the name. It was the one he expected; his contact.

"Hola, amigo!" came the call from the bow of the approaching fishing boat. "Como esta?"

"Que pasa?" Hauke called back. "Hable Engles, okay?" he commanded in a friendly tone.

Everything seems to be all right, he noted. In fact, the greeting seemed to be more friendly than usual. Maybe it's just my imagination, he added, forcing his caution to take hold. The dude's probably been hitting the Ron Rico again, he mused.

The fishing boat pulled alongside. Hauke tossed a line to the dock hand, and as soon as the two boats were secured to each other, he climbed over the deck of the ocean racer to step aboard the Cucaracha.

"Amigo," Milagro called to Hauke "Como esta hoy?"

"Today?" Hauke responded, surprised by the man's good humor. "Tonight, man, I feel just mucho bueno."

"Bueno, bueno," Milagro smiled broadly. He motioned for Hauke to follow him as he led the way into the main cabin.

Hauke followed, and the cause of Milagro's cheerful mood became evident.

In the forward bunk area just off the main cabin, the area he knew to be Milagro's, he spied the form of a woman through the half-open cabin door. She was lying on the bunk, and it was obvious from her prone posture that her hands were tied together behind her and her leg was chained to the bunk.

What is this, he asked himself, at the same time being careful to not let Milagro see the dislike in his expression. Jeez, he thought. Only Milagro could get off by keeping some woman tied up like that.

The woman's mouth was covered with a dirty cloth gag. Desperation and fear showed in her eyes. A slight trace of hope followed by pleading flashed across her face as she recognized Hauke to be someone from outside the crew.

Hauke couldn't respond to the pleading eyes, though. He was well aware that Milagro wouldn't tolerate any sympathy for the girl. That would be a show of weakness, and Milagro hated weakness. It was something to be preyed upon in his mind, something to help him show his misdirected Latin machismo. A weak man was as good as fish bait to Milagro. Hauke had no intention of ending up as fish bait.

He shook his head slightly as he turned to sit on the bench that served as a seat for the galley table. He forced a cynical grin and turned to Milagro as he reached for the rum bottle the man had set out. He poured himself a hefty slug of the brown liquid into a greasy glass, took a long swallow, then readied himself for confronting his host.

"Well, Dude," Hauke began. "What kind of stuff you got for me this trip?"

Milagro grinned broadly. The cabin's light illuminated his rotten teeth. "Same old theeng, amigo," he said in heavily accented English before taking a second swallow from his glass. "Cocoa gum. Viente kilograms."

"Twenty ki's!" commented Hauke with surprise. "Of pure gum? man, that makes maybe two hundred, two hundred twenty pounds of street grade stuff, depending on how they cut it. Hey, that's great!" He was quick to generate enthusiasm for the news as he mentally calculated the street value of the shipment. "Jeez, dude! That's maybe four million bucks worth. Man, that ought to keep them suckers happy."

"Si," Milagro agreed. "And there is one leetle theeng more," he added slyly as he turned around on his bench to open the door to his cabin to its fullest extent, fully exposing the girl on the bunk, dressed in rags. "You like theese, eh?" he asked, grinning even more broadly at Hauke.

Hauke was prepared for this show. He was very careful with his expression. "Yeah, man. I dig it a lot," he lied the obligatory response. He knew Milagro was offering the girl for his pleasure. Milagro liked to see his associates become as corrupted in his twisted pleasures as he was. That way he could see their weaknesses and gain a slight edge, if he ever needed one.

Hauke wasn't going to get caught in that trap, though. He had put a lot of thought into his dealings with Milagro, and that paid off. He knew how to reject Milagro's offer without making his reply a rejection of Milagro, and without making Milagro angry. He considered the possibility of Milagro's anger, and the thought was not appealing.

"Yeah, man," he repeated. "I dig it a lot." He turned to take another long look at the girl, pretending to leer at her defenseless form, then turned to look at his watch with obvious concern. He shook his head with a frown.

"Damn," he swore. "How come when there's fun to be had I'm already a half hour late? Damn it, dude. I'd like to, but I gotta get outa here. I got a long way to make tonight."

Milagro stared intently at Hauke for nearly a minute, then turned his suspicious gaze into an obvious frown full of disappointment. "Okay," he said at length. "Better you make the run on time. Better we make the money, eh?" He emptied his glass with his last words.

"Yeah, right," returned Hauke. "So? Where's the stuff?"

Milagro reached around into a cupboard and extracted four, square packages, each neatly wrapped in brown wax paper and tied with twine.

Hauke reached for the packages, but Milagro withdrew them and held up his hand to deny possession. "Uno momento, por favor," he said, again grinning broadly. "There is one theeng more. One leetle theeng, amigo."

Instantly Hauke was on guard. He knew that manner. It was a ploy for hiding sinister intent. "Hey, man," he said slowly. "There's no need for an attitude. What one little thing?"

"Dinero. Money," Milagro replied, continuing his grin.

"You get your bread same as always," Hauke cautiously responded. "You know I ain't dumb enough to carry that kind of cash with me on a deal."

Milagro knew that the money was always forwarded by another carrier at a later date through a preset routine, after Hauke returned safely to Belize. It had always been that way. That way there couldn't be any double deals, no rip-offs. More importantly to Hauke, it was his guarantee of a safe exit from the deal.

"Yes. That ees so. I weel get my money, verdad. But one leetle theeng. The money. Eet ees not enough, now."

"What do you mean, man, not enough?"

"I mean, amigo. The money. Eet does not, how you say? Pay my 'spenses, now. The Nostra, Coca Nostra, they want a leetle more of the money, now."

Hauke stared intently. He recognized the ploy to be a grab for more money by Milagro, not by the cocaine suppliers. He was going to say that, then thought better of it. To call Milagro a liar was dangerous. "The Coca Nostra wants more money?" he cautiously asked, instead.

"Si."

"man, I ain't got a say so there. How much more?"

"Tres mil dolares."

"Tres mil," Hauke whistled with astonishment. "Three thousand? Per kilo?"

"Si. Per kilo." Milagro had carried his broad grin throughout the interchange without so much as a break while speaking.

"You know I can't make changes in the deal for this package," Hauke protested. "It's too late, man. The deal's already been set."

"Si," Milagro said, nodding for effect.

"Then give me the stuff."

"Si, amigo. You will get theese package. But next time, the price, eet ees more. You weel tell El Tigre, si?"

Hauke relaxed ever so slightly. "Yeah," he said. "I'll tell El Tigre what you want. Next time the price is three grand per ki more. But he ain't going to like even hearing that, man."

"There weel be no choice, no?"

"Don't count on that, Dude," Hauke responded.

"Ah, amigo," Milagro said as he handed over the packages wrapped in wax paper for waterproofing, and leaned back. "But we have no reason to fight, no? Here," he added as he lifted the rum bottle. "Take another of my drink. Hey, take my woman. Drink. We are friends, no?"

Hauke didn't particularly like the suggestion that he and Milagro were friends, but he never said so. Instead, he said, "Your woman? That ain't how it looks to me. Being all tied up like that, held against her will, that don't make her your woman."

Milagro let the challenge pass. "But she is mine," he said. "How you say in America? Possession? She is nine point of the law, ees eet not?"

Hauke didn't answer. He repeated his remark about being late, and reached for the packages. He stacked them on top of each other, hefted the weight, then got up and headed for the companionway leading to the deck. With great effort he managed to ignore the mental pleas of the girl on the bunk behind him.

As soon as he was off the trawler and back aboard his ocean racer, Hauke lost no time in getting under way. As he pulled away he saw that the trawler's running lights were being turned on, and noted the one light inside the cabin where the girl was kept. He shuddered with the thought of what was going on in that cabin.

The run back to the cove where the outboard was kept was no more eventful than the run out, and after he had tied the mooring line to the front of the ocean racer - there was no need for quick dunking this time - he retrieved the outboard, carried the contraband aboard, then returned to the racer.

He made sure all the waterproof seals were secure, that the engines, gear and tanks were sealed, let the air out of the buoyancy tanks, and opened the quick scuttling scoop. The air rushing out through the escape vents on the air tanks whistled to him as he scrambled back aboard the outboard.

The ocean racer again settled slowly to the sand bottom of the cove, to be recovered for another run.

Chapter 15

Mikel Bear slept late the morning after his return from Belize. When he awoke he checked the time and wondered if his sleepiness had been based on his feelings of relief. Those feelings had developed after he made a decision on what to do about the Flyin' Penguin detectives.

At last he had devised a plan to rid himself of that thorn, those two thorns, in his side, and thinking of that fact gave him some personal pleasure. He was sure the plan would work, and he smiled as he got out of bed at 9:30 a.m., heading for his morning shower.

His pleasures were short-lived, however. After he emerged from the shower, the telephone rang. He looked at the instrument with some consternation. He wasn't expecting anyone to call this morning, and foremost among the things he hated were unexpected calls. They were always bad news. He stared at the phone, and finally answered it in the middle of the ninth ring. "Yeah," he growled into the receiver.

"Yeah. It's me," was the response.

"Who the...? Oh, Hauke?" Mikel said, at first confused, then relieved when he recognized his minion's voice. "Is this important?" He wanted to know whether or not it would be necessary to refer to the codebook and select the proper telephone booth for receiving the call, a booth that would protect the conversation from wiretaps. He hated to do that, though, because that meant at least a twenty minute trip to wherever that phone would be.

"Naw, man. This is just a friendly call. Sorry I missed

you yesterday, man," Hauke said in a friendly tone. "What made you make a trip down here without notice? There ain't nothing I ought to know about, is there?"

Mikel Bear chuckled. Of course there was something Hauke should know about. He wondered how the man could be so naive. Did he think that a trip to Belize and back was something done for the fun of it? "God damn rights there something you should know about," he again growled, less pleasantly than before.

"Yeah? Well?" Hauke responded.

"Yeah?" Bear echoed Hauke's words. "Well what? You got the message I left with Manuel, didn't you?"

"Yeah, man. Part of it. Something about Penn and PZ."

"That's God damn right. They're down there snooping around. They paid a visit to the yard, you know."

"I heard."

"And I don't know what that idiot, Manuel, told them."

"Hey. He didn't tell them nothing. He ain't that dumb."

"Don't bet on it. Anyway, I don't like their snooping about." Mikel hadn't considered Hauke's call as part of his plan, or even the fact that the call might offer another opportunity to reinforce his plan to get rid of the two thorns in his side. "Something's got to be done about them," he added after some thought, expecting Hauke to get the hint.

"Hey, man. I was thinking that was what you were thinking," Hauke carefully responded.

"So?"

"So? So what, man?"

"Don't fucking play games with me, Hauke. You know damn well what I mean."

There was a slight pause on Hauke's end before he answered. "Yeah. I guess I do, and you know what I mean when I say I ain't going to do it."

"What do you mean, ain't?" Bear angrily retorted .

"Look, man. I know I owe you some favors, and all that, but no way I'm going to... ah, ain't no way I'm going to do that."

"What?" the Bear almost shouted. "If you don't, then you damn well better make sure it gets done, hear?"

It wasn't Hauke's refusal to commit cold blooded murder that bothered Mikel so much as the refusal of his minion to blindly obey his command. Such an objection to his wishes showed a crack in the man's devotion, the type of devotion he expected from those who were to continue as favorites in his eyes.

Hauke said he heard, but he still wasn't going to have anything to do with such an activity. He also said, in the most confronting tone that he had ever used so far in speaking to his boss, that if such an activity was to take place, then the Bear had to see that it gets done himself, and without his knowledge.

"What the hell are you talking about?" Mikel nearly yelled into the telephone. "You already know about it."

"I don't neither know nothing of the sort, man," came the angered response.

"Hauke!" Bear roared. "I don't like anyone telling me how to run my affairs."

"Cool it, man," Hauke shouted back. "Before you fly off the handle, there's something else you want to know."

"What?" Mikel was caught off guard. "What else?"

"Milagro's wants more bread, for one. And the other, he's got a broad with him."

"A broad?" Mikel nearly exploded. "Look! I don't give a damn what he does with his spare time. That's his business, girl or no," he paused to regain his self-control. "But what's this crap about an increase? He wants an increase?"

"Hey, man. You better give a damn about the broad," Hauke responded, undaunted. "She don't want to be there.

She could be trouble, man"

"I don't give a sh..."

"She's American," Hauke interrupted.

Mikel paused, digesting the information. "You mean to tell me," he continued at length, "that S.O.B. has gone and grabbed, ah, got an American broad? And he's keeping her on his boat?"

"Ain't that what I said?"

"That idiot," Mikel yelled again. "Doesn't he know what that means for him if...?" He caught himself, remembering they weren't speaking on a secure phone.

"Yeah, I suppose he does know what that means," Hauke said. "I guess he don't care."

"Jesus!" Mikel exclaimed. "We got to do something about him." His thoughts returned to the other part of Hauke's message. "More money? He wants more money?"

"By three," Hauke confirmed.

"Three thousand per kilo?" the Bear yelled. He lost his temper and forgot his rule about sensitive information and phones.

Hauke had not lost his self-control, though. "That's what the dude said, man," he quickly interjected. "Three thousand per kilo-ton of Mahogany sawdust, FOB San Francisco, full freighter loads, through customs."

Mikel paused. "Oh," he said, realizing Hauke had covered his security breach. "Okay," he continued, regaining his self-control. "Tell the shipper I'll take the request to the board. Tell him I'll let him know as soon as the decision is made."

"You got it, man," Hauke said.

"And that other thing," Mikel went on. "You're off the hook on that. I'll take care of the arrangements, myself." His tone softened. He expected to hear some concurring response from Hauke, but only silence greeted his ears. "I'll tell you what," he added. "I think you had better get your tail out of there while those Flyin' Penguins are screwing around. That faggot, Bund, is catching the next flight up here for, ah, business. Why don't you get on the same plane? I don't want those guys to get too nosy and end up being lucky. If they get a handle on you that just might happen, so do as I say. Manuel can handle the next run." Without waiting for a response he hung up the phone.

He didn't want to give Hauke a chance to reply. He had known Hauke wouldn't have a hand in eliminating someone the way he had hoped at the beginning of the call. That's why he made other arrangements to that end at the last minute before leaving Belize. He had made them through other contacts.

"Yeah," he said aloud after hanging up the phone and returning to the bathroom to resume his shaving. "I'll take care of the arrangements, all right. I already took care of them," he chuckled at the thought. "And they're damn good arrangements, too." He smiled at the prospects of success with those arrangements.

"That God damn Milagro," he said as he returned to Hauke's message. "Where the hell does he get the balls to try that stickup? Three grand per kilo? What the hell's he thinking? I'll give him three grand, all right, but it won't be dollars. It's time I got another messenger, anyway. I'll take that up with the board, too. Him and his damn American woman. He probably snatched her from some boat in the area. That God damn idiot. All I need is for Penn Gwinn to get wind that someone connected to me pulled a stunt like that, all for one damn white piece of a..."

He stopped in mid-sentence, stunned by his realization. "Didn't Morri Bund say that Penn Gwinn had asked him some questions about some woman who was missing?" He put his razor down. "And now Milagro turns up with some broad captive?" The association passed through his mind. "No. That can't be. That idiot

Milagro couldn't have grabbed the same broad that Penn was hired to find, could he?" He stared at himself in the mirror. "The God damn odds against that are impossible." He continued his stare absentmindedly, thinking of the odds. "But God damn it," he concluded with a shaking of his head, not wanting to believe his conclusion. "Stranger things than that have happened."

He spent the next several seconds thinking of the odds for and against such a happening. He also considered the uncanny abilities of the Flyin' Penguins. That damned penguini, as he called Penn. After a minute or so he decided the odds were too high, the possibilities too rare, and returned to his shaving.

"But then," he argued with himself, again stopping in the middle of his shave. "What else could Penn be doing in Belize? He sure as hell isn't there to check on me."

He continued his argumentative soliloquy for another few minutes, then finally concluded that the odds were, truly, too slim. The scare from the possibilities did reinforce his desire to have the two detectives eliminated, though. He was fully aware of the talents they had for digging up information with lousy leads. His thoughts returned to Milagro. "Since Milagro could be a problem for the big boys," he said to himself aloud. "Maybe I can tie that Penguini in with him and get a little assurance from them that the problem would be taken care of professionally. That would be an easy solution, taking care of the Penguini and Milagro at the same time. That would be just the insurance I need, just in case my earlier arrangements fall through." He grinned at himself in the mirror.

Satisfied with the completion of his plans, he finished his shaving. He had a meeting in three hours with the board, as he called his associates in his cocaine running operation, and there wasn't enough time to put the polish on the plan, but he would make his pitch anyway.

At one thirty that afternoon Bear had parked his Jaguar in the parking lot for the Acapulco Restaurant in Larkspur Landing Circle. He then made his way past the hostess at the entrance, to the table where his associates were waiting.

He closed his ears to the music of the mechanical mariachi bands blaring from the loudspeakers posted about the upper perches of the fern bedecked open effect ceiling, and took his customary seat at the table. The table was in the rear corner of the room, and he sat with his back to the wall, as was his custom. That way no one could sneak up behind him. Once seated, he directed the patiently waiting waitress to serve him one of the triple Margaritas that had made the restaurant famous.

The others at the table said nothing when Bear sat down, and he glanced at each of them in turn. The first man he noted was Tom Keany, the sole Agent in Charge of Western Operations for the Drug Enforcement Administration. He nodded hello with a faint smile that indicated a sharing of information to the exclusion of the others, and then turned his attentions to those others.

One of the other two Bear recognized, even though he knew the man only by the name of Ollie, and didn't know the man's connections. He had been dealing with Ollie since the operation began, and he believed him to be the all-important man. Bear suspected he might be associated with the Mafia, or with something else as well organized and ruthless. He thought Ollie had once said something about an organization named the Quad Lateral Council, but he hadn't been able to yet pin that down. That was one of those things that he had always kept in the back of his mind as something he was going to have to find out about sometime.

About the only thing Mikel really knew about Ollie was that he handled the money the operation took in from the street vendors. He usually stayed away from these meetings and sent one of his men, one of his bagmen, who would arrange the money transfers. Ollie would only show up for critical planning meetings. Mikel liked to think that this was a critical planning meeting.

The third man Mikel had never seen before. The man seemed out of place in a white suit, white shirt, yellow tie and white Panama hat. Bear assumed he was associated with Ollie, but he seemed to be too alert to be just another bag man. There was something in his eyes that sent a twitch of alarm down Mikel 's neck. He didn't like the man. Nor did he like the unexpected intrusion of the man, but he was wise enough to let his objections pass. He would demand to have the man identified at some later time.

Mikel glanced again at Ollie. He stared in silence for several thoughtful seconds, enjoying the effect his staring created, or at what it would have created in any lesser man. It had no effect on Ollie, who returned an icy stare.

Mikel was the first to speak. "This must be an important matter for you to get personally involved," he said to Ollie.

"Ollie's here at my request, Mikel. You should know that," Keany interjected.

Mikel smiled. "Yes, I would guess that. I wasn't trying to be unfriendly," he said. "And you know that," he countered with a friendly challenge.

"Good," Ollie said. "Since we're all friends here, let's get down to friendly business, shall we?" He reached for a cigarette from the pack of Pall Malls unfiltered that was resting in the center of the table.

"You like to live on the edge, don't you," Mikel joked as he pointed to the cigarettes. "No filter, or anything?"

Ollie responded to the second challenge with another icy stare. He continued the stare as he carefully struck a match, lit his cigarette, then stubbed the match out against the palm of his other hand.

Mikel winced at the thought of the pain the burning match must have caused. Jesus, he thought. The guy's an animal.

"What's life but one chance after another," Ollie said with a slight grin. "Anyway," he continued. "You want to take care of business or make jokes?" He slowly blew out a puff of smoke while waiting for Mikel 's answer.

Further discussion was interrupted by the return of the waitress with her tray full of Margaritas. She placed four on the table without comment, and continued onto the next table.

The men reached for their drinks simultaneously, and then politely toasted each other before taking the first sip. Mikel drank most of his in the first gulp, and noticed that the stranger in the Panama hat barely took a sip.

"We have a problem," Tom Keany began the serious discussion as he placed his glass on the table.

"We have two problems," Mikel added.

"Our problem..," Keany continued, clearly ignoring Mikel 's interruption, "...concerns coverage."

"Coverage?" Mikel asked, not understanding the meaning of the expression. "Coverage of what?"

"You don't have enough men on the streets to handle the stuff you're bringing in."

"That's not my problem," Mikel challenged. "That's your problem. You're the one who's been saying who I can or can't use." He half sneered with egotism, sure his answer gave the upper hand on that topic.

Ollie looked again at Mikel . His demeanor demanded attention. "Are you going to stay on that high horse of yours, or are you going to get off it and get down to common sense? We have some serious things to go over, and this game playing of yours is nothing but bullshit. Know what I mean?"

Mikel didn't expect the challenge, and he didn't care for the subtle threat. He had enough common sense, though, to know the threat was serious. He knew Ollie didn't make idle threats, and that made him change his attitude. He had put a lot of time in this operation, and one bad word from Ollie to whoever the man's superiors were could bring it all to an abrupt end. "I'm sorry," he politely apologized. "I'm just a bit touchy this afternoon. I was just handed a little problem that I don't like."

Ollie nodded his acceptance of the apology. The man with the white Panama hat kept silent in the background.

"So? What's the problem?" Mikel asked in a much softer tone, looking at Tom Keany. "We ought to be able to gather a couple more people off the streets who want to make some easy money. I suggested that in the beginning, but you had to use only specially cleared snitches who don't even have file jackets. I always said the street people were the best ones to move the stuff. Your people don't speak the right language. At least, not those that we have been able to convince of the importance of their keeping secret about what they're doing."

"That is why," Tom replied, "I'm going to take you up on your suggestion, after all. You get me a list with positive ID's on the people you want to use, and if they don't have a rap sheet I'll okay their use."

"Come on, Tom," Mikel protested. "You know better than that. Nobody without a rap sheet is going to be dirty enough to take up this trick. If they don't have a rap, or at least some kind of file jacket, you don't have a handle on them. You can't twist them to get them to do what you want. You know that."

The DEA agent thought about Mikel 's reply, then was forced to agree. He knew the type of men who were needed to sell cocaine. They would have to be the type who were dirty enough to know something about dealing, but who were also straight enough to give good tracking of the money they took in. Only then would they be provided immunity from prosecution on any cocaine trafficking charges, if they were caught by some other task force. He also knew that Mikel was the one who could locate the type of men needed and make that part of the operation function without the press getting their hands on it. "All right," he said at length. "I suppose you win. But Christ, make damn sure this keeps covered."

"Hey," Mikel answered with a smile of confidence, having just won the point. "I can't afford to let it get out any more than you can."

"You do realize, of course," Ollie said, "That if this does ever get out, my organization's part in this operation will not only be terminated, but absolutely denied."

Mikel turned his confident smile on Ollie. "Just like in the movies," he said.

"Just like in the movies," Ollie replied. "And, just like in the movies, we want more money for our part."

Mikel sat up with a start. This was more than he had expected. "What?" he asked. "What the hell are you talking about?" He lost his smile. His anger rose.

"My organization feels that under the circumstances we need to make more on our end to cover our needs," Ollie responded simply.

"Your needs," Mikel growled as he began to see the squeeze play. "Just what the hell are your needs?"

"The Contras are not going to be re-funded by congress," Ollie answered without emotion.

"So? What's that got to do with me?" Mikel was still upset, but more controlled.

"Come off it, Mikel ," Tom Keany interceded. "You know damn well the entire purpose of this operation is to supply the Contras with money so they can buy arms and ammunition to use against the Sandinistas."

Mikel turned to stare at his friend for a few seconds before responding. "What I know damn well about this operation," he began slowly. "Is that the amount of money it develops is not enough to supply a whole God damn army, so don't give me that crap."

Ollie exploded in anger. "Are you really so damn self centered," he asked, "that you think your little smuggling operation is the only one we have going? Jesus, you egotistic blustering blob of shit. We let you set this thing up just like any one of the dozen other operations we have going solely because we need more money. Now, don't for one minute think that you are the only person we can use for movement in this part of the country. You can be replaced any damn minute I feel like it, so when I say we want a bigger cut, I'm not asking you, I'm telling you. I'm telling you that your percentage is cut by five percent, beginning on the next run." He sat back and reached for another cigarette in order to quell his ire.

The stranger in the Panama hat smiled calmly.

Mikel glared at Ollie, then at the stranger. "Who is this other guy, anyway?" he demanded, sublimating his anger at Ollie. He well knew that Ollie had the power to not only cut off the operation, but to also cut off him, literally, if desired.

"He's here with me," Ollie said. "That's all you need to know."

"Who is he?" Mikel persisted.

"That's all you need to know about him, Mikel," Keany interceded in a conciliatory tone. "Take my word for it."

Mikel glanced at his friend, started to say something, then shrugged his shoulders instead. He wondered if he had any real allies after that answer. He evaluated his position once more, and decided he had better apply utmost tact.

While Mikel was weighing his options he realized his one possible advantage, also. He went over the recent outburst by Ollie, and saw his opportunity. If he made an overt effort to show that he agreed with Ollie's order, then with a little more quick talking he could make Ollie feel just enough embarrassed about the loss of self control to perhaps be more inclined to consider the request he would make about Milagro. If he was lucky, maybe he could get Ollie to include that damn pesky Penguini, too.

His mind was racing as he next spoke. "Okay. I'm not going to fight the cut, if you think that is best," he said. "After all, I didn't just set up the operation, recruit the manpower, develop the importing part of the business, and cover our tracks with customs and the local police to make any money." He hoped his sarcasm wasn't too offensive. "What the hell?" he continued. "It's all for mom, apple pie, and Chevrolet, right?" He phrased the last of his statement with a jaded grin from the left side of his mouth.

"I think you're beginning to get the picture," Ollie replied.

"But we still do have a problem that has to be handled," Mikel continued, pushing his advantage.

It was Ollie's turn to smile sarcastically. "What?" he asked. "You mean there's a problem that you can't handle?"

"If it was just my problem, I would handle it, but it isn't. It falls in Keany's territory."

"What?" Keany asked, surprised.

"The captain of the boat that makes the run from Honduras to the pickup point wants more money, too."

"That's impossible," Ollie flatly stated as he reached for his Margarita.

"I said the same thing when I heard the God damn request," Mikel responded. "That's why I think he should be discovered, so to speak, and replaced."

Ollie stopped in mid-drink and stared at Mikel. "You mean you want his boat taken off the endangered species list?"

"Yes," Mikel nodded. "And, along with that, there are two nosy private dicks that are looking into, ah, trying to look into the log importing business. They are going to have to be taken care of, too."

Tom Keany looked at Mikel while absorbing the request and the apparent purpose behind it. "The one reason you were chosen for this job," he said at length, "is that you are supposed to be able to cover your tracks without our help. I think those two private dicks, as you call them, are your problem. They're certainly not the DEA's. We're not going to be part of any personal squabble. And besides," he added after a slight pause, "I thought you had something set up for controlling just a situation."

Mikel had expected his friend to come up with such an objection. In fact, he had counted on it, all except about the remark about controls. He had to ignore that comment at the moment. "Then it's up to you, Ollie," he said, following his plan. He knew he was pushing a little too hard, but he had to take risks.

Ollie slowly reached for another Pall Mall, lit it just as deliberately, then after blowing out a smoke ring, sat back and smiled a grim little smile at Mikel . "That was a nice try, Mikel ," he said. "But you really don't know who you're playing cards with, do you? No, it is not up to me. It's just like Tom said. You were selected because you made the noise about your abilities, so now face up to it. You settle your problem all by yourself. And don't get the agency implicated. I don't think that would be too good for... ah, such a good idea, if you know what I mean."

Mikel was taken back. He knew exactly what Ollie meant, and that was the first blunt threat anyone had ever made to him. He bristled with the thought of letting it pass unchallenged, but his common sense prevailed. He wasn't about to get himself in hot water with Ollie's organization.

"As for Milagro," Tom Keany interceded once more. "I can't make that decision. It has to come from our control agent in the area. I don't know whether or not an immediate replacement for Milagro is at hand. If there is one readily available, then I'm sure the agent will go along with the change you want, and let you know the new codes. If not, then you'll have to wait until there is."

"In the meantime," Mikel complained. "I have to take the loss that this problem solving might cost me?"

Tom Keany silently shrugged his shoulders.

Mikel turned to Ollie, looking for one possible last hope on that point. None came. The man was stone faced.

The man in the Panama Hat continued his relentless controlled smiling; smiling and watching.

"Okay," Mikel said in defeat. "Then I'll just have to take care of the Penguini myself, and you'll take care of Milagro. I'll make the call and request the name change tonight. When that control agent of yours gives the okay, it'll all take place. All right?"

Keany looked at Ollie for confirmation.

Ollie glanced at the man in the Panama hat, then returned a nod to Keany.

"Okay, then. That's how it is," Keany said.

"Good enough," Mikel responded. "I'll be looking for a call from your end." He added that he thought it was good to have had the meeting, and then got up from the table.

He shook hands with the Ollie and Keany, ignored the man in the Panama Hat, and strode out of the restaurant. He had lost too much of his confidence in that meeting, and he hoped it didn't show in his failure to exhibit his usual swaggering walk during his exit.

Chapter 16

Mikel Bear arrived back at his house and pushed the button on his automatic garage door opener. The gate in the wrought iron fence surrounding his front yard opened with the garage door, and he drove inside the garage. He was deep in thought. He never noted the man in the two door older model Mercedes parked half a block down the street.

He got out of the car and entered the house with his thoughts focused on what final touches he might add to his plan to eliminate Milagro. At the same time he tried to think of a way to polish his plan of eliminating the Flyin' Penguin detectives. He wondered if it had been wise to give Manuel that responsibility.

"Embee!" he shouted as he entered the kitchen. "Get me a beer."

Embee Bear reluctantly left her couch, coffee and TV to get the beer. She poured it in the Bear's favorite glass while he plopped himself down in his seat at the large kitchen table, the table that also served as his desk. She put the glass on the table in front of him and returned to her couch. Through the entire movement she never bothered to say hello.

And he never bothered to thank her for her efforts. He took a long draft from the glass, wiped the beer suds from his mustache, and grabbed the phone to dial an international number.

When the whirrings and clickings of various international exchanges ended, the phone was answered on the other end. "Buenas dias," the voice flowed into the receiver. “Que quieres?”

“Qiero hablar a El Tigre,” Bear said in his unpracticed text book Spanish. He was aware that his voice would be recognized, but he followed the routine anyway. After all, it was set up by him. He developed it especially as a means of disguising any request for a change in operations that he may have.

“Un momentito,” the voice said.

After a short pause, another voice came on the line. He recognized it as belonging to Morri Bund. “Si?” the voice replied.

“Este es por El Lobo. Quiero comprar los articulos de las historicas, por favor,” Mikel awkwardly read the words from his pre-written coded sentences. *I want to buy some historical artifacts,* he mentally translated. The name El Lobo was the key. That meant the operations name was to be changed from what it now was, El Tigre, to El Lobo. That also meant a change in some operatives, namely from Milagro, the present carrier, to the next person in line.

“Si, Senor. Muy Bien. Muchas gracias. Y cuantos articulos?” the voice asked. *Very good. How many items?*

“Cuanto tienes?” Bear asked. *How many do you have*?

“Yo mirare',” the voice answered. *I'll look.*

“Bueno,” Bear said.

“Bueno,” the voice said before hanging up.

Mikel also hung up, then sat back and waited. He glanced over at his wife, again engrossed in her soap opera, and shook his head. “How the hell can you watch that crap?” he demanded.

“It's better than the alternative,” Embee responded sharply.

“What alternative?”

“Not watching it.”

Mikel considered telling her how he felt about smart

ass answers, but decided it would only provoke another quarrel. He quietly avoided the issue, keeping one eye on her and the other on the TV out of boredom.

Approximately fifteen minutes later the phone rang. "Hello," he growled into it.

"Hello," responded the caller. It was Morri Bund, now speaking in English. "I would like to speak with Mr. Bear about an investigating matter of the most urgent nature, in private," the caller continued.

"Sure. When?" Mikel asked.

"At your convenience," the caller replied. The coded response meant that the name change ordered earlier was okay, and what was needed now was only a final starting time to put it into effect.

"Would tomorrow be good?" Bear asked.

"That would be fine," the caller said. "Shall I come alone?"

The question meant was another shipment to be made? "Yes," Bear replied. He did want another shipment to be made.

"Very well. At ten, say, tomorrow?"

"That'll be fine," Bear okayed the meeting time. The meaning, though, was that the shipment was expected to be ten kilos. "Oh, come to think of it," he continued. "Better make it Friday, at about 3:30. That okay?" That was the shipment time that Bear wanted.

"That time would be perfect. Where?"

Mikel quickly thumbed through his code book to select some appropriate coordinates for the shipment transfer. "Well, let's see. The place I usually use for confidential meetings is no longer so quiet." Meaning the previous rendezvous point is no longer valid. "We'll use another location, say at 17588 North West Street," he replied. The numbers were the longitude and north latitude of the rendezvous site: 17.5 North by 88 West.

"Fine," the caller said. "See you there." The caller

hung up the phone.

Bear was pleased with the results of his call. Milagro would sail to the expected rendezvous with Hauke at the old location, only Hauke wouldn't be there. The Coast Guard would be there, instead. Hauke would be at the new coordinates to meet the other boat, the one that would replace Milagro's. If his plans worked out all right, that is. He saw no reason why they wouldn't.

Bear chuckled at the thought of his plans. That dumb son of a bitch, Milagro. Thinking he could rip me off for another three thousand per ki. He took another swallow from his beer, then thought about his recent meeting with Tom Keany and the others. I'll let you know when the change is ready to take place, he chuckled, remembering Tom's words. He took the final slug from his beer and set it on the kitchen counter behind him. "Poor Tom Keany," he chuckled some more at the thought of his own duplicit abilities. "He'd have a fit if he knew I controlled his control agent in Belize. Imagine him thinking Morri Bund would have enough balls to make a decision by himself. Bund's job is to take my request and coordinate it. Nothing more."

He glanced at his watch. It was more than the requisite one hour waiting time since the recent board meeting, so he picked up the phone to dial another number. This time it was a local call. "Yes?" came the answer to the call.

"Nine thirty for pizza?" Bear asked.

After a short pause, Tom Keany replied as Bear had expected. "Sure," he cheerily said.

Bear hung up the phone and told his wife that he was going to be out for the rest of the evening. "Don't wait up for me," he called, as he retrieved his coat from the hallway coat stand, put it on while striding through the door to the garage, and slammed the door behind him.

Embee Bear hardly glanced up as Bear left. She was glad the monster was going to be gone again for the evening. It gave her more time with her most recent lover. Jesus, she whispered to herself. I can't wait to get that man out of my life. She returned her attentions to the Days of Our Lives on her three foot projected image television screen.

* * * *

Yanks was the driver of the older green two door Mercedes that was parked down the street from the Bear's house. He had been parked there since three that afternoon, and was relieved to see Bear's return at 4:47 p.m. He was naturally surprised to see the man again depart the residence twenty minutes later.

"5:07 p.m.," Yanks spoke into his portable tape recorder, which was his method of taking notes during his surveillance. "The subject departed his residence alone in the above reported Jaguar."

Yanks also made the following entries in his report for that evening's observations:

"7:18 p.m. The subject arrived and parked in the parking lot for DeJerki's Pizza, 440 Main Street, Guerneville, which he subsequently entered."

"7:25 p.m. This investigator entered the above noted pizza parlor and observed the subject sitting at a table near the rear wall. He was accompanied by a white male adult, subsequently identified as Tom Keany, an agent for the Drug Enforcement Administration."

"7:37 p.m. This investigator took a seat at an adjacent table open to the public, and in public access, where the conversation between the two above noted persons was heard. This conversation could be heard without overt efforts being made by this investigator to so hear, and without any mechanical assistance whatsoever."

"The elements of the conversation," he continued explaining to the imaginary transcriber of his tapes, "which could plainly be heard without excessive efforts, in public access and within the normal hearing range of the investigator, are as follows:

1. The subject said, 'Do you think Ollie is serious about upping his cut?'

2. The subject's companion responded, 'Definitely.'

3. The subject was heard to say later on, 'El Lobo is going into effect, ah, subject to your approval, of course. I spoke with your man down there. He has another one ready.'

4. Excessive noise in the environment over rode their conversations for several minutes. The subject was heard to say later on, 'That damn Penguini should be gone, taken care of, by that time.'

5. The subject was heard to say later on, 'Bund wants another date up here. I guess I better get someone for him. Maybe someone we can use in a movie, again. Got any ideas?'

6. There was some more conversation which couldn't be heard due to noise interference from other patrons.

7. The subject's companion was heard to say, 'I don't think so. Besides, he's got friends in Washington, you know. I haven't been able to do anything about him at all, except get him sent down there to Belize to get him out of my hair.'

8. The subject was heard to say later on, 'I got the latest report from McIvers. There are still no official investigations into this area that would involve us. Not through the San Francisco Police, anyway.'

9. The subject's companion was heard to say, 'Good. Then I guess I better clear our Mr. Bund for the time off for one more of his visits, if you can keep the heat off any consequences that may develop.'

10. The subject was heard to respond, 'I think I can.'

11. The subject's companion was heard to say later

on, 'Well, then I guess we have to pay that place a visit to make arrangements, as much as I hate to.'

12. The subject was heard to respond, 'Look. We're getting half the profits from that little house of S and M, so what are you complaining about?'

13. The subject's companion was heard to respond, 'Maybe so, but I don't have to like it, do I? Damn it. Getting involved with smuggling to help the government I can handle, especially when it has White House sanctions, which I sometimes wonder about. I can even reconcile siphoning off a little of the profits for our own use, but I still don't have to like what goes on in those movies we're financing. Even if it does increase our take.'"

"No more conversation was heard past this point in time by this investigator, as I was forced to retire to my vehicle to prevent compromising the investigations by being discovered to be listening to the subject's conversations."

"8:39 p.m. The subject and his companion emerged from the above noted pizza parlor. The subject got into his vehicle and drove from the area followed by the above noted companion."

"9:00 p.m. The subject, followed by his companion, arrived and parked in front of a private residence at 63419 Old River Road, in the Guerneville area. The house at that address is removed from the others by several hundred yards along the road, and surrounded by Redwood trees and shrubbery. The house is located on the up-slope of the hill to the south of the road, and is of several levels, at least three thousand square feet in size, estimated."

"At the time of the subject's arrival several other vehicles could be seen parked in the vicinity, most of them late model American and some late model German types. The license plates could not be recorded without fear of compromising the investigation at this time."

"9:22 p.m. Lights could be seen inside several rooms of the house. No inside activity could be seen through the normal methods of observation from a suitable surveillance position."

"11:09 p.m. This investigator attempted closer observation of the above noted residence. At this time a walk past the front of the residence on the side of the road as close to the building as possible without violating rights to privacy and trespassing laws, was made. Sounds of music, laughter, and general sounds of merriment could be heard emanating from inside."

"11:12 p.m. During the walk past the house a rear area side window, which was in clear public view, revealed the interior of a back room. It was plainly visible from public access grounds, and without trespass upon the property, without any aids to vision, that inside the room a white male was held standing with his hands above his head, possibly being held there by some form of restraint. This person was visible from the waist up. It should be noted that an excessive amount of light was about the room, as though it was being illuminated with something brighter than normal house lights. The purpose for this great lighting was not directly observed, although it appeared to be adequate light for indoor film exposure."

"11:45 p.m. The subject and his companion emerged from the above noted residence accompanied by two other males, one Caucasian, one black. They stood on the front porch for several minutes, apparently engaged in discussion, before the two un-named males returned inside the house. The subject, with his companion, then returned to their respective vehicles and each drove from the area."

"1:00 p.m. The subject arrived back at his residence where he entered the garage, out of view."

"2:00 a.m. Since all lights but one inside the subject's residence were extinguished, surveillance was

terminated."
report tape was eventually transcribed by Lara, the Flyin' Penguins' secretary, and relayed to Penn, personally.

Chapter 17

Sol's paprika ball rose over Belize City two hours earlier than it did over Danville, California where Bear was sleeping in as the result of his late night's trip to the Russian River area.

At the same time, Penn in Belize found the sun's heat penetrating his mosquito netting to glare across his face. He got out of bed and walked to the opened windows. They were the old-fashioned colonial type windows that opened the full height of the wall, floor to ceiling, and swung outwards on either side to leave an opening designed to walk through. Assuming, of course, that a man would want to walk through them and climb down two stories to the ground.

Penn stretched his cramped muscles and yawned. His view covered the harbor, and his gaze fell upon the small outboard runabout, which he had learned belonged to Hauke. It was the one Hauke used for his many overnight fishing trips.

He was relieved to see that the boat was still in the harbor where Hauke had berthed it after the return the previous morning. That meant Hauke was still in the area, and probably could be located for questioning, if circumstances dictated.

Penn quickly showered and dressed, then placed a wake up call, which he knew would not be enjoyed, to his partner in the next room. He thought of using the outside verandah beside the swimming pool for his morning's ingestion ritual, but changed his mind. The day was already too hot for outside eating.

As he walked down the hallway, he noted the soft closing of the door several rooms down the hall, but made no reference to it. He cast aside the observation, thinking the activity was probably a hasty retreat made by a woman tourist who didn't want to be seen getting the morning paper from the hallway while dressed in nightgown and curlers.

PZ strolled into the dinning room an hour later, after Penn had consumed the last bit of his omelet, drank his third cup of coffee, and worked the crossword puzzle in the foreign edition of the San Francisco Chronicle.

He took the seat across the table, ordered his usual filling breakfast of Coca Cola, and grinned in response to Penn's continuing disbelief of the his standard breakfast. "This is how I keep my trim figure," he said in defense.

Penn studied him for a second. "What I can't understand," he said, "is that all you ever eat is that crap while I try to eat a balanced diet. I'm not any taller than you. I wear a belt size two inches shorter than yours, and yet, you weigh twenty pounds less than I do. What the hell is your secret?"

"Mind over matter," PZ answered while taking another sip of his Coke.

"I think it's just because you're a coke head," Penn said.

"A what? I don't use cocaine!" PZ quickly and adamantly defended himself.

"I'm talking about coca cola, Turkey," Penn said. "I think the difference between us is that while I'm full of substance, you're full of hot air."

PZ shrugged off the barb.

Further jousting was barred by the approach of the hotel's Maitre D' carrying a telephone.

"Mr. Gwinn," he said in the typical suave and polished tone of a man who made a career of his position. "A telephone call for you. Would you care to take it here, or would you prefer to have it transferred to the privacy of your room?"

Penn glanced at PZ, then reached to the handset being held in front of him. "I'll take it here, thanks," he said to the Maitre D'. "Hello," he responded questioningly into the telephone.

"Penn? This is Yanks," came the caller's greeting.

"Yanks?" Penn responded with surprise. "What's up? I didn't expect to hear from you so soon."

"Listen," Yanks replied, conveying a sense of urgency. "I'm glad I caught you. Be careful down there."

"What?"

"I said watch yourself. I followed Bear last night. I gave Lara the notes on my tape. But the important thing is, Bear met Tom Keany, and he made some remarks about having you and PZ taken care of."

"What? Keany of the DEA?" Penn shot a glance at PZ. "Are you sure? I mean, are you sure you heard him say that?"

"There's not a mind in my, I mean, not a doubt in my mind."

"How in hell did you ever hear something like that? Where?"

"Well, this is the way it went down. I tailed him to a pizza parlor in Guerneville, where he met Keany, and I heard them talking. Bear said, and I quote, 'PZ and Penn should be gone, taken care of, by this time.' Unquote. Now, that's pretty sure to me."

"What makes you think that means..."

"Look," Yanks hurriedly interrupted Penn. "I sure can't be knocking to know, I mean, I can't be sure he means to knock you guys off, but I do know from the voice sound, I mean, from the sound of his voice, that is sure as hell what he sounded like he meant."

"Okay. Okay," It took a second for Penn to sort out Yanks' sentence. "I understand. And I appreciate the warning, but give me a little more to go on, will you? Take a deep breath, calm down, and think about this: Did he say how? Or when?"

"No. But he did say something about a guy named El Lobo being in operation. And he did say something about somebody named Bund coming up here. And get this, they said some things about an S house of M, I mean, a house of S and M, and I guess that's where I tailed them to."

"What?"

"A house of S and M. You know, pain. Whips and chains, and all that cr..."

"I know what S & M stands for. What I'm talking about is the Bear. What the hell was he doing there?"

"Like I said, he and Keany made arrangements for the Bund to, I mean, for the visit of the guy named Bund."

"What?" Penn repeated. He shot another confused glance at PZ, who was by then also thoroughly confused by the half of the conversation he heard.

"That's right. You heard right." Yanks affirmed.

"Good Christ," Penn said, letting the news sink in. "Okay," he added. "Good work, Yanks. Look, keep on him, will you? Keep in touch with Lara if you can't reach me here. I can't tell you how important this news is, Yanks. Thanks. You did a good job."

"Yep. I thought I did. Bye."

"Bye." Penn put down the receiver, looking pensive. "You're not going to believe this," he said to PZ. He recited what Yanks had said.

PZ whistled before taking another drink of his breakfast Coke.

"Yeah. That's how I took it," Penn agreed with PZ's surprise.

PZ whistled again after putting the glass on the table.

"You already said that," Penn commented.

PZ shook his head and nodded in the direction of the

entrance to the dining room, which was behind Penn's back.

Penn turned to follow PZ's nod. What he saw made him want to whistle, as well. He would have, too, had he not been reared under more gentile family auspices.

Entering the verandah was Morgan Baletta, dressed in her swimsuit. The full-bodied woman in her minuscule blue bikini was barely covered by the orange terry cloth toga that she wore draped over her left shoulder and under her right arm. Her long blonde hair, olive tanned skin, and blue eyes that matched the splashing blue of the tiny swim suit, made her stupefying. She smiled as she approached the two, nodded hello, and sat in the third chair at the round glass top table.

"Well, good morning. What a pleasant surprise," Penn greeted.

PZ was too awed to say anything.

As she sat, her toga fell to one side, toward Penn, and he could read the label. 'An original by Lelia', it read. Nice, he thought.

She began her conversation simply. "We've received word that Milagro has been given instructions to get another load of merchandise."

Penn and PZ studied her with even greater interest.

"How did you get that information?" Penn asked.

"I can't tell you that, I'm afraid, but this time the code name was changed to El Lobo from El Tigre."

"Code? What do you mean, code?" He paused to think. "You mean, El Tigre is a code word? Not a person?" He flashed on Yanks' recent telephone call.

The woman raised her left eyebrow slightly before replying. "I thought you knew that, already. Yes, El Tigre was the old code, and now it has been changed to El Lobo."

"Okay, so it has been changed," Penn said. "Why is that so important?"

"Because, every time the code name is changed, the boat, in this case Milagro's Cucaracha, makes its last trip. It is either picked up by the Coast Guard for carrying contraband, or is never heard from again."

"You mean that this is going to be Milagro's last trip?"

"It looks that way."

"But, how about Hauke? Is he going to make the trip?"

"I don't see how. He got on the plane for the States this morning." She turned her head to watch the TACA Airlines jet slowly passing from view through the arches of the verandah. "He should be on that plane right there."

PZ finally regained enough of his poise to want to appear constructive. "Then that sure as hell shoots our theory to hell, don't it?" He glanced at the plane, finding it hard to look at it and the girl at the same time.

"Doesn't it," Penn corrected.

"Ain't that what I said?" he shot back.

"Maybe it doesn't," Morgan said. "This El Lobo call had another surprise."

"Oh? What?" Penn asked, hoping his skepticism wasn't being noticed.

"Well, the call made some reference to a person called number two being given the opportunity to take number one's place."

"Number two? Penn asked.

"Right. That would have to be Manuel," she said. "He's probably taking Hauke's place."

"Then," Penn added, "If Manuel takes the boat out, that supports our, your, drug case against Mikel Bear. And Morri Bund, as well. At least you would have enough to question him with."

"It might not be that easy. Bund is on that plane, too."

"Wait a minute," PZ sounded confused. "What's going on here? Why's everybody skipping town?"

"That's just what I'd like to know," Morgan replied.

"And I was hoping you two could find out for me, since it just might resolve your problem at the same time."

The comment dropped like a bomb on the two investigators. "What do you mean?" they asked in unison.

"There was something else that I didn't tell you the other night. I didn't want to say anything until I could put the pieces together, but here it is: Hauke placed a call from Hard Loggers yesterday morning to a telephone in Danville, California."

"Bear's telephone?" Penn asked.

She nodded. "Anyway, in that call, Hauke told Bear about the white woman Milagro had aboard his boat."

"Jesus!" Penn sat up with a start. "You knew this and you didn't tell us?" He made no effort to hide how upset he was with the delayed delivery of the news.

"I didn't have the information verified then. It would have been useless to give you anything that wasn't true."

Penn sat back and stared at the girl. His sixth sense tingled, the sense that worked in his favor when something was amiss. He suddenly felt that Baletta's message was too pat, too patently rendered. There was something about her explanation that didn't fit.

"All we gotta do," PZ said. "Is follow Manuel to Milagro. With any luck, we can get the girl out, and we can get back home and forget all about this place."

"She may not be Allie, you know," Penn cautioned.

"Maybe not," PZ defended his position. "But then, too, maybe she is. The timing is right, and even if she isn't, at least she ought to be rescued."

"You're presuming she wants to be rescued, aren't you?" Penn countered.

"What do you mean?"

"I mean, she doesn't necessarily have to be on Milagro's boat against her will, you know."

"Oh. I never thought of that," PZ conceded. "But Hey," he perked up. "We sure as hell have to find out."

"That is true," Penn agreed.

"Where is Milagro's boat?" PZ asked Morgan.

"That's just the problem," she replied. "We don't know."

"What's wrong with the Coast Guard? Can't they find it?"

"They probably could, if they had orders to. But, also, the problem with that is that if Milagro does have a girl aboard against her will, do you think she would still be aboard by the time the Coasties arrive on the scene, charging in like Gang Busters?"

"I see what you mean." Penn looked disconsolate. "Can't they just find the boat for us?"

"Not without orders. Besides, there are other complications outside the realm of our function."

Penn perked up. "What the hell does that mean?" he asked.

"It means, that for some reason, the coasties don't want to be very helpful on this particular problem with Milagro. There seems to be some upper echelon inter-agency workings in this thing that we don't know about."

Penn's intuition stirred more heavily. He wondered what she was up to. Was she suggesting they find Milagro themselves? "But we're talking about a person's life, here," he continued. "Not just smuggling. Doesn't the Coast Guard know that?" Then he answered his own question. "It's the same old story, isn't it? No proof that anyone's in danger. They're always looking for a way to get out of doing what they're supposed to."

"Exactly," she responded. "Like you said, there's no proof that the girl is there against her will. Actually, there's no proof that the girl is on the boat, at all. Anyway, the particular agency involved here, which seems to be controlling the Coast Guard, doesn't place much value on any one individual's life when compared to their overall objectives."

"Hell," interjected Penn. "That sounds a great deal like someone I used to work for."

Morgan's eyes questioned Penn.

"I used to work for an agency like the CIA," Penn explained. "Only they were worse. It was the Defense Intelligence Agency. That sounds one hell of a lot like something they would do,"

"You mean," PZ interjected, "that the Coast Guard and the CIA are working together? For what?"

"Well, hell," Penn said. "That's easy. What does Milagro do? He runs cocaine. Who watches him run cocaine? The Coast Guard. Who is tied in with the Coast Guard down here, if our presumption is correct? The CIA. And the DEA keeps their back turned because the CIA wants them to."

"Jesus," PZ said. "The DEA, CIA and USCG? It sounds like alphabet soup."

"Don't forget our friends Hauke and Bear," Penn added.

"And Morri Bund," Morgan said. "Plus some organization called the Quad Lateral Council."

"You mentioned them before," Penn said. "Are you sure you don't mean the Tri Lateral Commission of Rockefeller and the Chase Manhattan bank fame?"

"No. I mean the Quad Lateral Council. The Q4C, as they are known by the initials they use," she replied. "They're even more ruthless than the Tri Lateral Commission."

"They're a new one to me," PZ interjected.

"This thing sounds more like a Hollywood script the more we get into it," Penn said with a shaking of his head.

"It all fits, though, don't it?" PZ said. "So we don't have a chance, like I been saying. We're wasting our time here."

Penn glared at his partner. "Look," he said. "I'm not going to argue with you on that point again." He took a sip of his morning's orange juice, then continued in spite of PZ's obstructionism. "This is the way it stacks up: Milagro picks up the coke in Nicaragua, or Honduras, or even Panama, or somewhere down there that is a trans-shipment point from Colombia, delivers it to Hauke, who delivers it to Bear, who sells it, and the various government agencies keep their backs turned, or even help in the concealment. The Coast Guard gives protection to the boat, Milagro's in this case, and the DEA covers the problem with customs and importation, while the CIA takes some of the money to sustain their interests in the area."

"Money? The CIA needs to smuggle coke to get money?" PZ asked with skepticism.

"Not the CIA themselves. They're well funded by congress. But someone they are trying to help would need the money without the congress knowing about it."

"The Contras," PZ concluded. "They're funding the Contras with the money they're getting from the smuggling."

"That's the way it seems," Penn agreed. "However, there's a problem with that conclusion."

"Right," agreed Morgan. "We still haven't been able to prove the Hauke-Milagro connection for sure, and I don't think we can unless we catch them in the act."

"Then we're gonna follow Hauke, or I mean, Manuel, right?" PZ asked.

"That's liable to get tough," cautioned Morgan. "There's probably a lot of firepower involved."

Penn studied Morgan. She actually does want us to follow Manuel to meet Milagro. But, why? What's there that I'm missing? Aloud, he said, "It'd only be tough if Milagro sees us."

"Ain't that the idea?" PZ said. "To catch him in the act so we can get on his boat."

"That, though, is just the problem," Penn explained.

"If Milagro sees us, then the girl's as good as dead, same as if the Coast Guard found him."

"I would have to agree with that one," Morgan responded.

"We gotta follow Manuel to catch Milagro, and if we gotta check out this broad he's carrying," PZ said. "He's bound to get going pretty soon if he has so damn much ground to cover, I mean sea to cover, to get to where he meets Milagro."

"You're probably right," Penn agreed.

"Very well," Morgan seemed to sigh as she got up from the table. "I'll go change, and be back here in one hour."

"What?" Penn responded. It hadn't occurred to him that she would want to help look for Milagro. That didn't fit too well with his understanding of her role in the plan. Why would she want to be there when we find Milagro? What's she going to do, arrest him? Not likely. I don't think she has any powers of arrest. Then what? Shoot him? Protect him? Who from? Us?"

"This is my game, remember?" she said over her shoulder as she strode from the room.

"Damn," Penn whispered.

"Oh, oh," PZ said. "Don't say that. Every time I hear that, we end up in trouble."

"Can't help it," Penn replied. His sense of danger had again been alerted. "Come on," he added as he got up from the table and tossed a five-dollar bill down to cover the breakfast.

PZ followed Penn through the dining room and up the stairs quietly, not being able to add much to their recent discussions.

It was in their favor that they both had been quiet as they continued down the carpeted hallway towards their room. They were soundless as they approached the door to Penn's room. It wasn't out of an overt desire to be quiet, but merely because they were both deep in thought.

Penn slipped his room key into the lock. The door slowly opened in response to the push. It had been opened already, and was left ajar.

Penn glanced at PZ, and with reactions based on experience, they quickly stepped to the side and out of sight of anyone who might be watching the door from the inside.

Penn cautiously pushed the door all the way open and peered around the opening. The bedroom door was also open, and a shadow crossed the floor as a figure moved about inside that room with a quiet and seemingly deliberate manner, busily engaged in some activity not clearly comprehensible to the two detectives.

The two detectives glanced at each other, exchanged signals declaring their respective parts in the surprise they were going to give their intruder, and crept inside.

Penn suspected that the intruder was connected with Yank's recent warning, and might be the result of one of Bear's plans. He suspected that since Hauke had left Belize that morning, it might be Manuel.

Penn peered into the bedroom and saw the shadow of the intruder as it crossed the floor and approached the very door he was peering through.

With a signal for PZ to follow, Penn rushed through the door and pounced on the unsuspecting intruder, forcing the hapless victim to the floor.

The intruder let out a blood curdling scream, certain that she was being attacked by some monster.

Undeterred by the screaming, PZ moved quickly through the door and piled on top of Penn, who was now actually struggling to let go of the person.

Penn had realized that the mysterious intruder was the hotel maid on her appointed rounds.

The woman was still screaming as though her virginal reputation was at stake. She didn't stop until the two

Americans got her to her feet and unceremoniously escorted her out of the bedroom and into the hallway where the other guests were poking their heads out of their doorways wanting to know what was going on.

Just as the two were about to shut the door to Penn's room in defense of the piercing looks, PZ noticed a head protruding from the door of the adjacent room. “Hey! Wait a minute,” he yelled as the head quickly retreated behind the shutting door. “That's my room. Who are you?” He sprinted out of the room and down the hallway to his room with Penn hard on his heels, as the guests shut their doors, reluctant to get involved.

Penn and PZ's adrenaline was already pumping from their escapade with the maid, who by now was scampering down the hallway and around the corner to safety. They both crashed into the door to PZ's room without so much as a second thought, before the retreating person could get it locked from the inside.

The door smashed open, and running across the room was a real intruder.

Penn tackled the intruder in full run, and suffered a nasty rug burn on his elbows for the effort when he slid across the carpeted floor.

Chapter 18

Penn turned the intruder over. It was Manuel.

Manuel had started complaining when his face hit the floor, but after Penn turned him over, he quieted. His eyes darted wildly between PZ standing over him, and Penn, who was fighting to restrain him.

"What the hell are you doing here?" PZ yelled at the man as Penn struggled to his feet.

Penn yanked Manuel to his feet and twisted his arm back behind his shoulders. Penn shoved him up against the wall, forcing his face against the plaster with a thud. At the same time, Penn grabbed his little finger and bent it back against the wrist. "Ever had your finger broken," Penn threatened as he gave the finger a slight twist for effect. "It hurts like hell for more than a year."

Manuel stifled a scream.

"You're going to give me some answers, or you're really going to feel that finger." He added another twist to the finger for emphasis.

"Yessuh! Yessuh! " the Creole cried.

"What are you doing here?" Penn demanded.

Manuel stammered with his answer. "She...ah...she tell me she mean fa da me to...ah, give fa da you da message, Suh,"

"Message? What message? Who is she?" Penn demanded.

"She say that she mean fa da you fa da clear out. She be mad fa da you fa da buttin' in she's business. She mean fa da you fa da get out 'fore she say you get da hurt."

"Who?" Penn demanded again, applying more

pressure to the little finger. "Who's she? Hauke?"

"She say I fa da let on who she be, she fa da kill me, for true!"

"That might be," Penn said in anger. "But for sure right now you're going to get a broken finger if you don't answer."

Manuel was afraid of pain, but it was clear he feared whoever 'she' was a lot more than the pain of a broken finger. He violently shook his head 'no'.

Penn resigned to not getting the answer. He turned Manuel to face him while maintaining the Ju Jitsu hold on the man's little finger. "Okay, then," he said. "There are some other questions you can answer."

"Yessuh," Manuel responded with relief. "Yessuh."

"When Hauke makes his run, how does he do it?" Penn asked, strengthening his finger grasp.

Manuel grimaced. "Okay. I can tell you dat. She go wid da runabout, out dere." He nodded towards the window as he spoke.

"But that boat is not fast enough, is it?" Penn gave the finger another twist with the question.

"Yessuh, Yessuh, it is," the Creole quickly replied. "Only..."

"Only what?"

"Only, she don't take it all de ways. She gets de other boat."

"Other boat? What other boat?"

"De other one. De fast one. She keep at Nose Cay."

"What the hell are you talking about?" Penn demanded. "There isn't any other boat," he added, remembering his conversation with Morgan on that subject.

"Dere is, Suh. Dere is. It cain't be saw fa da account it be in de sea."

"What the hell does that mean?" PZ asked as Penn thought about the man's words.

"In de sea, Suh," Manuel answered PZ. "Under de water near by Nose Cay."

"Under the water?" Penn questioned the man's answer. "How is it kept under the water?"

"She float it, mon, Suh. When she get it, she make it come fa da sea, and go away, fast."

"Hauke takes his runabout to Nose Cay, then gets another boat out of the water that is faster? And continues in that one?" Penn asked, piecing together the riddle.

"Yessuh. Ouch! Yessuh, Yessuh, that's how she do it, for true!"

"I'll be God damn," PZ said, realizing the solution to the once seemingly insurmountable problem of time and mileage on the water. "An ocean racer. They keep an ocean racer under the water at Nose Cay, and use it for the fast run. No wonder it didn't figure. No wonder it couldn't be found on any island. Hell, it's too fast to be spotted while in use, and even if it is, it gets dumped back into the ocean where it never gets found. What an idea!"

"That seems to be the answer," Penn agreed, although with some skepticism. Then another thought crossed his mind. "When is the next run?" He asked, putting pressure on the finger again.

"Friday night, Suh. She say Friday night."

"But, it can't be Friday night. Hauke's gone, isn't he?" Penn gave the finger another twist, then backed off to let the man answer without screaming in pain.

"But fa da me do da run now," Manuel replied.

"You make the run? Then you have the information on where Milagro's boat is to meet you?"

The Creole's eyes rolled in fear. He suddenly realized the importance of the information he revealed. He began shaking his head slowly from side to side in indecision, not wanting to answer, but afraid of the pain in his little finger.

"Do you know where?" Penn re-asked the question.

Getting a better grip on Manuel's finger, he again demanded, "Where?"

"It be in me head," Manuel responded fearfully.

Penn shook his head. "I mean where are you supposed to meet Milagro? And who told you to make the run? Was it the Bear?"

Manuel began shaking his head in negative reply. "No. No, Suh. No be fa da Bear."

"Not the Bear? Then whom?" Penn pushed the finger almost to the breaking point.

"Aieee," the Creole complained. El Lobo!" he nearly shouted. "El Lobo! She be who say who make da run."

"Who is this El Lobo?" Penn continued his demands. "And where are you supposed to meet Milagro?" He began applying steady twisting pressure on the man's finger, expecting to hear it snap at any minute. He regretted causing such unending torture, but he needed the answer.

"El Lobo?" Manuel's eyebrows lifted. "She be...."

There was a pause in his reply as he looked past Penn at the door. Then his eyes opened wide with terror. "No! No!" he shouted in a panic, pleading.

Two sounds broke the silence that followed his pleading. They were muffled sounds. Sounds like air being forced through a narrow tube, a tube like a silencer on an automatic pistol. "Pffft! Pffft!" The hissing pierced the air.

Penn recognized the sounds and he heard the whine of the bullets as they passed his shoulder. He also recognized the two red spots that appeared on the left side of Manuel's chest. He watched the two red spots grow and merge into one big one as Manuel sagged to the floor with blood gushing over the entire front of him.

Penn let go of Manuel and sprinted to the still opened door, with PZ close behind, but they were too late. Whoever had fired the shots that killed Manuel had disappeared.

Realizing they had no chance of finding the assailant by that time, they returned to Manuel. "Whoever did this sure as hell's no amateur," Penn said, looking down at Manuel. "Whoever it was knew how much time was available for the shooting and for the escape, and timed his moves perfectly."

"Shit," PZ said, nearly as an afterthought. "Now what?"

"Well. In the first place, we don't want this to get out," Penn responded, not certain he was answering PZ's question.

"I mean now what the hell do we do? It's for damn sure we can't follow him to meet Milagro."

Penn glanced at his partner. "That, unfortunately, is a fact," he agreed. "But right now that's not the important item on our agenda. Right now we have to figure out what to do with this little problem."

"I think I can take care of that," Morgan Baletta interrupted from the doorway. She entered the room and shut the door, continuing across the room to get a closer look at the dead man. "That's Manuel, I presume," she said.

"That's him," Penn confirmed. "But where'd you come from?"

"I just got off the elevator around the corner as some guy pushed his way into it. He nearly knocked me off my feet in his rush, but he managed to get in just before the door closed."

"Then why didn't we see you when we went after him?" Penn asked, skeptical of the story.

"I guess it's because I first went into the wrong room around the corner to find you. The desk clerk apparently gave the wrong number to your room. I just got chased out of it, then came around here and heard you two talking, so I came in."

"Some timing," PZ commented.

"You never know, I guess," she responded with a shrug of her shoulders.

"You said you could take care of this mess?" Penn asked her, returning to her first remark.

"Sure. I'll call the Prefecture of Police and give him some story about a robbery, or something. He'll take my word for whatever I tell him and not get too pushy. Especially when it becomes clear that Manuel is Jamaican, and not a Belize citizen. That'll make it a lot easier for the Prefecture. He won't have to file any papers on the problem. He'll just let it go away. Provided, of course, that you have the money to pay for the funeral. Belizeans are very careful about that point. They don't want to use state money to pay for burying someone who never paid taxes to the country in the first place. They only want to cover their citizens, not careless tourists."

"Well, I guess we can cough up enough to pay for the funeral," Penn sighed. "And, I suspect the funeral would be one hell of a lot more expensive for Manuel than for a citizen. Particularly when there are such circumstances as this to be ignored, right?"

"I think you got the picture," the woman said. "If I am not mistaken, about two hundred, American, ought to handle the problem. Do you have that on you?"

"I suppose," Penn said as he looked to PZ for agreement, more out of ritual than of necessity.

PZ shrugged his shoulders in assent.

"Good," Morgan said, and she picked up the telephone. "I'll make a call and have a few friends of mine take care of the body after we leave."

"It's a good thing he told us the secret of the faster boat before he so inconsiderately kicked the bucket," PZ said, trying to break the ominous silence the followed Morgan's words.

Penn wished PZ had kept his mouth shut, though.

Damn Turkey, he thought. I wanted to see just what steps Morgan would have taken from this point, assuming she didn't have any idea that Manuel had revealed the fast boat secret. But that possibility was blown, now. "Okay. Let's get out of this place," he said. He was resigned to the take the next step in the process, whatever that process was, in spite of the fact that he wanted to remain on the offensive and in control. Also, he was beginning to feel uneasy about this woman, and he knew that whatever steps were to be taken, they had to include keeping a close watch on her. He was familiar, too damn familiar, with the loyalties of field agents. They were all the same, regardless of the name of their agency. They were first loyal to themselves, and then to their cause. They couldn't always be trusted. For some subconscious reason, he was beginning to distrust this one very much.

"What do we do now?" PZ asked.

"I'm not quite sure, yet," Penn replied. "Besides getting out of here, that is. Then, if you want to try locating Milagro by hit or miss, I suppose we might give that a try."

"Oh," PZ responded.

"I don't suppose you happen to have any information just lying around your place that would solve this problem of Milagro's whereabouts, would you?" he asked Morgan with a slight tone of sarcasm.

"As a matter of fact, I don't," she replied, noting the detective's developing distaste for her.

"So, again I ask, now what?" PZ was being persistent.

"I think," Penn added thoughtfully, "that it might not be a bad idea to take a look at Hauke's office."

"That might prove to be a good suggestion," Morgan agreed, appearing to want to redeem herself. "Just what might you be looking for?"

"I don't know, for sure," Penn replied. "There might be something there of value. Maybe there's something that will tell us where he's going in the states. We might be able to locate him and force him to come back here to complete the run." Penn already had a pretty good idea where Hauke had gone. Where else would he go but to visit Mikel Bear? He'd be easy enough to find there, but he didn't want Morgan to know that, not just yet. Anyway, he wanted to get into Hauke's office for whatever other leads it might reveal.

"Of course," PZ followed up. "Not only that, he might have left something around that gave Manuel the directions for the run."

"Exactly," Penn smiled as he lead the trio out of the hotel.

"Guess I'll call on the Prefecture of Police to take care of this problem," Morgan said as she left Penn and PZ hailing the taxi waiting in front of the hotel after having just disgorged some more moneyed American tourists.

Penn gave the driver directions to the Hard Logger's yard, climbed in with PZ following, and sat back silently thinking as the cab bounced over the potholes and part-whole parts of the road.

When the cab braked to a stop in front of the gate surrounding the Hard Loggers' yard, Penn paid the driver and asked him to wait for them. "There'll be a five dollar tip in it, if you do," he offered as a bribe as he turned to join PZ, who was already halfway across the yard to the small cement block office.

Penn was surprised to find the office door unlocked, and without any interference from the yard employees in the area, the two entered the small two-room building that smelled of mahogany sawdust and mildew.

They rummaged through the drawers and closet shelves in the office, then in the back room that served as Manuel's part time living quarters. Two .38 caliber six inch barrel revolvers with matching white imitation pearl grips were found in a drawer of the small table beside the rumpled single cot, but nothing was found that appeared like written directions to the Milagro meeting place.

Penn made note of the location of the revolvers in case they were needed at some later time.

"There's only two," he commented about the weapons.

"Yeah. Too bad there's not one for Morgan," PZ responded.

"Why? She already has one of her own, remember?" Penn reminded him, remembering how she so skillfully trained her .357 Magnum on his and PZ's chests when they intruded into her front yard.

"Oh, that's right," PZ said. "I forgot."

After half an hour of searching without finding anything related to their primary purpose, Penn said he thought the search was turning out to be mostly fruitless.

PZ agreed.

"You think we can go back to the hotel by now?" PZ asked, bored with the search. "I could use a drink. How about you?"

"I suppose so," Penn replied pensively.

Back at the Fort George once more, they went directly to their favorite table in the lounge. It was nearly noontime, and they had made sure they didn't return from Hauke's office for almost three hours after first leaving that little mess in PZ's room. Even now they weren't sure they were in the clear. They settled in, though, and after ordering their drinks, they sat for another twenty minutes, neither speaking. They weren't entirely positive they weren't going to get pounced on any second for one of those insufferable rounds of third degree questioning that everyone reads about taking place in the various banana republics of Central America.

By one p.m. they were on their third drink.

"Now what?" PZ asked, breaking the near record silence between them.

"You turkey," Penn replied. "This morning our only

chance of ever locating Allie got blown away. We didn't find any clues in Hauke's office, which means we have to go back to the states to pin him down, and all you can do is ask now what?"

"Aren't you the touchy one?" PZ responded.

Penn sipped his drink. He had been touchy, he silently agreed. He was already pondering the probabilities of either sitting here to wait for Hauke's return, or go back to the states to locate him. He considered the odds of getting some information out of Hauke in time to get back to Belize to get to Milagro before the Coast Guard does, or before Milagro got caught in whatever plot was hatched to make this his last run. If they missed him they would never be sure whether or not the woman who was with him was Allie or not. That was the problem making him touchy. "If we did go back, then what?" he asked.

"What's the matter with you?" PZ asked. Penn's demeanor surprised him.

"Actually, I suppose, since I told Yanks to put a tail on Bear, if Hauke gets together with Bear, we'll know where they are. All we have to do is find out what they're up to so we can do something to make them return here, so Hauke can make the run and we can follow him."

"Hmmm," PZ reluctantly agreed. "I guess you're right."

"That's the only possible line of action now that Manuel's dead."

"Suppose he won't return?"

"I said we would make him return."

"How?"

"How the hell do I know? We'll cross that bridge when we come to it," Penn was becoming impatient with PZ's reluctance. "Actually," he added. "Manuel's death in itself might force Hauke to return to make the run."

"That's a possibility, and it's probably a good possibility. At least it's one we can try. It's for sure we haven't gotten anywhere down here."

"Okay," Penn said at length. "You go get our bags, and I'll make the reservations for this evening's flight back. The evening flight goes to Miami where we'll have to catch the late night red eye flight to Oakland. That way we can be home by morning. That's better than sitting around here until tomorrow's flight, at least. That okay with you?"

"Sure," PZ said with some enthusiasm. He finished his drink and headed for the stairs.

Penn headed for the now familiar telephone booth, preferring to use it rather than returning to his room. He wouldn't have been surprised had the airline clerk told him that the evening's flight was booked full, so when he realized their reservations were confirmed, he began feeling more positive about things in general.

His second call was to Yanks. He didn't expect the man to be home, and at best hoped his answering machine was on. He wanted to tell Yanks to put even more emphasis on Bear's tail.

He had guessed correctly. Yanks wasn't home, so he left the message on the machine.

His last call was the important one. It was to Lara to let her know he was on his way back home. By the time he had finished that call, PZ had returned carrying the two overstuffed travel bags that they used whenever they went out of town.

"You know something?" Penn asked PZ once they were firmly ensconced in their coach class seats leaving Belize International for Miami.

"Here we go again," PZ responded with a touch of sarcasm. "No. I don't know nothing."

"Anything," Penn corrected. "You don't know anything."

"Thanks."

"Actually, I was just thinking about the Aquino case.

Remember that one?"

"How could I forget?"

"Do you remember how, during that entire case, we actually didn't solve anything?"

"What're you talking about? Vallerga got his, and Marcos kept his, and also, I suppose, Yletta got hers, unfortunately."

"Well, that's true. But what I meant was, that in spite of all we did, we actually didn't do anything. I mean, we were really led along by the events, not resolving the problems."

"How can you say we didn't do anything? We stopped Vallerga from taking over the government, didn't we?"

"That we did. But more as followers than as doers, know what I mean? All the events played themselves out while we just watched, neither causing them, nor being able to stop them for that matter."

"Yeah. I guess that was so. But what's so important about that now?"

"Because, I have the damnedest feeling in the back of my head that once again we're just following along. We're following along watching things happen instead of making them happen to resolve anything."

PZ didn't comment. Instead, he flagged down the flight attendant and ordered an individual serving of vodka and one of Kahlua, along with a glass of ice. He had his Black Russian in the making.

Penn wondered why his partner had more of a look of anxiety than normal. He put it down to relief at having gotten out of Belize without having to face the third degree from the local police.

Chapter 19

The midnight red eye flight from Miami had tired Penn and PZ, but there was one thing in their favor when they reached the Oakland International Airport. They didn't have to go through customs again. They already spent two hours with that chore in Miami. It took less than half an hour to find their bags, and to wend their way through the lobby to the sidewalk.

Penn had asked Lara to collect his car from the airport parking lot the day after he and PZ left for Belize, and she had been expecting Penn's call to tell her when they would be back. He was relieved to see her right on time, as usual.

"Well, good. There's Lara," he commented as he spied her pulling into the curb lane of traffic, barely missing a much too long white limousine that pulled out in front of her. "Let's get the hell out of this place. I'm a bit tired of anything airline connected right now."

"Yeah. Me, too," PZ added as Lara pulled to a stop.

Lara reached over to unlock the door just in time, and Penn was greeted by her infectious, "Hi, Love," as he got in.

Before he could answer her greeting, though, she leaned over and threw her arms around his neck, then smothered his mouth with her lips. "Ummmmh," she purred, obviously losing interest in all else at the moment.

"Hey! Lady!" the parking control officer called as he stepped up to the car door. "I can tell you're glad to see the guy, but you can't hold up traffic just for that."

Penn peeled Lara's arms from around his neck and

peevishly grinned at the cop. “Give me a break, will you?” he called back through the open car window. “I've been gone for a while.”

“Sure you have,” the cop replied with cynicism, not moving, waiting for Lara to drive away.

She shrugged her shoulders, laughed lightly in that special way that Penn loved, and stomped on the gas pedal. The Beast squealed and belched a cloud of black smoke in the officers' face for his lack of consideration.

“Well,” she said after she had negotiated the exit from the airport and was well on her way down Hagenberger Lane to the freeway. “Did you get a lead on Allie?”

Penn glanced at her from the center of the front car seat where he had been riding, enjoying the closeness of her. “A lead, maybe,” he responded with exasperation. He didn't want to have to return his thoughts to the problems of the project, yet. He wanted to remain in the pleasantness of the moment.

“Yanks called and said he would meet you at the Peppermill in Corte Madera at ten. I know that's your favorite place, visually speaking, but are you going to be up to it? You don't look like you got too much rest on that plane.”

Penn grinned at her once more, appreciating her use of the words 'visually speaking.' The Peppermill could be a visual delight to some people, the way the waitresses are dressed. He also noted the sarcasm as well as the touch of jealousy in her words.

“Ah, we'll be all right,” PZ intervened from the back seat.

Penn smiled at PZ's interjection. He knew PZ enjoyed playing the Rambo type in front of Lara. It was PZ's way of dealing with the jealousy that troubled him whenever he faced the affection Lara expressed for Penn. Penn knew PZ secretly wished for the same form of affection and devotion from some woman, at the same time overtly pretending the predisposition of the macho predator. Penn decided to not answer Lara's question, though. It really didn't matter how tired he felt at the moment. There was work to be done.

Less than an hour later Lara dropped the two detectives off at the Peppermill, then reluctantly took the car home. Yanks would provide transportation from there.

The Peppermill Lounge was the most pretentious plastic coated playground for the polyester clad purveyors of pleasure in Marin County. The decor consisted of gaudy colors and plastic plants. The cocktail waitresses wore red polyester gowns that reached to the ankles, with wide venting slits from the hips, and which were loosely strapped off the shoulder tops.

Visually delightful? Penn thought of Lara's comments. To PZ, possibly.

The lounge was dark, though, which was well suited for clandestine meetings. It was also furnished with soft cushioned couches, and fitted with a Musak System designed not to drown out the hushed conversations which took place between the hustlers and the hustled who patronized the place, but to give them just enough noise for cover.

Yanks was already sitting in a booth in the corner farthest from the entrance, trying to keep the attentions of one of the lounge hostesses.

It appeared that he wasn't having much success, though, for she walked away briskly as PZ and Penn approached, displaying a Pepsodent smile that glared through too heavy make-up. She had the smile that was often plastered on the countenances of women who were paid to exert themselves in a contrived friendly manner.

PZ tried his line on the waitress as she passed, but with pretty much the same results Yanks had. His thrust was thwarted by her professional verbal sidestepping, and he sat down unperturbed in spite of being unsuccessful. He was familiar with the game.

"Hey, glad you guys made it back safely," Yanks greeted them cheerfully as they plopped down on the low couches beside the too short cocktail table.

"Yeah, we made it back safely," PZ said, showing an unusual lack of patience with Yanks' patter.

"Thanks, Yanks," Penn returned the greeting, at the same time noting PZ's temperament. He wondered why PZ wasn't taking the woman's rejection in stride. He put the thought aside, though. "I hope you have some good news to tell us," he added to Yanks. "We need to hear something good right now."

"Well, guess what?" Yanks began his story.

"We don't pay you to make us guess," PZ interjected.

"Okay," Yanks returned, unruffled by the rebuke. "Then I guess I'll tell you. Bear and Keany are at the S & M place in Guerneville. Marena and Manny Bolton both are there, too."

"Marena?" PZ asked, his interest picking up.

"The same and one-ly, I mean, the same one and only," Yanks replied. "I guess Lara hasn't had a chance to relay my last report to you yet, hunh? When I called you I told you I followed Bear and Keany up to their place in the Russian River where they make the flicks, right?"

Penn nodded.

"So, that's where she makes them, hunh?" PZ interjected again, as though he had forgotten his and Penn's recent encounter with the Mitchell Brothers palace of porn. "I saw her in one of her S & M movies, once," he added, ready to continue the dissertation of several days earlier on the same topic.

"Yeah," Yanks replied, interrupting PZ. "I checked around some while you were gone. You know, with nothing better to do, and guess what I found out?"

"Like I said..." PZ returned to his complaint, frustrated by Yank's interruption of his story.

"I know," Yanks again interrupted PZ, casting a glance at him. "I'm not getting paid to make you guess. Okay. I found out that some of the heaviest S & M flicks, the kind with Marena in 'em, come right out of that place in Guerneville." He paused for effect, grinning while watching Penn absorb his report. "What's more," he continued, "a few snuff flicks have been made in that place, too."

"Snuff flicks?" Penn asked.

"Yeah. Like porno flicks that really kill. A sick part of S & M, the ultimate, is to carry out the game until the victim, the masochist, gets snuffed out. Killed. That's why they're called..."

"Snuff flicks," PZ butted in.

"And Mikel Bear's running the place, like I told you," Yanks added.

"Good Christ. If Bear is running a porno operation, an S & M operation, with Marena and Bolton..."

"Bolt-on," PZ interrupted with a chortle. He placed the emphasis on the first syllable, Bolt. "A bolt-on is what he'd need if he had to get Marena excited enough to make good porno flicks."

Penn glared at PZ. "You seem to know a lot about Marena. Is there something you want to tell me?" His challenge was meant to be a humorous way of getting the man to shut up.

PZ didn't respond as planned. "Hey!" he defended himself. "I read the papers, you know."

Penn didn't have time to refute PZ's slightly exaggerated claim of having ever read a newspaper, so he returned to the information Yanks continued offering.

"Not only that," Yanks was saying, "but there's some guy there that Bear picked up from the airport yesterday. The guy flew in on TACA Airlines."

"Morri Bund," PZ again interjected.

"Morri Bund," Penn echoed, thinking.

"Well," PZ came up with another chortle. "All we need to complete the picture is for Sergeant McIvers to be there, too."

"I don't think that'll happen," Yanks said.

"Really? You sound quite definite on that point, Yanks," Penn said. "Why is that? I thought McIvers and Bear were good pals."

"They ain't been so good lately, from what I hear," Yanks explained.

"Why?"

"Well, the streets have it that McIvers has been giving Bear information from working police files, and Giddings heard about it."

"No kidding?" Penn wasn't surprised that Captain Giddings had heard of that going on. What was surprising was that it took so long for him to learn it. "What did Giddings have to say?"

"Well, I guess he called McIvers on the carpet and told him to straighten that out or he'd be back on the street in uniform," Yanks explained. "Word is, that McIvers is more than a pissed little, I mean, a little pissed at Bear for letting that one get out."

"I guess. How did it get out, anyway?" Penn wasn't sure he believed everything he was hearing.

"I guess from that DEA agent, Keany," Yanks added. "Or from someone else, maybe someone that wasn't entirely happy with the Bear's operations here. Someone who would like to toss some kind of wrenched monkey, I mean, monkey wrench into them."

"Who?" Penn asked.

"I don't know. Hell, if I did, I wouldn't tell, ah, I mean, wouldn't I tell you? Oh, by the way, Keany's in on part of the action, too."

Penn could only stare at Yanks. He suspected that this final piece of information had been held out for effect, for the last bit of glee Yanks could get from it. He knew

Yanks could intuitively feel the impact the information would have, and enjoyed playing the game. "Is there anything else you haven't told us, yet?" he asked flatly.

"Well," Yanks said, playing the line slowly, almost expertly.

"There's more?" Penn asked with a tone of demand.

"One thing more," Yanks admitted, plying the bait. Then after seeing both fish were hooked, he said, "Hauke is supposed to get himself back to Belize to take care of the logging business, whatever that is. It's apparently safe for him now that you two are out of there."

Penn was too surprised with the news to do anything more than sit back and stare at Yanks. "How hell did you find that out so quickly?" he asked.

"Hey," Yanks said. "I have my sources."

"Hah!" PZ chortled. "I bet I know who she is." He sat back and grinned mischievously.

Yanks ignored PZ and sat back, while grinning triumphantly.

The cocktail waitress arrived with her plastic grin, and asked if she should bring another round.

Penn nodded assent. The momentary interruption allowed him to start putting together the pieces of the puzzle. "You tapped Bear's phone, didn't you?" he asked Yanks.

"Just a little tap,'" Yanks replied, expecting a reprimand for the illegal stunt. "But you wouldn't know what you know now if I hadn't," he defended his actions.

Penn shook his head. He was afraid something like that would be done by Yanks, but he knew such drastic steps were needed in this particular case. His reprimand wasn't forthcoming, much to Yanks' relief. "Is the tap still on?" he asked, instead.

"No. Not really," Yanks replied evasively.

Penn saw the answer for the lie that it was. He knew Yanks was aware that the tap should have been removed when it was learned that he and PZ were returning from Belize. He also knew Yanks could play the game right up to the hilt and would know just how valuable the information was. He was somewhat annoyed, though, that Yanks always played the game so effectively. Then, too, that was partly why he felt Yanks was a valuable employee. "Just what was the extent of the tap?" he asked at length.

"Well," Yanks began his explanation. "The timing was a bit tricky, so I only got a few calls, that's all. The first call was taken by Embee. I guess she takes messages for Bear. Anyway, the caller said El Lobo was ready, and it was okay for Hauke to come back to take care of the logging, again, since the two detectives, you two, were on their way back to the states, and also since number two, whoever that is, is no longer in the running. Embee sounded surprised about that, though. Then she said something which I guess meant that Bear didn't expect you two to ever come back, and then the caller said something about number two missing his chance, or something to that effect. Then the caller said two number, ah, number two was dead. Embee was surprised. Then the caller said Bear would have to find another man to take his place.

"Jesus, you memorized all that?" PZ commented as soon as Yanks stopped to take a breath.

"And more," Yanks added. "Then Embee said that Bear said that from the way things looked to him, he was going to have to take care of a few things up here, then take Hauke back to Belize, himself. That he was going to have to figure out a way to get that damned Penguini, you, again, back there where you could be handled by him, personally. Then she made some remark about his having to take care of another nasty detail, too. Something about an increase in prices of supplies, I think was said. Anyway, the conclusion was that Bear was certain that the mess could be cleared up only by himself. And that was it."

"That's a mouthful," PZ said.

"I quite agree," Penn said. "The caller was a woman?"

"How did you know that?" It was Yanks' turn to be surprised.

"Because a certain luscious broad named Morgan Baletta," PZ explained, "was the only person who knew we came back here when we did."

Penn glanced at his partner. He nodded his confirmation in response to Yanks' questioning gaze.

"Were there any other calls?" Penn returned to the topic of the telephone tap, wondering if there might be just one more item of information Yanks was holding back for effect. There was.

"Well, there is one other thing, but I don't think it really related to this thing," he said, casting his eyes downward to avoid Penn's scrutiny.

Penn knew the man's ploy, knew he was lying. "Okay, Yanks," he admonished. "Enough of the suspense. What the hell is the rest of the story?"

"After Embee hung up from the first call, Bear must have come home. He called some guy and explained that he needed more street venders...."

"Who'd he call?" PZ interrupted.

Penn thought it unusual that PZ was so anxious to know if the other man on the call was identified.

"I don't know," Yanks responded. "He didn't give a name. Anyway, the other guy said he'd get right on it. Then he asked Bear if McIvers knew about the increase in men, or if he had to worry about McIvers finding out. Bear chuckled and said that he had McIvers under control with the stories he's been telling that, get this, 'dumb-ass cop.' He said that dumb-ass cop couldn't find his ass with his pants down, so he doubted if the man could find out about the venders, and that the other wouldn't have to worry about him. Then the other guy said okay. And Bear hung up."

Penn looked intently at Yanks innocent expression of satisfaction after the tale was related, then asked, "You're sure you don't know whom this other guy is?' he asked.

"No. He never gave a name."

"That figures," Penn remarked. "Tell me, Yanks. Did you do this taping with a tape recorder, or did you listen in?"

"Tape."

"Then, you still have the tape?"

"Sure. Why?"

"Because, I think I have an idea," Penn replied. He reached for his drink and took a sip, then again leaned back to think.

"Were there any more calls?" PZ asked.

Penn believed PZ asked the question out of a desire to contribute something to the conference.

"There were more calls, I'm sure," Yanks answered, "but I didn't tape them. I couldn't. Did I do good?"

"I think you did well enough," Penn concluded.

"Yeah, I'd say so," confirmed PZ, seeming to relax slightly.

"PZ," Penn said after several minutes of silence among the trio, broken only by the ever-insistent Musak system and a sprinkling of laughs and giggles of the hustled responding to the hustlers throughout the room. "Why don't you go over to that pay telephone, and see if you can get in touch with Sergeant McIvers, of the Ess Eff Pee Dee?"

PZ first questioned the suggestion, then shrugged and got up, heading for the telephone.

"Where is this tape?" Penn asked Yanks.

"In my car. Why? You want it now?"

"I do, and I also want your portable tape recorder to play it on. Do you have that with you, too?"

"Sure."

"Then go get them, will you?"

"Sure, Chief," Yanks aped PZ's response, and left the room. He returned four minutes later with the tape and the recorder. PZ returned five minutes later to say McIvers was on his way, and sat down with a concerned expression.

"Something troubling you?" Penn quizzed, casually.

"Hunh?" PZ replied. "Oh, ah, no. Not really."

Chapter 20

Penn waited for the cocktail waitress in the revealing gown to suggest another drink order. As she bent over to retrieve the empty glasses she made an attempt to display herself in a manner that was calculated by the management to induce interest in spending some more time in the lounge. He considered that the tactics must have been imported from the sin centers of Nevada, where the Peppermill Lounge chain got started.

He had some time to kill, and he idled it away by surveying the lounge and the crowd, appraising the various customers, while PZ took the opportunity to try connecting with one of the single girls at the bar. Nearly half an hour later PZ returned to the booth in disappointment.

Penn was about to comment on PZ's lack of progress, but was interrupted by the entrance of Sergeant McIvers.

Yanks had been ordered out of the building before the sergeant's arrival. It wouldn't have been prudent to let McIvers know of the meeting between Yanks and the Flyin' Penguin Detective Agency. That wouldn't have fit in with the plan.

"Sergeant McIvers," Penn greeted as he stood up and offered his hand for the ritualistic social stroking handshake. "I'm glad you could find time in your busy schedule to reply to my request. I'm sure you'll be glad you did, too."

"Yeah?" the cop challenged. "So what's so important that it could effect half the cases I'm working on? Provided, of course, that I am working on anything that you would know something about."

"Hey," Penn responded affably, in spite of the intent in the remark. "Are we going to start off with chips on our shoulders? Or, are we going to get together for the solution to what most likely, although I am sure you don't realize it yet, is our mutual problem?"

"That sounds too confusing for me," McIvers responded without emotion. He was wielding his police mentality style self-protection. That was something all police officers are trained to do, and he was a typical cop. "Look," he continued. "The captain said it would be a good idea to get my ass down here to talk to you. I don't happen to like the idea, but I just work there, know what I mean?"

"Sure. I know," Penn responded in a friendly tone. "And I also know that you have a thing going with Mikel Bear that is about to make you out one God damn big fool."

The sergeant sat back in surprise. He was caught between the acceptance of Penn's first soft approach and contrasting sudden directness. "Just what the hell are you talking about?" he demanded, trying to retain the upper hand.

Penn saw the sergeant's anger rising, and wondered if it was caused by a sense of awareness, or a precognition, of the upcoming predicament, one in which the man might not appear to be the knight in shining armor he liked everyone to think he was.

"Well," Penn continued, being careful not to sound too over confident with seeing a chink in the cop's armor. When dealing with the typical policeman's mentality an almost subservient position had to be established right up to the moment of reality, up until that moment that the cop would realize he was had by the cajones, as they would say in Mexico. "I think that first, you should sit back and let me make my position clear. Then, I think you should listen to a conversation on this tape recorder here, that would be of most importance to you. I think that then we should discuss what we should do."

The sergeant looked suspicious. "I'm not sure I like your innuendoes," he said. "But since it's the captain's wish I should listen, what do you have on your mind?"

"What I have on my mind is this: I think that Mikel Bear persuaded you to give him certain information on files that deal with ongoing investigations. I don't know what he used to persuade you, but I do know that he has no respect for you, and that he is using you as a source solely for his own good. If he made any promises to you for that information, then I think you should know how he deals with people he makes promises to, and for that matter, with people in general. That's what's on my mind."

The sergeant said nothing. He only glared. He was already half expecting the conversation would not be to his liking.

Penn saw his advantage, and continued his thrust. "My sources have it that Mikel Bear got you to give him the status of the investigations on the Russian River S & M activities, the homicides that every once in a while show up on the streets of the Tenderloin or in the South of Market Street area, the street dealing investigations, and the heavy importing of stuff right under the noses of the Vice Squad. I suspect he gave you some story about being able to help you solve most of those cases, when what he was really doing was making sure he could protect his own neck with the information. And, knowing Mikel Bear as I do, I suspect he promised you the world in a gold cup for your help. Am I not right?"

It was a subtle change in Penn's attitude from reticence and subservience at the beginning of his speech to one of forthright control at the end.

The change wasn't yet detected by the sergeant, but his

face turned white by the time Penn had finished. He looked like he had been caught with his hand in the cookie jar.

When he at last replied, it was nearly automatic, without thinking of his response, as though it was a response from the trained underling answering his boss rather than from one who was supposed to be the inquisitor. "He said I could have the credit for breaking the cases. That I could have the collar and the credit, maybe to get my lieutenant's bars, if I helped him in his investigations." He reached for a cigarette, tried to light it with a shaky hand, then took one long puff. After blowing it out, he seemed to regain some of his self-control. Looking at Penn, he added, "But how did you know about that?" he asked.

"To be honest, I didn't know all of it," Penn responded quietly. "But I do know Mikel Bear, like I said. I know his style. He promises what his marks want the most, and then plays on that want until the last, when the mark sees the game. By then Bear's the only winner. The mark is the loser. By that time he's had it all set up for no other way."

The sergeant furrowed his brow in consternation.

"But," Penn continued, "I also know how you can pull this thing out, and at the same time get your revenge, if you want to call it that, on the Bear for duping you."

The sergeant took another puff on his cigarette. It was a long puff, nearly drawing the ashes down to the filter in one breath. The nicotine helped him regain some confidence. "I'm not saying that there is anything that I have to be helped out of, mind you," he said, "but, if I did want to make certain adjustments, or, that is, if I were to accept any recommendations for changes in my ongoing investigative procedures, what would you suggest?"

Penn tried not to show his satisfaction in realizing he had won the day. He knew then that the sergeant was guilty as suspected. He also knew that he had the man by the Mexican term. "I would suggest that you first listen to this tape," he said as he reached over to turn on the machine. He then handed the earphones to the sergeant so that only the man could hear the recorded conversations of Mikel Bear. He hadn't listened to the tape himself. He didn't think it necessary, since Yanks was usually pretty thorough on his verbal transcriptions. He watched intently as the sergeant put on the earphones and turned on the machine.

As the officer listened to the tape, his face went first red in embarrassment, then white in anger. His pulse raced at about the time that he would have been listening to the remark about not being able to find certain parts of his anatomy.

"That son of a bitch," he swore when he took off the earphones and set them on the table. "That son of a bitch," he repeated while staring at the tape recorder as though he found what it contained was unbelievable. "That bastard. He has been playing me for a fool."

"Exactly as I said, isn't it?" Penn said. "But I have a way out of this dilemma, for you, if you would like to hear it," he said.

"How?" the sergeant said quietly. He was hard spent to ask without showing a loss of pride.

"How long would it take you to get warrants for a Russian River address?"

The question was not what the officer had expected. He frowned, but didn't question Penn's intent, only the place. "You mean for that place in Guerneville that Bear was talking about?"

"Yes."

"Too long," he said. "I would have to have an affidavit filled out and sworn. Then I would have to coordinate with the Sonoma County Sheriff's Office, since the Russian River area is unincorporated, and that would take some time."

"There's no way to have it by this evening, then?"

"This evening? No. No way."

"Okay, then, how about this? If you can't go in with a warrant, how about if you were in hot pursuit?"

The sergeant grinned, ever so slightly, seeing some plan for revenge developing. "Sure. I could get away with that. I don't think anything I would see that's not related to the hot pursuit could be used, be admissible, though," he said.

"Okay. Suppose the person you were pursuing appeared to be associated with the activities that you observed after you followed him into the house? Wouldn't that work?"

"Possibly. Then I could write it up as material, I guess. But the D.A. would have a fit, and the people who got busted would have a good cause to come back on the department for false arrest, illegal detention, all those good things the department dearly loves to have thrown at them."

Penn grinned at the sarcasm. "Not if they were guilty," he said.

"Even then," the sergeant corrected.

"Legally, yes. But, being guilty, they couldn't afford to expose their information and their connections by pursuing such a course of action. They would, instead, have to get out of Dodge, so to speak, and that would do three things. It would first relieve you of your complicated mess. Secondly, it would make a local hero of sorts out of you, which I'm sure you wouldn't object to. And thirdly, it would get the perpetrators of a particular crime I'm working on, out in the open. Does that sound like a good idea?"

"No cop in his right mind would even think of going along with your plan, you know that," he said in rebuttal.

"Probably. But drastic problems require drastic solutions. What's more, once you do get these guys behind bars, then you would have 72 hours to hold them on suspicion. That would give you enough time to get your warrant for the house, search it, and file a complaint charging them all with violations of the Health and Welfare codes, as well as conspiracy, or whatever."

The sergeant looked at Penn in the eye. "There's one more thing," he said. "This thing you're working on. What is it? How can I be sure that what you're doing is not the same thing that the Bear did, only with a different twist?"

"I'll tell you how you can be sure. First, you can call Captain Giddings and ask him if I've ever been anything other than straight forward with the police. Second, I'll tell you what we're after right from the start."

"Well, since it was the captain's order that I follow up on PZ's call, I guess I can take you at your word. What're you after?"

"You haven't forgotten about that small time hood, Hauke, have you?"

The sergeant was again caught by surprise. "What do you mean?"

"I'm sure you know him from somewhere else besides that tape right there," Penn said, nodding at the tape recorder. "I seem to remember something about a few dollars of your own money being made off with in an unusual way some time ago." Penn showed half a grin with the words.

"How do you know about that?" the sergeant demanded, a little embarrassed.

"That's not important. What is, is that he's involved with the Bear."

"Shit. I know that," the sergeant said without enthusiasm.

"He's also the prime shipper of the cocaine under Bear's direction, that hits your streets. I'll bet you didn't know that," Penn challenged.

The sergeant nodded. "I didn't know that," he agreed.

"And the reason Bear wanted the files on the street vendors? Going back to the tape, again, do you remember the conversation between Bear and that guy about the street vendors?"

"Yeah," the sergeant began to see Penn's point.

"Doesn't that answer the question?"

"Yep. I guess it pretty much does. More than just one, too. That's for sure."

"Not only is Bear responsible for selling that crap on the streets, but he's the one who set up that Guerneville operation, and unless I miss my guess, the money for that set up came from the money from the coke dealing."

Penn sat back to let his words sink in. At the same time he shot a glance at PZ. He noted his partner's face showed a great deal of concern, but hadn't time to wonder why, not while in the middle of persuading the sergeant, anyway.

"And the reason I think the place ought to get busted as soon as possible, and this wasn't on the tapes, is that the porn flicks they make up there get pretty damned heavy into the S & M game. That's the reason he wanted information on the Tenderloin and South of Market murder investigations. Their S & M games sometimes get too rough, and bingo, another body is anonymously dumped where the least amount of suspicion would be attached to them. After all, that area is known for being frequented by all sorts of strange people, and what's another body, more or less? But the point is, they come from Guerneville more times than I would like to think."

"Jesus!" the sergeant exclaimed. He hadn't put that association together.

"And," Penn continued, "that's where Marena makes most of her money. She's not only working the Mitchell Brothers as a showgirl, but she deals heavy in the back rooms, not only in coke, but in black market information.

She sells her ability to keep her mouth shut, so to speak. She is a principal player in those movies, because she has one damn strong need to display her sadistic nature. The Bear is taking advantage of that need by making movies of her and her perversions."

"Jesus," the sergeant said again, somewhat louder.

"And if you want more. There's Manny Bolton."

"The artist?"

"The artist. He gets his ideas for that morbid crap he paints from the goings on in that place. He even takes part in some of the movies. And..."

"Jesus! There's even more?" the sergeant interrupted. He was wide eyed by this time.

"There's more," Penn affirmed. "Tom Keany. Ever hear that name?"

"You're kidding? Not the head of the local DEA?"

"Him. He's involved with the Bear. That's another reason why Bear wanted..." He let the sentence drop.

"The files on the DEA connections with our drug task force," the sergeant completed Penn's statement. "This is getting pretty heavy, you know?" By now he had recovered from his initial shock and was developing a cop's interest in the details, typically tempering that interest with a professional touch of skepticism.

"Also involved is a field agent for the DEA who just arrived here from Belize. As a matter fact, I have reason to believe he is in the Guerneville house right now. That's another reason for expedient action."

"Jesus," the sergeant said, finding he had no alternative but to revert to that one word.

"And, there is a control agent somewhere, we believe he's in Belize, who runs the entire drug importing network, from the producer through the street sales. We believe that control agent is the one who set up Bear in the operation in the first place."

"How the hell did you come up with that? We've been

trying to pin a tail on the connection between Belize and the stuff on the streets here for nearly a year."

Penn grinned. "Well," he said. "It's no surprise that you haven't been having any luck. The God damn donkey was being told where you were pointing the pin holding the tail. No wonder you kept missing. Bear's been the connection, and he's been moving around one step ahead of you all the way. Thanks to your information." Penn completed his recitation with almost a sigh of relief. He reached for his glass and sat back to enjoy watching his words take effect. He only hoped that what he presented as the truth, which in fact was largely speculation and presumption, was at least half true.

The sergeant watched Penn intently for several minutes. During that time he lit another Marlboro, only this time he stuck the un-filtered end in his mouth. He lit the filter without thinking, and it wasn't until the second rapid puff that he discovered his error. He coughed, swore, leaned forward and stamped the butt in the ashtray, then leaned back while pulling out another one, all with one motion, pre-occupied with his thoughts.

"There's still one thing you haven't told me," he said, after lighting the second cigarette with greater care, and after taking a long puff.

"Those things are going to kill you one of these days," Penn commented, avoiding the officer's comment.

"What?" PZ asked. He had been mostly distracted during the conversations. The word kill attracted his attention.

Penn glanced at his partner. "McIvers and his cigarettes," he explained.

"What is the case you two are working on, and how does it affect that little hood, Hauke?" The sergeant asked.

"Quite frankly," Penn answered. "We are hoping that this little shakeup we're talking about making in

Guerneville will force Bear's hand, and the hand of the control agent in Belize. This in turn will lead us to the connection, whom, we have reason to believe, is the one who will lead us to a certain girl we've been hired to find. As the icing on the cake, PZ and I believe the whole mess is behind the recent murder of a certain private investigator friend of ours."

"Blaise Markham?" the sergeant asked.

"The same," Penn said.

"I see," the sergeant said. "In that case, maybe we ought to get started. How do you propose we set up this little cat and mouse game of hot pursuit?"

"That," answered Penn, "is the question."

"I don't think it's possible," PZ commented without enthusiasm.

Chapter 21

Penn sat back in his plastic covered cushion. For a few minutes he stared at the fire floating in the water of the imitation rock well built in the center of the room. He wondered how the flame burned just on the surface of the water. "Interesting effect," he said. "Everything in this place is staged," he mused. "All the world's a stage."

"So now we get Shakespeare?" PZ quipped. "It'd be a lot better if you gave us a way into that place in Guerneville. I still don't think it's a good idea to go there at all, but if you say we have to, as you're thinking we do, then you better come up with a God damn good plan." He sipped his Black Russian. "The only reason I can see for you wanting to go there at all, is to get something going so that Hauke will have to get back to Belize to make his run and lead us to Milagro, right?"

Penn nodded. "I think," he said, "that I just came up with the way to get us in there."

"Well, you going to let us in on it?" PZ asked.

"Sure. What we need is a mouse who won't mind being chased into the trap, and won't mind being booked right along with all the fat cats that are trapped in the net. It has to be someone who could make good use of the few hours he'll spend in detention with those cats until the booking is completed. It has to be someone who can get as much additional information out of them as he can before he's ushered out the back door when they get sent to their holding cells."

PZ shot a questioning glance at Penn. "You mean somebody who's been through that before?"

"Exactly."

"Hey," Yanks said as he returned to the lounge and barged into the conversation. "What a coincidence, seeing you here. Mind if I sit down?" He grinned at the trio.

"Talk about auspicious omens," Penn smiled at Yanks, who had plopped himself down in the same seat he had vacated earlier. "I was just thinking about you."

"Me?" Yanks asked. He half expected Penn to be upset by his unauthorized return.

"Yeah," PZ chirped. "Just the guy we need."

"Maybe I showed up at a good time," Yanks commented. "But I'm not sure it was a good time. For me, that is. What's on your mind?"

"Ever been in jail, Yanks?" Penn asked.

"Of course he has," PZ said. "Didn't he spend time in several, ah, guest houses courtesy of the feds for his part in the Watergate affair?"

Penn grinned at Yanks. He brought up the question purely as a means of impressing Sergeant McIvers with the idea that Yanks would be a good man to use in this game.

Yanks shrugged his shoulders.

"How would you like to make a little extra cash?" Penn asked Yanks.

"Hey, anytime. Who do you want knocked off?" He joked.

After the chuckling quieted, Penn explained the plan, and Yanks agreed to be the mouse.

"So, here are the important details," Penn continued. "Sergeant McIvers is going to be chasing you on a full run as you barge into the house. I don't know how fast you can run, but I suspect McIvers will be about one step behind you as you open the door. Once inside, you will have to play the thing by ear. You will have to find the room where the activity is taking place, and let McIvers bust you in that room. That'll give him, and whatever men he can round up to handle this thing with him, the chance to look over the place, and bust the whole damn bunch, especially Bear. Do you think you can handle that?"

"Sure," Yanks replied coolly. "Sounds like a piece of cake to me. For a hundred I'll do that, easy. One big one in advance, that is," he added with a smile.

Penn had to admire Yanks' chutzpah. Not only for being willing to be the mouse in what could be a dangerous game of cops and robbers, but also for the way he slipped in the request for the money. He frowned at Yanks, maybe a little more than he should have for appearances, then reached into his pocket for a hundred dollar bill, which he handed over.

"Hey," Yanks remarked as he grasped the money. "I think I'm going to have to carry a caper on this piece, ah, I mean, carry a piece on this caper."

"Wait a minute," McIvers interrupted. "I don't like the idea of any shooting. Not if we can avoid it."

"Well," Penn replied. "I think some shooting is necessary to make the thing look real. Besides, you don't have to worry. The last time I went shooting with Yanks, he beat me by at least fifty points. I'm sure he won't have any trouble missing you, or your men." He grinned as he reached for his drink. "As for PZ and myself, we both have concealed weapon permits. In a situation like that, we'd be armed."

The sergeant said he still wasn't sure he liked the sound of that, but he offered no real objection.

Penn continued with the plan. "Okay," he asked the sergeant. "Who can you get to go along on this exercise?"

"I can get two detectives from the squad. I can trust them well enough."

"Good. Then we'll all meet at the junction of River Road and Highway 116, in Guerneville, and from that point we'll start the chase. The house is about a mile up the road from there, according to my sources." Penn glanced at Yanks. "By the time you get there we will have scouted the area and made the route secure, so there won't be any foul ups. So, let's meet there no later than, say, six thirty this evening?"

"Sounds good to me," McIvers said. "I have to check with my men, though. Where can you be reached if they can't make it?"

"Right here, I guess," Penn said as he glanced at PZ. "At least for another hour or so. There's not much else we have to do until this thing gets done, anyway." He looked at his watch. It was already a quarter to one, and add another two hours waiting for McIvers' call would make it nearly three. That would allow enough time to drive to Guerneville and check out the place before anything happened.

"Good," McIvers said. "Okay. If you don't hear from me within two hours, it's on."

"Okay." Penn agreed.

"Yep," PZ chimed in.

McIvers got up and left as Penn looked at Yanks. "You sneaky dog," he said. "I'll take my hundred dollars back, now."

Yanks grimaced, but returned the bill. He made a light-hearted complaint about the risk he was taking, and how much he thought the job was worth. "After all," he said. "You expect me to go barging into a house where at least two DEA agents are playing, all armed, to say nothing of that wild man, Bear. How do you know that I won't get shot? Isn't that worth an extra hundred or so?"

"No," Penn replied. "And the reason it isn't, is because PZ and I are going to be right behind you, not McIvers. I didn't want to tell this part of the plan to him, but he's going to be chasing all three of us, and we'll make sure no one gets shot. At least, not one of us. Besides, Keany and Bund are federal officers. They can't fire their weapons without getting written permission from headquarters first." Penn grinned with the comment. He knew it wasn't true, but he enjoyed poking fun at the way federal agents are so tightly controlled.

PZ and Yanks both eyed Penn with questioning gazes. They didn't appear overly amused by the witticism.

"Well," said Yanks. "If you guys are going to be around here for a few hours, I think I'll take a run downtown to get a few things before we head up the river, so to speak. I'll catch you back here around three?"

"Sure," Penn responded.

Yanks got up and followed McIvers' retreat.

"As long as we're gonna be here for a bit," PZ said, "I think I'll go call a friend or two of mine." He smiled as he got up and headed for the telephone. "Maybe they can come over and keep us company while we wait."

Penn watched his partner get up. "You know, PZ," he said, shaking his head. "If you were stranded on a desert island you'd want a woman more than you'd want food."

"Why not? They're a lot more fun to...."

"Don't say it," Penn interrupted, chagrined. He should have known better than to give PZ that much of an opening.

The cocktail waitress came around to pick up the empty glasses on the table, and Penn order his third Myers's with ginger ale of the day. "This is about the last one, I think," he said, surprised by how energetic he felt in spite of the long day. "All I need is to be so looped that I won't be able to find the front door to that place tonight."

The waitress returned with the drink, including another one for PZ, which Penn had taken the liberty of ordering. She sat the glasses on the table as PZ returned. "Just in time, Turkey," Penn joked. "You can pay for this round. I paid for the last two."

PZ assented, with a frown.

"You don't look too enthusiastic," Penn said as PZ sat down. "What happened? Get turned down?"

"Nah. That never happens to me," he said with exaggeration. "Just can't get through to anybody. Nobody's home."

"Sure," Penn chided with sarcasm.

PZ shrugged his shoulders as he received his change from the waitress. "What're you doing later, Sweetheart?" he asked her.

She looked at PZ straight in the eye. "Something more interesting than you can come up with, I'm sure," she replied.

PZ coughed, then retrieved the dollar tip he had placed on the table for her.

She smiled a self-satisfied grin as she walked off.

"Well," PZ added. "We didn't want any more service in this joint, anyway."

"Poor PZ," Penn again chided. "You're ego's taking a beating today, isn't it?"

"Look, Buzzard," PZ responded somewhat testily. "I got no problems in that line. Everybody expected me to be out of town for longer, that's all. Besides, I'm not back in true form yet from all that hot weather in Belize. It stunts a guy's style, you know."

Penn hoped PZ's style was all that had been effected by their visit to Belize. They still had to go back there, and he wanted PZ to be along, since he expected the next trip to be a dangerous one.

The next two hours went slowly, and would have been much more awkward if they had spent them in the lounge, but after their last drink they decided they had better spend some time in the restaurant before the night's game playing. They wanted at least to be in condition to play the game.

Yanks returned at 2:30 to join them for coffee, and at nearly three, without having heard from McIvers, they climbed into Yanks' car for the ride north.

Guerneville is a little more than thirty miles northwest

of Santa Rosa, and the trip took less than two hours at the speed Yanks drove in his green two door 1962 Mercedes sedan. It seemed incongruous to Penn that a successful surveillance investigator like Yanks would keep such a relic. The green color was faded to olive drab, the once tasteful touches of chrome had long since transmogrified to spotty orange rust upon dull metal, and the smoke from the diesel engine revived understanding of the reason for pollution laws. Even so, Yanks took pride in his 'Vintage Machine', as he called it.

But the vehicle rolled along the freeway with a smoothness which extolled the precision engineering, to say nothing of the quality of second rate Bridgestone tires he always kept on well balanced, shiny new chrome plated rims.

The wheels and tires were the only items on the vehicle that exhibited any sort of maintenance. Yanks had won them in a poker game, a fact that was neither a testament to his ability to play the game, nor to his ability to play with the right adversaries, since the wheels were put up as a bet in place of hard cash. It seemed to Penn that if you were going to play poker, you would want to make sure the other people in the game had the money to back up their game.

Yanks did take pride in his vintage carriage, though, and in spite of its age, it managed to get them in the vicinity of Old River Road effectively and efficiently. "There's the house," he said finally, as he nodded towards an old three story semi-Victorian style structure. It was half hidden among the tall redwoods, but placed away from the trees as though the fire inspector had recently ordered a clearing of all brush for several yards from the structure just to make his job easier, should the need for his services arise at some time.

Parked in front of the house were half a dozen cars, all conspicuously out of place.

"Well," Yanks added after driving past. "What do you think?"

"I think," Penn replied, "That you exaggerated a bit when you reported that you managed to look in the rear window without trespassing."

"Hey. No way," Yanks defended himself. "If you stop right about, right about here," he added as he slowed the car to a stop, "you can see between the trees and right into the window there along the side near the back."

Penn looked where Yanks pointed. "I'm supposed to think you managed that view without binoculars?" he asked suspiciously. The window was nearly forty yards from their car.

"Well," Yanks relented. "Who's the difference, I mean, who's to know the difference, anyway?"

PZ chuckled.

Yanks had stretched the facts a bit, but Penn had to approve, no matter how reluctantly. "Okay," he said as Yanks turned the car around. "How should we handle this affair?"

Yanks shot a surprised glance at Penn. "I thought you had this caper figured out."

"Just an idle question," Penn mused. "Anyway, for now I think we should get back to somewhere near the intersection of this road and the highway. That way we can watch for any of these cars leaving, and wait for McIvers arrival at the same time. When you go back by the place, though, I think PZ and I had better get down out of view. I wouldn't want any stray eyes to recognize us."

The idea seemed to have merit with Yanks, and he looked relieved as he wended his way past the mansion once more. He glanced at the parked cars while passing, did a double take, then slowed nearly to a stop.

"What's wrong?" Penn asked.

"Nothing," he said. "Nothing, if you consider the fact that the Bear's Jag isn't here, is nothing, that is."

"You're kidding?" Penn sat up from his hunched over semi-concealed position in the front seat. "Was it here before?"

"Last night it was."

Penn looked at the group of cars. "God damn it, where the hell do you suppose he went?"

"Just our friggin luck," PZ butted in. "Now we gotta locate the S.O.B."

"You think he got word of our coming?" Yanks asked.

"I'm not going to think anything, right now," Penn replied. "But I know one thing. If McIvers played us for fools and told Bear, he's got another game coming."

Yanks got the car moving again, and crept slowly down the road out of the area. He finally parked at the intersection of Old River Road and Highway 116, as Penn suggested.

"I suppose it was unrealistic to hope that the Bear would be here for this thing, anyway," Penn tried to console his disappointment. "After all, he does have a home to go to. There's no real reason for him to spend all his time up here."

"Except that he was supposed to be up here for a few days, this trip," Yanks explained.

Penn wondered how Yanks had gotten that piece of information, but hadn't the time to ask. A car came down the road from the direction of the house.

"One of the cars from the house," Yanks noted as it approached. "That one was parked nearest the door."

"Recognize anybody?" Penn asked, as he again slipped down out of view.

The car passed, and Yanks carefully studied the driver. "No one I've ever seen," he said as it pulled out onto the highway and sped off around the corner. "Must be just one of the customers," he conjectured.

"Well, we have another hour or so to kill before McIvers shows up. Maybe we'll get lucky. Maybe Bear will show up, after all," Yanks commented.

"And maybe I'll win the lottery, too," Penn said.

Not much else was said until Sergeant McIvers arrived accompanied by his two detectives in an unmarked squad car.

"Let me handle the talking," Penn quietly said as he got out of the car. "Hey," he called to McIvers as the sergeant got out of the rear of the police car. "You and I have a little meeting to attend to, right now."

McIvers was noticeably surprised by Penn's demeanor, but said nothing as he joined Penn at the rear of the two vehicles out of earshot of the others. "What the hell's your problem?" he demanded. His police mentality had again taken control of his temperament.

Penn began his complaint in quieter and more conciliatory tones once the man came within hushed speaking distance. "I wanted you over here so we can talk in private," he said. "There's no need for the others to hear what we have to say, right?"

"That depends on what you have to say," the sergeant responded, still on the defensive.

"We have developed a little problem," Penn calculated his attack. "Mikel Bear's not here." He watched the sergeant's expression closely. He looked for some indication that would reveal the sergeant had warned Bear, but there was none.

"Son of a bitch," the sergeant said, disappointed. After a few seconds, he added, "I could put out an APB on him."

"Except," cautioned Penn. "The way I see it, you don't have a reason, yet, even to stop him, let alone arrest him."

"I guess you're right," the sergeant said.

"Did you tell anyone else about this plan?" Penn asked, continuing his attempt at reaching an understanding of what had happened.

"Not a soul, except for McUther and McNuttin. They're the two with me. I never told them a damn thing until after we got underway, and we haven't stopped since leaving, so there's no way they could have let it out."

"Well," Penn sighed. "You still want to go on with this thing? Now that the big apple is missing, that is?"

"How about you?" McIvers responded.

"Damn right!"

"Then let's ride, Red Rider," the cop replied with his face showing an ever widening grin with the prospects of the roundup about to take place.

Jesus, Penn thought. Nothing makes a cop happier than the prospect of making an arrest. He led the way back to the cars to fill every one in on the changes in the plan.

His plan now was to park Yanks' car on the road out of view from the house. Yanks would run up the road with he and PZ following. When the three approached the house, McIvers and his men would start chasing them, and when they got to the house, they would be running as hard as they could, as though trying to lose McIvers.

At that point McIvers was to order them to stop, and then fire at least one round into the ground.

Yanks would in turn fire into a nearby tree, or somewhere harmless, and then run into the house through the front door, with Penn and PZ still following.

Once inside, with the element of surprise, they would quickly run through the various rooms to witness the activities, and return to the area near the front door to be ordered to stop. Then they would be placed under arrest by McIvers and crew.

It was a good plan, and appeared to be workable to all concerned, so five minutes later, at 6:30 p.m. exactly, Yanks and company were charging up the road to the house.

The McIvers' Players were doing their part, and the sergeant fired the expected first round after calling for them to halt.

Yanks returned the fire, hit a nearby tree trunk, and charged up the stairs of the house, bent on bursting through the front door. He grabbed the doorknob at a full run, expecting it to open with one quick twist.

But the greatest of plans are often foiled by some insignificant detail overlooked in planning. The door, quite naturally, was locked, and Yanks slammed into it without being able to stop.

The surprise of slamming into the impenetrable wooden slab broke his concentration. He took little time to react, though, and quickly drew his .38 revolver. He fired three shots at the doorknob and blew it somewhere down the hallway inside the house. He then charged at the door with renewed vigor, with Penn and PZ nearly on top of him.

Their weight was added to Yanks' force against the door, and they tore the panel off its hinges. It slammed down the hallway after the door knob with the three of them running full tilt behind it, stumbling and falling over each other in their rush.

The door rebounded against a man inside the hallway who had come to see what was happening, and he was knocked back down the hallway, confused. With each awkward step he tried to regain his balance, but ended up falling into the laps of a half dressed man and woman who came running out of the first side room, also wanting to know what was causing such an uproar.

Meantime, Yanks' momentum carried him into the hallway. He saw the couple and bounded up the flight of stairs to the left of the door.

Penn and PZ regained their footing and continued down the hall with the McIvers team close behind.

A scream was heard from the rear of the house, and a man charged through the rear door of the hallway with a gun drawn. He looked at McIvers, and pointed his revolver in the cop's direction.

It was a quick lesson in probabilities for the man. If you point a gun at a cop, you're going to end up dead.

McIvers fired while on the run, and the man fell back with blood spurting from the left side of his chest. He dropped his gun and stared with disbelief at his wound. Then, with glassy eyes, he staggered, and fell.

By this time several doors could be heard slamming upstairs, and footsteps were heard running up and down the hallway amid a mass confusion of yells, questions and oaths.

More shots were fired that sounded like rapid fire from an automatic rifle, and one body came tumbling down the stairs headfirst.

It wasn't a victim, though. It was Yanks, and he was now rolling down the stairs with arms and legs flailing.

The cops had sounded the words of arrest by then, but that caused even more confusion.

PZ, who had slowed down to assess the situation, spied a man running down the hallway and into a side room. With a sudden spurt of energy, he chased him. The door slammed shut after his entry, and shouts were heard behind it. "You?" the voice shouted. "What the fuck are you doing here?"

Then gunshots were heard.

Penn turned with the sound of the shots. "Jesus! That sounded like PZ's .44 Magnum," he shouted as he ran for the door, crashed through it and landed on his face, gun up, facing PZ.

PZ was standing over a dead man on the floor. He was cursing the man, still nervously pointing his gun at the body, as though he expected it to get up and shoot at him again. He looked at Penn. "The son of a bitch almost killed me," he yelled in defense.

Penn took little notice of the pile of white powder on the table near the bed. He knew it was cocaine, but he hadn't time to be concerned with it. "God damn it, PZ," He shouted. “He's dead! Come on! Let's get out of here!”

PZ looked back at the body as though he was just realizing what had transpired, then nodded and ran after Penn, who had stepped back into the hallway.

Penn turned to his left to head for the front door, but out of the corner of his eye he spied PZ on the run again. This time on the heels of someone who had slipped into another doorway down the hall.

Penn lunged after PZ. When he got to the doorway he saw PZ bounding across the room to grab the feet of a woman who was scrambling head first out the window. The feet belonged to Marena Bloeswell.

It was typically PZ's luck to have nabbed that particular quarry. The feet were covered with high heels, but the rest of her body was totally nude.

Luck, though, isn't always good. In this case it was PZ's misfortune. Marena was full of rage when he pulled her back into the room. He became the focus of her rage and she initiated him into the danger that could be wielded with the high heels worn by an angry woman. She stomped her foot down and pierced the top of PZ's shoe.

The details of the confrontation which ensued were too rapidly occurring to be clearly remembered, but when it was all over, Marena was lying face down on the floor with PZ's knee centered in her back, and with his belt wrapped tightly around both wrists behind her. Her mouth was forced against the floor, stifling a steady stream of profanity. One had to wonder whether or not PZ was pleased when Sgt. McNuttin rushed into the room to place the handcuffs on the woman's wrists and cover her nude form with a blanket from the nearby bed.

Shouting, warnings, and more shooting in the upper rooms of the house drew Penn's attention from PZ's bout with Marena. “Jesus!” he said to no one in particular as he ran from the room. “This sure as hell is not the way this thing was supposed to go down. What the hell's going on now?"

Then he saw what was going on. Or at least he saw part of what was going on. Sergeant McIvers had elected to take Yanks' earlier route back down the stairway from the second floor. When he tumbled to the bottom he rolled into the doorway and saw Penn. "Jesus Christ!" he shouted. "What the hell are we doing here? You didn't tell me that much firepower was in this place."

Penn hadn't time to ask the man what he meant. A burst of automatic weapon fire sprayed down the stairs.

McIvers jumped back into the room with Penn pushing on him. Penn slammed the door and faced the quizzing, suddenly silenced stares of Marena, McNuttin, McIvers and PZ, all in the middle of the room.

Penn began explaining that he had no idea what was going on, either, when another burst of automatic rifle fire was heard. Splinters flew as the bullets penetrated the walls and wood casings of the door.

Penn fell to the floor with the rest of the group, hoping it would give sanctuary from the spraying bullets.

That was when Marena saw her chance. She got up, and with one great leap, cleared the open window, headed for the ground outside.

McNuttin saw his quarry getting away, and amid another burst of gunfire, went out the window like Tarzan, screaming, "Stop! Damn it. You're under arrest!"

McIvers was next through the window.

Penn turned to PZ. "Where the hell's Yanks?" he shouted over the increasing racket of shouts and small arms fire that was now emanating from the other parts of the house. It seemed as though everyone in the house thought every one else was an enemy, and had decided to shoot first. They could ask questions later, if they got out alive.

"How the hell do I know?" PZ shouted back as he lunged for safety behind the table he had just turned over, ignoring the sanctuary of the open window for the moment.

The shouts from the hallway interfered with Penn's question about Yanks. "Someone's down there," a voice yelled just outside the doorway. "You cover him and we'll take the guys in the front room."

Penn recognized that voice, but the recognition did nothing to relieve his worries. "That's Tom Keany," he shouted to PZ. "Christ! If he finds out who we are, he'll have to make sure he gets rid of us to protect his own tail!"

PZ nodded, anxiously.

"Christ!" Penn repeated again, under his breath. It was no longer a question of police protocol, worrying about warrants or no warrants, it was a matter of survival. He crawled over to PZ's position of safety, and unfolded a plan. "What we had better do," he said, "is get the hell out of this mess, then regroup and come back to get Yanks. You agree?"

PZ looked up and started to say something.

However, without allowing PZ the luxury of argument, Penn got to his feet. With a running forward dive, he went through the window, clearing the sides without effort.

PZ followed and landed on top of Penn among the shrubbery. To his delight, when he looked up, he saw the angry Marena staring at him, nude and not the least bashful about it. McNuttin was standing behind her, holding on to her by the handcuffs.

PZ grinned maliciously. "I never thought about it before," he said to her, "but you don't look so good up close."

"Fuck you," she sneered.

Sgt. McNuttin had watched Penn and PZ land. Then, when some more shots rang out from the house and sprayed the surrounding trees, his eyes darted about quickly. He spotted a huge tree, and tried to run for the cover the tree afforded, but Marena wasn't cooperating.

She turned and kicked him in the groin, instead.

PZ and Penn both made for the tree, and neither had seen the interaction between Marena and the cop. When Penn reached the tree, he noted that the cop was there alone, groaning, and looking back. The last they saw of Marena was her bare behind weaving in and out of the redwoods in full flight.

About ten yards away, in the other direction, he spied McIvers and McUther, both crouched behind another tree. He waived his arm to call them over. They shook their heads 'no'. They wanted to stay behind the tree, safe from the occasional stray bullet that ricocheted out of the house.

"Look," Penn shouted to them. "We have to get Yanks out of that mess, fast. Come on!"

Without waiting for replies, Penn started for the rear part of the house. PZ followed dutifully, while the three cops decided to beat a hasty retreat.

Penn plopped himself down behind another tree trunk, then looked back to see the cops going the other direction. To reform and regroup, he surmised.

"Bastards," PZ swore. "A few gunshots and they turn coat. What the hell do they teach them guys in police school, anyway? It sure as hell isn't close combat."

"That's a fact," Penn agreed. "Come to think of it, talking about close combat, who the hell was that guy you just took out? It sounded like he knew you, from the way he yelled at you when you entered the room."

PZ looked startled, then quickly explained. "I don't know who the bastard was. All I know is that he looked surprised when I entered, then he started shooting up the place. Hell, I had no choice but to fire back to save myself. I was the better shot, I guess."

Penn studied him, pondering his answer.

"How the hell are we going to get Yanks out of that place?" PZ asked, changing the topic, nodding in the direction of the house.

Penn was forced to consider the question. He was also wondering how to accomplish that feat, and his anxiety was beginning to rise, with good reason. During the interlude outside the house, the interchange inside the house had become more excited. The place had gone wild. Shooting came from all sections.

"God damn it," he whispered loudly to PZ as he peered around the tree trunk to look at the rear of the house. "Come on," he said as he got up on his hands and knees.

"Come on?" PZ asked. "Where the hell are you going?"

"To the back door, Turkey," Penn responded, as he slowly crawled around the tree. He needed all his past combat experience to force himself to crawl the short distance to the house in the face of what he expected to find there. Or rather, in the face of what he didn't know he would find there. It was always the unexpected that got you killed.

The one thing that Penn did know, though, was that there wasn't time to worry about the unexpected for long. He believed Yanks was still inside the house, and if that was true, the chances of Yanks getting out alive diminished in direct proportion to the amount of time he was left in there alone.

That, in itself, was enough impetus to overcome the fear of the unexpected, and he formed his plan of attack while he crawled for the back porch.

But then the unexpected did happen. It was one of those tricks of fate. Fire billowed out of the upstairs windows. Within seconds as he watched, it spread to the downstairs part of the house with explosive force.

"Jesus," PZ called. "The free-basing! They must have been free-basing their coke. The fire they were using must have gotten out of control. It set the house on fire!"

Penn agreed with PZ's assessment. But whether or not PZ was right, the fire was not only the unexpected, it also was an opportunity. If it grew unchecked, the people inside would be too busy getting out to worry about Yanks. Then Yanks could be rescued, if he hadn't already gotten himself out, or worse, already gotten himself killed.

Penn concentrated on that thought as he crept up the steps to the back porch. Most of the shooting had stopped, no doubt due to the common enemy of fire.

He reached the back door as he heard more shouting and yelling accumulating in the front yard. Several cars were starting, and some were tearing down the driveway.

Penn felt more daring, and slowly pried open the door. It was the same door he had seen at the far end of the hallway when he had entered the front of the house before all the fireworks started. He didn't know it at the minute, but it was also the same door that Yanks passed through to get clear of the house at about the same time PZ was confronting Marena.

Nor did Penn know that Yanks had completed his plan of action even before entering the house. Much to Penn's later consternation, he learned that Yanks had planned on simply running through the house and fleeing out the back door before anyone had a chance to realize his presence. He had no plans to remain inside, but something had gone wrong with his plan, too. When he had entered the house he saw the people standing in the hallway. One of them was Marena. It was Yanks' intrusion that forced Marena into the bedroom where PZ found her, and it was Marena's presence that forced Yanks to detour, at the last minute, up the stairs to his fateful meeting. After he had tumbled back down the stairs, he saw his chance to continue down the hallway and out the rear door, as planned, which he did. By the time the shooting had started he was a hundred yards away, watching the scene from the safety of another redwood tree.

It was the three hoods around the mountain of cocaine in the upstairs room that forced Yanks' hasty retreat back down the stairs. It was their guns and trigger happy nerves that began the entire shooting spree inside the house.

"Free-basing!" was Yanks' surprised uttering on opening the door.

"Set up!" was the only yell he heard from one of the hoods.

As Yanks told it later, the last thing he saw before slamming the door shut and jumping for the stairs was an Uzi being raised in his direction.

It was the free-basing like PZ had guessed, as it was determined later, that had caused the fire. It started upstairs, and within minutes had penetrated the downstairs, engulfing the entire house in less than twenty minutes.

In less than twenty five minutes the ancient and dry lumber of the structure had nearly burned to the ground.

It was thirty five minutes after the first flames were spotted that the Guerneville Station of the Sonoma County Fire Department arrived on the scene. They were just in time to put out the first of the redwood trees that began smoldering from the nearness of the flames. Had they been even five minutes later, the Fire Marshal's earlier demand of clearing all the shrubbery from around the house in case of fire would have been all for naught. The forest would have become one large inferno. As it was, the house was the sole loss.

Unless, of course, you wanted to count numerous paintings officially listed with the contents of the house. All the paintings were the property of the less than renowned modern painter, Manny Bolton. It was Bolton who was later identified as the owner of the mansion. It was fortunate for him that the plastic used for porno video tapes was combustible. The fire destroyed any evidence that might have been amassed in defense against his claim of illegal entry, the entry, which later supported his suit against the San Francisco Police Department for violating his constitutional rights. He made a fortune from that case, five years later.

That was the sole loss, that is, if one didn't count the four bodies later discovered among the ashes. Two of the bodies were found bound to some metal contraption that had confused the fire and arson investigators, according to the official accounts later filed.

It must have been a terrible way to die, the newspaper accounts later read, for the two were chained to the burning building in their restraining contraptions, having to watch the smoke and flames quickly consume the building, and them, while having no possible escape.

The ultimate in masochism, the underground newspaper S & M Weekly would print when mentioning the passing of one of the more notable underground sites in which to ply the practice.

The third body was dead before the fire, of two .44 caliber gunshot wounds in the heart, both placed within three inches of each other. They surmised that shooting was done by someone with a professional background, possibly someone with something to hide. They even ventured some guesses that the entire fire had been the result of events surrounding that particular shooting.

Penn kept quiet about that matter. He would have a hard time trying to prove that PZ fired in self-defense. And PZ kept his mouth shut. He even declined discussing it with Penn in private, so Penn didn't pursue the topic after his first comments the night it happened.

The only capture of the evening's episode had been Marena. But she had escaped, and since they really had nothing to charge her with, they never tried to relocate her. She wasn't even mentioned in the police report.

"A damn shame," Sgt. McIvers would later say while filing his report on the incident. "It's a damn shame that one of the four unidentified men was found in the same room where I last saw the fleeing felon I chased into the house during hot pursuit." That regret was supported by two other sergeants, McUther and McNuttin.

"At least," the sergeant's official report continued, "the fire destroyed one of the leading distribution points for cocaine smuggling in central California."

More than a few street vendors and hustlers later wondered what happened to their supply of street grade merchandise. A number of them vowed to never get involved with the Bear or his contacts again. Too many problems, they said.

"It was believed, based on the evidence," the sergeant's report also read, "that the unidentified white male subject which he and his team had chased into the house, had recently been seen involved in a felony sale of a controlled substance. He was also suspected to be a major kingpin in the distribution of more that fifteen million dollars worth of cocaine in the San Francisco bay area in the past four months, alone."

But Penn and PZ had not waited for the official reports and findings of that night to be completed before continuing their assignment. They still had the problem of the missing Allie, and time was not in their favor. For their intents, the entire Guerneville episode was a flop.

PZ, especially, thought it so.

Chapter 22

"Well, Chief, what do we do about that mess?" PZ asked sarcastically, after he, Penn and Yanks had fled Guerneville just ahead of the arrival of the fire trucks. They were safely ensconced in the sanctity of Penn's fifty-three foot ketch rigged motorsailer, the Flyin' Penguin, which was moored in the San Rafael canal. All three were trying to calm their nerves after the hectic evening, and the boat was a safe haven.

"Hell," Penn rationalized. "McIvers knows what he's doing. He can handle it without our help.

"I suppose that's good enough for me," PZ said with a frown as he reached for his home made mixture of Kahlua and vodka. "Some night though, hunh?" he added "I told you it was a stupid idea."

"You said that three times, already," Penn replied. "And what the hell was all that shouting about that I heard in that room between you and that guy you shot? It sounded like he knew you."

"Hey," PZ replied angrily in defense. "I told you once, already. I don't know who he was. He was yelling at me like some crazy weirdo. Then he started shooting. He was some pusher, that's all."

"How do you know he was a pusher?" Penn asked.

PZ's nostrils widened, and his eyes squinted ever so slightly with his rising ire. "God damn it! I..." Then with a change of thought, he softened his response. "Hell," he said. "What else could he have been? Christ, what is this, the third degree? I just guessed he was a pusher, that's all."

"I don't suppose you already knew he was a pusher?" Penn asked, not fully satisfied with his partner's explanation.

"What's that supposed to mean?"

"Well, look," Penn said, now on the defensive. "You don't make a secret out of the fact that once in a while you have a little snort or two, especially with the women you hang around with. I just thought that you might have seen the guy before, that's all. And God damn it, anyway. You know me better than that. If I had meant anything more serious I would have said so. I wasn't making any accusations."

PZ glared, then took another drink of his alcoholic coffee to subdue his anger.

"Hey, kids," Yanks intervened. "If you two are going to fight, I'm going home."

Penn and PZ glanced at Yanks. In their spat they had forgotten him, and were surprised by his interruption. He never interrupted them before.

It was at that point that Penn decided he better change the subject. "All right," he sighed. "I guess I'm still upset over the way things turned out. Hell, everyone else in that Great Guerneville Shoot-out will be just as much on edge for some time to come, with all the explaining and re-explaining that will have to be done."

"Yeah," PZ agreed, losing his edginess.

"As a matter of fact," Penn continued. "I hope they spend enough time in that process to enable you and me to get on with what we have to do. And that's another thing. I hope they don't try to give us any trouble about the part we played."

"Hell. They won't be able to put us in that place tonight, not based on any evidence. We're in the clear," PZ said with some of his unperturbability returning. "McIvers is going to have one heck of a time proving we were even near there at all, if we all back each other's alibis, that is. Anyway, we were right here all night, right, Chief?"

"You know, PZ. The more I think of it, the more I think you're right. McIvers sure as hell can't say that the plan was ours. How would that look on the record of a sergeant who's trying to earn his lieutenant's bars, his following some half baked scheme a private investigator came up with? And if you can put up with your conscience about the man you took out, then who's to complain?"

PZ shot an angered glance at Penn.

"Hey," Penn said. "I never said you were to blame, okay?"

"Well, okay," PZ sighed before taking the last swallow from his cup. "I guess."

"At least we got out in one piece," Penn went on, "but we're not any closer to the solution of this Allie problem then we were when we started that mess. What I want to know is, why wasn't Bear there when we made that raid? How did he find out about it in time to flee the coop? And also, where is he now?"

"I don't know about that, but aren't you forgetting about our original reason for the raid? I think you can count that as another thing we don't know about."

"Oh, right. Hauke. Where is he now?"

"You think he could be back at Bear's?" Yanks interjected hopefully.

"Good chance of it, I'd bet," PZ responded. "But how do we find out?"

"I thought you were supposed to be an investigator," Penn chided.

"What's that supposed to mean, Buzzard?" PZ quickly replied.

"What else could it mean, Turkey? We go there and find out."

"We couldn't just call?" Yanks again interjected across

the top of his rum and coffee.

"And if he answers the phone, what do we say? Do we ask him how he got out before the raid? Or what?" Penn answered.

"I see your point," Yanks conceded.

A lull in the conversation developed, and Lara retrieved the coffee pot from the galley stove to pour some more coffee for Penn and Yanks. She handed the Kahlua bottle to PZ, and returned to her seat beside Penn. "Didn't you say that Yanks had a tap on the Bear's telephone?" she asked.

Penn glanced at her, then at Yanks. "That's right. I don't suppose..." he began, then stopped. He didn't expect that Yanks would have left the tap on the phone, knowing the dangers, especially after all his repeated objections to the violation of law.

Yanks said nothing and cast he eyes down at the table.

"Yanks?" Penn repeated his questioning glance.

Yanks looked up again with the expression of a puppy that had just been caught pulling a steak off the barbecue.

"I thought you told me that you took off that tap," Penn said.

"I didn't say that, exactly," Yanks replied with trepidation.

"Don't quibble, Yanks. Is that tap still on or not?" Penn demanded.

"Well, sort of," Yanks again replied, though less timidly.

"What the hell do you mean, sort of? Is it or isn't it?"

"I don't know, really."

"What? How in hell could you not know?"

"Well, because, " Yanks began slowly, "it isn't a tap. It's more of a recording."

"What the hell's the difference between a tap and a recording," Penn persisted.

"Well, one's on the outside line, and the other... is..."

"Is what? Where?"

"Sort of on the inside." Yanks almost whispered the answer.

"How in hell did you get a tape recorder in Mikel Bear's house?" Penn asked. The thought of Yanks accomplishing such a stunt simply astounded him.

Another lull developed in the conversation when Yanks was reluctant to answer.

After a few seconds PZ began grinning. "You degenerate bastard," he quipped. "You've been dicking Embee. That's how you got the recorder in there." PZ was beside himself with amusement.

Penn was beside himself with surprise.

Lara was beside herself with PZ's coarseness.

Yanks was beside himself with the embarrassment of being discovered. "I wouldn't exactly call it that," he demurred. "We're just good friends, really." He didn't want to tell the truth, that Embee was trying to get him to fill her in on all the going's on with the Flyin' Penguin Detective Agency. He was certain by now that was her only purpose for their relationship, as non-fulfilling as it was.

"Whatever," Penn said. "So, all we have to do, you have to do, is go back there and get the tape?"

Yanks shrugged his shoulders.

"I guess that means yes?" Penn asked.

Yanks nodded slightly.

"There is one problem," Penn added. "What do we do if Bear's there?"

"I thought that was what we wanted," PZ said with a confused look.

"Good point," Penn said, sitting back to think. "But, Bear's not going to be there," he decided. "Not now. It's only been three hours since the raid, and I'll bet he's either still trying to find out what happened, or is trying to build a cover story. Hell, he could even be out hunting for us right this minute."

"Or on his way out of Dodge," PZ suggested

After a few more sips from his cup, Penn leaned forward. "Okay. Here's the way I see it," he said, putting down his coffee. "We will have to pay Bear's house a visit. If he's there, or if Hauke's there, then so much the better. Then I guess we'll have a face-to-face. God help either man if they had anything to do with Allie's disappearance. If they aren't there, then maybe Embee might know where they went. Or maybe the tape will show another call on Bear's phone that would give us something to go on. If all that fails, then we're headed back to you know where because we're running out of time. That's the only other place that Hauke could be. Besides, if I remember your report, Yanks, you said that one of the calls told Bear that Hauke could return to Belize since we had left there, right?"

Yanks nodded.

"So that's it, isn't it," Penn said as he got up from the galley table.

"Jesus," PZ objected as he too, got up. "I thought you saw enough of that damned Fort George Hotel by now."

Penn ignored the comment. He gave Lara a quick kiss, grabbed his coat, and with an order for Yanks and PZ to follow, headed out the hatch to the dock.

With Penn driving, it took exactly forty-three minutes to cross the San Rafael Bridge, pass through the Caldicott Tunnel into Diablo Valley, and enter the small town of Danville, south of Walnut Creek.

Mikel Bear's house, an imposing structure of wood and masonry put together with some architect's distorted concepts of mixed neo-colonialism, Gothic, and Tudor styling, was dark upon their arrival.

"You suppose anyone's home?" PZ asked as Penn pulled to the curb and switched off the car.

"Embee is home," Yanks assured them as he looked at

his watch. "It's 1:30 in the morning, and that's her car in the drive."

PZ grinned again, but Penn's quick glance cut off any remark that might have been added to earlier comments about Yanks' extracurricular activities with the Bear's wife.

"Do you suppose Bear's home, too?" Penn asked Yanks.

"No way," Yanks responded.

"What makes you so sure?" PZ asked with skepticism.

"Because no lights are on," Yanks replied.

"What's that mean?" PZ asked doubtfully. "Don't they turn their lights off when the go to bed like everybody else?"

"Bear doesn't," Yanks said.

"What?" PZ asked. "Why?"

"Bear's afraid of the dark," Yanks chuckled as he answered. "He never turns out the lights in the house. He always leaves at least one light on in each room. Each room but his bedroom, that is."

"Bear? Afraid of the dark?" PZ again asked.

"That's not being afraid of the dark," Penn dispelled PZ's confusion. "That's being cautious. If all the lights are on, then anyone entering and moving about the house can be clearly seen. He keeps his bedroom dark because he wants any intruder to think that's where he's sleeping, when in reality, he's probably in some other non-conspicuous part of the house. Or, if not, then when his bedroom is dark, he can easily see anyone entering from any other room that's lit. Am I right, Yanks?"

"How'd you know that?" PZ asked with surprise.

"Because it's an old trick I learned in the intelligence trade, way back when," he explained. Then he turned around to look at Yanks in the rear seat. "Tell you what, Yanks, old boy. You go in and get the tape, or any other information you can, and we'll wait for you, say, at the end of the block, down there," Penn nodded in the direction of the corner about fifty yards away. "If you have any trouble, we'll see you coming and we'll pick you up. Otherwise, when you leave the house, leave under a normal walk. Okay?"

"Well, I suppose," Yanks reluctantly agreed. He then got out of the car forcing PZ to lean forward while opening the single side door in keeping with exiting a two door hard top sedan.

"Don't slam the...." Penn began his warning.

Slam went the door after Yanks' exit.

"...door," Penn completed his sentence too late.

"Well," PZ commented. "If that doesn't wake up the neighbors, nothing will."

Penn frowned as he let the car coast down the hill to the nearby intersection.

Twenty minutes passed before Yanks came strutting back down the street sporting a smile. It was hard to determine whether the smile was from having just seen the object of his illicit affair, or from his containing some important information, again playing the cat and mouse game.

"Don't slam the...." Penn again tried to caution Yanks as the man got into the car.

Slam!

"...God damn door," Penn sighed, his order trailing off feebly.

"Oh, well," PZ consoled. "If the neighbors aren't awake by now, they'll never wake up. What the hell."

"Right," Penn said with sarcasm as he turned to face Yanks getting comfortable again in the rear seat. "What happened?"

"Like I said, Bear isn't home. He's still out somewhere, according to Embee. She heard from him, but he's not expected back for a few days or so. Something to do with Belize, apparently. He has to take care of some supply problem. As she pointed out he had said, he has to make arrangements to take care of that nosy private dick, someone he calls that damned Penguini. Some word, hunh? He said that damned Penguini is going to have to be taken care of, either here or there, if he ever goes back there," Yanks took a breath before continuing. "You got any idea who he means by Penguini?" He chuckled.

Penn ignored the taunt, although he did wonder why Penguini was singular, meaning just himself, as opposed to Penguinis, plural, which would include PZ. "How about Hauke?" he asked. "Did she have any information about Hauke's whereabouts?"

"Yep. He's with Bear."

"What about the tape? Does it reveal anything?" Penn was getting anxious, now being certain that Hauke was back in Belize. He guessed Hauke was probably getting ready to make Friday's coca run.

"Jesus. How should I know if it has anything on it," Yanks retorted. "You think I had the time to play Embee, ah, I mean to listen to Embee's story and play the tape too?"

"To say nothing of other things," PZ butted in.

"Well, damn it, a gotta guy's, ah, a guy's gotta be a little smooth about these things, you know. I can't just go barging in to get the tape. I gotta little smooth bit, ah, gotta be a little bit smooth."

"Did you get the tape?" Penn asked, impatiently.

"Here," Yanks handed the cassette sized recording to Penn. "You can stick it in your..."

"In what?"

"...in your car stereo," Yanks continued, pleased with himself.

Penn grabbed the tape from Yanks' hand and jammed into the car's cassette player. While waiting for it to rewind to the beginning, he started the car and headed back to the freeway. He wasn't making his intentions obvious, but he was heading directly for the Oakland International Airport. He was planning to be on the very next plane for whatever connecting flight there was that could be made from anywhere to Belize City.

The tape clicked completion of the rewinding, and Penn pushed the play button as he entered the freeway.

The first sound from the machine was a dial tone. It was immediately followed by an abrupt silence, which might have been due to someone turning off the recorder. Then another dial tone came on, but it ended with other sounds that indicated the phone had been replaced on the receiver without dialing.

The next sound was yet another dial tone, followed by fifteen touch-tones.

"Fifteen numbers," recounted Penn. "That means an international call. Three digits for the international access code, two digits for the country code, three digits for the city or area code, three digits for the prefix, and four numbers for the telephone number."

"You want to know what the numbers are?" Yanks asked, a broad grin once more appearing across his face, playing the game.

"You have a dial decoder in your pocket?" Penn asked with surprise.

"Nah. Not so complicated," Yanks responded. "Embee told me the only international calls he ever makes are either to Belize or to Nicaragua."

"Nicaragua?" Penn was again surprised.

"Yeah. But the call wasn't to Nicaragua. The two tones after three international call digits. They're the same tone. Nicaragua has two different tones. So, that leaves what?"

"Belize," PZ predictably responded.

"I don't suppose you know where in Belize?" Penn hoped Yanks might have some information that would cut down their searching time in Belize. He was pretty sure the call was to some control agent, and he was beginning to have a strong suspicion as to whom that man, or in this case that woman, might be.

"No," Yanks replied, "but according to Embee, there are several numbers that he calls down there. It could be any one of them." He paused. "Speaking of Embee," he continued, "I'd like to get back to her before she has a chance to, ah, get involved with something else. Know what I mean?"

"I know what you mean, Yanks," Penn replied. "Okay. You can drop us off at the airport and be back to your monkey business before we even get off the ground. Only make sure my car gets back to Lara before she leaves the office tomorrow. Okay?"

"Sure," Yanks responded with enthusiasm.

"Airport?" PZ asked with some somberness. "Jesus. Don't' we even get a chance for a break?"

Penn had to chuckle. He got a lot of pleasure from the idea of Yanks and Embee. It was satisfying to him to think that his employee was besting his old nemesis, doing the same thing that his nemesis had been trying for years to do to him.

Chapter 23

"You know how much time we've spent on damned airplanes alone, on this ridiculous chase?" PZ asked as he came down the aisle of the Continental Airlines 1011 wide body jet. He had taken a few minutes before boarding to make a telephone call, and had let Penn go on board before him. Now he was getting to his seat, the last person to board. "We've spent more than fifteen hours getting back and forth from Belize already. And this isn't even a direct flight, this time. We're going to put in another five hours by the time we get there. man, I'm getting air logged."

"Hey, Turkey, don't start your complaining again," Penn responded testily. "At least you'll get to see Morgan again, won't you?" It must have been some telephone call, he thought. It took him long enough. "Who'd you call?" he asked. "All your girlfriends, to let them know you're going to be out of town again for a while, so that they could play around with someone else if they needed the money?"

"Look, Buzzard," PZ retorted. "I got things to take care of, too, you know. As for Morgan Baletta, there's nothing special about her. Besides, the way I see it, if we do see her again, getting in bed with her is going to be the last thing on my mind."

Penn shot a skeptical glance at his partner.

"Well," PZ added. "Maybe the second to last thing."

"Nothing changes much, does it, Turkey?" Penn responded. He was in good humor, in spite of having to pass the rest of the night in an airplane seat instead of his comfortable bunk aboard the Flyin' Penguin with Lara, and in spite of having to listen his partner's complaints, as well.

Penn's good disposition lasted until they reached New Orleans. It didn't begin eroding until they completed their two hour's wait to change planes from the luxurious Continental 747 to the TACA Airlines twin engine prop-jet Lockheed Electra. TACA's new 767 was out of service with some type of engine trouble, and the only back-up plane they had for that route was the old prop-jet. The change wasn't a pleasant one.

During the entire period of waiting, PZ managed to express his reluctance to return to Belize no less than ten times, in spite of the fact that he would admit it was the only lead they had for locating Allie. It seemed to Penn that PZ's greatest objections were related to the fact that Mikel Bear was supposed to be in Belize, also. He wondered just what special phobia PZ was developing about the Bear.

"Jeez," PZ commented after seating himself next to the window over the front wing of the Electra. "Now I know what TACA stands for: Take A Chance Airline. I thought they banned these things years ago. They're not the most stable planes, you know."

"I didn't know," responded Penn, growing somewhat weary of PZ's complaining. "And I don't particularly care to hear about it at the moment."

PZ quieted down, and in spite of his skepticism over the antiquated airplane, the flight was uneventful. Two hours later they landed in Belize City, touching down only ten minutes past their scheduled 2:33 p.m. arrival time.

They again cleared customs by handing the agent an American five dollar bill to reassure him that the one bag Penn and PZ each carried weren't in need of searching, and then headed for the first taxi in line in front of the dilapidated terminal building. Penn directed the driver to take them to the Fort George Hotel.

They were less than three blocks from the terminal when the taxi driver peered at them through the rear view mirror of the small, older model Toyota Carolla. "Are you Mates being followed for any particular reason?" he asked in a typically Australian accent.

"Why would you say that?" Penn asked, not turning around to look out the rear window as PZ did.

There wasn't time for the driver's answer, though. The rear window was suddenly splattered all over the inside of the car, and all over the two detectives, by a shotgun blast from a car behind them.

"God damn!" exclaimed the cabby in his impeccable English.

"Get the hell out of here!" commanded Penn as he and PZ ducked from two additional blasts. The second of the two blasts took out half the front window, as well.

The driver needed no second command. He floored the gas pedal and flipped the car into a sudden right turn to enter a narrow alley. As he turned, the car's bumper bounced off the side of the building that formed one side of the alley.

The squealing of tires on the pavement meant that the car behind them had slid to a stop before it hastily backed up, and turned into the alley to follow.

Penn looked back through the windowless opening and saw the car. It was a four door black Mercedes Benz, and it was accelerating with a roar.

By then, though, it had become a worthless chase. The taxi driver knew the ins and outs of the old colonial buildings and back alleys of Belize City. He had turned into an alley, one that got increasingly narrower as it progressed between two brick buildings. The little Japanese car scraped its sides on the walls as it squeezed between them. Penn quickly identified the trouble the larger and wider Mercedes was getting into.

A crash of fenders against brick, followed by breaking glass, greeted Penn's ears. The Mercedes had wedged itself between the two brick buildings.

The alleyway turned sharply to the left and ended in a set of double doors. For a fleeting minute Penn wondered if the cab driver had run out of luck, and had hit a dead end. He thought it would be only a matter of minutes before the men wielding the shotgun from the Mercedes came bounding around the corner of the alley on foot to finish off their game.

The cab driver hadn't run out of luck. He knew full well what he was doing. He slid to a stop nearly hitting the double doors, jumped out of the cab, and then quickly pulled the doors open to drive the cab through them before once again getting out to shut them.

Then just as hurriedly, he opened another set of doors in front of the cab and drove the cab out onto a main thoroughfare.

Before the Mercedes could disentangle itself and race around the block, the cabby had his passengers safely out of the area and on their way out of the city to the safety of the country.

"Jesus!" PZ exclaimed, finally regaining enough self control to remark about the incident. "What the hell was all that about?"

"That," Penn replied thoughtfully as they bounced along the rutted Western Highway leading from Belize City to the surrounding jungle, "is one God damn good question. And the trouble is," he added before lapsing into a period of thought, "is why? Why would anyone be waiting for us? Who the hell knew we were coming here in the first place?"

"Hey," PZ added. "Nobody knew we were coming here but Yanks. He sure as hell wouldn't tell anybody, I don't think."

"I don't think he would, either" Penn agreed. "But,

someone told someone, that's for sure. Unless," he let the sentence drop, and furrowed his brows, thinking.

"Unless what?"

"Unless the Bear put out the word to keep an eye out for us, thinking we might be coming back."

"How would they know who we were, I mean, what we looked like, though?"

Penn glanced at PZ. "Are you kidding?" he asked. "With my bald head and beard, not to mention your curly hair that runs all the way down to your chin? Who would fail to recognize us if someone had the right description? You've even given our description when we had to meet a new client somewhere, haven't you? You've said it yourself, we'd be hard to miss."

PZ frowned. "There's something else that's been going around in the back of my head," he said.

Penn gave him an inquisitive glance.

"Remember what you said about the way things seem to keep happening? That things didn't happen on a case because we made them happen, but we only happened to be there when they did happen?"

"And?" Penn asked.

"Well, I been thinking. Maybe these things are happening because we are here. I mean, because someone is making them happen to us."

Penn stared at his partner. "I sometimes wonder which end of your body you do your thinking with," he responded. "Of course someone's making them happen to us, Turkey. Who is making them happen to us is the God damn question."

PZ went on undaunted. "What I mean, Buzzard, is that the someone who is making these things happen is someone who knows where we are, and what we're up to."

"Sorry to interrupt, Mates," the taxi driver said. "But I think you should know that we can't go forever in this direction. What do you say I turn around and get to wherever you two would like to be staying? I mean, I would like to do something about the windows in this cab, you know."

Penn looked at the driver in surprise. Up until then his attention had been focused on the events. "Sure," he answered at length.

"Begging your pardon, mate," the driver continued. "But sure what? Where would you be going now?"

"To the Fort..." Penn began. Again he let the sentence drop. He had to think about that question. "I'm not really quite sure, now," he said. "I don't think we want to go to the Fort George, the way things look. Do you have any suggestions for an out of the way place, one that's not too, ah, how do I say this, native?"

The driver laughed. "You mean one that would be suiting to your American standards?" he asked.

"Right."

"Well, look. I can see that you boys are in a spot of trouble, are you not? I mean, there seems to be someone out there to do you harm, ain't there? And my cab is a bit short of perfect now, ain't it?"

Penn saw the man's point. Pieces of broken window were spewed about the inside of the taxi. "What are you trying to say?" he asked, defensively.

"I mean, you mates aren't in any trouble with the law, or anything like that, are you?"

Penn didn't answer. Instead, he reached into his rear pocket and retrieved his Marin County Special Deputy Sheriff's identity card that was given to him by his friend, the newly elected Sheriff of Marin County. He showed the card to the driver and returned it to his pocket before the driver could read the words printed in red across the front of it. The words read 'Non Sworn'. They indicated it really carried no police powers, and that the bearer was nothing more than a personal friend of the Sheriff. It was a courtesy card the kept the bearer from getting traffic tickets, mostly.

The driver glanced at the green letters that spelled Sheriff, said, “Oh,” and then slowed down. He quickly turned the car around and proceeded back towards town. “I suppose,” he added after making the turn, “that what that means is that if I want to get paid for the damages on my cab, that I have to send a bill to your Sheriff?”

“No. Not really,” Penn consoled as he reached into his pocket and extracted two hundred dollar bills. He gave them to the driver. “Here,” he said. “This should pay for the damages. Okay?”

“The driver took the money and smiled. “You're all right, Mate, yes, Sir! Now, where did you say you wanted to go? Just say where and I'll get you there, windows or no.”

“As I was saying,” Penn responded. “I'm not sure.”

“Well, as I was saying,” the driver said, mimicking Penn. “Since you don't want to stay at your regular hotel, I might have a suggestion. Mind you, it's just a suggestion, but it might do you a bit of good.”

“I'd listen to any suggestion right now,” Penn said.

“I have a boat in the harbor that would be a safe place for you. No one would be able to find you there, providing, of course, that you don't want anyone to find you there. I could let you rent that for, say, a few days.”

“What kind of boat?” Penn's curiosity was aroused. He wondered if perhaps fortune was turning in their favor. A boat might come in handy this trip.

“It's a sport fishing boat,” the driver answered. “A Cape Hatteras. I bought it from a guy who had a heart attack trying to land a Marlin one time.”

“How big?”

“Nearly 150 kilograms, that'd be nearly 350 pounds in your country, as I recall.”

“Not the Marlin,” Penn said with exasperation. “The boat. How big's the boat?”

"Oh. The boat. She's about fifteen meters, ah, about forty five feet. Twin Caterpillar diesels, too."

"How much?"

"I could let you mates rent it for as little as, say, forty dollars a day. American, that is."

Penn smiled sardonically. He studied the driver's hopeful expression in the mirror. "Are you sure you aren't a New Yorker?" he gibed. "That seems a little expensive to me."

The driver shrugged his shoulders. "Hey," he said. "A guy's gotta do what he's gotta do. The money's where it's at, you know, mates?"

"Not to change the subject," PZ interrupted. "But what I meant a minute ago, was, and I know you're not going to like the sound of this, but Yanks did go back to see Bear's wife after we left, didn't he? He might have let it be known that we were heading back down here."

"Yeah," Penn agreed. PZ was right. He didn't like the sound of it.

"Hey," PZ continued. "I said you wouldn't like it, but who knows? Maybe he said something he didn't mean to say, or without knowing it. A woman can do that to a guy."

"You should certainly know," Penn conceded. He had already considered that thought in spite of its distaste. He didn't like thinking of Yanks as being untrustworthy, or even careless. "Look," he said. "I appreciate that you're thinking about this case, and I have to admit that you could be right. It's also true that it's not an idea I like, but there are other possibilities."

PZ took Penn's apology as assent to proceed, and expressed more of his thoughts. "The truth is," he said, "That if Yanks did say anything to Embee about our coming back here, then that means that Embee told Bear, and he had to have set this up, and that's why we got our little reception committee."

"Someone else could have told Bear," Penn proffered.

"What do you mean?" PZ asked.

"I keep thinking of what Yanks said before dropping us off at the airport. Something about wanting to get back to Embee before she had a chance to get involved."

"You mean you think she's not only screwing Yanks behind Bear's back, but there might be someone else, too?"

PZ was simply delighted by that thought. It pleased him to think there might be some other person on this earth as degenerate as himself when it came to sexual matters.

"But," Penn said after some thought, "if there is someone else, and she's been talking about us, that would still mean, unfortunately, that Yanks had to first tell her we were coming back down here."

"Yanks might have let that slip out when he got back to her last night," PZ conjectured. "But who can that be, like I also asked?"

"You mean," Penn said. "Who else does Embee know, who knows Bear's business well enough to want us out of the way?"

"Jesus," PZ jumped. "You don't think..."

"Hauke?" Penn interrupted the answer with another question. "Don't you think that would be a little too obvious? Besides, if what we know about Hauke is true, he's not smart enough to be that high up on the ladder of this operation. Remember, he's Bear's minion, not the other way around. Bear is the mastermind in this game, not Hauke. Or, at least, I think it's Bear."

"Yeah. That's right," PZ said, disappointed his conclusion was too obviously in error. "Wait a minute. What do you mean, you think it's Bear? If not him, then who?"

"That's where we left off before, isn't it?"

"I don't want to interrupt again, mates," the driver said

as he veered to the side of the road to make room for a passing truck that was overloaded with chickens and careening precariously from side to side all over the road. "But do you want the boat or not?"

Penn was glad for the interruption. "Sure," he said. "We'll take it. It'll be a good idea to keep out of sight until we can figure out just who is calling the shots."

"Good show," the driver said with enthusiasm. "We'll be there in a shake of a Roo's leg."

Penn brushed some of the broken glass from the rear seat. Damn good thing it's so hot down here, he mused, or the wind blowing through the broken windshield would be a hell of a lot more uncomfortable. He turned to watch the assortment of people walking along the road, at the same time trying to relax.

The driver negotiated the return to the city without being intercepted, which was no easy feat, considering there were few roads to be traveled in a country as small as Belize. Now they were nearing the waterfront close to the mouth of Haul Over Creek.

"Well," the driver said as he pulled his cab to a stop beside the harbor. He got out and cheerfully opened the door for his two passengers. "What do you think?" he asked, pointing their way along the docks to the Wavy Lady, the boat of which he was so proud.

Penn took in the boat with one quick glance, and assessed that her owner needed to spend much more time on her paint and varnish, but other than that, she appeared sound enough.

"Jesus," PZ responded as he followed Penn and the driver down the jetty. "I didn't think a forty five foot cruiser would be so damn small."

Penn glanced at his partner, remembering PZ's dislike for anything resembling marine activity. "Turkey," he said, "since when did you know anything about boats at all. Hell, the only reason you take showers is so you won't get seasick taking a bath."

The cab driver laughed as he jumped onto the deck and opened the side rail to let his guests board. "She's a lot bigger than I need, actually," he explained. "The only reason I have her is because I inherited her from a mate who died of a stroke down here. The last thing he said was for me to take care of his little sweetheart. And since he had no apparent heirs, or at least none that knew the boat was down here, the Prefecture of Police considered those last words to be a will. So, here it is. Some day I'm going to trade her off, though. I would really like to have something a little faster, a little racier. Like maybe one of those Cigarettes that I've been reading about, or a Donzi, some kind of ocean racer. Ninety knots over the ocean. That would be some wiggly croc, now wouldn't it? And the sheilas? Hey, more sheilas than you can shake a stick at, as you Americans say, with one of those."

"Sheilas?" PZ asked.

"That's woman in Stryne," the driver replied.

"What the hell's Stryne?" PZ asked, more confused.

"Stryne. Strawlia, Mate. That's where I'm from. Darwin, to be exact. Like I said, I'm an Aussie. From the land of Aus, as we say. You people call it Australia, actually," he replied.

"Oh," PZ looked chagrined. "I thought you were English."

"I thought you said you got this boat from a guy who died while marlin fishing?" Penn asked with an amused grin.

"Marlin fishing? Did I?" the driver responded with a furrowed brow.

"You did," Penn confirmed.

"Oh, well. Whatever. Same difference."

A short tour of the boat followed, and enough of the rental money changed hands to cover the first three days. The driver then returned to his cab, leaving Penn and PZ alone on the boat, which much to Penn's pleasure, turned out to be better kept and more conveniently fitted out below decks than the exterior indicated.

Penn went forward into the cabin to get a beer, while PZ grabbed a deck chair.

Returning from the galley several minutes later with a bottle of Belikin Beer, he glanced at PZ.

PZ was sitting in the deck chair firmly holding onto the two arms, turning pale. The rocking of the boat, which was caused by Penn's rummaging around below decks, along with the rise and fall caused by the swells from the Caribbean less than fifty yards past the docks, was taking its toll on him.

"You don't look too well, PZ," Penn said, trying to show some sympathy for his partner.

"I don't feel to good, either," PZ complained. "I'm not going to like staying on this damn thing."

Penn sat in the other deck chair and gazed at PZ. "Why do you get seasick here, but not on my boat?" he asked.

"I get sick on all these tiny boats. Yours is a helluva lot bigger. It don't rock so much."

"Well," Penn said at length. "You could go to the Fort George, if you want. That way, when you get shot at again, maybe we can tag some kind of identity on who is doing the shooting."

PZ sent back a resentful glance. "Look, Buzzard," he said testily. "I could get the hell back home, too, you know."

"Back home? We just got here and you want to get out again? What's wrong? Really? Did that little incident with the taxi scare you?"

"I can't believe you said that. Damn right it scared me. What d'you think, I go around all day letting some dude shoot at me? And with a 12 gauge? Jesus!" He shook his head as he finished the statement. "Besides, damn it," he added as he sat up slightly, obviously weighing odds against having to hang his head over the side rail as a result of the boat's continuing movement, "I'm not getting paid to let somebody take pot shots at me. This is your gig, remember? You're the one that offered we do it for free."

PZ's onslaught made Penn's anger rise. He was tired, and his patience was short, particularly with his partner, in light of all the objections and mental roadblocks PZ had been throwing into this investigation since it began.

"I'm tired of this whole thing. This hotter-than-hell hole, getting shot at, skipping back and forth across the country so much I can get airsick just thinking about it. Not to mention all the damn time we're spending down here while our clients at home are getting disgusted because we're not getting their cases done. On top of all that, now I gotta stay on this rocking stinkpot? It's bullshit. You know that? That's what it all is, bullshit."

Penn was taken back by PZ's outburst. It's true, he thought, the constant traveling and the humidity of the Belizean tropics was oppressive, but it hasn't been that bad. "Bullshit?" he shot back. "You think looking for Allie is bullshit, do you? Well, I tell you what, Turkey. Why don't you just grab your bag and head back to the airport? I can handle this thing myself, anyway." He blurted out his challenge without thinking, and was wondering if he was going to be sorry for it. After all, he and PZ had gone through a lot together. Hell, he reconciled his thoughts. It's just the combination of nerves and weariness.

He took a long swallow from the beer. The cold liquid was refreshing. He decided to put the little spat out of his mind.

But PZ wasn't going to let the argument drop. "All right, damn it," he nearly shouted as he got up. "All right. That does it. I've had it with this shit. If you think you're good enough to do this thing by yourself, then do it. I'll be at the office making some money, for a change. See you when you get back." He grabbed his travel bag beside his chair, crawled up the ladder to the deck, over the rail onto the dock, and stomped off in the direction of land.

Penn watched him, too stunned to rally with any quick apology. He got up and was about to shout after him, but caught himself. What the hell, he thought. Something must really be bothering him. We've had arguments before, but we've always been able to resolve our differences.

Penn sat down again. It can't just be this case, he said to himself, pondering his beer. Something has been bothering him ever since last night, since the great shoot-out. He took another drink. Of course! That's the problem. The shoot out. It's got to be it. He's upset about having to put away that guy who shot at him. Hell, that's normal. I should have realized that was it.

Penn shook his head over his lack of understanding, with letting his lack of patience and weariness get in the way of his thinking. He got up, headed for the galley, and got another beer before returning to the settee. Well, hell. He'll get over it, he thought. Besides, he's right. Someone should stay home to get the rest of the work done. Insurance companies aren't too forgiving when their work gets delayed because you've been wrapped up in someone else's project. If they're not satisfied with your work they go to some other investigator. Damned competition. That's the trouble with this business. Too much competition. He took another swallow of beer. Too damn much headache, too, he added while recalling the need for the constant promotion, public relations, and staying on top of all the insurance cases that were being worked at the same time, ready to spout off the progress on the investigation when a client calls. Yeah. Too damn much headache and not enough antacid.

He took another drink of his beer, surprised at how quickly the five percent alcohol content of Belikin, the Belize Temple beer, reached his mind. He was feeling a little light headed. Ah, Hell. It's just as well. I could use a good drunk right about now. He quickly finished the remainder of the contents, then returned for a third bottle.

There's something else about this entire thing, to tell the truth, he continued in his musing. PZ has been against trying to find Markham's murderer ever since we started. And this thing with Allie. PZ was never whole heartedly for it. Especially when he found out it had something to do with Mikel Bear. Penn stared vacantly out the porthole, over the water, going over his thoughts, as he finished his third bottle of beer.

A coastal freighter entered the harbor. The sound of its horn, accompanied by a tug boat's responding toots, blasted his thoughts away. The blasts and toots continued through the twilight of evening into the darkness of night, and through Penn's sixth bottle of Belikin.

When the show was over the tugboat proudly chugged out of the harbor.

Penn decided he had enough excitement, to say nothing of beer, for one day. He closed the hatch, bolted it out of force of habit, and collapsed on the bunk. As he drifted off to sleep a faint roaring of engines of the last flight of the night leaving Belize International floated into his thoughts. That must be PZ's flight, he mused as the twilight of half awareness passed into oblivion of sleep.

Chapter 24

The knocking on the companionway was loud and persistent.

"Who? What?" Penn mumbled as he turned to peer up at the closed hatch. He wished whoever was causing the knocking would quit and simply go away.

He realized he was expecting too much when the knocking became a pounding, so he rubbed his eyes and sat up. Hell, it has to be the cab driver, he thought. That's the only person who knows I'm here. "Okay. I'm coming," he called. He was half awake when he reached for the deadbolt on the hatch. He wanted to get rid of the annoyance so he could return to his dreams.

But, he never got the chance to return to his dreams. He ended up in a nightmare, instead.

"What the hell's the racket about?" he demanded, reaching the hatch deadbolt.

The hatch was forced open from above when he unbolted it. Somebody mumbled something incoherent as the hatch was slammed all the way back, then something hard hit him in the side of the head. In his drowsiness he decided he must have hit his head on the side of the companionway when the boat lurched.

The flash of moonlight that glinted off the blue hard steel of an automatic pistol proved him wrong, though. The person doing the knocking had tapped him on the head with the pistol barrel to gain his attention.

Something else was said above him, then someone was tossed through the hatch to land on top of him, sending him sprawling back against the bunk.

He struggled against the weight of the person, who was just as valiantly struggling to get off him. As soon as they cleared each other, Penn stood up to take a look at what was going on, but he was shoved back down on the bunk again by unseen hands.

A bright beam of a flashlight flooded his eyes, blinding him. It was a professional maneuver that made it impossible for him to see for several minutes.

"Just stay on that bunk, and everything will be okay," ordered a voice from behind the flashlight.

Adrenaline flooded Penn's veins, quickly dispelling the lulling effect of too much beer. He came to his senses.

From the light of a second flashlight near the hatchway he saw the barrel of a .45 automatic.

He heard another voice. He concentrated on it. It was unmistakable. The drawl carried the words with a nasal tone that only came from that part of the U.S. The pronunciation, though, was precise. It implied education, polish. It was the same polish and education he heard in Markham's office when he and PZ faced Mr. Martin and the Texan.

The light flashed on the person who crawled onto the other bunk. It was the cab driver, and he had a cut over his right eye. It was a cut shaped by gun barrel.

The driver looked at Penn. "Sorry, Mate," he said. "I guess these blokes had my cab number, or something. They were at my place waiting when I got home. I had to show them where you were, or else."

Penn shrugged his shoulders in response. That hardly seemed to be a relevant point to him at the moment. He knew how persuasive people could be when they had guns.

"Now, you two just relax," the Texan said. "We're going for a little boat ride."

As he spoke, the twin caterpillar diesels that powered the boat were brought to life. The other person, whoever he was, must have known a great deal about boats, or at least a great deal about this particular boat. The engines were started without the hunting and fishing for the right controls and buttons that would have been the routine of someone less knowledgeable.

The boat's mooring lines had evidently been released before the two came aboard, for no time was taken to free them after the engines were started. The boat cleared the harbor in the dark as though the pilot knew the area.

For nearly three hours the boat bounced and jostled along the open water. Penn calculated that the speed had to be in excess of 25 knots, considering the size and weight of the boat, and from the sounds of the powerful engines.

Then the boat slowed, soon stopping dead in the water. The engines were turned off, and nothing was heard in the sudden ominous silence but soft slapping of wavelets against the hull's sides.

The night was beginning to warm with the glow of dawn, and the sky was turning orange eastward over the Caribbean. The light filtered through the curtains on the cabin portholes.

Penn looked around again, as he had with every chance that availed itself during the trip. He had looked for some escape route, but none had been evident.

During the trip the Texan remained seated on the companionway ladder, sternly surveying his two victims. Every time Penn tried to speak to the cab driver, the Texan interrupted. The man's words were direct and to the point. "Shut up," he said with calm control.

To Penn, the man's expression, to say nothing of the way he handled his gun, was proving a prudent master. Penn had shut up.

When the boat stopped, the Texan stood, looked up the companionway, nodded, and backed back up the ladder to the cockpit, keeping his gun poised all the way. He shut the hatch without so much as a good bye.

Penn glanced at the cab driver, then they both returned their glances to the hatch. They slowly got up. They headed for the hatch together, being careful and cautious, not sure the Texan wouldn't be coming back down any second.

Penn stopped to listen to the footsteps on the deck. It seemed odd to him that he and the cab driver would be left to their own devices so quietly, so quickly.

Eight shots were fired from a .45 automatic. Two of them sounded like they went into something metallic. The shots were close by, and they were followed by the sound of some other inboard engines being started. There had been another boat alongside the power boat. The sounds of the engines were followed by those of a man jumping from the cruiser to the other boat as its engine accelerated.

Penn lunged for the hatch. He exploded through it, and fell onto the cockpit deck. He got up and, looking over the stern, saw the other boat fading into the distance. The early morning's sun returned glistening shafts of mirrored sunlight off the chrome plated hull trim as it glided away over the swells.

"They're running away!" the cab driver remarked as he joined Penn at the side rail. "Why, Mate?" he added.

"I'm not sure," Penn replied as he turned to survey the boat. The hatches over the engines were open. He rushed over to look into the engine compartments, fearing the worst. He stared into the engine holds, and his fears were realized. "Damn it!" he swore.

"What?" the cab driver asked, as he joined Penn to peer at the engines. "The block's have been holed," he said, stunned, eyeing the oil seeping out of the bottom of them.

Penn wasn't only peering at the engines, though. He was also peering between the engines. He was peering at the water flowing in through the gaping six inch hole in the bottom caused by six of the .45 slugs. The Texan and his companion sabotaged the boat before leaving. "That was what they fired at just before they left," he explained.

"My God!" the cab driver exclaimed. "We're going to sink!" Then, after re-thinking his statement, he said, "We are sinking!"

Penn quietly laughed at the simplicity of the man's conclusion.

"The life jackets, Mate," the driver said, heading for the hatches under the cockpit benches.

Penn knew better. He knew there wouldn't be any life jackets left on board. The Texan would have thought of that. And the bunk mattresses wouldn't stem the flow of water through such a big hole. How simple, he thought. What a simple way to get rid of us. Just take us out to deep water, let the boat sink, and let the sharks do the rest of their dirty work. No problems, and no mess. The boat was fiberglass, so there wasn't an accessible piece of wood on board that would float to remain as evidence. There wasn't even a piece of wood aboard big enough to make even a toothpick. Making a raft for survival was out of the question. "Damn," he finally added, still staring at the rising water. .

He walked to the bow and back, assessing the situation. On seeing the continuing rise of water already edging close to the cabin floors, he reconciled himself to some of the despair the cab driver was showing. "Well, friend," he said. "Unless a boat comes along in the next half hour or so, it looks like we're going to get wet."

"I was afraid you'd say that, Mate," the man responded disconsolately.

"At least we can climb up onto the fish spotting tower," Penn added. "That way we can stay dry a few minutes longer, I guess." As he spoke he began climbing the aluminum ladder that ran from the cockpit past the flying bridge to the fish spotting deck that was perched about twenty feet above the water.

Most all sport-fishing boats in the Caribbean were fitted with a fish spotting deck. It wasn't the most comfortable place to be when the boat was moving, but it's an ideal height for spotting something in the distance. Now Penn was hoping to use the added height to spot something, anything, in the distance that might give them a break.

When he reached the top of the ladder his frustration heightened, and his expression showed it.

"Nothing, eh, Mate?" the cab driver said as he began his climb up the ladder.

Penn slowly shook his head from side to side. There was nothing in view within the horizon, anywhere, and the horizon from that height was at least twenty five miles away. "Hell, if there was a boat out there, do you think you could swim long enough for it to find us, if it ever did? Damn it!" He again shook his head in frustration, and looked down at the boat.

The bottom of the engines were awash by then, and the cab driver was perched on the ladder just beneath the one-man spotting platform, obviously wishing Penn would move to let him gain a little more altitude, a little more distance from the rising water. Or rather, from the sinking of the boat.

Penn watched, at a loss for words as the boat kept slipping slowly downward, inch by inch.

Water soon covered the engines. As the boat inched slowly downward the water began rolling in little rivulets across the cockpit decks. The gentle rocking of the boat as it settled sent water cascading over one side deck, then the other, and in minutes, it poured over the sides to fill the cockpit.

The cabin became awash, and the water began inching up the sides toward the cabin top.

The cabin top passed under water less than twenty

minutes after the Texan and his companion left. Penn wondered how long it would take for the boat to become top heavy in the relatively calm seas and turn over, dumping them from the top of the lookout into the sea, and how long it would be before the sharks came.

The boat was sinking rapidly now, with the entire hull under water.

Penn was thankful it was at least sinking in an upright position. "Some luck," he consoled himself. "Of all the times for that lucky bastard PZ to jump ship."

When the water covered the second rung of the ladder he thought of Lara. He regretted that she would have to worry about him, forever wondering what had happened.

Chapter 25

Mikel Bear stared at the public phone as it rang. He let it ring at least ten times before answering. He waited for it to ring enough to be sure it wasn't someone mis-dialing. After the tenth ring he picked it up. "Yeah?" he growled into the mouthpiece. "What's so important now?"

He waited for the explanations added, "What do you mean Milagro is still operating? The code was changed. I cleared the change, the Belize contact was notified." He waited for the caller to explain. "Well God damn it! Who's running things, anyway? I said he wasn't to be protected any longer.... What? Well, God damn it! Well, okay, then. He'll make this one run as El Lobo, but that's all." He slammed down the phone in anger and stomped out of the booth to his Jaguar parked at the curb. As he got in he reviewed recent events.

That God damn Penguini! The crap he pulled in Guerneville, and the way he slipped out of the set up I planned with Manuel just out of pure luck. And now, back in Belize, he slipped out of the trap again, even when the hit men not only had a perfect description, but knew exactly when they were arriving at the airport.

He lit a cigarette, then started his car, still reviewing the events.

Hit men? Hah! Where the hell did Ollie come up with two dudes that are such duds? They couldn't hit two guys sitting in the back of a cab with a shotgun at twenty feet on a clear day? Jesus! He shook his head. Well, their latest stunt with the boat better work. I don't know how PZ slipped out in time, but what the hell. I wasn't after him, anyway.

Twenty minutes later the Bear was again sitting at his kitchen table with a cup of coffee in front of him, again reviewing the recent events.

"One ounce of coke it cost me, but it paid off," he said as though Embee, sitting on the sofa watching television, was listening to him. "It gave me the best possible source of information on Penguini's moves."

Knowing he had at last bested Penn Gwinn gave him a stirring in his loins. The syndrome of getting his rocks off by putting down his competition, was a thrill to him. He laughed out loud with pleasure, slamming his coffee cup down on the table.

"God damn," he said, again exacting pleasure from his success. "God damn," he said again, though with a change in tone, becoming suddenly serious.

"God damn bastard," he added, now frowning. "How the hell that bastard Milagro escaped the trap with the Coasties is beyond me. Now I gotta take care of him. I ought to let him feed the sharks, too." He smiled again as the thought penetrated his ego. "That's for sure what I ought to do, feed him to the sharks, too." He grinned again, after realizing there was no reason why he couldn't do just that.

He tried to take another swallow of coffee from his coffee mug, then found it empty. "Embee!" he bellowed to the woman who was sitting less than fifteen feet away on the couch watching television. "Get me some more coffee."

Embee Bear turned her head from her TV. She stared for several seconds, then reluctantly rose to walk past the table to the coffeepot on the kitchen counter less than three feet away from the Bear in the other direction.

Her expression was complacent, but her thoughts were less than placid as she poured the coffee. She knew what the caller Bear talked to, had said. She had even known it in advance, but she wasn't going to let the Bear know that.

The Bear, she silently laughed. A God damn Grizzly, she added with contempt. "So, now what are you going to do?" she asked, feigning naiveté.

She knew what his answer would be. She always knew, since she had long ago figured him out. His ego was the summation of his being. But she asked the question just to continue playing the part, to act the dumb little wife, as always. It was a role that got her what she wanted, and it was one she was going to continue playing so long as it was of benefit to her.

"So now what?" Bear growled his response. "So now what the hell do you care? So now I'm going back down there to do that little job with a certain boat captain, that's what." He rose from his chair to stomp out of the room and up the stairs to the bedroom.

Embee heard him plop himself down onto the bed, and she winced. She knew what he would want next.

"Embee!" he bellowed. "C'mere," he ordered.

Embee grimaced again. This was the one thing she hated more than anything else about living with Mikel Bear.

At one time she enjoyed making love with the man. She had even enjoyed giving him pleasure orally, and he seemed to enjoy that so much. In fact, he began to enjoy that more than anything else, so she continued giving him pleasure that way. She continued until she realized that this demand was his way of subjugating her. It wasn't a sharing of emotion for him, she soon learned. It was his way of showing his dominance, his machismo.

Then one day she met her special friend, thanks to her brother, and it was that friend who opened her eyes to a whole new world. It was a different world. One where she could think and do the things she had only dreamed of doing before. Her friend taught her how to get back at her beast of a husband.

She began putting together operations that took advantage of her husband's resources. They were small operations at first, then as her experience grew, she planned bigger and bigger moves. It had been easy for her. She could listen in on all the telephone calls. She could find the telephone number, discover whom he was calling and whom he was doing business with, then apply her line of persuasion. It was easy to out-think Bear's macho over-confidence and set things up to her satisfaction. She had learned that she could live her own life in spite of the Bear, and she did.

How easy it is to work people, she thought. Once you know how. Even a guy like Yanks. He was a good contact. He had been surprisingly compliant for a man of his talents. At times she did enjoy him, that was true, as much as she enjoyed any man, that is, but it was his wire tapping talents she needed.

She developed her contacts, and worked them into damn good profits. Some of those contacts she liked, some she hadn't. She even made love to more than one of them, knowing the male ego was prey to a confusing presentation of sex and business. It was a simple enough price to pay, and it worked. Before long she would have amassed enough money in her own account to not only tell Mikel Bear where to get off, but to hire the manpower to protect herself from him if she needed to. Or better, to have him taken care of, if need be.

It wasn't quite time to do that yet, though. She had a few more details to resolve, then she would be the one going to Belize again, not Mikel . Her trip wouldn't be business, though. Not that time.

Still, for a while, when Mikel called, she would have to perform his dirty little deed, so she turned to trudge up the stairs.

* * *

Hauke unlocked the door to the Hard Loggers office and surveyed the mess. "God damn," he said. "What the hell has been going on here? man, I go away for a few days, and the place falls apart. I knew I shouldn't have left things to that jive ass Manuel."

Manuel's dead, though, he told himself. And those God damn honky snoops have been taken care of, so I can get back to making my bread on this gig. Before long I can be on my own again. Hell, then I can tell Bear where to put it, if I want. It's been a long time, he continued his thoughts as he reached for a cold Corona Beer from the refrigerator. Yep. It had been a long time since he developed his plan, since he got the idea that he could do a little behind the scenes importing as well as Mikel Bear. His advantage, he knew, was that he could keep track of the Bear's steps every bit of the way, because of the way he had played on the Bear's wife, Embee. He felt she had a strong feeling for him, and he knew that he had played his cards right in that regard. He knew it, because he could feel it.

She had consented to go along with him almost at once. It was almost as though she had thought of the idea herself, when he brought it up to her. Hell, it was like the idea was really hers in the first place. But he kept telling himself that it couldn't have been. It just fit into her plans, that's all, he rationalized.

"So," he added to no one in particular, looking about his small office with pride. "So just a few more runs, and I'll be talking that honky sugar into spending time down here. Then where'll Bear be?" He laughed at the idea.

Where'll he be? He chuckled again as he sat in his office chair and leaned back against the wall, putting his feet up on his dusty desk. If he bothers us, man, the dude'll be six feet under. I've never done anybody in before, and I wouldn't be able to do it to Bear, but Embee said she'd take care of him, if it was needed. And I God damn do believe the bitch would.

"But now," he said aloud as he slammed his chair down and sat up. "Now I gotta get this operation back into gear, make Bear think I'm still working. I got to keep things working smooth until I got a little more bread to work with. I got to get my dudes back here to work again. I got to make another run tomorrow. I can have them all back here when I return."

He picked up the phone and began calling the numbers that he stored in his memory. They were the telephone numbers of the people he knew he could trust to come back to work, to do the plugging and the hole drilling in the special logs that would soon be again coming into the logging company.

* * * * *

Mikel Bear arrived in the Belize City International Airport. He was wishing his little fruit fly, Morri Bund, had greeted him with the air conditioned limousine, but he knew the man was too busy to run errands now. He was too busy back in the states still answering questions about his involvement in that mess at the Russian River.

"Hah," he said to himself, thinking of the explanation Bund must be trying to provide. "That'll fix his little dinker up good. Hell, I didn't really need him down here, anyway. They only thing he did was keep the Prefecture of Police off my ass when things first started up. The Prefecture doesn't even worry about me, now, so he's sure no worry to me." He put his bag on the counter for the Belizean Customs agent to paw through.

The agent recognized Bear, and passed him through with no more than routine opening of the bag for the sake of the letter of the law. "Oh, mon. I don't need to worry none about you. Have a good day, Mr. Bear." Mikel thanked him for the courtesy.

"But there is someone who does worry me," Mikel found himself saying out loud as he exited the airport building, still dwelling on puzzles at hand. "That God damn Milagro, and he better damn well worry about me 'cause I'm the biggest thing he's ever going to have to worry about." He finished his resolute remark as he climbed into the rear of the first cab in line in front of the building.

As the cab pulled away from the building and headed for the Hard Loggers' office in accordance with his directions, Bear noted the few pieces of broken glass on the floor board. He glanced at the driver's taxi permit posted on the back of the front seat and noted that the picture on the permit showed a white man, whereas the driver was black.

Hunh, he said to himself. Probably stole the damn cab from someone. What the hell do I care?

At the logging office Mikel had the cab stop long enough for Hauke to come out and join him. "I presume you're going to get things working all right again?" he growled.

Hauke nodded his head in nonchalance, like a self-assured subordinate speaking to a boss who was not thought to be so superior. "Yeah, man. Of course," he replied.

"Good," Bear said before telling the cab driver to drive on. "I'll keep in touch," he added as Hauke shut the door to the now moving cab. "To the Fort George Hotel," Mikel said to the driver.

It seemed to Bear that everyone stayed at the Fort George Hotel when they were in Belize City. The reason for that was simple, he rationalized. The Fort George was the only good hotel in the entire country, except maybe for The Villa directly across the street. But he had never stayed at The Villa. Besides, the Fort George is usually full of tourists, and they're good cover, he added to his thoughts as he got out of the cab in response to the doorman's opening of the cab door in front of the hotel.

He made his way to the elevator that would take him to the third floor, and failed to notice the man in the white suit with the Panama hat, who was sitting in the cane chair near the elevator door.

The man was holding a newspaper in front of his face for cover. It wouldn't do for Bear to see him.

Mikel tossed his suitcase on the bed after making sure his room door was locked. Then he picked up the telephone, got the desk clerk and ordered a call placed to a local number.

After a minute or so, the clerk managed to secure an outside line and rang the number.

To Bear's disappointment, though, the line was busy. He slammed down the receiver in his impatience, and looked at his watch. It was only eleven fifteen in the morning. He had a while to wait until dark, so he had plenty of time to make that call after all, he decided. "Anyway," he said. "I may not even want to tell anybody until it's over with. No use stirring up things unless I have to."

He took off his shirt, then laid down on the bed to rest, and to think. After a few more minutes he picked up the receiver again to get the desk clerk. He wanted to place an order for some personal services that he knew were available for the right price. Right then he considered that he would be willing to pay the right price.

"God damn sharks," he chuckled. "That's what the women are down here. God damn sharks, snapping up your money."

He thought about Penn, and how he expected Penn had dealt with the sharks. The thought of getting eaten by sharks made him shudder. Sharks! I hate God damn sharks. In his worst nightmares, the ones that kept coming back, he was eaten by sharks time and time again.

Then he chuckled with another thought. "But here I am," he chuckled. "About to get eaten by sharks myself, right here in this hotel room. I hope the shark they send up is a good looking one this time." He got up, took off the rest of his clothes and stepped into the coolness of the shower.

Several hours later he chased the tired native girl from his room, again showered, put on his clothes and left the room. It was time to meet Hauke.

* * * *

After the elevator doors closed behind Bear's exit, the man in the white suit smiled softly, got up, and walked to the telephone booth to place an international call.

He had to remove his white Panama hat as he fit his girth into the telephone booth, but that gave him no trouble. The trouble arose when he tried to hold the hat in front of him. It nearly slipped from his grasp when he had to use both hands to operate the telephone; one to hold the receiver and the other to insert the coins.

"Damn monkey machines," he swore as his hat slipped and he almost dropped it again. He grabbed it and stuffed it under his arm, holding it by squeezing it between his elbow and his side. As he raised his arm carefully to slip another coin into the slot, the hat slipped again, this time landing on the floor.

That made him lose his usually unperturbable temper. In anger he stomped on the hat. He made sure it wasn't going anywhere this time.

After listening to the coins jingle their way down the myriad of crevices inside the machine, the dial tone finally returned, and he dialed his number.

"Yes?" came the response after the third ring.

"He got here about two hours ago," the man

responded. "Had a broad sent up to his room. She finally left, and he just went out a few minutes ago."

"A few minutes ago? Why the hell didn't you follow him?" the voice demanded.

"Because I know where he went, that's why."

"Where?"

"To meet Hauke."

"He's going to make another run?"

"Yeah. He went to meet Hauke to set up the details for tomorrow's departure, I would imagine."

"The last run, I venture to guess," the voice said with a chuckle.

The man in white joined in with a laugh of his own.

The other voice then became serious. "I don't need to tell you what will happen if there's a slip op on this one."

The man in white stopped laughing. "There won't be any slip ups, and you don't need to remind me. I already alerted Milagro about what the Bear probably has in mind. He knows how to handle himself. He'll be ready for him, and that'll make things easier."

"Good. Call me when it's over."

"Will do." The man in white hung up the phone, stepped out of the booth, and with great effort, bent over to retrieve his white Panama hat with his footprint neatly outlined on the flattened crown.

"God damn dinky telephone booths," he complained, blaming his shortcomings on something else, as was his habit. "No," he added as he brushed off and reshaped his hat, "there won't be any slip ups this time."

He walked out of the hotel while reviewing the last meeting between Bear and Keany. He had thoroughly enjoyed watching the Bear go through his contortions during the squeeze. Complaining about not being able to run things his way. Hah! The dumb ass. If he only knew how close he was to the person that was really running things.

* * * *

Morgan Baletta was busily weeding her garden of native Belizean plants that grew behind her high walled patio, when her telephone rang.

She hurried inside and glanced at the wall clock. It was after 2:00 p.m. Because she was weeding in the privacy of her own patio, she hadn't yet bothered to put on any clothes, and now that she was inside, she had no need to dress before answering the phone.

"Hi, hon," she responded to the caller's greeting. "Hey, you caught me at just the right time. I'm standing here talking to you stark naked."

She laughed at the expected reply, and playfully carried on the descriptions to delight her caller's imagination for several minutes before her caller turned to more serious business, the reason for the call.

"What you're saying," she responded after hearing the message, "is that there's a good probability that the Bear is going to arrive in Belize anytime? Well, not to worry. He's already here.... What kind of adjustment was he talking about?.... Milagro....? No. I agree. That doesn't sound as though he's talking about suspender sizes," she joined in her caller's humor. "I was afraid that would happen, sooner or later. That's just what I was expecting when the last change in call signs was made at his request.... What? Yeah. That's the one, but we're now using La Ursa. That ought to make him sit up and take notice, don't you think?" She laughed at the joke being shared by her caller.

She reached for a cigarette on the nearby table while the caller talked, lit it, and blew out several smoke rings in semi diversion.

"Okay, Hon," she said at length. "Not to worry. I think your timing is just about right. I think this run will be the last. Okay. See you soon."

She hung up the phone and lingered over it while thinking about her caller, cherishing the moments she had spent talking for a few more seconds before heading to the shower. After that, she knew, she would have to take care of more serious business on the telephone.

"Mira, mi hermano," Morgan Baletta spoke into her telephone an hour later. "Look here!" Sometimes she had to treat her brother with tact, but there were other times when he could take anything she had to say to him with brotherly affection and understanding. This time, though, in this operation, she had to be most delicate.

Damn Latino machismo, anyway, she thought to herself while listening to Milagro's objections to her recent order.

"Look, my brother," she repeated herself when she had the chance to break in. She switched to English, deferring the Latino idioms, to be able to speak from a position of power. "I know what you're saying, but you will have to do this my way. You know there are other things we have to consider besides the Bear in this. We don't want to get things too stirred up down here if we can help it. We don't want my, ah, office to cancel out this contract, now, do we? Where would we be then, hunh?"

She listened to her brother's response. "Si. Yes," he said. "I see you have the right reasoning, again, big sister. Just like you always have. Yes, I will let the worm make this pickup, and as you say, the next run will be with a different boat. I will get rid of the name, maybe even the whole boat this time. And also, I will get rid of the muchacha, as you say. Yes, the money is more important, I think."

Morgan completed her instructions to her brother with a satisfied smile. She knew he would always do as she said, even if he didn't like it. He was smart enough to see the advantage in her connections with the American CIA.

After all, she thought after hanging up the phone. It

was her association that saved him in the most recent change from El Tigre to El Lobo. She had a hard time convincing her brother to change the name of the Cucaracha, but he did. He changed the name to another that she had selected from the operations list, just in time.

Good, she added, satisfied the right choices had been made. It has taken me too long to set up this operation to let that egotistic idiot Bear interrupt things with his petty anger with Penn Gwinn. After this run I'll notify Keany that the Bear is to be replaced.

Or, she continued with conjecture, if that doesn't work, I'll just get the hell out of this business. God, but that would feel good, to just lounge around all day, laughing, loving, living. I just hope to hell nothing goes wrong with our plans at this late date.

Chapter 26

"The God damn ocean's the only thing I hate more than sharks," Mikel Bear said while leaving the harbor with Hauke in the small runabout the next morning. "How in hell did I let you talk me into this, anyway, Hauke? And the one thing I hate more than being on the ocean, is being in it. Nobody in his right mind likes the ocean," he added. "Fish shit in the ocean."

This time he was forced to be on the ocean, though. It was against his better judgment, but Hauke had demanded that he be present to do his own dirty work.

"You're here 'cause I asked you to be," Hauke said in response to Bear's inquisition. "You know I ain't gonna have anything to do with taking out Milagro. If you want that problem taken care of, then you got to do it."

"You ungrateful son of a bitch," Bear retorted. "I take you, a flunky who never knew anything better than how to heist an empty house, and I teach you the ins and outs of an operation like this, introduce you to the finer workings of international style, and I still got to do the hard work myself?"

"You got it, man," Hauke replied, testily.

Bear sat back in the rear seat of the cockpit, thinking about that conversation. Mutiny, he called it. Pure mutiny. But he had to admit that he couldn't have managed to get this business off the ground in Belize without someone like Hauke to help run the day to day aspect of the operations. He fully resented Hauke's growing independence, though. He didn't like anyone being independent when he was supposed to have control.

Like that damn bitch, Baletta. Who in hell does she think she is, trying to tell me how to handle my affairs? I made it clear to her that Milagro had to be dumped. He was demanding too much. He was demanding too much money and he was demanding too much control in how the stuff should be carried from Honduras to Belize. And if that wasn't enough, he had demanded to keep that broad on his boat in spite of my telling him he had to get rid of her. She's nothing more than a damned invitation to trouble. Damn it, anyway.

He braced himself against the splash of spray that bounded back over the bow of the runabout.

A God damn invitation, he continued. And a damn engraved special invitation for that Penguini. Christ, of all the snatch to grab, he had to snatch the one snatch that put the friggin Penguini on his tail. Gold damn it! If it hadn't been for the way things were finally handled with that damn snoop, I'd be in deep doo doo now.

"C'mon, man," Hauke called from the wheel to interrupt Mikel 's dour complaints. "Don't be so damn brooding. Take a deep breath, the salt air's good for you. Here, have a beer." He tossed a can of Tecate back as he finished the statement.

Mikel let the can fly past him with no attempt at catching it, and watched as it splashed in the water. The sinking can quickly passed from view in the boat's wake.

Turning back to Hauke, he chuckled, pleased with himself with his show of superiority over his subordinate's tone.

He concentrated on Hauke, then thought about the boat that they were on. It was the same one Hauke always took when making one of his runs.

He considered the run they were making. He knew this was going to be a very short run, and a very efficient one, if his plans worked out. It would take two hours to get to the cay and raise the ocean racer. It would take four hours more at high speed over the water to meet Milagro, five minutes to get the stuff he's carrying, and another two minutes to hand him the wrapped package with the phony money and the special surprise grenades inside. It would take another couple of minutes to get the hell out of the way before he opened the package, four hours back to sink the ocean racer again, and two more hours back to Belize City. By the next morning there'd be another boat lined up in Honduras to take Milagro's place. That's the way he wanted it, that's how he planned it, and by God, that was how it was going to be!

He gently handled the package in his hands. He didn't want it to go off accidentally. He reached into his pants pocket to feel the other grenade he had stuffed there, making an ominous bulge. He felt safer with the second grenade. A follow up, he called it, just in case the first one was discovered. He believed he could toss the second one in Milagro's boat in case of emergencies. He always liked to have a back-up plan. That gave him control.

Just like I planned with El Tigre, or El Lobo, or what the hell is it now? La Ursa? The Bear thought about that. Where the hell'd they come up with that one? He leaned back in response to another unexpected bounce over a wave. And how did they make such a change without my approval in the first place? He dodged another wave.

What is it? Am I losing control, or what? Where did they get this La Ursa idea? Are they trying to laugh at me? Me? The one who set this whole damn operation up? Where the hell would they be without me? They think someone else could have done this? Hell, he frowned as he braced himself for yet another bounce.

Hauke throttled back on the outboard and the runabout came to a stop near the cay where the ocean racer was sunk. He walked over to the side of the boat and looked down. "Jesus, he said with a smile. "Look at all the God damn sharks!"

"What?" Mikel said with a start. "Where?"

Then Hauke laughed. There were no sharks. At least there weren't any visible to him at the moment. Even so, just to be careful in case a man-eater was lurking about somewhere near, he made arrangements to use the shark cage, as normal.

"Screw you, Hauke," the bear defended himself against the barb when he realized Hauke was making fun of him. "God damn it, you're getting a bit too big for your pants," he warned. "Just like that damn Milagro," he added. "That won't do in my operation."

Hauke had heard the threat before, and shrugged it off, like he usually did. He busied himself with the shark cage and with the routine of raising the ocean racer.

Mikel returned his thoughts to Milagro. That God damn Milagro. How in hell does he do it, anyway? I gave the order for the change to El Lobo just to get him caught, but somehow he managed to change the name of his boat at the same time. He must be one of the luckiest bastards alive. You'd almost think he knew when the operations name had been changed. And now, one more run with the new name, I'm told. Damn his luck. Well, he's running out of luck now.

* * * *

Bear's operation? Hauke silently pondered the term. There's more to this operation than he knows about. There's something else going on here. Like, somebody else is giving the orders, but not so that Bear knows it. I wish to hell I knew who that is. Someday I'm going to get Embee to find out. She'll tell me.

Hauke's thoughts quickly fell on Embee and the last night they had spent together. That was just a few nights ago when the place in Guerneville was attacked and burned. When the Bear came home earlier than expected, for some reason.

"He's one lucky dude," Hauke had said to Embee, after they had learned of the attack. He never thought about it at the time, but now that he did, he wondered who the caller was who had given Bear the news about that attack. He remembered telling Embee that Bear must have a guardian angel, or something, to get himself out of there just in time.

Embee had agreed. Mikel had returned just after she and Hauke had risen from the bed and had gotten dressed, prior to Hauke's departure. They had just sat down in the kitchen, with Embee making the coffee, when they heard the front gate and the garage door creak and groan as they opened for Bear's arrival.

I damn near got caught that time, he chuckled to himself. He remembered how close it was with him going out the back door as Bear came in the front. It was nearly one of those husband-finds-his-old-lady-with-another-man situations. He had been lucky, too, and he had made it to the airport, ready to get on the first plane out of town, before calling the Bear to find out what was going on. He had no idea what had happened that night in Guerneville when he talked to Bear. And he didn't argue when Bear told him to get on the first plane back to Belize to get things going again because the Penguini was back in the U.S., and things were safe again in the operation.

Damn, but that's one good woman. He reaffirmed his pleasure in his boss's wife. I just wished she would spend as much time thinking about me as I do about her. Sometimes I think she might have somebody else, the times when she gets that far away look in her eyes.

He laughed lightly again, keeping his expression concealed from Bear. Another source of laughter flashed through his mind. He was amused by the thought of how every time Bear was fucking over someone, his wife was doing the same thing to him behind his back.

Hauke's thoughts returned to the task at hand. Maybe I'll get lucky this time. Maybe the ocean racer won't start, or something. Jesus, I hate to go through with something like this. The run, okay, but the surprise for Milagro? I don't like it. There ain't no call to take the man out, even if he does want a bigger cut. Hell, he's got the hard part of the job, running the Coast Guard lines and such. Shit, it'd be easier to give him the extra money to keep things running smooth like.

* * * *

Penn looked to the east and watched the sun as it rose ever so slowly over the Caribbean. He felt its warmth and wondered if it would be the last warm day of his life.

He studied the water that was steadily ascending the boat ladder to his perch since the break of daylight, when he and the cabby were stranded by the Texan. He noted something odd. "Wait a minute!" he cried, his voice rising on each syllable. "Wait a God damn minute! Hey! The boat has stopped sinking. God damn! It's stopped sinking!"

The cab driver looked up at him, showing an expression that recited his obvious belief that Penn had lost his mind to think a boat could stop sinking in the middle of the ocean after the decks were completely under.

Penn wondered, too, for a second, whether he had gone mad. Then he took another look. "God damn it! The boat has hit bottom! Look!"

The cab driver looked downward, half in hope, half in fear.

The water had reached the fourth step, but no further.

"Son of a bitch, Mate!" the cab driver exclaimed. "Son of a bitch!" he shouted at the top of his lungs. "You're bleeding right, Mate! I can't believe it!"

"Well, I can believe it," Penn shouted back. "She's hit bottom. Those bastards were too sure of themselves. They were so sure that the boat would sink this far out from land that they forgot they were in the Caribbean. They forgot these waters are full of reefs and coral heads. I bet, no, I know, the water is no more than fifteen feet deep. Look! That's all the farther the boat sunk!"

"The boat is on the bottom." The cab driver had to state the fact just to believe it.

Both of them looked at the water for several minutes more, fearing they might be wrong, and the boat would resume its sinking.

The cab driver looked back up at Penn. "She's stopped all right, Mate," he said, frustration and disappointment showing once again in his expression. "Now what? We still can't get off it."

"Now what?" Penn said, glaring at the man for his lack of imagination. "Now what? Now we at least know we're not going to drown, don't we? Now we at least know that we have a chance. Now we have time to deal with things. That's what."

"With what things?" the man asked pessimistically. "Things like dying of hunger. Or worse, Mate, of thirst?"

"Look, we're not so bad off. At least there's a canvass canopy over our heads to keep off the sun."

"Yea?" the cab driver said with skepticism. "But what about food and water. They're what's important out here in this heat."

"Come on," Penn coaxed the cabby. "There's some cans of food, meat and beans, and the like, in the cabinets. The sea water won't have hurt them. All we have to is dive down and get them. And there are some glasses, pots, even fishing poles and lines. We might not be in such bad shape, if we can get some water, that is."

"That's about what I said," the cab driver replied, leaning back against the ladder from his perch on the next to top rung and casually glancing out to sea.

"We can use the water glasses," Penn argued. "We can make solar stills with them. The sun will provide enough heat to create steam in the glass if it's turned upside down, and the steam can be condensed for fresh water."

"Sounds like a job that'd take a bit of time, Mate," the cab driver responded.

"Perhaps, but what else have we got right now?"

"Well, you go right on ahead and do that if you want, but I don't think I want to go through the work."

Penn glared at the man. He found the objections unfathomable in their circumstance. "So, what are you going to do? Give up and die of thirst?"

"Me, Mate? Die of thirst?" the man quickly responded with a smirk.

The smirk confused Penn.

"No," he continued. "I think what I'll do is wait for that boat right over there," he nodded to the East, "to come pick us up. They'll have a bit of water and tucker on board. That's water and food to you, Mate," he added with a grin.

Penn look startled for a second before glancing in the direction indicated. "I'll be God damn," he said. "There is a boat over there. She's headed this way, too, by the looks of the smoke from her stack."

"How long, do you guess, before they reach us, Mate," the cab driver asked with a satisfied smile, putting his hand over his eyes to shield the sun's glare as he peered at the boat.

"I don't know, but she seems to be making pretty good time. She must have passed over the horizon within the last half hour, or I'm sure I would have spotted her earlier. I guess we just wait and find out, hunh?"

"Right, Mate,"

The boat was making good time, as Penn predicted. It took a little over an hour for it to come from the horizon to within hailing distance. It took only another forty minutes for Penn and the Australian to climb aboard the forty two foot cruiser which was being sailed by its Bahamian owner and his Jamaican one girl crew on a sail around the Caribbean.

By that afternoon they reached the same harbor in Belize City that their own cruiser had departed the fateful night before. They docked the boat in the same slip, since it was available.

The captain considered the likelihood of having to make a report of his arrival to the port authorities, since he hadn't stopped at the transient dock, but Penn and the cab driver convinced the captain it wouldn't be necessary. Since their boat had hit an uncharted coral head and put a hole in the bottom while fishing in the shallow waters, and that since the boat was from that harbor, it wasn't required to report the sinking, they explained. It would just cause more red tape than was necessary, and would only serve to delay their efforts to go back out with another boat to patch the hole and raise the boat again.

"Besides," they argued in favor of their position, "since you and your girlfriend still have some pot on board which hasn't yet been smoked, it's probably just as well you spend the night unnoticed and slip out again before dawn."

The captain agreed with them, and with many thanks, Penn and the cab driver left the boat.

"Great cruise, eh, Mate?" the cabby said as they walked up the dock. "Now what?"

"I suppose," Penn answered, "that the best thing for us to do is find a place to stay. Then we sit down and do some serious thinking about what we should do next."

"Well," the cabby said. "I don't think I can do all that just now. I mean, I am missing my cab, you know. Maybe we first ought to find it? Then we can get to where we might want to be heading and sort things out like you said?"

"That is a good point," Penn responded. "That's probably a good way to get things back in order. Where'd you leave it, anyway?"

"Well, Mate, if I knew that, I wouldn't have to find it, now would I?"

"That's also a good point," Penn added with slight suspicion. "How do you know it isn't where you left it last, anyway? What makes you think it's gone?"

"Because where I left it is where we're standing right now. Right beside this telephone booth. And it sure isn't here now, is it, Mate?"

"Fantastic," Penn responded dryly. The night's ordeal was taking its toll, and looking for a lost cab was the last thing he wanted to do. Right now he just wanted to get some decent rest, maybe a drink to calm his nerves, and get some place where he didn't have to be on guard for a while, to think and then figure out how to find Hauke. Looking back at the cabby, he added, "So now we have to find your cab?" His desire to do nothing of the kind was evident in his tone.

"Hey," the cabby with surprising enthusiasm for the situation. "That's really not so hard. We start looking for it by calling the central dispatch in the city and asking for an old mate of mine. He can check around with the other cabs and see if anyone has spotted mine. After all, you know, an orange and white Toyota cab is not going to be too hard to find in a place the size of Belize City."

The driver made his comment as he headed for another one of those mechanical monsters installed by Belizean Bell to reach out and touch someone. Only the reaching took a little more patience than normal. The booth was half fallen down. The black and yellow paint was chipped, and the telephone needed several good bangings on the side to make the connection after feeding it a few Belizean coins as tribute to the Telephone God.

Once the call went through, the cab driver began speaking into the handset in excited tones.

He was too far away for Penn to listen to the conversation clearly, even if he had wanted to, but he did overhear a few yeah's, where's and Mate's. He also heard the cabby call someone by the name Georgio before hanging up.

"Well?" Penn asked without expression as the man came back.

The enthusiasm the cabby had before the call was now on the wane. "My cab's been seen being driven by some black chap."

"What's so surprising about that? We knew it was stolen, didn't we?"

"Yeah, but by now it could damn well be repainted, re-tagged with a new license, and be sold to some high rolling bureaucrat."

"Don't be so pessimistic," Penn cautioned. "Hell, for all we know it could be parked in someone's back yard, too. Anyway, who's this Georgio you talked to?"

"Georgio? He's a mate, a good friend. He's going to pick us up here, then I'll talk him into taking us to where he last saw my cab. I think that would be a good place as any to start. Don't you agree?"

Penn didn't agree, but he had no choice in the matter if he didn't want to stay sitting beside the dock of the bay for the rest of the day.

It wasn't more than five minutes later that Georgio arrived and slid his Nissan Stanza to a stop less than five feet away from the two.

"Jesus," Penn commented, shaking his head while watching the other cabby's antics.

"So, he's in a hurry, Mate," the cabby said. "Hey, Georgio," he continued as he opened the front door of the Nissan, "You don't really want to run us over, do you?" Without waiting for a response, he jumped in beside the man and signaled for Penn to climb into the rear seat.

Penn complied, and they were off at a hare's pace. Penn wondered if Georgio knew any speeds besides full go and full stop.

Even though he sported a Latin name, Georgio was from the land down under, too. His accent was even heavier than the first cabby's 'stryne.

"G'Day, Mate," Georgio said with typical Australian enthusiasm for anything living. "Sorry 'bout that, but I think I just saw your cab, Mate. Get a move on and we can hunker the cob, Mate."

"We can what?" Penn quizzed as he was forced back against the seat by the cab's acceleration.

"Catch the man," the cabby translated.

"Another Aussie," Penn responded.

"Stryne as a 'roo, Mate," Georgio said as he turned around to speak to Penn. "Georgio's the name, driving's me game. How d'ya'do?" He tipped his cap as he spoke, and damned near ran off the road while looking back.

Penn wondered which hand the man was using to steer the car, but he couldn't afford the luxury of guessing for long. The cab lurched back onto the roadway, then once again lurched as it rounded a corner. He had to reach for the side straps to hang on.

"I just seen your Holden, Mate," Georgio said as he turned his attention back to his driving, now that he was half way around the corner, careening madly. "About an hour ago, it was. Parked off the side of the Southern Highway, just behind the garage of some high roller's house, I suspect it was. I had to turn around to take a second look, you know. I thought to myself at the time that it was strange you'd be parking there that way, and leaving your cab empty. I was going to update dispatch, but it wasn't but a few minutes after that when your call came in about having to find it. Right lucky, now, Mate, I say it is."

Penn noted the Aussie's penchant for nonstop talking and smiled. He mused at the reason the man called what was obviously a Toyota, a Holden. It was due to the fact that all the cars made in Australia are made by the Holden Motor Car Company under special license by the true manufacturer. The name has become nearly synonymous for car in the land down under.

Another ten minutes brought them to the house in question. Georgio slowed to a normal speed and drove past the front of the house, then turned down the side road to pass the side yard and the garage. The car was parked beside the garage.

"Sure as hell," the cabby said as they passed it at a little more than a snail's pace. "There's mine, all right. Stop the car and let's get it."

"Uh," Georgio interjected. "I don't have any problems with that straight away, Mate. But don't you want to think about this a little first? I say, don't you want to know just who stole the blinkin' car? Besides, the keys are probably inside the house, don't you think, Mate?"

"That's probably right," Penn chipped in.

"Okay," said the cabby after thinking. "So what do we do? Just knock on the front door and walk in like bloomin' guests? Not very bloody likely."

"You've got a point," Penn proffered. "The best thing to do is probably play this hand with a little more caution. Keep driving and go a block or so down the street, at least far enough to be out of view before stopping. Then let's put our heads together and come up with a plan."

Georgio nodded and sped up to reach a wide spot in the road between the two wood shacks about a block and a half farther down the road. He parked between three Creole kids in their pre-teens, all dressed in faded denim overalls without shirts or shoes. They were getting great pleasure out of playing the American game of marbles in the dust beside the road, and they paid no attention to the cab, engrossed as they were in the agate shooting exploits of the larger kid.

"I don't suppose you have your pistol with you, do you, Georgio?" the cabby asked, after Georgio stopped the cab.

"Pistol?" Penn asked

Georgio looked at his friend. "Sorry, Mate," he responded.

"I'm glad you thought of that," Penn interrupted. "I know just the place to pick up something in that line, if they're still there, that is."

"Yeah?" the cabby asked as he turned to Penn.

"Yes. At the Hard Logger's office. It's a mile or two..."

"I know where that is," Georgio interrupted, putting the car in gear and once again tearing up the dirt road in mad acceleration, without waiting for Penn's explanation. "We can be there in a jiff."

The jiff turned out to be more like fifteen minutes, Penn noted as they finally arrived in front of the main gate to the Hard Logger's yard.

Penn got out of the cab followed by the cabby. He was somewhat confused by the fact that there wasn't anyone around the yard. He remembered it from the last time he was here, that it was a busy place, but now the place looked deserted. He was relieved to find it that way. That meant it was less likely he would be discovered.

They approached the front door and found it firmly locked.

Penn led the way around to the rear of the building and tried the one window that opened into the rear room. He peeked cautiously into the room, half expecting someone's face might suddenly stare back at him in spite of the front lock.

But there was no one inside, so he gently tried lifting the windowsill. It gave, and slid open with surprising ease.

With a jump Penn threw his head and shoulders

through the window. With a slithering motion like a bloated Python, he wiggled inside, but he plopped onto the floor without any resemblance to the smooth sliding motion of a snake.

"What I need," he said to himself as he began looking about the room, "is to find... Ah, there it is." He spied the same table that he and PZ had seen on their earlier visit, the table that stored the pistols with the matched plastic pearl handles.

He quietly opened the drawer as though someone was yet to catch him in the act. "Good," he said as he found the pistols, grabbed them one at a time, checked the chambers to insure they were loaded, and stuck them into his waistband. He was about to shut the drawer, but his hand stopped with the drawer half closed. Something had caught his attention in the drawer.

On the bottom of it was a photograph. A woman was standing on a small quay. She wore something less than a bikini swimsuit, but that was not what caught his attention, it was the woman herself, silhouetted against a large yacht in the background, a yacht with four letter C's painted in each corner of a square on the side of the yacht's smokestack.

The yacht was unfamiliar, but the woman he knew. He would have known her even if the note scribbled across the bottom of the photograph hadn't been signed Embee.

"Someone's coming," the cabby loudly whispered through the window.

Penn hastily shut the drawer and scrambled back out the window to the ground as a car drove past the gate along the road.

The driver seemed unconcerned with their antics at the office, so Penn and the cabby strolled back to Georgio's cab, straining to look nonchalant.

"Okay," Penn said as they got back into the cab. "Let's go get your taxi."

"Right on, Mate," Georgio said as he again raced off down the highway.

"What are you planning to do with those things, anyway?" the cabby asked.

Penn ignored the question. "I think the plan is that I'll scout the place where the cab is parked, since I have the experience with that sort of thing. Then, if it looks clear enough, I'll find a way into the house. You keep an eye open," he said to Georgio. "And when I wave my hand over my head, you drive the cab up to the front of the house and make some noise. Maybe honk the horn a couple of times, as though you're signaling someone to come out, like you've been called to pick up a fare there, or something. But whatever you do, make as much noise as possible. I want the people in that house to put all their attention on you for at least several minutes. Can you do that?"

Georgio glanced at his counterpart, then at Penn, and said, "No problem, Mate."

Penn wondered what their shared glances meant, but he decided he was too busy to be bothered by the question at the moment.

The party arrived back on the side street past the garage where the taxi had been spotted, and Georgio stopped as quietly as he could, in spite of the squeaking disc brakes on the front wheels.

"Okay," he whispered, as though their every word was now being monitored.

Penn grinned at the typical responses of the amateur sleuths. Amateurs always exaggerated the unnecessary. Who the hell is going to hear us out here, anyway? "Okay," he replied to the cabby. "Do you know how to use one of these things?"

"Me, Mate?" the cabby said as he smiled at Georgio. "Old Georgio here and me, we were mates in the Aussie Scouts in Southeast Asia. I suspect I do, Mate," he added with a smile as he took the pistol proffered by Penn.

Penn grinned again. There was no doubt in his mind that the cabby would know which end of the thing was which.

Penn slipped out of the cab, followed by the cabby. Cautiously they darted behind the nearest shack for cover while making their way to the white stucco house where the car was parked.

"I hope you know what you're doing, Mate" the cabby cautioned as they made for the house.

"So do I," Penn called back in a hoarse whisper.

"Has it occurred to you that there could be more than one bloke inside that house?" the cabby asked.

"It has."

"And?"

"And what?"

"Fantastic, Mate," the cabby said in consolation, realizing he wasn't going to get any answer of substance at the moment.

They rounded another smaller shack near the house, and the only resistance they met was a barking dog that wouldn't get out of the shade of the shack to support his yelping. They approached to within fifty feet of the house before their cover disappeared. There was nothing between their last shack and the house but scraggly wild lawn.

Penn looked back to be sure Georgio could still see them, and glanced at his new found assistant.

"Just as I thought, Mate," the cabby chided. "You've got just about as much a plan as I have. So now what?"

Penn grinned. "If you were my partner, PZ, making that comment, I'd say you gobbled like a turkey with the damnedest questions."

"That's because I don't like ending up with my head on the chopping block. That's why I do, Mate,"

"There's the back door," Penn said. "The steps leading

up the rear, there."

"You plan to have Georgio raise enough commotion in front of the house for us to burst into the rear?" the cabby asked, disbelieving.

"Exactly," Penn replied as he waived at Georgio.

Georgio quickly drove to the front of the house and began his incessant horn honking.

"Come on," Penn whispered. "This is it." He lightly ran for the porch, closely followed by the cabby.

"I surely hope it isn't locked, Mate," the cabby said, close on Penn's heels.

Penn ascended the stairs with the cabby breathing down his neck.

"I surely hope it isn't locked, Mate," the cabby repeated, only more hopefully.

Penn grabbed for the doorknob and twisted. It wasn't locked. The knob turned easily, and both stepped through the door to find themselves in an outdated kitchen, near an old four burner gas stove and an old fashioned refrigerator, the type with the cooling coils on top.

Penn stood motionless. He placed his finger against his lips to signal for quiet.

The cabby complied, standing at the ready with his pistol pointed out in front of him as though playing some part in a B grade western.

Penn wondered if his assessment on the man's ability to handle the gun was too quickly made.

They listened to the continuing commotion in front caused by Georgio, and then they heard a voice.

Chills went up and down Penn's spine as he glanced at the cabby.

The cabby's eyes were opening wide at the sound of the voice. It was the Texan.

Penn took his pistol out of his waistband and held it up in front of him just as the Aussie was, silently hoping that he was improving on the quality of the B grade movie.

He slowly pulled back on the hammer and motioned for the cabby to follow as he crept over to the doorway leading out of the kitchen.

Penn half expected whoever the Texan was speaking to would come charging through the door to see what the noise was in the kitchen. But after waiting for a few seconds without incident, he felt secure enough to take a peek around the doorway.

The subject of the Texan's questioning was looking out the front window at Georgio's cab, and the Texan was sitting in an armchair with a newspaper in his hand, waiting for an answer.

The man at the window turned to respond to the question. That was when Penn recognized that man, too, and the back of his neck tingled. It was none other than Martin.

Penn's plan had worked. The two men were focusing their attentions on the noise coming from Georgio's cab, and the back door intrusion wasn't even noticed.

Penn boldly stepped through the doorway and went into a half crouch, holding the pistol in both hands out in front of him. "Put your hands in the air and don't so much as flinch," he ordered coolly as the cabby came in behind him to stand just to his right.

"What?" the Texan shouted as he turned his head to Penn.

"How the hell'd you get back here?" Martin asked as he recognized his antagonist.

"I'll ask the questions, if you don't mind," Penn countered. "Now you," he added as he pointed towards the Texan. "You get up. And you, you bastard," he said to Martin. "Just dare make one move to give me an excuse to shoot you."

Martin started to move in spite of the order.

"Just a bit further, Mate," the cabby challenged as he covered Martin with his pistol. "Just a bit further and I can blow your bloody head clean off."

Martin froze in his tracks.

The Texan grinned with a touch of sadism, and shook his head in defiance of Penn's order to get to his feet.

"I don't have to remind you that shooting both of you right now would be more than justified by what you tried to do to us last night. Now both of you get down on your God damn knees with your hands behind the backs of your heads." He fired his first round into the chair.

The Texan jumped to his feet.

Georgio was still honking the cab's horn.

"Open the door and tell that cab driver he can stop the honking now," Penn said to the cabby. He refrained from using Georgio's name to protect the man from some possible repercussions at some later date.

The cabby stuck his head out the front door, keeping one eye on the men on their knees, and waived at Georgio.

Georgio gave two short toots, and drove off.

Where the hell is he going? Penn wondered. But he had no time for puzzles, he had his hands full with the two in front of him. "Watch these two bastards real close," he said to the cabby, "while I search them."

The cabby nodded, holding his gun out in front of him, peering intently as though waiting for one of the two to make the slightest threatening move.

Penn stuck his gun in his waistband, and with experienced thoroughness, traced the outline of the Texan's body from under the shoulders, down both sides, and around the waist line.

"Well, now," he said as he reached under the man's arm from behind and extracted a Walther PPKs .380 automatic. "Mr. Texas has a toy."

He placed the gun into his own waistband beside the pistol, and continued the search to include both sides of the man's legs, and both ankles under his socks.

Finding nothing more, Penn turned his attention to

Martin.

Martin snarled. "Touch me, fucker," he said, "and you're a dead man."

Penn shrugged his shoulders in feigned disinterest, raised the .380 he had taken from the Texan, pointed it directly between Martin's eyes, and slowly pulled back the hammer. "Okay," he said with a calm that hid his bluff. "No neverminds to me. I can just as easily put you out of your misery first. Hell, that'd even make it easier for me, anyway."

Martin's eyes went wide. "You wouldn't," he stammered, pleading.

"Why don't you give me the chance to prove that to you," Penn added with a sneer. He fired a round into the wall beside the man's ear.

"Jesus!" Martin cried in panic. "Jesus!" he cried again, nearly out of control. "Okay! Okay!"

"That's what I thought," Penn commented as he stuck the gun back in his waistband and went around behind the man. He then began the same methodical search that he went through on the Texan.

He found Martin's gun, too. It was a .45 automatic, just like the one that was used to blow the hole through the bottom of the cabby's boat.

Penn continued his search with typical professional thoroughness and uncovered another gun. This one was a Hi-Power .22 caliber Charter Arms two shot derringer that was carried in the side of the man's right shoe under his sock.

"Must have one hell of an athlete's foot problem to need this kind of cure," Penn chided as he pulled out the gun.

The man glared.

"Haven't you had enough of this play, Mate?" the cabby asked at length. "Why don't we just go ahead and shoot these blokes? Didn't they try to drown us?"

"That's just what we will do if they don't come up with some answers," Penn threatened, grinning at the opportunity to expand the subject the cabby introduced. "Now, you bastard," he said to the Texan as he came around to face the man, raising his gun to a ready position. "Just who the hell are you?"

The man said nothing. Instead, he furtively glanced at some point behind Penn, and began to sneer.

That was Penn's warning. He quickly turned, and saw the black man on the stairway behind him. The man had been upstairs during the commotion, and had listened to the entire episode. He had descended the stairs slowly, and was pointing his blue short nosed .38 at Penn's back.

Penn ducked and fell to the floor just before the man fired. He rolled over and fired back three rounds in quick succession.

His intelligence agency training was still effective. The black man tumbled down the stairs head first with blood oozing from three holes in his chest into his heart.

Penn got up and saw that the cabby was following his part as back up. He was lying on the floor with his gun pointed at the Texan, just in case the man tried to take advantage of the intrusion and make some move. At the same time he was keeping his eyes on Martin.

The Texan hadn't moved, though. He only stared. He was too well trained to not know how quickly another trained individual could respond. He knew he wouldn't have had a chance under those circumstances, so he stayed quiet.

Martin was not going to move, either. He wasn't going to move again, ever. The black man's round missed Penn, but it hit Martin in the head, killing him instantly. His body hit the floor like a sack of concrete.

Penn regained his feet and approached the Texan. "Well," he said calmly, straining to retain his cool appearance. "I guess that means you have to give me what

I want to know or join your friends. What'll it be?"

The Texan looked into Penn's eyes for a few minutes, then looked at the floor. He knew he was beaten. "What do you want to know," he said, resolutely.

"Who do you work for?"

"Morgan Baletta."

"What?" The answer stunned Penn, but he regained his composure and continued the questioning. "She's supposed to be with the DEA. Is she?"

"She was."

"Now?"

"Someone else."

"CIA?"

"No. She has contacts with the Company, but I think she works for someone else."

"And she hired you to kill us. Why?"

"She didn't hire us to kill you."

"Then who did?"

"Someone, I didn't get the name."

"Why did that someone want us out of the way?"

"You were getting too close to the answer."

"What answer?"

"Markham."

"Markham? What did he have to do with this?"

"You're a friend of his, or you were, anyway. You were getting too close to finding out who killed him."

"What's that got to do with this down here?"

"He found out about the house in Guerneville."

"Jesus," Penn responded in surprise. "This keeps getting deeper and deeper. Mikel Bear was behind the house in Guerneville, what's that got to do with you, or Baletta, for that matter?"

"That dumb ass Bear's not smart enough to run things in Guerneville. He was set up to think that he was, but he wasn't."

"Then who was smart enough?" Penn wondered just

how long this story was going to be. He wondered just how long he could push his luck, keeping this man talking.

"Baletta's boss, that's who."

"Now we're back to that. Who's Baletta's boss?"

"I don't know."

Penn raised the gun. "How can you two work for the same person without knowing who it is?"

"Hey," the man's eyes gave the first show of fear. "You got to believe me. I just take my orders from her. I don't know who the boss is. You got to believe me on that one. I'm telling you the truth. All that I know."

"Okay," Penn relented. He lowered the pistol. "Then you killed Markham?"

The man shrugged, but didn't answer.

"Why?"

"I didn't say I did."

"Who did, then?"

"Some one else. Some guy Bear uses in the states."

"Name?" Penn demanded.

"I don't know."

"What's he look like?"

"Hell, like any body else. How do I know? I never saw him."

"Then why was Markham killed? He was getting too close to the Guerneville thing, was he figuring out what it was all about?"

"Yeah. He knew too much. He knew the reason for the house."

"You mean making porno movies? That's why Markham was killed, to keep the lid on a porno operation?" Penn was angered by the thought that his friend was murdered to cover something so worthless.

"No. That's just a cover. The porno was a sideline for the Bear. It was something to keep him busy. The real reason for the house was to be a shipping point. A distribution point for the stuff that get's brought in."

"Stuff. Cocaine?"

"Yeah."

"Okay. I know that, but how is it being brought in? Through the logs he imports?"

The Texan nodded.

Penn sat down in the chair and leaned back to think, still pointing the gun at the man kneeling in front of him. "Look," he said after a short pause. "This thing's too complex. Just start at the beginning and tell me all that you know."

"If I do, what do I get?"

So that's it, Penn thought. He's been setting up a basis for a trade all along. That's why he's been so talkative. "What do you get?" he asked. "I'll tell you what. I'll be fair. You get a chance to walk out of here with your skin in one piece, that's what."

"A chance?" The Texan's eyebrows lifted.

"Right. I'll give you an even chance to make it to the front door before I start shooting. Then it's up to you."

"That's not much of a chance."

"Better than nothing."

The Texan looked up again, then back down at the floor. It was now clear that he feared for his life, but he saw the chance for escape. He decided to take it. "Okay," he said. "The CIA with the White House Staff buys coke from the Coca Nostra in Colombia, ships it to Honduras, then it goes by boat..."

"The CIA?" Penn interrupted.

"Yeah..."

"Milagro's boat?" Penn interrupted a second time. The boat was more important to him at the moment than any machinations of the most sinister branch of the government.

"Yeah. By Milagro's boat to somewhere off the coast of Belize where Bear's flunky, Hauke, meets him, makes the buy, then brings the stuff back in here. He puts it into those logs and ships them to Frisco. They take it out of the logs on the freighter and drop it off the coast near Jenner, near the Russian River. Some fisherman picks it up and takes it up the river to Guerneville where it's picked up by some more of Bear's men and taken to the house where they make the movies. That's where they divide it up to sell on the streets. Or did before it burned down a couple a days ago."

"So the porno business is nothing more than a cover up for the coke distribution?"

"That, and like I said, for Bear to keep himself busy with. Besides, he said he needed the business to keep his sources and contacts happy."

"Sources and contacts?"

"Yeah, Morri Bund and an agent by the name of Keany. He's into the S & M movies for the money he makes from them. He splits the money with Bear and the broad that does the dirty work."

"The broad. You mean Marena?"

"Yeah, that's her."

"I see," Penn responded as he paused again to think. "How did this involve Markham? How did he find out about all that mess in Guerneville in the first place?"

"Easy. He was Marena's half brother."

"I'll be God damn," said Penn in amazement. "That's how he got the names on the list I found in his office. Marena couldn't keep her mouth shut, right? And Markham was the one she did all the talking to. That's how he got the names."

"Something like that."

"That was what you and your friend, here, were doing in his office. The same thing we were doing, only you knew about the list and we didn't. You were looking for it, only you weren't smart enough to look in the right places. I found that list."

"Like I said..."

"Right. Something like that. Only, you said you didn't kill Markham."

The man shrugged his shoulders, stealing a glance at the cabby as a diversion of his thoughts.

The cab driver had been sitting silently through the entire exchange. He took the opportunity to add his thoughts. "I'll be a croc's crapper," he said. "What have I gotten myself into, Mate?"

Penn smiled reassurance at him. "Don't worry," he said. Then he turned his attention back to the Texan. He wanted to get more out of him, especially about Markham's murderer. "You didn't kill Markham, but you know who did, don't you?"

"Like I said. No. I don't know. It was the brains behind the operation who wanted him out of the way."

"The brains? The CIA?"

"No, I don't think so. They were just involved in the coke trading for the money."

Penn decided the man was telling the truth about not knowing the name, or who the so-called brains behind the operation was, so he began another line of questioning. "The CIA was involved for the money, you said?"

"Yeah."

"How did they collect it from the street sales, anyway?"

"That was Bear's job. He collected the money and gave it back to the Company. They used it to buy guns for the Contras."

"Guns for the Contras? Come on. Bear couldn't have moved that much stuff, enough to finance the Contras."

"Bear wasn't the agency's only source."

"That's impossible. The Coast Guard would have intercepted too many boats going through that route. There couldn't be enough runs to make enough money for that large an operation."

"The Coast Guard has a certain list of boats that they

aren't to interfere with."

"List? Who makes that list?"

"I don't know. The Company, or someone from the White House. I don't know everything, damn it."

"Markham knew everything, didn't he?"

"Almost, but that's everything I know."

"You still haven't answered the big one," Penn decided to push as far as he could. "Who's Mr. Big? The man behind it all? The President?"

"President? Hah. I doubt that. The only things he knows are women and cigars. I don't think he's aware enough of anything to know what's going on behind his back."

"Someone in his administration?"

"Hey! Like I said. I don't know who in particular."

"Who does know?"

The man shrugged his shoulders.

"I would hate to think that was your answer," Penn warned.

"Look," the Texan said desperately. "I told you too much already. If I knew that and told you, or even if they think that I told you, do you think it would do me any good to get away from you? Jesus, I'd rather you kill me here on the spot than have to wait for them to catch up to me. Nobody ever gives up the names of the men in the Company and gets away with it, they're worse than the Mafia. They hunt you down like a dog." He started shaking his head in defeat. "You can't tell anyone where you got the information I gave you. I don't ever want to go through what they'd do to me. I couldn't go through that."

Penn stared at the pathetic figure kneeling before him. The man was shaking, broken. He had reached the point where nothing more could be gleaned from him. His last plea had been from a man who had lost hope. "Okay," Penn said quietly. "You can go."

The Texan looked up. He looked confused. He shook his head slowly from side to side as though finding his release beyond his comprehension, as though it was some sadistic trick.

"Look" Penn said. "I told you to get out of here," he added with his voice rising. "Now go, before I come to my senses and put one through your head. Get the hell out of here." He shouted the last command in frustration.

The man stood, slowly. He looked about, then turned and started for the door. He faltered, then straightened, clearly expecting to be shot in the back at any step. The closer he got to the door, the quicker his steps became.

He opened the door, stared outside while standing stiffly, then slowly stepped through it, as though he was sure it was an impossible barrier.

Once through, he closed the door softly. His footsteps could be heard as he ran off the steps and disappeared down the walkway.

"Was that a good idea?" the cabby asked.

"What'd you expect? That I could kill the bastard in cold blood?"

"I might have, Mate,"

"Bullshit," Penn replied with distaste.

"So now what?" the cabby asked.

"Now?" Penn answered. "Now I think we get the hell out of here before that guy regains his courage and comes back to haunt us."

"I was hoping you would say something like that, mate," the cabby responded as he headed for the door.

"Hold it," Penn cautioned. "I'm not so sure it would be a good idea to go rushing out of here that way."

"Why?" The cabby was confused.

"There's one part of this puzzle about your cab that's been bothering me."

"Puzzle? What?"

"Are you sure Georgio is a good friend?"

"Well, he's been a good bloke all along."

"Then you tell me how he managed to spot your cab parked beside the garage outside when he was supposed to be driving down the Southern Highway? I don't know if you noticed, but it couldn't be seen unless you turned down the side road, just like we did when we arrived."

"Oh, shit," the cabby said. It was the first non-Australian slang Penn had heard from him. "Then we can't go out the back door?"

"Not the back nor the front, I suspect. They both can be seen from the same spot down the road."

"Crap. Then how're we going to get out of here?"

"That," Penn replied, "is a good question. But the number one question at the moment is where are the keys to the cab?" As he spoke he walked over to the black man and began rummaging through his pockets, at the same time he told the cabby to search the other dead man.

"Damn. We'll have to look around the house for them, Mate," the cabby said, not finding the keys.

"Maybe not. They might still be in the cab's ignition," Penn responded. "But if they're not, then we do some walking."

Chapter 27

"How do we get out of the house?" the cabby asked.

"I think I have an idea," Penn responded as he crossed to the couch and sat. "How about calling a taxi?"

"Another cab, mate?" the cabby asked. He thought about the suggestion, then smiled at the brashness of the idea. "Sure. That'll make things a bit of a go, won't it?" He found the idea amusing.

Penn reached for the telephone on the end table. He dialed an 'O' and asked the operator to connect him with the Belizean Cab Company.

After a minute or two the connection was made. He ordered the cab and instructed that the driver honk his horn loudly in front of the house to signal his arrival. "Yes," he assured the dispatcher, "I'll come out just as soon as I hear the horn. Thank you."

He smiled as he replaced the receiver. "Well," he added as he got up and went into the side room. "Let's see if we can get this plan off the ground."

He carefully lifted the window at the side of the room and checked to make sure there was adequate cover on that part of the yard to keep them from being seen during their escape. It was less then five feet to the ground, and the side of the garage was less then twenty feet away.

The cabby's cab, the one they had come to retrieve in the first place, was just to the rear of that garage, and there was no one in sight. He wondered if that was because the other cab driver was sitting down the street in front of the house with the Texan, waiting for him and the cabby to come confidently striding out the front door.

But he had no idle time to ponder that question. It was

more important they get out of there as soon as possible. He motioned for the cabby to follow, and slipped out the window, cautiously making his way for the cover of the garage and the parked cab. He opened the front door and slipped behind the steering wheel, keeping down, careful not to put himself in view.

"We're in luck," he whispered as the cabby slid in through the rear door on the same side. "The keys are in the lock."

"All right, mate," the cabby responded with enthusiasm.

"Now, if our plan works..." Penn let the sentence drop as they patiently waited for the arrival of the cab that they called. In the tenseness of the moment Penn didn't consider the irony of him setting himself up to do the driving with the cabby as passenger in his own cab.

Their wait was short, and soon a loud piercing horn was heard from the front of the house Penn had the cover he needed to start the Toyota, and as he expected, in tribute to Japanese engineering, the engine fired up on the first try.

He depressed the clutch and shifted it into first gear, then as he sat up, he popped out the clutch and stomped down on the gas pedal.

The little car leaped like a jackrabbit and screamed out from behind the garage, across a short expanse of open field, and onto the dirt road.

The kids playing marbles in the middle of the road leaped back from their game as the speeding car raced through their circle, scattering their marbles.

The only danger Penn and the cabby passed during their escape was the flying marbles bouncing off the rear of the car, launched by angry kids.

Three miles further down the road the cabby raised his head to peer out the rear window. "Doesn't look like we're being followed," he commented as he climbed into the front passenger seat.

"Doesn't look like it," Penn agreed.

"Now what, mate?" the cabby asked as he grabbed the panic handle on the dash board to keep from being tossed around while Penn jockeyed the speeding car through a tight turn.

"Two things. First, we find Morgan Baletta. She is the only person who can tell us where Hauke is supposed to meet Milagro. At the same time we can find out just who the hell is at the bottom of this mess. I now know why Markham was killed. I think I do, anyway. But I don't yet know who did it, and that's the important thing."

"Ah, begging your pardon, mate, but who is this Markham bloke? A mate of yours?"

"Well, not that good a friend, maybe, but certainly a friend of a type. More of a co-worker, I guess. A damn good investigator. There aren't many of them left now days."

"And you just found out why he was killed?"

"Right. The Texan back there just let me know Markham was killed because he knew too much, or was finding out too much about the Bear/CIA/DEA/Coast Guard/Guerneville pornography operation back home. The states, that is. And he was killed before he had a chance to finish his case, or before he had a chance to put it all together."

"Oh. You mean he was done in to keep him from telling everybody he knew about that mess, eh, mate?"

"Right, but from telling who? That's another question."

"He hadn't given his information to who it was that hired him, I gather."

"Not as far as I can tell. As a matter of fact, I don't even know who had hired him, or if he had been hired by anyone at all."

"That is a Roo's leg, then, ain't it? How many players

are there in this mystery, anyway. Tell me about them. There's nothing I like better than playing a little Agatha Christie once in while. Maybe I can be a little help, eh, mate?"

Penn glanced at the cabby, then back at the road to pass a slow moving truck that was hogging the center line.

After settling back on the right side of the two lane pothole infested asphalt, Penn decided it wouldn't hurt to have some fresh thoughts on the case, so he recited the cast of players. "Well, you're not going to know any of these names, but what the hell? There's Mikel Bear, Morri Bund, Marena Bloeswell, Morgan Baletta, Milagro and Hauke, whose real name is Mantee Beaulleiu. And Manuel, whose last name I don't know, but he's dead, so that lets him out. Also, there's Manny Bolton, who's too much of a wimp to do anything that requires guts."

"Well, now, mate. That's a bit of an oddy, ain't it?"

Penn shot the man another glance while keeping one eye of the road. "What's a bit odd?"

"Those names, mate. Ever notice them?"

"Notice them, what do you mean?" He went over the list. Then as recognition dawned, his mouth dropped in surprise. "I'll be damned! Talk about a riddle. Every one of those names start with either an M or a B."

"That's just about what I meant, mate."

Penn went over the initials again. "M. B.? MB? No. It can't be."

"Can't be what?"

"Mikel Bear's wife is named Embee."

"Mikel Bear's wife? Just who is this Mikel Bear, anyway? Funny name for a bloke."

"He's... well, never mind. He's the main problem in this case. Has been to me for a long time. Anyway, his wife's name is Embee."

"That's some coincidence, eh, mate?"

"Coincidence? Maybe. Or, how about it being the

sense of humor of a criminal genius?"

"I suppose," the cabby added. "There's been stranger ones than that now and then, I hear."

"I have to thank you for your input," Penn told the man. "I think that right now a telephone call to the states is in order."

The cabby added nothing more as he sat back in his seat and watched as Penn piloted the car into the center of town, then finally to a stop behind the Four Fort Street Guesthouse, around the corner from the Fort George Hotel.

"I hope you're not planning to stay here," the cabby commented as he got out of the cab behind Penn.

"No chance. I just want to use the telephone, and they have the best one in town. I parked here for cover."

"Oh," the cabby added as he followed Penn around the corner at a fast pace, into the Fort George hotel.

As they passed through the front doors, they ignored the white suited man with the Panama hat who passed through the opposite door outward bound, too intent on where he was heading to look at anyone.

Penn listened to Yanks' excited responses to his questions over the telephone. "Damn it, Penn. I've been trying to get hold of you for three days. You got to know. The woman that called about your leaving Belize back then, that I got on that tape? She's been daily to, ah, talking to Embee almost daily. You're not going to believe this, but Embee told her to, get this, Embee told her she had made arrangements for guy some, ah, some guy in Belize to tell Milagro to down gun Bear, ah, gun down Bear on the next run."

"Now, wait a minute, Yanks," he responded. "Slow down. You're telling me that Embee Bear gave orders to someone in Belize to get rid of Mikel Bear?"

"Yep. And she's been giving orders all along to that broad called, ah, Baletta, I think she called her, among other things. I thought we had a going thing, ah, a thing going, Embee and me, but she's got this thing with that dame in Belize."

"Embee Bear and Morgan Baletta?" Penn was taken back by that surprising piece of news. "Are you sure?"

"Yep, and whoever La Ursa is, too. And El Tigre, or El Lobo, only I think El Lobo's real name is La Ursa."

"Jesus Christ," Penn remarked as he took in the meaning of Yanks' message.

"What?" Yanks asked anxiously, as though he hadn't heard clearly.

"I said Jesus Christ," Penn repeated.

"Yeah. He's probably involved, too," Yanks said.

"Listen, Yanks," Penn ordered. "I want you to keep an eye on Embee. And damn it, this could be the most important job you've ever done for me, so don't let your emotions get in the way of doing what you're supposed to do. Don't let her out of your sight. I don't care what you have to do to do that, but stay with her. Keep an eye on her until you hear from me. Check in with Lara at the office every morning. Before long I may give you enough evidence to get Captain Giddings to arrest her, and I want to know where she is if I do. Got that?"

"Well, sure, Boss, I got that. Besides, I can do that just to see what she's really up to, playing me along like she has."

"Don't feel bad, Yanks. If she's been playing you along, take some pleasure in this: Think of what she's been doing to Bear."

"Hey. That's right. Okay. I'll keep in touch with Lara. You be careful, now, hear?"

"I hear. Thanks." He hung up the phone, going over the news. "Embee put out a contract on her own husband," he said to no one in particular. "That's certainly a strange twist, but it sure as hell falls in line with recent developments, doesn't it?"

The cabby perked up his ears as Penn stepped out of the telephone booth, talking to himself. "Excuse me, mate," he said to Penn, "but did I just hear you say that one with the funny name, Embee, and some other sheila got together to put this whole thing together?"

Penn glanced up. "Something like that, yes."

"You mean to tell me, that this guy we just let go, that Texan as you called him, wouldn't talk because he was afraid of what two sheilas would do to him? Come on."

Penn thought about the man's remark. "That doesn't sound too convincing, does it?"

"Not really, mate."

"Then, the only recourse is to think that there's someone else involved, someone who they're connected to that's really in power."

"That sounds more likely, mate."

"Or, there is another possibility. Maybe they have someone working for them that is capable of such actions."

"MB," the cabby was obviously mulling over that thought. "Maybe. But two sheilas running things like that? I wouldn't be too sure."

Penn was amused by the man's chauvinism. He wondered if it was typical of Australians. "You admit, it has got to be a possibility. Anyway, it's time to pay a call on Morgan Baletta. Come on." He headed back to the cab. "Tell you what. You can drive this time. It's your cab, after all."

* * * *

The man in the white suit held his slightly mis-shaped Panama hat in his hand as he got out of the taxi in front of Morgan Baletta's house. He paid the driver and put on the hat as he threaded his way through the front iron gate into the courtyard amid the squawks of the watching parrots.

Morgan was lounging in a chair on the porch just out of the sunshine line. She was drinking her favorite drink, a Pina Colada, from a quart sized glass.

The man in white admired the woman's trim figure and ample breasts that were barely contained under the skimpy bikini top. He wondered why it was that he could never get close to her. "Just not her type, I guess," he mumbled, taking his handkerchief from his pocket and wiping the sweat off his rounded face before stepping up on the porch.

Morgan casually watched his approach.

"Afternoon," he greeted with a friendly nod as he sat in one of the chairs at the table.

"Afternoon," Morgan responded with a smile. She held up the glass as though to offer the man a drink. "The Pina Coladas are good, this time," she told him. "Not as much pineapple as before. It shouldn't give you the runs this time." She smiled as she concluded her offer with that barbed reminder of his last visit when he imbibed too much of the laxative concoction.

"I spoke with your brother," the man said, jumping directly into the reason for his visit. "He says the operation will be performed as ordered."

"Well, good," Morgan replied. "I would have to say your plan seems to be workable this time."

"I take that as a compliment," he smiled as he loosened his shirt collar. "Maybe I will have one of those after all," he added as he picked up a glass from the several on the table, then struggled out of his chair to amble over to the refrigerator where the pitcher of pineapple juice, coconut milk and rum mix was kept cold.

"I'm going to call Embee and tell her things are going smoothly, then," Morgan said as she got up and entered the house.

The man watched her as she leaned forward to get out of the chair, exposing most of her breasts with her movements. He silently gulped a bit as he watched her move, but he was careful not to stare. He didn't want to offend this woman. She was too close to the Quad Lateral Council and to the person running this operation. He was sure that since they had enough confidence in him to put him in charge of getting rid of Mikel Bear, that now they were going to offer him the job of taking over the Hard Logger operations.

He had laughed when the discussion came up earlier about whether or not he was capable of handling such an operation. They had no idea just how capable he was. The logging operation would be a secondary job for him, but it would pay him more than his primary assignment with the Company. The operation would put him in a position to make himself rich, either directly from the operation, or maybe as Bear did, by using some of the money to finance other things.

First, though, he had to make sure the two men the Company had assigned him through Morgan had taken care of those bothersome detectives. Then he had to arrange Bear's demise. And now that it was all over, or nearly all over, he could begin to relax and make plans. Maybe he could even sway Morgan's attentions, if he had the money from the operation at his disposal, that is. He smiled at the thought as he took a long draft from his glass, ignoring the taxi that passed in front of the house.

The Aussie cabby parked several hundred yards down the road from Morgan Baletta's house, as Penn suggested. Penn didn't want anyone who might pass by to be aware of their visit, and that meant parking far away then sneaking back to the house along its blind side.

Penn wasn't sure how they were going to get into the house without all those noisy birds alerting Morgan, but he considered that they would cross that bridge when they came to it.

When they approached the wall on the side of the

courtyard, Penn thought it odd that the birds were not as noisy as he had remembered. After listening a few minutes, he realized why. Voices emanated from inside the courtyard.

"Well," Penn heard Morgan say. "Embee's delighted with the turn of events. She agrees with me. Now that the little problems of the detectives and Bear are out of the way, not to mention Morri Bund, though she admits that was just a stroke of luck, we can go ahead with our plans and re-institute the shipping of logs."

"Good," Penn heard the man respond.

"And," Morgan continued, "I'm sure you will be glad to hear this, you will be responsible for the Hard Logger operation not only from this end, but also from the San Francisco end, as well."

"Fantastic," the man responded with enthusiasm.

"Do you think you can handle it?" Morgan asked. "I mean, Manuel's dead, you know."

"No, I didn't know that," the man replied. "How did that happen?"

"Well, to be honest, he was getting a little too big for his shorts. Then on top of that, he started to blab his guts to those damned detectives. I had to get rid of him. Just in time, too. He was in their room at the hotel, about to let out everything he knew."

Outside the wall Penn shot a startled glance at his companion. The cabby didn't understand the full meaning of what they had heard, but he looked sufficiently enough impressed for Penn's liking. "So that was how she managed to show up so soon after Manuel's shooting," he whispered, as though the cabby would know what he was talking about. "She's the one who did the shooting."

The cabby gave a small smile of acknowledgment.

"Tell you what," Penn continued whispering. "I think it'll be best if we do this the easy way. Can you get yourself on top of this wall to cover me without their knowing you're there?"

The cabby gave the wall a quick once over, then responded, "Easy, mate. Just watch me."

"You're sure you won't have any trouble with that gun if things get nasty?" Penn asked, realizing he had never relied on the man's ability to actually use it.

"No problem, mate," the cabby was positive. "What are you going to do?"

"I'm going to walk right in there and yell boo! Like any self-respecting ghost would do. They think I'm dead, remember? The shock of seeing me ought to give us the advantage, don't you think?"

The cabby grinned and nodded then turned to face the fence.

"When I get in there, I intend to get them flat on the ground, faces down, as soon as I can. That's where you come in. If they cause any trouble, make yourself known from up there."

"Right, mate," the cabby whispered as he began his climb up the stone wall.

"Don't forget, these two can be dangerous," he cautioned, also in a whisper, which he hoped hadn't been too loud.

The cabby nodded.

Penn headed for the gate. With an aggressive thrust he slammed it open and strutted into the courtyard.

Morgan jumped when she saw Penn, and dropped her glass. It splattered broken pieces over the tiled porch.

The man in white turned to see what had shocked her. "What?" he shouted as he spied Penn. "You can't be! It isn't possible! You're dead...!" His words trailed off.

"It is, and I'm not," Penn retorted with smiling calm. "Don't get any funny ideas, Morgan," he warned as he pulled the PPKs .380 he took from the Texan, out of his waistband with his right hand, and drew the .38 from Manuel's office, which was also in his waistband, with his other hand.

The man in white, though, was not completely overcome by the shock, and he was extremely fast, faster than Morgan. He never struggled to get out of his chair. He merely reached into his coat and pulled out a snub nosed revolver. He fired at Penn with a single motion that had the touch of years of practice.

But Penn was even faster. When he saw the man reach into his coat he lunged for the ground to his right.

They fired at the same time, only the man's shot missed his moving target and splattered one of the parrots off the perch, making feathers fly, while Penn's bullet tore through the man's mid-section.

Penn rolled over to watch Morgan's movements as the man in white fell back in his chair, desperately grasping at his chest to stop the crimson fluid oozing over his once white shirt.

Morgan had risen slower than the man in white, but she was methodical. She reached under the table while she got up, grabbed the gun she kept there, and shot at the still rolling Penn.

Her first shot ricocheted off the tile, singing into the air over the nearby jungle. She took aim for another shot as Penn took aim in return.

The cabby on the wall was the next person to shoot. He fired a round from his wall top vantage point, only his aim wasn't that good. He hit the porch in front of Morgan and the tile splintered in all directions, some cutting her leg.

The splintering tile broke Morgan's concentration, though, and she fired her second round wildly into the air. she spun to face the cabby, who was getting ready for his second shot. That was her mistake.

Penn took the time to make sure his aim was exact. His next shot was fired an instant before Morgan's. Her shot missed the cabby, while his went through the side of her chest and destroyed her heart.

Chapter 28

Penn got to his feet. The adrenaline's after effect was beginning to show as he walked over to inspect the once beautiful woman's form now grotesquely sprawled across the bloodied porch tiles.

The cabby jumped down from the wall. "I sure wish she hadn't tried that, mate," he said.

"That's a fact," Penn agreed with a sorrowful expression.

"You needn't feel to badly, mate," the cabby added. "After all, she was trying to kill you, wasn't she?"

Penn shrugged his shoulders. "I guess she was, at that," he said. "Besides, she killed Manuel, too."

"Who's this Manuel bloke, anyway?"

"Who was Manuel?" Penn responded with a frown. "Manuel was just some poor soul trying to get by, doing what he was told, that's all. He had the misfortune of getting involved with one of Bear's schemes."

"Bear? That bloke that again?"

Penn looked at the cabby. "Yeah. Mikel Bear. I guess he still doesn't mean all that much to you, does he?"

"Afraid not, mate. It's a bit too confusing, everything that Texan bloke blabbered about, and all those M. B. names."

"No matter," Penn said as he turned his attention back to Morgan's body. "She was involved with the smuggling, and that means she was probably involved with Allie's kidnapping, too."

"Smuggling? Kidnapping? I thought you were bugging that ocker about some bloke's murder? Isn't that what this is all about?"

"Some of it."

"Some of it?"

Penn glanced at the cabby. "I know. You're confused, and it's too damned involved to explain now. No matter. I guess you don't really need to know, anyway. It's better that way."

He turned to the man in white who was still staring down at the red spot gradually growing on the front of his shirt. He was breathing heavily. He was still conscious, but he was about to go into shock.

Penn stepped up to him, and stuck the muzzle of his gun against the man's chin.

The man's eyes were wide with fear. Pain throbbed through him. The bullet that entered his chest hadn't come out the other side.

Penn saw the wound wasn't in a place likely to do any lasting damage. "You'll live," he said as gruffly as he could. "But not for long if you don't give me some answers."

The man's eyes went even wider. "Get me an ambulance," he rasped. "Please! I'll bleed to death."

"You just might, at that," Penn replied. "Or you might not. I won't give a damn either way, but first you're going to tell me where I'll find Milagro."

"I need a doctor," the man moaned.

"You'll need an undertaker if I don't get my answer," Penn persisted.

"He's on his boat," the man in white moaned.

"Damn it!" Penn swore. "I'm tired of fooling around with you. Now this is your last chance. Where the hell is he?" Penn raised the barrel of the revolver to the man's face and pulled back the hammer.

The man focused both eyes on the gun, looking cross-eyed at the end of the barrel. "He's near the rendezvous. He's heading to Sa..." He coughed, then gasped for breath.

"Where?" Penn demanded. "I swear I'll kill you now

if you don't tell me."

"Nose Cay... hundred miles...Nose Cay... Please... Get an ambulance," he said, gasping..

"Who do you work for?" Penn raised his voice.

The man rolled his head back. "CIA," he whispered.

Penn failed to show his surprise. "Markham," he bellowed, instead. "Did you kill Blaise Markham?"

"Please, I can't last much...." the man rasped.

"Did you kill him?" Penn shouted.

The man's eyes closed and he gasped for air. He would soon pass into the protection that unconsciousness offered.

Penn grabbed the man by the hair and shook his head. "Did you kill Markham?" again he shouted, demanding his answer.

The man's eyes opened and stared into Penn's. "No," the man mumbled feebly. "Please..."

"Who did?" Penn continued his shouting.

The man shook his head slowly and closed his eyes.

Penn shook the man's head again, harder. "Did the Company order him killed?"

"Wha..."

"Did the Company kill him?" Penn shouted to pierce the man's consciousness, trying to keep him from passing out. "Why was he killed?" He hoped any answer from this man might lead to who committed the murder.

"No. Not Company... He... was going to.... police."

"Police? With what?"

"With... please... ambulance. Coca Nostra. Guerneville. Morgan. Quad... company. Can't let him, had to.... Can't get out... President." The man's words came in staccato fashion before he passed out.

"Jesus," the cabby whispered. Up until then he had been silently witnessing the event. "The Texan mentioned the President."

"The President," Penn said quietly as he turned,

repeating the word as though he wasn't sure of what he had heard.

"That's what he said, mate," the cabby responded. "Did he mean the American President?" he asked, awed.

"I don't know. Sure sounded like it, though, didn't it? Jesus, the President, the CIA, the DEA, Coca Nostra, Cocaine," Penn repeated the relevant names. "Jesus," he said again, shaking his head.

"What have you gotten into, mate?" the cabby asked. He glanced at the man in white. "It doesn't look like this bloke's going to be much more help now, does it?"

"I don't suppose so," Penn responded.

"Going to call an ambulance for him?" the cabby asked.

"I guess I'd better," Penn responded as he reached over the man for the telephone resting on the table. "Nose Cay," he repeated as he dialed the "O" for operator. "You have any idea where Nose Cay is?" he asked the cabby.

"Sure, mate. Just off Ambergris Cay towards Turneffe. It's about a hundred kilometers out, I'd say. Not much of a cay, though. Nothing but sand and a few coconuts."

Penn responded to the operator's question, requesting an ambulance be sent immediately to the house, giving the description and location as best he could, then hung up the phone.

"There's going to be some stink about all this, you know, mate," the cabby said as he turned to follow Penn's lead out of the courtyard.

"I know," Penn responded. "But I think I know just how to get things wrapped up so that we're in the clear. He began walking at a quicker pace back to the cab. "I'm going to get some answers to give to the Prefecture of Police for some questions that he hasn't even thought of yet. That'll clear us with this mess."

Back in the cab, after making a U-turn and heading back to the city, the cabby ventured to question Penn's intentions.

"I was thinking," Penn responded, then paused to let the sound of the siren of the passing ambulance fade away, "that I should get a fast boat. But you know what? There's a helicopter at the airport. I saw it when I last came in."

"A helicopter, mate?"

"Yeah," Penn said with a grin. "I think the best way to catch Milagro is by helicopter to Nose Cay. His boat will be easy to spot from the air."

"That's another question, mate? Who is this Milagro bloke, anyway? What part's that ocker play?"

Penn stopped for a moment to think. The cabby hadn't been involved in all the details of the chase. He still didn't understand the complexities of it. "I guess I don't have time to give you all the details now, but take my word for it, we have got to catch up with Milagro and his boat."

"Okay. So what's his boat? What's it look like?"

"Milagro's a fisherman, supposedly. Or at least, that's what his boat is supposed to be, a fishing boat of some sort. That's what I have to look for, and I should find it somewhere near Nose Cay, if that guy was telling the truth." He hoped the man was telling the truth. He didn't like to think about it, but somehow he knew Allie's life depended on what the man in white had said.

* * * *

Mikel Bear watched Milagro's boat approach the ocean racer. He was glad this part of the plan was going well. He was so jostled and bounced from racing over the ocean that his insides felt as though they had been run through a mixer. I'll feel a hell of a lot better when this is over with, he reasoned. As soon as I get rid of this bastard, Milagro, I can replace him with another carrier, no problem. Even if whoever is supposed to be covering for him down here doesn't like it, that's what's going to happen. God damn it! I don't like somebody else trying to tell me how to run my business. Hell, there's at least a dozen guys who'd love to have this job, with the runs protected, and all. They'd do it for one hell of a lot less money, too.

"What're you thinking about?" Hauke called back, not liking Bear's grave expression.

"Nothing," Bear shouted back. "Nothing at all," he added, trying to display a smile of self-confidence as he continued to fondle the specially prepared package in his lap. And another thing, he continued his thoughts. Who the hell set this trip up to be run in daylight? My orders are to never hold a meeting in the daylight. He shook his head in frustration. Somebody's screwing up, here.

"Milagro must have added some armament to his boat," Hauke said, interrupting Bear's thoughts while pointing to the approaching fishing boat. "That looks like one hell of a gun mounted on the fore deck. It looks like a 30 caliber machine gun."

Mikel peered at the approaching fishing boat. He studied the gun. The sight of it alarmed him.

"There's a guy standing just in front of it forward of the pilot house. He looks like he's moving it around, or something," Hauke added.

"Sure as hell," Mikel said. "That bastard's got some extra firepower with him now, but why? He certainly doesn't keep it there for protection. If the Coast Guard saw it, they'd open fire without asking questions when they stopped him for a search. That thing's nothing but trouble. God damn, he ought to know that. Shit, what the hell's he up to?"

Milagro's reasoning suddenly dawned on him. "Jesus!" he shouted to Hauke. "Turn this thing around. We've got to get out of here. That guy with the gun is taking aim..."

His words were interrupted by a burst of machine gun

fire. He saw the flame shoot from the muzzle of the gun before the sounds were heard across the water, barely audible over the roar of the ocean racer's engines.

Hauke needed no directions, though. He saw the flame, too. He turned the boat just as the rounds hit all around their boat. "Damn it!" he shouted. "What the hell's he doing that for, man? Jesus!"

"Damn it, Hauke," Bear shouted in fury. "Get out of range!"

A second burst was fired from the machine gun.

Hauke had the ocean racer heading in the opposite direction by then, and the second burst fell short.

Within minutes the racer was out of range, or at least out of accurate firing range. The gunner stopped shooting.

"Okay," Bear shouted to Hauke. "Slow down and let me think for a minute."

Hauke frowned at his boss. He didn't want to stop so near the danger.

"Hauke," Bear began anew. "I think I got just the answer to this little problem. Get me that M-16 rifle you keep in the hatch for shark shooting, then you get this boat going again, and this time you keep it right off Milagro's stern. Don't matter what he does with his boat, but you keep off his stern. That way, that gun won't be able to shoot at us without hitting the wheelhouse. That'll give us protection. Got it?"

"You're fucking crazy, man. There ain't no reason some other dude with a gun won't come around to the back of the boat and pick us off."

"God damn it, Hauke! You do as I say. You get me that rifle! I'll take care of anybody that wants to play games shooting at me. Then I got a little surprise package for that bastard Milagro here in this bag, and I'm going to give it to him soon as we get close. That's the way we can solve this little problem."

"No it ain't," Hauke retorted as he reluctantly retrieved

the rifle, his voice rising with his frustration. "We can get the hell out of here. Nobody gets hurt that way," he nearly shouted as he threw the rifle to the Bear.

"God damn it, Hauke!" Mikel Bear roared as he checked the breech of the rifle to make sure it was loaded. "You're a God damn coward! Get this fucking boat turned around again and you come up on Milagro from the rear, hear? I'll show you what the hell a man does in this situation. That rummy on the bow won't have a chance to get a bead on us, if you do as I say. Get close enough for me to get a good shot." Bear lifted the gun to practice his sighting. "You come up on them from behind, like I said. We're not turning tail and running. Not for one God damned minute, we're not!"

"Piss on you," Hauke retorted in resentment.

"What?" Bear shouted back. "God damn you! You get this boat going like I said, or you'll be the first to get it." He turned the barrel of the M-16 on Hauke.

Hauke glared, then turned back to the controls. He thrust the throttles forward as quickly as he could, resigned to doing as he was told, for the time being.

* * * *

Penn wasn't surprised by the cabby's refusal to get into the helicopter at the Belize Municipal Airport.

"I'm not getting into that contraption, mate," the man had said while walking with Penn to the machine.

While boarding the chopper, Penn reflected on the events that caused the meeting between he and the cabby, and the succession of events that led them to that point. The cabby had been so consistently enthusiastic in his efforts to help prior to now. It was almost as if the man had enjoyed the excitement as a change in an otherwise dreary routine of cab driving. But to be afraid of riding in a helicopter after what they had been through seemed totally inconsistent with the man's character. He dwelled on that point as he took his position in the co-pilot's seat and buckled his seat belt. He couldn't help wondering if the cabby was really only a cab driver. Hell, he said to himself, barely noticing the crescendo-ing whine of the turbine engine that began rotating the overhead propellers. You're getting too damn paranoid in this mess. Calm down.

Penn shut the side door and listened as the pilot told him to sit back, that their flight to the vicinity of where he expected to find the boat they were looking for would take about two hours.

Penn nodded in response. He waived to his new friend standing on the ground a dozen or so yards away as the helicopter lifted off the ground. It lifted with a slight wobble, then a slight turning from side to side before dipping forward to pick up speed, ascending at the same time.

The increasing noise of the engine and blades inhibited further conversation with the pilot without having to shout, so he tried to relax, and peered at the collage several hundred feet below of coral reefs, atolls, small islands, and glass clear water.

More islands and cays came into view as the helicopter skimmed over the waves breaking on the reef. Penn turned his thoughts to the beauty of the Caribbean, sparkling blue in the deepest parts, dotted with gleaming white sandy cays. "How unbelievable," he thought. "Such breathtaking beauty, yet it hides the ugliest of men; the ugliest of scams, of crooked dope deals and murderous junk running; death and destruction. The same time weary tales of human selfishness and greed." He wondered if humans would ever change.

He also thought of the man in the white suit and Panama hat. He went over the man's words, and his mood turned from maudlin romanticism to harsh reality. The

President. The words rang from the back of his thoughts. The CIA? Jesus, the CIA is running cocaine to the states to raise money to fund the Contras in Nicaragua. He frowned. Hell. Why should I be so surprised? Wasn't it the same government that had promised not to bomb Cambodia after they had already dropped the bombs? Maybe not the same people, but the same government. Isn't it the same government that complained about the French selling arms to Iran when they were doing the same thing behind everyone's back? And now this. Who ever said there was honesty in government?

He frowned again, with more disgust, then returned to the problem at hand. If the clown in the white suit didn't kill Markham, then that question still had to be answered. One more thing, who the hell hired Markham in the first place?

His thoughts were interrupted by the sight of the trawler plowing through the flat waters several miles to the left front of the speeding helicopter. He noted the ocean racer rounding the side of it, heading for the stern.

He nudged the shoulder of the pilot, pointing to the boat. "I have to get a closer look at those two boats," Penn shouted to him.

The pilot nodded, then leaned the joystick to the left and forward. The helicopter swayed as it changed directions, and soon they were passing less than two hundred feet over the two boats, near a small sand island that jutted up from the reef.

Penn continued watching the two boats, and was confused by their circling game. The faster ocean racer was trying to approach the fishing trawler from the stern, and the trawler was turning in a tight circle, trying to keep the racer off its side.

The racer was the winner in the game. As the chopper approached, the racer had made two complete closing circles on the trawler, and was within a hundred yards or so of its stern.

"Good Christ," Penn said aloud as he stared at the water borne bout of speedboat against slow plowing trawler. "Wasn't that the flash of gunfire from the trawler? From the man on the forward deck? A mounted machine gun?"

* * * *

Hauke was expertly maneuvering, dodging the machine gun mounted bow of the turning trawler to keep approaching from the stern. When he was within half a football field's distance from the stern, Mikel Bear ordered him to slow down. Bear needed a less rocking platform from which to take aim with the rifle. The break in the bouncing and bobbing while they slowed was just enough to allow quick sighting before squeezing off a shot.

Bear's aim was good, and the round entered the wheel house dead center, putting a hole through the bare chest of the Honduran crewman who was steering under Milagro's command. The trawler momentarily stopped its circling course.

Bear got what he wanted, the chance to approach to within a few yards of the stern without the machine gun brought into firing position.

As the racer came to within five yards of the trawler, Bear tossed the rifle to Hauke. "Take this!" he shouted. "If anyone comes out to take a pot shot at us, you nail him first!" Bear grabbed the package with the hand grenades from the seat beside him. He ripped it open and retrieved one. He quickly pulled the pin and made ready to throw.

Hauke held the rifle with one hand, keeping his other on the racer's steering wheel, watching the Bear's movements with confusion. He wasn't afraid to ignore Bear's orders, but he was afraid of having to kill someone, anyone, even someone who was setting out to kill him first. He stood perplexed, swaying back and forth with the boat's motion as he watched another of Milagro's crewmen emerge from the rear of the wheelhouse, rifle in hand.

The crewman raised his rifle and aimed as Mikel drew his arm back to throw the grenade with all his might, carefully judging the distance between the two boats.

"Ain't no way nobody gets wasted when I work a job!" Hauke shouted with sudden decisiveness. "Watch out!" he yelled at the crew of Milagro's boat as he spun the wheel of the racer around. "He's got a grenade!" He never thought of the futility of his words in the tenseness of the situation. He could only think of his code: Nobody gets wasted when he works a job.

The Bear threw the grenade just as Hauke shoved the throttles forward. "That'll fix those bastards," Bear shouted as he threw. But the sudden lurching of the racer at the moment of the throw made the grenade miss the mark.

The crewman saw the grenade coming and dropped his rifle to retreat to the safety of the wheel house, to get as far away from the explosion as he could, as fast as he could.

Bear lost his balance and fell over on the cockpit seat, grasping his package with grenades in front of him. He looked up at Hauke in amazement, not believing what Hauke had done.

The grenade bounced off the rear of the trawler's wheelhouse and landed in the aft gunwale. Hauke counted the seconds before the grenade's explosion, as the boat shot forward in a bouncing arc.

The gunner on the trawler's fore deck smiled as he watched the ocean racer bouncing into view. As it came into firing range he grinned broadly, placing the ocean racer in his sights.

Six seconds after Bear threw the grenade the machine

gunner pulled his trigger. He fired nearly twenty rounds in the direction of the fleeing ocean racer. The first rounds sprayed into the water off the stern of the racer, leaving a trail of water spouts as they traced their path up the wake, up the stern, across the deck and across the steering position.

While standing at the steering wheel, swearing no one ever got wasted on one of his jobs, Hauke got wasted.

Mikel Bear regained his footing long enough to shout at Hauke. "What the hell..." He caught himself in mid sentence and stared. Hauke slumped over the racer's wheel, then dropped to the cockpit floor with blood spewing from his body in too many places to count.

Eight seconds after throwing the hand grenade, Bear turned to Milagro's boat. He stared in disbelief. The boat was still afloat and the man at the machine gun was firing another burst. He saw the flash of flame before he heard the sounds. He watched the mounds of water splash into the air one by one, as if in slow motion. They crept up the racer's wake, punctured the stern of the boat, blew out one of the two engines, and continued up the hull to where he braced himself against the side rail.

Ten seconds after he threw the grenade, Bear saw the explosion on the trawler. The aft portion of the trawler's wheelhouse was blown away along with the aft gunwale section.

Then one of the rounds from the machine gun found its mark. It hit Bear squarely in the middle of the stomach.

Planks and fishing gear were blown fifty feet into the air as the trawler wobbled from side to side, slowed, and settled. Fire broke out in the aft section.

The grenade didn't blow the bottom out of the boat as Bear had planned, because it landed against the gunwale and rolled into a steel bait box when it went off. The explosion was too high above the waterline, and too tightly contained to destroy the boat, but it opened some hull seams and started a fire. The water began flowing into it, and would soon sink it if the fire didn't consume it first.

* * * *

"Holy Christ!" Penn shouted against the chopping racket of the helicopter.

They had descended to nearly a hundred feet over the scene as the grenade went off, and the concussion sent the helicopter reeling for several seconds.

Penn watched the ocean racer speed off with Hauke lying on the floor and Bear clutching at his mid-section. He turned his attention to the trawler. He watched as flames shot upward from the aft section. The diesel soaked wood burned fiercely. "If Allie's on that boat..." he shouted. He never finished the sentence. In frustration, he turned his attention back to the ocean racer bouncing across the waves in a slow arc, heading around a small nearby sand cay.

* * * * *

Mikel Bear wasn't concerned with his destination at the moment, he was concentrating on his stomach. The pain was excruciating. He stared hard at himself for several seconds before he summoned enough courage to ask himself what happened.

"Jesus, it hurts," he mumbled. "But there's no blood. What?"

Several more seconds passed. The bullet hit him in the middle, but it hadn't penetrated. Instead, it was deflected by one of the hand grenades he carried in the package in front of him. The grenade saved his life, but now he was deathly afraid of it. He dropped the package, as though it was a pariah.

The package rolled to the stern of the cockpit, and opened. The hand grenade that saved his life broke free and rattled back and forth as the boat leaped and bounced.

Relieved and dismayed, he turned back to Milagro's boat. He had expected to put an end to the man and the trawler, but the trawler was still moving. He saw smoke billowing out from the rear of it. "The son of a bitch," he said flatly, as he turned and hobbled forward to grab the ocean racer's steering wheel, slipping in Hauke's blood.

The machine gunner on the trawler saw his chance, and fired one last burst at the fleeing ocean racer.

Mikel glanced back at the trawler as the burst was fired. Once more he saw the approaching water fountains marking the deadly approach of bullets. This time he was ready for them. He turned the racer's wheel from side to side to avoid them.

He was partially successful. The bullets missed him, but one of them hit the grenade rolling about the cockpit floor. It made a pinging sound as it broke the safety pin.

The ocean racer rounded the cay before the grenade exploded.

Chapter 29

"Put this thing down on that sandy cay," Penn shouted to the helicopter pilot. "Anyplace along the beach, or any clear spot."

The pilot nodded and headed for a sandy knoll about twenty yards from the beach. He landed the chopper with a bump that was harder than what an experienced helicopter pilot should have offered.

Penn unbuckled his seat belt, and shoved the door open.

The pilot held him back by putting a hand on his shoulder. "Hey!" he shouted. "I'm not about to stay around here with all this shooting going on. If you want to, that's your business, but I'm getting the hell out of here."

Penn glanced at the pilot, then out at Milagro's boat, which was now heading straight for the beach. He noted the name of 'Diablo' that was newly painted across the bow as it passed through a line of shallow breakers caused by the light trade winds. He looked back at the pilot and nodded. He had no choice but to stay, helicopter or no, and said so.

"It's your neck," the pilot shouted. "You want me to send back some help for you?"

"Yeah. Thanks," Penn shouted as he jumped out. "Send back the British Coast Guard cutter that's based in Belize City!"

The pilot nodded. Penn slammed the door shut, and the helicopter jumped into the air with the pilot gaining as much altitude as possible, as quickly as the machine was able.

Penn turned to face the trawler. He shook his head.

Your luck, he mumbled under his breath, as he watched the boat clear the waves and push itself up onto a small coral head just off the beach. Now you're out here with nothing but a mismatched pair of half empty handguns, and coming at you is a burning boat with a machine gun mounted on the fore deck. Some planning that is. He shook his head, chastising his lack of forethought. "Well," he reconciled aloud as he retrieved the .380 automatic and headed for the beach. "Better make the best of it."

He appraised Milagro's boat. The fire now engulfed the stern. Three men were attempting to fight it with buckets of water from over the side, but they were losing. While they fought the fire, the boat slipped onto the reef fifty feet from the beach. It shuddered and stopped with a scraping noise heard over the light waves crashing on the coral. Pieces torn from the bottom of it floated up as soon as it came to a stop.

Penn ran down the beach toward the trawler. He had no idea what action he would take, but he was driven by his fear for the life of the nurse he was sent to find. If she were there, he had to get to her before the fire did, or worse, before the boat sank with her on board. She had to be tied, or she would be swimming away from the boat by now.

The four crewmen looked helplessly at the fire for several minutes, then simultaneously jumped over the side into the water.

Penn stopped running when the men jumped off the boat and swam toward the beach. He watched as they crawled out of the water. They were covered with green sea grass, and smiled rotten toothed grins.

With careful and deliberate aim, Penn raised his pistol. He aimed it at the center of the three and went into a shooting crouch. "Milagro!" he shouted.

The rag clad men were to afraid of the fire on the boat to think about someone on the beach, so when Penn shouted at them, they stared at him in confusion. They didn't understand, but behind them was a boat on fire, so they warily continued up the beach.

The man in the center of the group, the dirtiest looking, leered at Penn with a superficial grin. "What ees theese?" he asked.

"Down on your face!" Penn shouted, anxiously looking over their heads at the burning boat behind them. Time was getting short. "Get down on the sand, now!"

They grinned, as though smiling was the only way to save their souls, and stopped walking.

"Is there a woman aboard that boat?" Penn growled as menacingly as he could, threatening with the pistol.

There was no response, only dirty toothed grins.

"Answer me!" he shouted.

The man in the center raised his hands in front of him in a friendly gesture. "We are no danger to you, I theenk, amigo," the man said. He resumed his walking up the beach, grinning and removing the seaweed from around his waist at the same time.

"Hold it right God damn there!" Penn angrily shouted, as he pulled back the hammer of the pistol.

The man, who Penn now guessed to be Milagro, kept grinning, as did the others. They all resumed walking, and Milagro reached behind him as though to remove more seaweed, but his hand returned with a revolver. He fired with surprising quickness. He was nervous, though, and his aim was poor. The shot hit the sand three feet in front of Penn.

Penn fired in response, in self-defense, an automatic reaction that was the result of years of training. He put three rounds through Milagro's chest quickly, expertly.

The other men stopped. They stared in disbelief at the sight of their boss face down on the sand.

"Is there a woman on that boat?" Penn shouted.

They lifted their heads and stared back with rotten

toothed grins, not heeding.

Then it dawned on Penn. They didn't understand English.

"Hay una mujere en la barca?" Penn shouted while glancing at the boat. It was now listing to one side, soon to slip off the coral reef that was keeping it above water. If that happened, it would sink backwards into the water. That would put out the fire, but it would also make it nearly impossible to save anyone who might yet be aboard.

When they heard the Spanish, the men's eyes lit up. "Si, Senior," they shouted in unison. "Si, Si."

"Jesus!" Penn cried. He hadn't actually believed it was possible for Allie to be on board until he heard it from the two. "Jesus!" he shouted louder as he stuck his gun in to his waistband, and ran for the water, his eyes fixed on the boat.

The boat was slipping, now. It rocked closer and closer to the reef's edge, ready to slip over at any second.

"God damn it!" Penn shouted once more as the boat rocked over, and slipped off the reef.

He ran waist deep into the water. His progress was painfully slow. The coarse sand and coral patches cut his feet until the water was deep enough for swimming; for full, frantic swimming.

He watched the boat sink as he swam the remaining yards to the small reef. Through the splashing water of each stroke he caught sight of the boat, of the steam that came from the fire that went out as it sank, of the cabin passing beneath the water, of the top of the radio antenna as it, too, passed beneath the surface.

He remembered little after that, except wondering how deep the water might be as he arrived over the sinking boat.

He gasped for as much air as he could force into his lungs while recalling all the underwater training from his agent days. He doubled over, raised his feet into the air, and let his body weight force him down while pulling hard with his arms and hands. He reached the boat as it settled on the bottom in twenty feet of water. He saw the main cabin entrance and headed for it.

He struggled through the hatch, frantic about Allie. Had she been able to gasp enough air in the last seconds before sinking to last this long? Would she still be alive? Was she even alive in the first place? Was it even Allie? Fears flooded his mind as he swam into the cabin.

Then he saw her, or what was part of her. He saw her legs dangling from somewhere in the cabin overhead, and he saw the chain that fastened her to the bunk.

Jesus! He shouted in his mind, struggling for lack of breath. She can't be dead! He fought against his reasoning, against knowing the girl's fate, and against his need for air. She couldn't have held her breath for that long, he argued. It had been nearly two minutes since the cabin went under water. Her body has to be floating up, dead. His rational mind fought exploding emotions. Drowned. Held down by the chain to the bunk frame.

He shook his head, desperately fighting his need to breathe. His lungs were straining. He had to surface.

He turned to swim back out the cabin and stopped. Did that leg move? It couldn't have. He must be delirious from lack of oxygen.

No! He answered his confused mind. The leg did move. No. It's some quirk of fate. The currents are moving her leg in some grotesque, devil's joke.

The leg moved again. They both moved. They couldn't have been moved by the water this time, because they kicked up and down. They were kicking, trying to swim.

Penn shook off his need for air. With lungs nearly bursting, with his every effort fighting his desire to open his mouth and gasp for air, for the air that was twenty feet above him. With desperate self-control he swam for the struggling legs.

He reached them, looked up, and stared at the wiggling bubble of air caught under the watertight cabin top.

He lunged upward as hard as he could for that little bubble, and surfaced beside the woman. She had been able to breathe life-giving air from that bubble during the entire time the boat was underwater.

She yelled in fear as Penn's face suddenly shot up in front of her. Her eyes filled with terror, then softened, bewildered, as she recognized her Godfather.

"Allie?" Penn said, surprised and elated. He was amazed he had so much self-control under the circumstances.

"Penn?" the girl asked, tears welling up in her eyes. "Is that really you? You're not a dream?"

"It's really me, Allie," he reassured her, remembering her struggle against the chain. "Now, we've got a problem with that chain, but I think I can solve it. Just take it easy," he consoled her. "We're going to get you out of this. Everything's going to be all right. I'm going back down to break that chain loose so we can get out of here."

He took several deep breaths, turned his head down and submerged.

He reached the chain and the wood strut it was wrapped around. He grabbed the chain near the strut. He placed both feet against the edge of the bunk and pulled up on the chain with all his might. Twice he jerked and pulled, but failed to break it loose.

Nearly spent, he spied a rifle lying on the floor several feet away, and lunged for it. He stuck the barrel behind the strut and wrested against it with all his remaining strength.

The strut loosened, then broke.

Penn lunged for the haven of the fresh air bubble and was greeted with Allie's elated hugs. "You did it!" She shouted. "You did it!"

"Easy," he again cautioned her. "There'll be time

enough for celebration after we get back on the beach. Can you swim?"

She nodded her head.

"Of course you can," Penn added. "I remember teaching you when you were only seven years old." He smiled his reassurance.

She nodded again, more fervently, with stronger resolve.

"Okay," he continued. "When you think you've got enough air, follow me. It'll be a short swim out of this thing and to the surface, then another short swim to the beach. Can you make it with that chain on your ankle?"

She nodded with even more enthusiasm.

"Good," Penn said. "Come on." He dropped beneath the surface.

He waited long enough to make sure Allie was following, then headed for the companionway out of the cabin.

Allie was a good swimmer. Penn had taught her well. Once out of the boat, she quickly outdistanced him on the short swim to the beach, even carrying the dead weight of the chain.

As Penn climbed out onto the hot sand, Allie was standing on the edge of the beach, staring at the crewmen sitting on the sand in the sparse shade of a coconut tree.

She turned to Penn. "I didn't think I was ever going to get out of there," she said, still heaving from the exertion of the swim, and fighting back tears of relief.

"You're safe now," he reassured her. "And soon you'll be back home."

"Gerald's dead," she said flatly.

"I know," Penn replied, not knowing what else to say.

"He killed him," she said, pointing to Milagro's body.

"I know," Penn responded.

"And you killed him?"

"He pulled a gun. I had to," he responded simply.

"Good," she said. "I would have, anyway, gun or not. The bastard." She strode to the man's body. She turned it over and rummaged through the pants pockets. She found what she needed, the key to the lock binding the chain to her ankle.

She spit on the dead man, then sat on the sand to unlock the chain. "These two," she said as she nodded in the direction of the crewmen who had remained seated, not sure what to do. "They're not bad. If it hadn't been for Santiago, there, I probably wouldn't have lasted this long. They're okay. The one that was bad, like that bastard Milagro, was probably killed by the people in that other boat, whoever they were."

Penn glanced at the man she pointed out as Santiago.He motioned to the man, calling him over. "Your shirt," he demanded of him. "Su camisa, por la mujere," he translated his demand.

Santiago quickly doffed shis shirt, and handed it to Penn.

"Tthis will make you look a bit more presentable," Penn said, delivering the shirt to Allie "Now, I guess the next important thing is figuring out how to get back to the mainland."

As Allie put on the shirt, Penn couldn't help but admire her self-control. He decided her strength must come from her father, and her specialized training in trauma nursing.

"How will we get off the island?" Allie asked, buttoning the last button on the shirt.

Penn admitted to himself that he wasn't sure how to accomplish that feat at the moment. He only hoped the British Coast Guard would believe the helicopter pilot's story.

To avoid answering her, he turned his attention back to the crewmen. He was about to suggest they retrieve some knife or tool from the sunken boat to use in cutting down the palms to make a raft, when sounds of a helicopter drifted in from the distance overhead. "That's a chopper," he said looking for the sounds' origin. "There it is!"

The helicopter dropped less than several hundred feet, descending rapidly. It was heading for the central sandy knoll where Penn had been dropped off less than half an hour ago.

It was the same helicopter. The pilot placed the machine on the ground with a bounce that again denied his experience, and waived at the group.

Penn grabbed Allie's arm, and with a cautious eye to the two crewmen, set out to cover the fifteen yards to the aircraft as quickly as he could, before the crewmen got any ideas.

"Hey!" Penn shouted to the pilot as he opened the rear door to the four passenger craft and helped Allie inside. "I thought you said you were getting out of here."

"I was," the pilot responded. "But, Hell. I never lost a fare yet. And I just couldn't run off and leave you out here all by yourself. I saw the whole show from a couple of thousand feet up, where I was safe. I figured you'd need some help, now, though."

"That's for sure. I was getting a little worried about getting off this place."

"You better worry some more," the pilot interrupted as he pointed behind Penn.

Penn turned quickly, alert. Not more than fifteen feet behind him was the less helpful of the crewmen. He had a piece of driftwood in his hand raised over his head, bent on striking a blow.

Penn quickly dropped to one knee and pulled out the .380. He cocked the hammer and took careful aim at the fast striding sailor. "Alto!" he shouted at the top of his voice, straining over the noise of the helicopter.

The man saw the gun and stopped in mid stride, nearly falling forward in his effort to check his body movement. He stared open mouthed at the muzzle of the gun, fear spreading across his face. He dropped the driftwood without bothering to lower his raised hand, as though it suddenly became red hot.

"Vaya! Vaya!" Penn shouted again, at the same time wondering if his weak textbook Spanish was good enough to make the man understand that he was telling him to go back. He hoped his pronunciation of 'go' was understood.

It was. The man stood for several seconds, then turned back to rejoin his comrades.

Penn watched him, then got into the co-pilot's seat while continuing to watch the three men.

"We have room for one of them," the pilot said as Penn shut the door.

"Yeah, but which one?" Penn responded. "No. I think the best thing to do is leave them. Let the Prefecture of Police worry about them. I'll make an anonymous telephone call to him when we get back, and report them. Besides, I don't like the idea of having to explain the dead body on the beach. As it is, they don't know who I am. I'd rather leave it that way." As he spoke he realized that the pilot, though, did know who he was. In self-protection, he added, "You saw the whole thing. You saw him pull the gun on me, didn't you? It was self defense."

The pilot looked at him and smiled. "You know, if I weren't such an agreeable kind of guy, I was an officer in the British Military before settling out here, I'd have to give you some argument about your responsibilities for this little affair, and all. But, yes, you can relax. You were justified. Besides, I don't want to have to go through the long explanations, and possibly end up as an accomplice, too. Don't worry. I don't have any idea what happened out here."

Penn grinned. "Thanks," he said quietly, barely audible over the engine noise.

As the helicopter rose out of reach, he signaled the pilot to wait, and opened his door. He called down to the two men. "Volveria!" he shouted. "Volveria con la policia hoy o la manana!" *I'll return today or tomorrow with the police.*

The men understood what he said. Santiago's eyes lit up, and he smiled. He was obviously glad that they weren't going to be forgotten on that deserted chunk of sand. The other man's expression, though, turned to a frown. He fended off Penn's words while turning away.

Penn nodded to the pilot and they roared off, bumping along as only a helicopter can do in response to the chop, chop, chop of the lifting blades.

The ride back to Belize City was spent in silence. Penn was glad for that. Even if the noise of the helicopter hadn't prevented worthwhile conversation, he was becoming too exhausted to contribute anything constructive. He appreciated the rest.

He looked over his shoulder at Allie from time to time, and wondered what her source of strength was. She had lost her husband, been kidnapped, tied to a bed, raped, beaten, and who knows what, yet she could turn a smile to her rescuer and plead for mercy for one of her captors. "Some woman," he said as the helicopter finally touched down at Belize Municipal Airport instead of the International, to hide their activities

"The first thing," Penn said to Allie as they climbed out of the machine and headed for one of the three cabs waiting at the entrance gate, "Is for us to get to somewhere with a telephone so you can call your father. I've been too damn lazy in my duties to keep him informed lately, and I couldn't think of a better apology than to have you call him for me."

Allie's eyes lit up, then moistened. "I..." she began.

"Don't," Penn interrupted.

She nodded and wiped her eyes, as they got into a waiting cab.

The ride to the Fort George took less than ten minutes,

and fifteen minutes later Allie took the telephone from Penn.

Before she spoke, Penn had to turn away. He felt a tug of emotion, hearing her first words, "Daddy?"

Penn secured two rooms in spite of the clerk's curiosity about the two thoroughly soaked gringos, then asked the clerk to make reservations for two on the first flight out the next morning to the states. He returned just as Allie was hanging up the phone.

She smiled faintly as he put his arm around her shoulders to lead her to her room.

He made sure she was comfortable, assured her he would be back for her in less than an hour, and gently closed the doormaking sure it was locked. He headed out of the hotel. He had a few things to clear up with the local authorities before he and Allie could leave the country.

Chapter 30

"Ah, Mister Gwinn," the Prefecture of Police greeted him with a smile as Penn entered his office. "I wonder? Do you have some explaining to do to me?"

Penn sat in the chair facing the Prefecture's desk. "I do have a few things to say," he smiled back, "that might answer a few of your miscellaneous questions. Providing, of course, that they are simple questions."

"Yes. I see. I think they can be simple questions." The Prefecture smiled in his confident manner.

"For instance?"

"For instance. It seems that someone left a dead person, Ms. Morgan Baletta, in fact, along with someone who was wounded, out at Ms. Baletta's house. I presume you wouldn't really have any answers to that, ah, what do you call it in the states, that situation?"

Penn continued his poker faced smile while thinking of the way the question was phrased. It was clear that the Prefecture wanted an explanation, but at the same time he didn't want any answers that would complicate what could otherwise be a simple solution. After an appropriate pause, Penn said, "If I did have any answers dealing with that, ah, situation, don't you think I would tell you?"

"If you did have any such answer," the Prefecture persisted, "What would it have been?" He again showed his knowing smile.

Penn rephrased his answer. "If I had any answer," he began confidently, "I would have said that perhaps the, what was it, one dead person and one wounded, is that what you said? I would have said they were part of a major cocaine smuggling operation involved with the

Hard Loggers business here in Belize, and that it would have been only a matter of time before the U.S. Government came in to ask a lot of embarrassing questions of the Prefecture of Police. I also would have said that the Prefecture should be glad to have that mess cleaned up for him, especially since the Hard Loggers business would now revert to state control, or possibly to the control of the Prefecture of Police for this city, since it obviously is a profit making business, when run legally, that is. And of course, if I had any other answers to any questions, and if I knew that I might be detained to provide some answers, then I would have to admit that since I am a U.S. citizen, the U.S. would have to step in and take control of the investigation, to say nothing of the Hard Logger business, since it, too, was American owned, and was involved in the smuggling of contraband. Also, I would probably have said that even the Belizean government would want to ask a lot of embarrassing questions concerning police matters and how they had been handled. That is, if any such detention had been initiated, and if I knew anything about the situation." Penn took a breath after completing what must have been the longest couple of sentences he ever uttered in his life. At the same time, he continued his self assured smile.

The Prefecture's smile waned, but his self-control was soon recaptured. "You would have said that?" he challenged.

"I would have said that, not to mention what I would have been forced to add. If I had any information, or answers, that is." Penn returned the game. "And, I think I would have said that there were two murdering criminal types who were also involved, who somehow met with an unfortunate demise in a house somewhere out the Southern Highway the other day, and that Belize is better off without them."

"I see."

"Oh, there is one other thing. If I had known anything about what was going on around here, then I surely would have related some information about some smugglers who are right now out there on an island called Nose Cay, and that to capture them would put a dent in the operations of smuggling cocaine into the U.S., which in turn, would surely earn meritorious recognition from the American Government for the diligence on the part of the Prefecture of Police who made the arrest, so to speak."

"Nose Cay, you say?" The Prefecture showed a change of interest in the game.

"Well, I might have said that if I had known that."

"If you did know about such things, would you take that knowledge out of the country as soon as you could? Like on tomorrow morning's flight?"

"If I knew such things, then I would probably take the information with me on that flight, yes." Penn accepted the 'get-out-of-town' request politely.

"Well, then, Mr. Gwinn," the Prefecture said with a broadening grin as he got up from his chair. "I must say that it has been a pleasure talking with a man of such little information concerning these questions as you seem to possess. It is indeed a shame that I cannot find any cause to detain you. Please, have a nice trip."

"I'm sure I will, Sir," Penn said as he got up and headed out of the office.

Back at the hotel Penn looked in on Allie, saw that she was sound asleep, and shut the door quietly. He headed for the bar, knowing he had some thinking to do.

The bar was much the same as it had been the last time he was there. The same bartender, the same not quite enough air conditioning, the same tourists, it seemed, sitting in the corner, soaking up the atmosphere. He ordered the same Myers's and ginger ale from the same waiter from the same table near the verandah, and sat back.

He was feeling good about having found his Goddaughter, but other things troubled him. He wondered about PZ, and why PZ was so adamant about going back home. Sure, he said to himself, the business needed tending, and at least PZ could accomplish that in his absence, to some degree. It wasn't like the man to avoid a fight.

The waiter came with the drink, and Penn decided to charge it to the rooms.

"Very good, Sir," the man said in well practiced high-English, and retired.

"The rest of the puzzle?" Penn continued to himself. "How about Markham?"

He dwelled on the elements of that problem, and came up with the same questions he faced before. Who killed Markham, and who hired Markham to do the investigation that got him killed?" He took his first drink down in two swallows, and called for another.

The name Embee suddenly appeared on the chalkboard of his mind. "Embee," he repeated the name.

As the waiter arrived with the second order Penn went to the lobby to use the telephone. He wanted to call Yanks.

Yanks answered his phone on the third ring.

"Yanks?" Penn said with enthusiasm. "It's me.... Yeah. Everything's fine. Better, in fact. I found Allie. She's okay, surprising for what she's been through. .. Yeah..... What....? You can't be serious....? Well, I'll be God damned." He thought for a minute about the news Yanks had just given him. "Okay, then. Listen. Allie and I are coming in on tomorrow's flight. Can you pick us up at the airport? Ask Lara to come with you. She can take care of Allie until her father arrives. Okay...? Thanks."

Penn hung up the phone and headed back to the bar. He sat down and went over Yanks' message. "Embee killed herself?" he repeated the news. He found it hard to believe. "When she learned of Morgan's death, she left a note saying she couldn't live alone any longer and shot herself in the head."

There was something about Yanks' message that troubled Penn, and he went over it again. Then it dawned on him. The problem with the message was this: How could Embee have found out about Morgan's death so quickly? Although it seemed like days ago that the events of the morning had played out, it was actually less than eight hours.

"That puts me back in the same hole," he said aloud, thinking. "That means someone called and told her, someone who I don't know about, who had to have been around just after it all happened. And that," he emphasized his thoughts by taking another swallow from his drink, "has to mean that Embee wasn't the Mr. Big, or Ms. Big, in this game."

He stared at his glass. "And that means you're back at square one, doesn't it?" He put down his glass and cursed. "Damn it. Who the hell is behind all this?"

Chapter 31

It was the following Thursday before Penn had a chance to concentrate on the final solution to the Markham murder mess, as he was calling it by then. The intervening time was spent welcoming Colonel Wilkins as he reclaimed his daughter, as well as catching up on all the office and business details left unattended by PZ in his absence. It took Penn three days to get things organized again, in spite of the fact that PZ had returned from Belize to handle just such business details. During that time he kept wondering just what the real cause of the argument was that PZ used for the excuse to return.

He hadn't yet found the time to enter that discussion with PZ, though. He had spent most of his free time filling in Captain Giddings about the Belizean elements of the drug smuggling operations.

It was that afternoon that Penn cornered PZ in their branch office, the Portobello Lounge. PZ had regained some of his positive attitude by then, and seemed willing to discuss the case.

"There's one thing I don't yet understand," PZ said over his second Black Russian of the day. "How in hell did Embee get the information concerning Morgan so quickly? And why was Morgan's death upsetting enough to her to make her commit suicide? That one sure blows my mind."

Penn replied after he took a swallow from his Myers's and ginger ale. "Or, in particular, how could that be such a stumbling block for her? We're not talking about just any normal woman. We're talking about a woman who had no trouble at all in dealing with other assorted killings, not to mention smuggling and a few other felonies. It just doesn't follow that she would lose it over Morgan's death, even if they were as close as they were supposed to be."

PZ gave Penn a pensive glance. "Hey! Are you saying you don't think she really committed suicide?" he asked.

"I wonder," Penn said with a wry smile. "Look. Who would be so upset over the loss of the operation in Belize that he, or she, would commit murder, or as the case seems to be, another murder? Who is so closely tied into Milagro, with the smuggling operation, with Morgan, too, for that matter, that they would find it necessary to do away with Embee? And why?"

"Or, to put it another way, Chief," PZ offered. "Who would know that Embee had so much information that she would be a danger to them? Her? Him?"

"Right," Penn agreed. "And that puts another slant on the question, doesn't it? To make that a valid question, though, you have to presume, as I think I already have, that Embee wasn't the head man, or person, after all."

"You mean that someone else was running things through Embee?"

"Exactly. Now, who would that be?"

"You're asking me?" PZ snorted.

"Right, Turkey. Who do we know that knows Embee. Or, who do we know that she knew? Or, better yet, who do we know that was associated with this entire mess?"

PZ's expression changed, as though he read Penn's intent. "Marena?" he asked with a frown.

Penn nodded as he took another drink.

"Well, hell," PZ said. "Why can't you just accept things the way they are? We got this case wrapped up, already, it seems to me. Besides, Marena sure as hell isn't smart enough to pull off a caper like that."

"What the hell's bothering you now, PZ?" Penn asked with surprise. "You're dragging your heels again."

"Dragging my heels?" PZ retorted. "Crap! I went

back and forth to that backwater country of Belize half a dozen times or so with you, didn't I? I wouldn't call that dragging my heels. Anyway, if you want to pay Marena another visit, it's no skin off my nose. Hell, she should have cooled off enough from that Guerneville caper by now to be talkative, anyway. Maybe."

Penn ignored PZ's forced change in attitude. "There's one thing we keep forgetting, though," he said. "Markham was working on the Guerneville mess, too. And if we go back to the photos we found under his desk, you'll remember that list of names. There were two persons on that list who weren't named, who were noted but not named."

PZ shrugged. "Sure. I remember. Those must have been Morgan and Embee, the way I see it."

"I don't think so. Morgan, possibly, but I don't think Embee. She was too close to Bear, too much in the middle of things for Markham not to have named her, if he had any idea that she was involved. No. I think it was someone else."

"Mr. Big, I gather."

"Maybe."

"Come on. Now we're going in circles." PZ frowned as he took the last of his drink.

"This entire case has been one big circle, PZ. As a matter of fact!" Penn added triumphantly as he sat up, putting his glass down on the table with enthusiasm. "That's the key. It is a circle. A damned tight circle. And that means we should look for the conclusion in the beginning. They're both the same."

"Now I'm going in circles," PZ said.

"Right. Who did we try talking to, first?" Penn asked.

"Marena?" PZ offered.

"Right. Why? Because Markham was related to Marena. But we figured the big operator had to be Embee, because of the initials thing. I guessed it might be the result of criminal genius. Well, I just thought of someone who could be that criminal genius, and who could have been in a position all along to know everything. If not directly, then through Embee, I'll bet, for sure. We were right there in the beginning."

PZ stared at Penn for several seconds before the name came to him. "In the beginning? You mean Taylor? Elzee Taylor? I don't see any connection between Embee Bear and Elzee Taylor."

"Neither did I, until something just went through my mind. I had a stroke of genius."

"Hah!"

"I can see you don't believe me," Penn responded to PZ's barb, getting up from the table at the same time, adding, "If I'm right, then we can wrap this thing up in a hurry. I think I've positively had a stroke of genius. I think I may have found the key to the whole mess."

He hurried for the door, threading his way through the later than noontime crowd. He said his hi's and bye's to friends, even dodged the hands of the playful pair, Donna and Denise, before slipping through the glass doors to leave the boompa boomp of the 50's juke box music behind. The doors nearly closed on PZ.

"Hey!" PZ called, trying to catch up. He barely made the passenger door of the Red Beast as Penn put the car into gear. "Remember me? I have to go along on this trip, too, you said."

"Only if you hurry," Penn smiled. "I said I had the key, and if I'm right, then we haven't any more time to lose. We've wasted enough time since I got back, as it is."

"Then have at it, Chief," PZ said as he buckled himself into the front seat.

Penn stomped on the throttle in his usual hurried manner. The machine squealed out of the parking lot as PZ grabbed for the side of the seat to hold on, ignoring the blue Mercedes forced onto the curb by Penn's reckless exit.

For their entire trip PZ made no comment. He was too busy maintaining his self-control while Penn rushed through town, through several red lighted intersections, and across the Richmond Bridge into the East Bay area.

"This is it!" Penn said enthusiastically when he found a parking space on East 14th Street in Oakland.

"The Alameda County Courthouse?" PZ asked. "You're checking on court records?"

"Exactly."

"What're you going to find?" PZ asked. "Someone's name with the word 'killer' written behind it? What're you looking for?"

"Come on, Turkey, and see for yourself," Penn answered as he jumped out of the car. He plugged the meter with the only thing close to change he had in his pockets, one of PZ's metal 3/8ths SAE washers. He bounded up the cement steps two at a time to enter the building, with PZ close behind, looking somewhat akin to a kid following an older brother.

"The County Recorder's office," PZ noted as Penn entered the first door they came to. "Don't tell me. Civil and Criminal Index?"

"Guess again."

"Birth records?"

That might work, but better yet..." he replied, letting the sentence drop as he reached into the shoulder high case to extract a leather bound tome.

"Marriage records? You're checking marriage records? Who for? Marena?"

"Close, but no cigar," Penn smiled as he opened the book and began thumbing through the list of married names.

"B's," PZ mused, watching. "Bear. You're looking for the name Bear," he added as Penn thumbed through the pages.

"Right. And here it is. Bear, Embee Bear, nee Taylor. I'll be damned. Just as I thought."

"Taylor," PZ said, astounded. "Embee Taylor? Jesus, she's related to Elzee Taylor?"

"Exactly," Penn responded. "That's the circle I was talking about. We were already there, we just didn't know it at the time."

"Elzee Taylor? You mean you think Elzee Taylor is the Mr. Big? The man with the criminal mind behind all this?" PZ didn't want to accept the supposition.

"There's one way to prove my theory," Penn replied as he returned the tome to the shelf. "Talk to his close friend."

"Who?"

"Who else but Marena, of course."

"Christ. We are going in circles," PZ responded as he turned to follow the already striding Penn on the way out of the room.

PZ again rode in silence, trying to hang onto his seat, as Penn raced out of Oakland and across the Bay Bridge into San Francisco. He merely winced as Penn nearly sideswiped a truck while hurrying to beat it through the stoplight at the 5th Street off ramp.

Penn reached the corner of Polk Street and Geary Boulevard in record time, considering the afternoon traffic. "Just in time for the end of the matinee," he said, parking in the red zone in front of the palace of porn. "Coming?" he asked, as he jumped out of the car and headed for the box office.

"Ten bucks is still too much for this crap," he told the cashier as he hurriedly purchased his ticket and started for the curtained entrance into the auditorium. "Damn," he added as he stopped and returned to the box office. "Here's another ten for this turkey, too," he said as he paid for PZ's ticket. "I should have known you wouldn't have any money with you," he added as he tugged on PZ's jacket sleeve to hurry him along.

PZ winked at the cashier and once more followed Penn through the door.

"Jesus," PZ whistled softly, looking at the stage, impressed by the double jointed antics of the couple acting there. "Do you believe that one?"

Penn was too busy threading his way through the seated crowd amid complaints and yells of 'down in front' to pay any attention to the center of attraction that afternoon. He realized Marena wasn't on stage, and that was all he needed to know for the moment. He was hoping that they could get past the guard on the door to the dressing rooms before Marena slipped away.

"Good," PZ said as he followed Penn though the curtains into the small room before hallway. "Mr. Muscles ain't here."

Penn nodded as he headed through the door leading to the hall facing the dressing rooms.

Halfway down the hallway on the right he found the door with Marena's name spelled across the top in gold printing. "Suitable for a star, I suppose," he commented sarcastically, as he stopped directly in front of the door to let PZ catch up.

They waited for a few minutes longer to listen for sounds from within, and since nothing was audible, Penn tried the doorknob.

It turned.

He pushed it open and stepped inside. PZ was nervously close on his heels.

PZ was so close on his heels, in fact, that when Penn stopped short, PZ bumped into him. Neither was expecting to be greeted the way they were.

Marena was the first person Penn saw inside the room. The second person was Elzee Taylor, and the last person was someone that could have been Mr. Muscles' twin, only this guy was much more neatly dressed in a blue suit and red tie. Penn assessed the tie and suit colors as power style dress.

The next thing they both saw was the .45 automatic Mr. Power Dresser held loosely in his right hand. It was pointing directly at the intruders, and it was clear from the way it was pointing that the man didn't like their intrusion.

"Oh, I see we're interrupting," Penn quickly remarked. "We'll just turn around and get out of here," he added as he started backing up, pushing PZ out behind him.

"That's quite all right, Mr. Gwinn," Mr. Power Dresser said, showing a wry grin. "Please come in," he added with sarcasm. "We've been expecting you, ever since you paid the cashier outside, that is." He motioned with his gun to direct Penn and PZ to return inside the room and shut the door.

Being of a mind to not argue with such formidable means of persuasion as a .45, Penn did as was requested.

"Damn," PZ remarked as he took his place standing beside Penn, facing the cannon sized hole in the end of the gun.

"To what do we owe the honor of this visit?" Elzee Taylor opened the interrogation with an icy tone. "You've met Monroe. Sometimes I have a problem holding him back, so I suggest you answer my question."

Penn considered his position. With the odds as they were, talking was his only choice of action. "I was hoping to ask you the same question, Elzee," he replied, forcing a grin.

"Do you want to explain that?" Elzee countered. "Or do you care whether or not I know what you're talking about?"

"I thought you might care," Penn replied, seeing what might be an opening. At the same time he scanned the room to find some sort of advantage that would enable their escape. "That's why we're here in the first place."

"Well?" Elzee asked.

"Well what?" Penn played.

"Oh, come, come, Penn. Don't play games with me. I'm sure by now you've figured out quite enough of what has been going on to have your reasons for being here. Now what is it that you want?"

As Elzee asked the question, he reached into the breast pocket of his coat and extracted a gold cigarette case. He carefully opened it, selected a 100mm cigarette, and closed the case with one hand while slipping the cigarette between his lips with the other in one smooth, well practiced motion.

Marena quickly grabbed a lighter from her dressing room table, and dutifully lit the cigarette for him.

Penn noted the initials Q4C engraved on the cigarette case, and it wasn't until that moment that Penn paid even a second's heed to Marena, but then he couldn't ignore her. She was dressed in nothing, or practically nothing. She wore a robe, but it was open down the front, concealing nothing. More aptly put, she was nothing-ly dressed, and not the least bit bashful about it.

Monroe kept his eyes solidly on the intruders without flinching.

"You know, Elzee," Penn said, deciding he could continue the talking game. "You're absolutely right. I have figured out what's been going on, and that's why I'm here."

"Well, how very interesting," Elzee responded with more condescension. "Just what have you figured out?"

"You set up this entire operation, didn't you?" Penn came directly to the point. He hoped PZ wouldn't get too antsy by being put into the delicate position of becoming a nuisance to Elzee, which now had to be eliminated. Just as Embee had been, and Markham, too, all to keep Elzee's secret.

"What operation would that be?" Elzee carried on the game like a cat toying with the mouse.

"There's only one thing I don't understand, Elzee," Penn went on, ignoring Elzee's attempt to appear innocent. "How could you be so ruthless that you could kill your own sister?"

Elzee frowned. "I see," he said. "This game is going to be over quite quickly. You do seem to know too much, I'm afraid. But not quite all, even so."

Ignoring the temptation to ask what else he didn't know, Penn pursued the weakness he sensed in Elzee. "How could you do that?" He persisted with his question about Embee, working on whatever guilt feelings Elzee may have felt about killing his own sister.

Elzee frowned again. "Embee? She lost her self-control," he began explaining. "When the Prefecture… ah, when I learned of Morgan's death, I went to see her to tell her. She lost control. God damn women, anyway. I wonder why they can't have the self-control a man has. If she had just maintained, then everything would have worked out all right. But no. She had to threaten me. Me! She thought I was responsible for Morgan's death because she knew I never liked Morgan in the first place. I didn't have anything to do with the bitch's death, but I couldn't convince Embee of that. She threatened the entire operation."

"The Prefecture?" Penn responded, remembering Elzee's stumbling over the word.

"What?" Elzee asked, absentmindedly. He had already passed from that topic to another in his mind, and had forgotten his remark that revealed another secret.

"You said the Prefecture. The Belizean Prefecture of Police?"

Elzee stared at Penn, gathering the necessary effort to come back to Penn's topic. "Yes. You do know too much," he said. "Ah, well," he sighed. "Yes. The Prefecture is an excellent source, and an excellent ally, I might add. Of course, nothing could have been set up down there by me in the first place if he hadn't been most cooperative."

"Bear didn't set things up?" Penn asked with surprise.

"Bear?" Elzee sneered. "Bear was only a pawn. He did set some things up that were useful, especially his distribution ring here, and the men he used for other sources of information. It was convenient to let him think he was the boss, but he wasn't. It was me and my connections."

"Why let the bastard run off at the mouth, Penn?" PZ suddenly interrupted. "Shut him up. Hell, he's only trying to worm his way out of this."

Penn glanced at PZ, but had to defer asking him what he was up to. Turning his attention back to Elzee, he continued. "Even the Guerneville operation?" he asked. He wanted to continue his questioning, since Elzee was willing to talk.

"The Guerneville thing? What do you know about that? You mean to tell me that you had a hand in that mess?"

"You didn't know it was Yanks who the police chased into the house in the first place? The laugh's on you on that one."

"Well, I must say, you ruined a perfectly good operation there, you know. I presume Yanks was working for you?"

Penn shrugged his shoulders, grinning.

"I even managed to get that smart ass Bear to give me twenty grand for Marena's contract on that set up," Elzee went on with a self-effacing grin. "Can you imagine the gullibility of that man?" he chuckled with self-satisfaction.

Marena joined the chuckle as Elzee returned to the topic at hand with typical pathological reasoning; without guilt, without remorse. "Oh, well," he said. "Of no importance. I'm sure you will pay for that, one way or another. Especially if Monroe gets his way. He has a special talent for taking revenge, or making amends, which ever you might call it. He learned that during his CIA training." He turned his head towards Monroe. "Didn't you?" he asked, not so much for confirmation as to illustrate his point.

The man grinned sadistically.

Penn appraised the man. "So that's it," he said. "You're the final connection with the feds on this thing."

"Not exactly the CIA," Elzee interjected. "Now he's with a much more proficient organization, the Quad Lateral Council."

Monroe widened his grin, saying nothing.

"A lot of agents go bad after training," Penn added, having to ignore the reference to that mysterious organization once more. He was too busy thinking, reaching for opportunities, watching Monroe. "They can't handle the delicate balance of good over evil. They just aren't grown up enough to tell the difference. Their infantile greed gets the best of them. How infantile is your greed?"

Monroe's face tensed.

"Tell me, big shot," Penn said with a sneer, seeing the effect of his thrust. "When are you going to grow up?"

Monroe's expression turned sour. He nearly drooled with hatred.

Penn hoped it was hatred and not anticipation.

Elzee was amused by the interplay. "Ah," he interrupted. "It's a shame we haven't any cameras. Your demise, shall we say, would make such an enjoyable movie. Especially with Marena, here, being part of the action."

Marena turned to Elzee. "What?" she asked. "What do you mean, part of the action?" Her eyes opened wide.

Elzee smiled back at her. "Ah, my Dearest. It's too bad, but you have outlived your usefulness. That's what I came here to tell you in the first place. Monroe will so enjoy you, too."

Marena was stunned. She stumbled back, bumping into a chair behind her. She realized Elzee had not only ended his relationship with her, but he planned to kill her, as well. She slowly shook her head from side to side, and started weaving in a faint. She leaned forward, then wobbled. She tried to hold her head up, but lost the battle and fell over backward, tripping over the chair.

Her feet flew up as the chair tipped over, and Elzee jumped to the side to avoid being kicked. The movement caught the attention of Monroe, distracting him.

Penn lunged for the gun. He grabbed it, and jammed his little finger between the hammer and the firing pin. That kept the hammer from closing if the trigger is pulled.

And the trigger was pulled. The hammer slammed down on Penn's little finger unmercifully, making him wince with the sharp shot of pain.

Confused by the misfire, Monroe stared at the gun, not believing it hadn't fired.

PZ, seeing his advantage, jumped across the prone Marena while holding his fist in the air straight out in front of him. He caught Elzee Taylor squarely in the sternum with the full force of his 190 pounds placed directly behind his outstretched arm.

Elzee gasped and fell to his knees, fighting for breath.

Penn continued struggling with Monroe over the gun, and tried to initiate a Ju Jitsu move that would have twisted the man's arm, but the movement needed more room. Instead, he tripped over Marena's body and lost his grip.

Monroe pulled back on the gun, and with the sudden release of restraint, he bounced against the dressing room wall with a thud.

Suddenly the door smashed open and in rushed three uniformed policemen.

Monroe rebounded from the wall and struggled to aim

at Penn again just as he saw the first officer. With nearly automatic reaction, he jerked the gun around and shot the officer in the chest. The man's action was nearly instantaneous, and tantamount to suicide.

Before the first cop hit the far wall, carried by the force of the bullet, the other two had riddled Monroe with their .38 service revolvers. He was dead before he fell.

The first cop rebounded from the wall, staggered, and shook his head. He felt his chest where he had been shot, and sighed with relief when he realized the .45 caliber bullet had been stopped by his bullet proof vest.

"Am I ever glad to see you," Penn yelled at Sergeant McIvers, who burst into the room after the three uniformed cops. "Where'd you come from?"

"Just like the calvary," PZ commented dryly as he picked himself up from Elzee Taylor's reclining form.

"Cavalry," Penn corrected with a light hearted laugh while straightening up the chair that was recently vacated by Marena, who was now beginning to show come signs of recovery from her shock. "How did you know we would be here, anyway?" he added to Sgt. McIvers.

"I've been following you ever since you made your report to the captain," McIvers explained. "I figured you had something heavy going down when you got back with that girl, and I sure as hell wanted some answers to everything that's been going on with this guy, Taylor. Especially since Bear's wife died under such suspicious circumstances."

"Well, whatever the reason, you sure showed up here in time. I don't suppose you had a chance to hear anything that went on before your Gang Busters entry, did you?"

"Naturally. That's why we came in when we did. We heard just about everything that was said since you closed the door."

"You're kidding," PZ interjected.

"I said we've been following you. What I heard just

about gives me the answers to all the questions I had."

"Great," PZ sighed as he sat on the floor against the wall near the door. "Then maybe we can get out of here and get a drink somewhere."

"You guys can go ahead. Oh, and the drink's on me," the sergeant said.

"Oh? Why?" Penn asked.

"Why? Well, because I think I owe you one. Not only that, but because of the irony of the way things turned out."

"Irony?"

"Yeah. The only reason I got into this thing in the first place with Bear was because he promised me some lieutenant's bars, remember? Well, Giddings is so pleased about the way I cleaned up this mess, not mentioning your help, of course, that he'll recommend those bars after all."

Penn didn't know whether to congratulate him or laugh out of exasperation. The man didn't seem the least bit bashful about taking credit for the resolution of the case. But what the hell, let him have the credit. If that's what it takes to get out of this place, then that's the way it is. "Congratulations," he eventually said, turning to the door and signaling for PZ to follow.

Chapter 32

Penn and PZ did have that drink with McIvers, after all. Only it wasn't until nearly three weeks later that the new Lieutenant McIvers came by the branch office at Penn's specific request to buy it.

"Here's to the best two P.I.'s in the business," the new lieutenant said as he lifted his glass.

"Yeah," PZ said with enthusiasm, always happy about receiving a free drink.

"Well, almost the best," commented Penn, looking into his glass.

"What d'ya mean?" McIvers asked, his glass half way up to his lips.

"We still haven't solved the original puzzle," Penn replied sullenly.

"I thought we, you, had. What are you talking about?" the lieutenant responded.

"Markham," Penn answered with a frown. "This whole thing started by trying to find out who killed him. Not only is that still unknown, but we also have the question of who hired him in the first place."

"Hell. Didn't I tell you?" McIvers offered. "We ran a background check on him, just to wrap up some of the details, you might say. You never knew who his connections were?"

"Connections?" Penn responded with curiosity. "I didn't know he was connected in any way. You mean to someone important?"

"You might say that," the officer replied with a grin before taking a sip of his drink for effect. "His uncle is Associate Editor of the Washington Post."

"The Post? The same Washington Post that started the

Watergate mess?" PZ asked in awe.

"The same," McIvers replied. "And Markham's uncle asked him to look into this cocaine thing, this Coca Nostra ring, here in the city. He did, and he got some answers, too. He came up with all the pieces, including names that weren't on that list you found."

"Answers? What answers?" PZ asked, nervously. "Like what? Who?"

"Like who was behind it, and all. Not only that, but like who Mikel Bear's operation included, who worked for him."

"What do I have to do," Penn added with exasperation, "drag it out of you? Who?"

"You can't guess? Really?" the lieutenant asked with a wry grin.

Penn glared at the man, thinking he disliked his smug and satisfied grin. He thought about the word game for a few minutes, and took a sip from his drink while wondering whether or not to try another tactic. Then the answer dawned on him. "Of course!" he quipped, setting his drink on the table. "If the Washington Post was involved, then the people behind it all must be..."

"Right," Lieutenant McIvers interrupted. "The CIA."

"The Company, and...."

"And the boys on the staff close to the Big man, himself."

"Jesus. You mean to sit there and tell me that this really does reach clear up to the Oval Office?" Penn asked.

"According to what we got in confidence, it probably does. There's some Marine Corps Colonel that's the main direction for the operation, apparently, and there seems to be another company or association that goes by the name of something like Quad Lateral Council, but unless I miss my guess, that means all the way to the top. Wouldn't you think so?"

"I'll be damned. Such a waste," he said sullenly. "Such a God damn waste."

"Yeah," PZ, for once serious, agreed. "Well, come on, Chief," he added, "I guess we don't need any more of this today. Besides, we got work to do, remember?"

Penn looked at his partner. "Sit down, PZ," he said solemnly. "There's something else we have to discuss."

PZ turned to Penn. "Look. I have things to do, and I'm going to go do them."

"Not right now, you're not," Penn challenged.

"What're you talking about?" PZ demanded.

"Tell me, PZ," Penn began quietly, painfully. "When were you busted on that coke possession charge?" He knew the answer. He had gotten it from Captain Giddings' sources with the DEA, just that morning.

PZ was stunned. He dropped both hands to the arms of the lounge chair and stared at Penn.

"Why didn't you tell me Keany and the DEA put a jacket on you?"

PZ still didn't answer.

"Is that why you were so reluctant to look into Markham's murder? Because you were afraid I'd turn up some information that you were one of Mikel Bear's dealers?"

PZ started shaking his head from side to side, slowly, disbelieving what he was hearing.

"That Guerneville raid. That pusher you shot. You had to get rid of him because he recognized you. You couldn't let that get out, so you shot him before he could say anything. That's what all the commotion was that I heard before the shots were fired." Penn frowned, hardly capable of going on, of piecing the puzzle together now that PZ was confessing through his silent staring, through his lack of denials.

It was hard for Penn to force himself to bring out all the evidence he had gathered against his long time partner, but he had to present it. He had to get the truth out. That was why he set up this appointment with McIvers.

"I now know how the Bear got warning of our intended Guerneville raid. You were obligated to call him with the information. You called him from the phone in the Peppermill Lounge while we were waiting for McIvers. I had a check run on the numbers dialed from that telephone on that day. Bear's number was called at that time."

PZ glared.

"It was the bust jacket that he held over you, wasn't it?" Penn continued.

PZ again shook his head in disbelief.

"The one thing that really bothers me, though, is that now I know who killed Markham."

"Yeah? Who?" PZ's anxiety was rising, and it showed.

"Someone he knew well enough to let get close to him."

"Who?" PZ demanded.

"You," Penn replied quietly, almost inaudibly.

Several seconds passed. Then PZ spoke. "You got any evidence to support this crap?" he hissed in anger.

"Some. Just what I mentioned, but not nearly so much as you've just given me by your question."

"Then it's all over, ain't it?" he said, staring at Penn, then at the lieutenant. Suddenly, he jumped up from the table and headed for the door, knocking over several other customers seated around tables.

"Hold it!" a voice shouted from in front of PZ, as two men in civilian clothes sprang to their feet from their table near the door, drawing their service revolvers.

The struggle lasted only seconds. PZ was grabbed by the two plain-clothes officers. He was wrestled to the floor, and handcuffed.

"Peter Zane Thomas," Lt. McIvers called, as he got to his feet. "You're under arrest. Take him outside and read him his rights," he added to the officers. "Then book him for murder one."

Penn got up and slowly followed the lieutenant and the two holding PZ as they left the lounge. He felt like he needed a rest, a long rest.

Two days later, after he had delivered his written report to the police department, Penn made plans to head for his favorite vacation spot, Baja California. Lara went to Hawaii for a week with her parents, and he had a lot of time to kill.

He looked forward to a long rest, and couldn't wait to get away. Had he been able to see what that trip to Baja California held in store for him, though, he would probably have spent his vacation isolated somewhere in Alaska, where it would have been mostly white with snow. It wouldn't have been green; green like a woman's cat eyes.